FriesenPress

One Printers Way
Altona, MB R0G 0B0
Canada

www.friesenpress.com

Copyright © 2021 by Brit Parker
First Edition — 2021

Illustrations: Michael S. Desjardins
Editor: Lindsay Smith
Book cover: Designed by Author. Original painting by M. S. Desjardins (Artist).

All the characters and events in this narrative are fictional, and no resemblance to real persons either living or dead is intended or should
be inferred.

All images, including the book cover are copyright protected and cannot be used, shared or copied unless given written consent by the Author.

Reference material for Navy destroyer, USS Midhurst, provided by friends of HMCS Haida National Historic Site, Hamilton, Ontario (Canada).

All rights reserved.

No part of this publication may be reproduced in any form, or by any means, electronic or mechanical, including photocopying, recording, or any information browsing, storage, or retrieval system, without permission in writing from FriesenPress.

ISBN
978-1-03-911327-5 (Hardcover)
978-1-03-911326-8 (Paperback)
978-1-03-911328-2 (eBook)

1. FICTION, ACTION & ADVENTURE

Distributed to the trade by The Ingram Book Company

***

He's trying to run me off the road! Brandon thought, as he floored the gas pedal. Grasping the steering wheel with a white-knuckle hold, he fought to keep control as the road twisted and curved down the hillside in front of him. Still groggy from hitting his head, he noticed the pursuing vehicle's front bumper gaining on him again.

***

Something about an ocean is calming. It will draw you toward it, with an almost alluring, seductive grasp, but if you're not careful it will eat you up and swallow you whole.

***

Reader review:

"Well researched and written. The action on
land and in the water is fast-paced and deadly.
This has everything I look for when choosing a new book to read:
mystery, great action, and truly likable characters.
I really enjoyed it and look forward to the next one."

Dedicated to my aunts,
Audrey and Betty (Elizabeth).

THE

BRIT PARKER

Acknowledgments

A heartfelt thank you to my parents for their continued love, support, and contribution during the publication of my first novel.

Special thanks to my devoted friends: Michael S. Desjardins – I'm happy that you were a part of this, and honored that you were the one that created the original painting for my book cover. Your level of professionalism serves as an example of someone who truly cares about his work. You've set this book cover apart from any other; Lisa Bayley – Thank you so much for your ongoing motivational support, guidance, and assistance with the building of this story. You helped make this novel shine, and gave me that extra boost needed to see this project through until the end.

Lindsay Smith – story/plot development editor;
Sheryl Desjardins - beta reader;
and Dean McConnachie of the Oakville
(Ontario) Dive Academy.

DETECTIVE CONSTABLE JEFF NORTHRUP
of the Metropolitan Toronto Police - 52 Division,
killed in the line of duty - July 2021.
You were a kind man and a true hero.
Thank you for your dedicated service,
and for your help.

Rest in Peace Jeff.

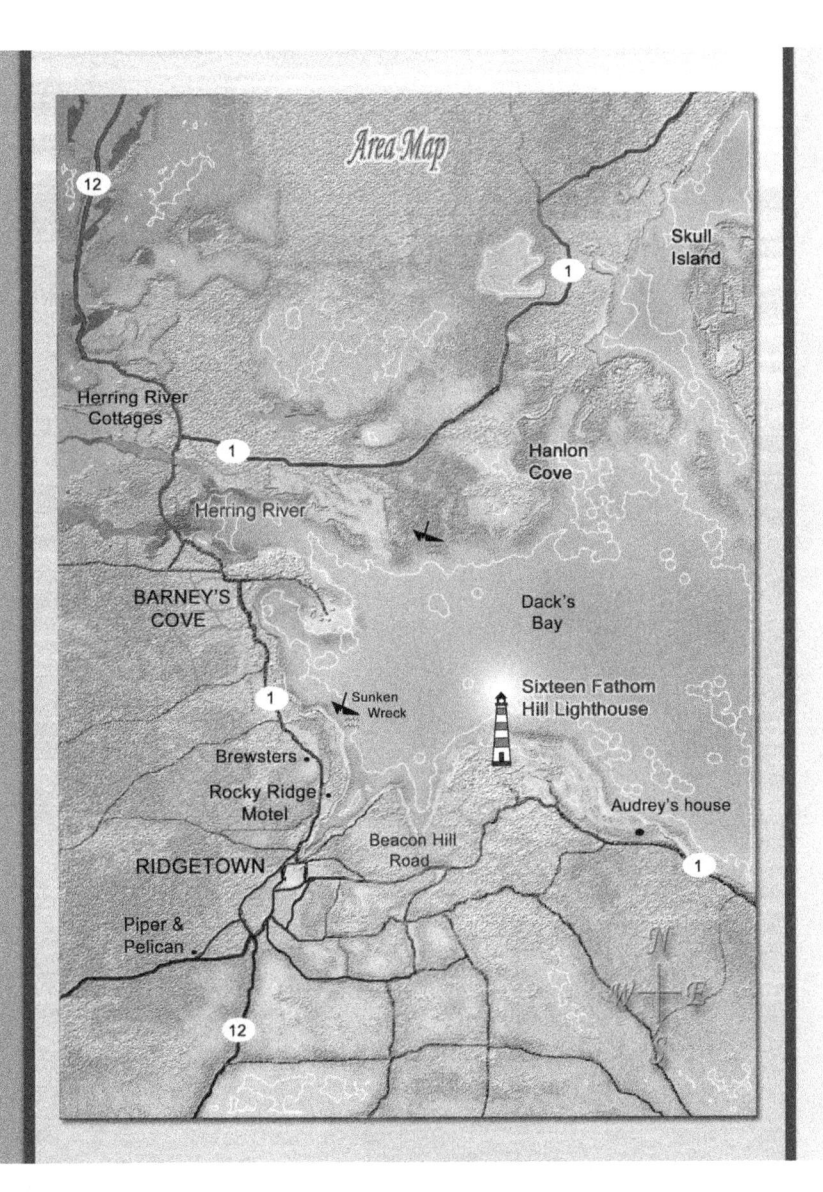

PROLOGUE

OFF THE COAST OF MAINE - JULY 1989

Waves angrily pounded against the port side of the 120 foot steel ship anchored a quarter of a mile offshore of the New England coast. Deckhand Dennis Cain watched from the shadows as a rope was thrown down to a small private yacht that had courageously maneuvered through the swelling waves to meet the salvage ship. Only hard rubber fenders, spaced out from stern to hull, kept the visiting vessel from slamming into the unyielding steel of the larger ship.

Dennis contemplated jumping overboard. The cold ocean wind did nothing to stave off the sweat that had formed on his body as he watched three men struggle to board the heaving ship. One man remained at the helm of the small private yacht. Dennis recognized the one with the designer beard on his face as Cy, a powerful man known to have funded some of the most successful salvage excursions along the Atlantic seaboard. Struggling seamen like Dennis fought tooth and nail to be part of a crew hired by Cy, as he paid quite handsomely for a good haul. That came with a price—once hired, men gave up their freedom to work as independent contractors. They belonged to Cy from that moment on, and if the rumors about him held even the slightest hint of truth, Dennis understood that not even God could help you if you crossed the man in any way.

He shivered at the thought. The salvage ship, under hire by Cy, had recently located and secured a nineteenth-century shipwreck believed to have gone down in a hurricane with a cargo of gold, silver, and rare museum quality artifacts. Cy had sent in a dive team and over the course of a few weeks they had recovered what was estimated to be a cool $550K worth of lost treasure.

Everything had been boxed and stored in the cargo hold until a proper inventory could be conducted on shore. In the interim, Dennis had grown curious. During a drunken night of celebration on board, he had slipped down to the hold to see for himself what exactly the treasure consisted of ... and if he might get his hands on a few trinkets for himself.

Armed with only a flashlight, he had managed to enter the hold unnoticed and make his way to the half dozen wooden crates bound for Cy's appraisers in New York.

The sound of metal scraping metal had startled him before he had an opportunity to inspect the load. He darted into the shadows to hide, nearly knocking over a large wooden barrel in the process. Scrambling to keep it upright, Dennis had thrown his weight on top of the barrel and held his breath.

The steel hold was as silent as a tomb. No further sounds came. After a few moments, confident he was alone, Dennis let out a slow sigh of relief and loosened his grip on the barrel. But the lid had come away, and as he stood it clattered noisily to the floor.

"Who's there?" a voice yelled out.

Dennis froze. He heard heavy footsteps making their way down the main aisle. A bright spotlight was weaving left to right, searching. Terrified, he had stumbled from his hiding spot and sputtered, "Cain, sir. We hit some waves. I was just checking the crates ... making sure they're secure."

The spotlight hit him full in the face and, blinded, he held his hands up to shield his eyes.

"This hold is off limits to crew!" an unfamiliar voice had gruffly replied. Dennis had felt strong fingers grip his neck and, without warning, he was thrust toward the entrance to the hold. "Get your ass topside," the voice had ordered. "I catch you down here again you'll wish you were never born."

The menace in the man's voice had been enough for Dennis to run all the way to his bunk where he stayed for the remainder of the night. What he had seen in the barrel in the split second before he had been discovered had him shaking with fear. They were scheduled to arrive in New York the following morning and he counted the hours as though they were his last, but at eleven o'clock the next morning the salvage vessel was still anchored at sea. Cy had come aboard instead, which was something Dennis had never before witnessed.

The Whiskey Lee

True, Cy may want to see their haul prior to landing, but Dennis felt in his gut that the boss was there because of what he had seen in the hold. And it was bad.

You stupid fuck, Dennis silently berated himself. *Why didn't you just mind your own fucking business?*

Dennis thought back to that moment in the hold, that single glance into the barrel before he had stumbled out. It had taken some time, huddled in the darkness of his cabin, for his brain to put it together. All of the strange things he had seen and heard while on the half dozen or so excursions aboard the ship were starting to make sense. It soon became clear to him what this ship was up to. And now, out of the blue, Cy—the boss man himself—was on board, the day after Dennis had been caught in the hold. He had never felt so threatened.

Ship's Captain Royer came out on deck and was greeted by grim, cold smiles from Cy and his associates. Dennis slipped deeper into the shadows and made his way to the starboard side, out of sight. Alone, he stared into the tumultuous sea, considering the plunge of ten or more feet and his chances of escape. The ramifications played out in his head. He could die from hypothermia before reaching the shore, a quarter mile away, or if he was lucky enough to survive the swim, he would surely be beaten to a pulp on the jagged rocks of the coastline. His choices were grim, but he preferred to lose his life to the sea than to a bullet to his head.

Dennis was jolted from his thoughts by Jackson, a fellow deckhand, who had appeared next to him.

"Captain's looking for you," Jackson said. "He wants you port side."

Dennis stared down at the gray-blue sea, feeling trapped. He fought the urge to vomit, and asked, "What for?"

Jackson shrugged. "Don't know. You do something?" he asked, jokingly.

I was hoping to, Dennis thought. His plan had been to feign illness once back in port, and then disappear—to hell with his pay. He would head west and gain employment on the other side of the country, but he had to get ashore for that to happen.

The sound of the midday meal bell broke the uncomfortable silence. Jackson moved to one side, motioning with his hand for Dennis to lead the way. As they reached the ladder that led to the lower deck where the mess hall was located, a stern voice snapped: "Cain!"

Dennis froze. *Run!* he thought, but there was nowhere to run. He had no way of avoiding the captain's summons, especially not with Jackson on his heels.

"Dennis Cain! Front and center!"

Taking a deep breath, Dennis slowly turned and faced Captain Royer. Cy and his men were with him. A snickering Jackson disappeared down the ladder.

"Thank you, Captain," Cy said quietly, dismissing him. As the captain walked away to join the men on the lower deck, Cy's men moved in closer behind their boss.

Dennis sucked in his breath, feeling Cy's cold hard eyes boring into him like two daggers. The boss's demeanor was disturbingly both relaxed and threatening—cool as a cucumber. Dennis' heart raced. He realized he could be facing his final moments and he silently pleaded with his God for help. With as much courage as he could muster, he met Cy's piercing green eyes and found he couldn't turn away. He had never seen such evil. *Those eyes. I can't escape those eyes. God, please help me!* he thought.

Cy and his men had positioned themselves so the center and stern passageways were blocked. With most of the ship's crew now in the mess on the lower deck, and the captain descending the ladder to join them, Dennis was alone with the three men.

"Ace, Evans, make sure no one gets through!" As Cy barked his orders at the two men standing steadfast in the passageways, beads of sweat rolled down Dennis's ashen face. He was trapped. "Yes boss," one of them answered. Seeing his captain disappear from sight, Dennis screamed inside his head. *Come back! Don't leave me here alone! PLEASE come back!* A choked sob escaped from his trembling lips before everything went black.

1

JUNE 2008 - OTTAWA, CANADA

Brandon was in the middle of transcribing his notes when the phone began to ring. *Machine will get it*, he thought. When the ringing finally stopped, he poured himself his third glass of red wine and sipped it appreciatively. He thought he'd be able to block out the sudden intrusion, but he was wrong. He placed the glass aside and leaned back in his chair, running his fingers through his thick brown hair. His height, confidence, stunning steel-blue eyes, high cheekbones, and killer smile seemed to pave a path for flirtatious attention from the ladies. Unmarried, the alluringly handsome man in his early thirties wasn't in a hurry to settle down. He was enjoying the bachelor life.

Brandon's work had picked him rather than the other way around. During his last year of high school, he had volunteered at the local newspaper as a grunt—filling coffee orders, proofreading, and eventually selling ad space. Although it wasn't a paid position, he had loved observing the uncertainty of the reporters' workdays—they covered everything from corporate events and fundraisers, to traffic accidents and drug busts. It was constant movement and, though not glamorous, Brandon was sucked in hook, line, and sinker. That September he enrolled in the journalism program at Algonquin College and three years later, had graduated with honors. A professor at the college who had become a mentor to Brandon got him some interesting work pulling together a memoir for an old sea captain that, surprisingly enough, made the best-seller list the following year. The success from that project afforded him some enticing, yet short-term job prospects; not completely confident, he decided to stick close to home and took an entry-level position at *The Ottawa Citizen* as a junior copy editor. As the opportunities presented themselves, Brandon was there—he wrote a weekly column covering up-and-coming businesses in the community; he shadowed a crime writer who chased police cars and inspired Brandon to write a six-part series on drug addiction. It was a chance encounter with a dumpster diver that led to an editorial about poverty in the city . . . and the rest was history. Brandon made the huge jump to freelance journalism and life went from interesting to great. He loved his job and the diversity of the subjects available in everyday life, but occasionally he yearned for something a little more adventurous . . . and perhaps dangerous.

When the transcripts were completed, Brandon retrieved the missed message. "Hey Brandon, it's Chad. I got some leads on some dive locations that you may be interested in. Call me back when you get a chance, okay?"

Brandon glanced up at the framed picture on his wall. A warm smile spread across his face as he remembered the day it was taken. He and his best friend Chad had just become certified open water divers. They had pooled their meager savings to travel to the Caribbean and charter a boat to gain some diving experience.

"We need warmth, my friend!" Chad had exclaimed, after a winter of negative double-digit temperatures. Brandon couldn't have agreed more.

For nine days the two friends had lost themselves in island life. Their first evening at the hotel's bar garnered them an introduction to Kai, whose family had been fishing off the coast of the islands for generations. Wearing nothing more than threadbare shorts and beaded dreadlocks, Kai took them around to some choice diving spots, pointing out shipwreck sites along the way. With his help, Brandon and Chad were able to book a two day diving charter, and the experience was worth a thousand times the cost of their trip.

They had known each other since they were kids. Brandon remembered how he and Chad would steal off on their bikes, without their parents knowing, to explore old brickyards and derelict buildings around town. They even spent a few summers snorkeling in the nearby lake, searching for hidden treasures lost beneath the water. Now Chad and his young family lived in Barney's Cove, Maine, where they ran a dive shop. Brandon had only visited once in the few years since Chad had moved there. Barney's Cove was one of the state's prettiest ocean-side villages. Homes and businesses along the shoreline were painted a variety of bright colors, reminding Brandon of his own country's charming fishing community of St John's, Newfoundland, nicknamed Jellybean Row. Much of Barney's Cove's charm came from the wharves and herring smoking sheds clustered around the tidal mouth of the Herring River. At any given time, seals could be seen perched patiently on nearby rocks for an opportunity to raid the heart-shaped fishing weirs. Nearby gulls anxiously awaited their chance to steal fish from unsuspecting victims. Barney's Cove sat within Dack's Bay. It was an area dotted with many small islands and rocks. On the other side of the bay, perched way up on the cliff, was a tall red and white lighthouse. At the bottom of that hill sat the town of Ridgetown.

Brandon had a passion for diving ever since he and Chad went south. His friend had turned him on to diving old shipwrecks.

Hearing Chad's message only fueled his excitement for the sport and he couldn't wait to phone his old friend back.

"Hey man," said Brandon cheerfully, when Chad answered. "Whatcha got for me?"

Chad laughed into the phone. "We're all fine, Brandon . . . thanks for asking! Jeeze! At least I know what to say to get a callback!"

Brandon blushed at the other end of the phone. "Ya got me there. Sorry."

"You still planning a vacation down my way?" Chad asked.

"For sure. I managed to free up some time two weeks from now, if that works."

"Wicked! Accommodations too? You know you're more than welcome to stay at our place."

"Thanks, but it's probably better if I grab a motel. That way my bachelor ways won't disturb anyone." He laughed. "I stay up late, get up at dawn, and make a hell of a mess in the bathroom."

After a few moments of catching up, Chad got to what really interested his friend. "There's material on shipwreck sites that I'd like to send you. Large vessel wrecks. I know a charter boat captain that will take out divers, but you need to reserve the dates with him ASAP."

Brandon felt excitement rising in his chest. "Wow! Fantastic!"

"Thought you'd say that. I'll fill you in once you're here, but there's one boat in particular that I've been searching for: *The Whiskey Lee*. It has some mystery and good ole folklore attached to it so it's quite up your alley. Maybe you'll have more luck finding it than I've had. I'll go out with you as often as I can, but for the days I'm stuck at the shop, my friend Lou can make himself available.

Lou knows the area well and he's a qualified wreck diving instructor. He wasn't living here the last time you visited, otherwise I would have introduced you guys. So, what do you think?"

"Sounds like the Hardy Boys meet Jacques Cousteau." Brandon laughed, truly thrilled by Chad's news.

Brandon hadn't had a real vacation in a long time, so he was able to bank a few extra weeks for this trip. He was growing weary of city life, and the stress of hunting down new stories and trying to sell them was not helping. Now he felt exhilarated, if not compelled, to hit the East Coast and embark on an adventure.

"Email me the charter's contact info and your schedule, and I'll nail down some splash times for us," said Brandon.

After hanging up, Brandon closed his laptop, eased himself back into the soft leather office chair, and put his feet up on his desk. He stared at the photo of him and Chad on the charter. All he could think about was the smell of a salty sea breeze and the thrill of underwater adventure. He imagined himself diving into murky depths, catching a glimpse of an old shipwreck, which would make the entire trip that much more worthwhile. He could barely contain his excitement. *Soon*, he thought. *Only two more weeks.*

After what seemed an eternity, it was finally time to head to the USA. Chad was hooking him up with all the required scuba gear, so Brandon could travel light. With typical bachelor thinking, he packed a toothbrush, a change of clothes, his laptop, phone, a credit card, and the required diving credentials.

Little did he know that his trip to the Pine Tree State would bring with it a level of danger he could never have imagined.

2

Ridgetown, Maine, was pretty much as he'd remembered it, with its plunging coastal cliffs and serene mountain tops.

Brandon parked his rented black Nissan Rogue SUV in the half-filled lot of the Rocky Ridge Motel and made his way to the office. Summer tourists were swarming the East Coast already and decent hotels were booked solid. Brandon had to make do with an out-of-the-way establishment normally geared toward construction workers on contract in the area. Upon entering the office, he noticed it sported the typical seashore motif found in most coastal motels—water color paintings of the town's wharf, and various views of the harbor, all courtesy of local starving artists. He checked in, attached his room key to his own set of keys, and then made his way to his room. When he opened the door, he was happy to find that the room was bright, airy, and clean. It was typical of a mom-and-pop motel: one queen bed, a small sofa from the seventies, a flat screen TV, a wooden side table, and two faded plaid armchairs. The space which probably used to be a closet now sported a sink, and a mini microwave that sat precariously on top of a dented bar fridge. Tired sheer curtains covered the large window, framed by heavy burgundy drapes. The oscillating fan hummed and creaked in the corner. Brandon pulled the sheer curtains aside, heaved open the window, and gazed out at the view.

The motel was perched high up on a rock face that overlooked a small inlet. It was low tide. Gulls circled over the exposed stretch of seabed, searching for stranded morsels. Somewhere beyond Brandon's line of sight, the mournful sound of a tugboat horn called out. He took a deep breath of the fresh air, closed his eyes, and smiled contentedly.

Half an hour later he entered Sea's the Moment dive shop in Barney's Cove. The first thing he noticed was how organized and professional the sales floor was. Displayed on the walls were assorted fins, snorkels, and mask; wet suits hung on steel floor racks and along the walls—thin neoprene suits for warm water; thicker for deeper, colder temperatures; dry suits for extremely cold or freezing waters, all in sizes and colors to satisfy a broad range of underwater enthusiasts. A heavy smell of neoprene hung in the air.

"I'll be right with you!" Brandon heard his friend's voice call out from a back room. The chime above the entrance door alerted staff when someone arrived; clearly Chad was unable to see who his new customer was, and Brandon was thrilled to be able to surprise him.

Moments later, Chad, a tall, gangly blond man, emerged. He stopped along the back wall to adjust a scuba tank that had slipped to one side, before looking up and seeing his old friend standing there. He broke into a huge smile, rushed across the store, and gave Brandon a bear hug.

"My God, you're actually here!" Chad exclaimed.

"In the flesh," Brandon laughingly replied. "Speaking of which, is that your security guard standing over there?" He jerked a thumb toward a pretty brunette clad in full scuba gear near the plate glass window.

Chad laughed. "Yes, and Lucy does a great job for minimal pay!"

"You named your mannequin Lucy?" Brandon answered, raising an eyebrow.

"I sure did. What can I say? I wanted to make the ladies feel welcome. Sherman's over there in the corner." He pointed to another mannequin. "Lucy's my most reliable employee. Always on time and has never taken a day off!" Chad remarked jokingly.

Brandon chuckled, looking around. "Nice outfit you got here," he commented, looking at the merchandise more closely. The store appeared to have everything—from masks, snorkels, and suits, to boots, gloves, weights, and tanks.

"Feel free to browse and make one or ten purchases." Chad laughed. "I just have to finish something in the back and then I'm all yours." He smacked his friend's shoulder gleefully before returning to the back room.

Brandon browsed the store. On the wall behind the checkout counter was a display of some modest treasures, labeled as having been found on dives over the years, with a "NOT FOR SALE – PLEASE DO NOT TOUCH" sign propped in front. There were several framed pictures of tourist group excursions, including

The Whiskey Lee

a beautiful underwater shot of divers exploring a shipwreck, with a reef shark lingering off in the distance. A locked glass display cabinet beneath the cash register offered dive knives with leg strap sheaths, underwater cameras, dive computers, watches, and other accessories for sale. A metal carousel standing near the front window caught Brandon's eye and he moved in for a closer look.

Old newspaper clippings detailing the mysteries surrounding local missing vessels had been carefully reproduced, wrapped in protective plastic, and put out for sale as interest pieces for $10 each. Brandon slowly twirled the carousel, glancing at the bold-faced headline of each story, fascinated.

"Some of those have since been recovered," Chad said, coming up behind Brandon and peering over his shoulder, "but some haven't, including this one here." Chad pulled out one and handed it to Brandon. "This is the one I mentioned on the phone."

Brandon scanned the first paragraph. "*Whiskey Lee*? What's so special about this one?"

Chad shrugged. "The guy was a local, experienced fisherman with a successful business, and a wife and kids. One day—poof! Gone."

Brandon raised an eyebrow. "Married men go missing all the time, for obvious reasons. Was this guy a saint or something?"

Chad grinned. "Probably not, but it was before my time. A couple years ago I was diving and found a lifeboat. No big deal, but what I could make out of the name, it looked to me like *The Whiskey Lee*. I took photos of it, and reported it, but the police more or less brushed it off. Guess they need a dead body before they're interested. I spoke to an Officer Flynn. He's mentioned in the article too. He oversaw the original investigation, but it led nowhere. We talked for a while, but basically, he said there wasn't enough supporting evidence at the time to consider it anything more than a ship lost at sea or a husband on the run. It remains an open case, but no one is interested anymore—wife moved on, people forgot. Even if the lifeboat I found did belong to *The Whiskey Lee*, chances are that maybe a storm took it out to sea and dumped it there, or some such shit. It's dead in the water. No pun intended."

Brandon smiled, continuing to scan the article.

Chad shook his head. "I wish all the letters were legible. You can still see the red paint. It hasn't faded completely, but enough. *The Whiskey Lee* was also red." He shrugged. "I guess it doesn't matter what I think, but I'm eighty percent sure it belongs to *The Whiskey Lee*. Trouble is, the longer it sits down there, the more faded it gets because of exposure. Yet if I bring it up to the surface, it would deteriorate faster, and the story would end there."

"So, it's still down there, where you found it?" Brandon asked.

"Still there, but I took lots of photos of it." Chad quickly crossed the store and pulled a box from the shelf behind the cash register. "Take a look at these."

Brandon shuffled through the box. Chad seemed to have snapped the boat at every possible angle. He pulled a few out and walked to the front window, tilting them in the light, squinting hard at the faded lettering barely visible through the murky water. "Hmm. Tough to make out. How far down?"

"About forty-five feet. The lettering is easier to make out when you're down there. It's just off a wall near a secluded cove north of here, which itself is a mystery to me."

"Why do you say that?" Brandon asked.

"Well, remember there are schooner wrecks in the area? One is in the small rocky bay, just south of where the lifeboat is resting. The other one is near the mouth of Barney's Cove. I took you out to those wrecks the last time you were here."

"Yeah, so what do they have to do with it?" Brandon asked.

"Well, I can see why the schooners sank—they were probably thrown around in a storm and smashed into the rocks, but the bottom of a lifeboat couldn't have hit that ledge or the rocks at Hanlon Cove. Any small boat can float right over the ledge. Mine did. It's well marked. Every smart boat operator knows to stay away from that area. Lots of hazards." Chad frowned. "It sunk on the deep side of the wall, and there doesn't appear to be any damage to its hull."

"Maybe it got away from the wharf where it was tied up, or was stolen by some landlubber," Brandon suggested.

"If so, why would anyone dump it in such a remote place? And why are there rocks inside of it? Weighing it down?"

Brandon raised an eyebrow.

Chad nodded. "Exactly! I found a shovel near there too. There's a lot of mystery surrounding this one, my friend. They never found Captain James Moreland, or his trawler. Not even a trace of either. What's weird is that most people around here won't even mention the name *Whiskey Lee*. Every time I tried to nose around, I got shut down. Some old salt told me they believe there's a curse surrounding it, or some such crap. Apparently, strange things started happening around here after the disappearance and, well, I guess the locals tied them all to *The Whiskey Lee*."

"What kind of strange things?" Brandon asked, flipping through the pictures again.

Chad rolled his eyes. "Ghost sightings, if you can believe it; a couple of suspicious deaths, and lights have been seen at the lighthouse on the point that's been shut down for years . . . that kind of strange."

"Really?" Brandon asked. "And people think these things are related to *The Whiskey Lee*'s disappearance?"

"So, they say, but I haven't really had the time to investigate further. The kids' ballet, hockey, soccer, and baseball became my new hobbies. As for a curse—bullshit. Lightening hasn't struck me dead yet and I'm two years into my search for answers. I haven't quit because that kinda shit only fuels me more. I can't resist a good mystery." He grinned, "And neither can you."

"Get out of my head." Brandon laughed. "Where to start, is the question."

Chad returned the photos to the box and put it away. "Good luck, buddy." He pointed to the article Brandon was still looking over. "Take it with you. Rest assured; you won't get bored out here."

"See what you've done now?" said Brandon, slapping the laminated story on the counter. "I'm already hooked on this."

"If you get some answers, the article is on the house. Otherwise, ten bucks and the cost of my beer tab at the local tavern." Chad grinned.

"Deal!" said Brandon, as they shook on it. "Challenge accepted and by the way, you'll be the one paying *my* beer tab."

Chad nodded and smiled. "Riiiiiiiight," he said.

***

Brandon had secured the charter boat dates with a hefty deposit via wire transfer, the balance to be paid in cash before even leaving the dock. He didn't like carrying that much cash on him, but Chad had explained that that was how business was done in Barney's Cove, especially on short notice.

An inventory snafu at the dive shop forced Chad to bow out of the first day's dives so, as promised, he arranged for his friend Lou to accompany Brandon.

Lou lived his life very much like a wandering Bohemian, and was more than happy to take advantage of free dives. Brandon could sense that the lean, tanned man in his early forties had lots of diving experience.

The two men met at the main—and only—wharf in Barney's Cove. Anderson, their charter boat captain, was expected to arrive soon after he finished fueling up at the gas docks. The morning summer sky was clear and a cool breeze floated in from the bay. Only a handful of small cruising boats were docked, sporting names such as *Owen's Idea*, *Screamin' Sally*, and *Babe Lure*. The local men who earned their living on the sea had sailed out hours before, eager to get a head start on the short fishing season the east coast weather afforded them.

Standing with their gear piled up at the end of the wharf, Brandon and Lou chatted about the day's plan, which was to explore the site of a 1950s passenger ferry that had sunk about five miles south shortly after WWII had ended. As their charter boat came into sight, Brandon pulled Chad's article about *The Whiskey Lee* from his backpack and handed it to Lou. "You familiar with this one?"

Lou pushed his sunglasses up on top of his head and took a quick glance at the headline: "FISHING TRAWLER, CAPTAIN, MISSING." The name on the pictured vessel read *WHISKEY LEE*. The article was dated July 15th, 1989.

Lou nodded. "Sure. Chad's baby." He grinned and handed it back to Brandon.

"What do you know about it?"

"Well, it's a strange puppy, I'll give it that. No evidence to prove it sank and no evidence to prove it didn't. Personally, I think the guy bailed on his wife and kids. At this very moment he could be sitting somewhere on a beach, sipping margaritas, and living the high life." Lou smirked.

"Whiskey," Brandon corrected him.

"What?" Lou asked.

"Whiskey. Sipping whiskey" Brandon smiled.

"Oh yeah! Whiskey, man!" Lou guffawed, slapping his knee as if Brandon had cracked the funniest joke on the planet.

Brandon could see why Chad liked this guy. Lou certainly knew how to keep things light. "What about the other stuff?" Brandon asked, drawing Lou's attention back to *The Whiskey Lee*. "The article reports that not long after Captain Moreland went missing, the local lighthouse keeper was found dead."

Lou nodded. "Shot, apparently. The news on that one died down quick for some reason. They shut the lighthouse down shortly after." Lou tapped the article. "Does it mention the girl?"

Brandon shook his head. "What girl?"

Lou raised his eyebrows. "Chad didn't mention it? Three days after the lighthouse keeper was found dead, fishermen pulled the body of a young pregnant woman out of the harbor not far from there. My aunt told me some arrogant reporter from the city had come in, nosing around, harassing both the families for a big scoop, hoping for some ugly scandal."

"Was there one? A scandal, I mean," Brandon asked.

"Nah. None that he found, anyway. My aunt was friends with one of the girl's relatives and I overheard them talking in the kitchen once, while I was over at their place giving my uncle a hand building the deck. The ladies didn't know I could hear them, but I believe the word *suicide* came up." Lou frowned, staring off into the distance. "You know, I haven't thought about that in years. I just remembered something else, talking about it now. That girl's relative told my aunt that the girl went missing the same night the lighthouse keeper was shot." He paused. "Makes you wonder."

Brandon followed Lou's gaze over the harbor.

"Some of the folks around here believe the old coot may be haunting the lighthouse now," Lou continued, "along with the girl. I have to admit that some strange goings on have been discussed over the years." Lou pointed toward the dilapidated lighthouse in the distance, perched up high atop a moss-covered cliff. "That's the conversation starter over there—Sixteen Fathom Hill Lighthouse, also known as Phantom Hill.

After the shooting, and then the discovery of the girl, no one wanted to go near it. It was eventually padlocked, mainly to keep the kids out. A more sophisticated navigational warning system was already in the making anyway, further out, so I guess the timing was right."

Brandon gazed at the white and red structure receding in the distance, his head full of questions. His thoughts were temporarily suspended by an approaching vessel. "Is that Captain Anderson?"

"Yeah, that's him," Lou confirmed, and then picked up where he had left off. "The strange thing is, I swear I've seen that lighthouse beam shining across the bay some nights. The inside lights seem to go on and off all by themselves too, once in a while. It's pretty spooky, even to me." He shivered.

At that moment, their charter pulled up to the wharf, tied off, and they got busy loading up the gear. As they headed out over the calm waters of Barney's Cove, and across the bay toward their first diving site, Brandon turned to gaze out over the ocean. It reminded him of something from an article he'd read in a diving magazine:

"Something about an ocean is calming. It will draw you toward it with an almost alluring, seductive grasp, but if you're not careful, it will eat you up and swallow you whole."

Shaking off the macabre mood Lou had created, Brandon turned his attention back to the day's excursion. He couldn't wait to get in the water. They quickly suited up after finding their dive site, and then lowered the anchor. "It's a good day to dive," said Brandon.

"It's always a good day when I'm diving." Lou beamed.

After setting the dive flag, the two men each did a giant stride entry off the back of the boat. The currents were a problem, especially near the surface, but once they started descending things got a little easier. Two sets of streaming breathing bubbles rose to the surface as they swam parallel to each other toward the ocean floor. Visibility was in the fifteen-to-twenty-foot range, and marine life was plentiful. Lou tapped Brandon on the shoulder and pointed to their right, where a small lobster scurried away, surprised by the two divers. Brandon nodded his appreciation of the sight and thanked himself for finally shaking off the confines of his home office and taking the trip to Maine.

At ninety feet, Brandon and Lou reached the sea floor. If the coordinates were right, they should be in the vicinity of the sunken ferry. After just a few minutes, a large, looming shape appeared in front of them, startling them both. The divers pulled up short, staring. Signaling with his hand, Lou began swimming toward the spellbinding shape before them.

The outline was unmistakably that of an old ferry. It was resting on its port side, its hull partially buried in sand. Mollusks and various plants clung to it; fine, feathery lichen, clinging to the structure, moved gracefully in the current, as if part of an underwater dance put on just for the divers.

Brandon eased closer with his camera, which was mounted on the end of an adjustable stick. Small fish and other aquatic life had already claimed this vessel as their own. From afar it resembled a small living reef. It was a peaceful scene, an eternal watery grave from yesteryear given a new lease on life as a natural undersea habitat.

Brandon's camera snapped incessantly, capturing images of a world many never got to witness in person. A past not forgotten.

3

REWIND – THE INVESTIGATION – 1989

Officer Flynn parked his cruiser in the gravel drive, grabbed his notebook from the passenger seat, and walked purposefully toward the two-story white clapboard house that belonged to James Moreland. The engine ticked loudly as it cooled. He ascended five wooden steps, to a dirty aluminum screen door, and knocked. Inside he heard movement and after a few seconds a tired-looking brunette in a yellow robe approached the door. The skin around her blue eyes was dark and swollen. She looked a mess.

"Mrs. Moreland? I'm Officer Flynn. I'd like to talk to you about your husband, James."

The woman pushed open the screen door and stood aside as Flynn entered the house. Out of courtesy, he removed his hat and nodded his thanks.

"You can call me Kathleen," she said in a husky voice, pushing stringy hair away from her face. "Living room is to your left. Can I get you a coffee or something, Officer?"

A week before, when the police had first responded to Kathleen's call about her missing husband James and his fishing trawler, they had been polite and taken down the few details that she could provide. Two young men who crewed for James part-time were also questioned. It wasn't common for the fifty-foot trawler to have more than one other person on board to help. It depended on how much of a haul the trawler was catching on weekly basis. Sometimes the numbers didn't make it worthwhile for the captain to hire an extra crew member, so he would go out alone.

A search party had been organized on both land and sea, with no results. The Coast Guard had been informed, along with authorities one hundred miles north and south of Barney's Cove, on the off chance that Captain Moreland or his boat should turn up. So far, there had been no sightings and Flynn felt tempted to believe what the rest of his department had already taken as the gospel truth—that the good captain had found warmer shores in which to moor his ship. Out of respect for the young mother of three, Flynn had decided to interview Kathleen Moreland one more time, on his own.

Officer Flynn sat on the edge of a faded blue sofa waiting for Kathleen to return with the coffee, which he'd politely accepted. He looked around the room, unimpressed. The walls were adorned with dark wood paneling that was coming away in spots. A floor-model television from the 70s sat in a corner, muted but tuned in to The Price is Right. Crocheted doilies and thrift store knick-knacks decorated the coffee table, leaving little room for the coffee mug she eventually brought to him. School photos of the kids sat atop the TV, but no wedding pictures of the Moreland's were in sight. Flynn waited until the woman had settled herself in the brown recliner to his right before he spoke.

"Mrs. Moreland—um, Kathleen—I want to tell you that my department is doing everything possible to locate your husband. We've got everyone along the coast on the lookout, and bulletins have been dispatched to every vessel, small and large, in hopes someone comes across *The Whiskey Lee* in their travels."

Kathleen nodded her head in appreciation but said nothing. Flynn cleared his throat, continuing.

"Can you tell me a little bit about James? His business, if he has hobbies, friends he hangs out with, that kind of thing?"

Kathleen took a deep drag of her cigarette and nodded again. "James had two hobbies: boats and drinking." She chuckled to herself. "I should have clued in when he christened that damned thing."

She explained to Flynn that James had started building his fifty-foot fishing trawler from a steel trawler building kit when he was in his early twenties. They had enough inherited land to accommodate the hulking cradle and trawler, so space wasn't a problem. On the other hand, the harsh winters were another story. It had been his dream to custom build a trawler and work for himself. The project had taken him eight long years to complete. James had worked full time during those years to support her and their growing family, while spending every spare moment in the yard working on his precious trawler.

Kathleen and their kids never saw him, save for mealtime or when he was passed out stone-cold tired from putting in all those hours.

"That must have put a tremendous strain on your relationship," Flynn commented. "Is it fair to say that you and your husband grew apart during those years?"

Kathleen noticeably stiffened in the chair. "Yes, it's fair, but what was I supposed to do about it? He was going to build that damned thing with or without my blessing, so I put up with it." She put her cigarette out and immediately lit another. She said in a quiet voice, "I wondered sometimes if he kept knocking me up just to keep me busy and out of his hair."

Flynn blushed, lost for words.

Kathleen gazed across the room at the TV. She said in a hollow tone, "I suppose you figure the same as everyone else in town . . . that I drove James out. That he ran off in some drunken fit, into the arms of a lusty, busty barmaid, to sail the seven seas. To hell with the wife and kids, the mortgage, the bills."

"Is that what you think?" Flynn gently prodded.

Kathleen turned and stared Flynn in the eyes. "Things were not good between us, I'll admit that. And though I can't prove it, something—or someone—had put a spring in his step these past months, and it sure as hell wasn't me." She leaned toward him now, her jaw clenched, her eyes wide. "But I can tell you one thing for sure, Officer Flynn—something had James so scared, so terrified these past weeks! He'd jump at the slightest sound, and nightmares . . ." She shuddered. "A few times he woke up screaming, his arms waving in the air like he was fighting someone off. It took all I had to wake him, to calm him down. I have no idea what could frighten a man so, but James doesn't scare easy, Officer Flynn. And now he's gone, without a trace."

Flynn's surprise was evident. "Do you know of anyone who might have wanted to hurt James? Someone he did business with, maybe?"

"I don't know of anyone who wanted to hurt him," Kathleen sighed. "He was a loner, spent all his time fishing. When he drank, he would sleep it off on the boat. No one ever came here to see him and he never went anywhere."

Flynn nodded and stood up to take his leave.

"Wait, I just remembered there was something else," she said nervously.

"What?" Flynn asked.

"James said he thought the trawler had been boarded a few days before he disappeared."

"What gave him reason to think that?"

"He said the cabin was a mess; things were strewn about like it had been ransacked or something. He swore he never left it in that condition."

"Oh? Was there anything missing?" Flynn asked.

"No. He probably would have mentioned if anything was missing. James thought he'd left the hatch door unlocked and maybe racoons got inside and tossed the cabin looking for food."

Flynn made some quick notes in his notebook. "Thanks. That may be of some importance. Anything helps. I appreciate your candor, Kathleen. I'm sure this is a very difficult time for you and we're doing all we can."

Kathleen walked him to the door. "I wish things were the same from when me and James first met," she lamented sadly, "but sometimes people change and there's just no going back. Me and the kids have played second fiddle to that boat from day one and we learned to live with it." She smiled tiredly. "I had sometimes wished over the years that there was another woman—she I could compete with, but not a boat."

Flynn said nothing. He opened the door and stepped outside.

"Find what scared him, Officer Flynn, and you'll find James." She turned and walked inside.

Kathleen had been right—after asking around, Flynn learned that James was a loner and didn't appear to have friends he chummed with. As a matter of fact, there was really only one thing people did know about him: Captain James Karl Moreland would never go fishing without having his lucky drink, whiskey on the rocks, the night before. *Old habits never die, but maybe this time the Whiskey found the rocks after all,* Flynn thought.

Kathleen's last words to Flynn had rattled him, and for some reason he couldn't accept a simple drunken accident at sea as the final conclusion to James's disappearance. Surely something from the boat would have floated to the surface and been found by now, or been washed ashore with the tide. He sighed with frustration, and headed his cruiser back into town. Flynn wanted to get a handle on James Moreland, the whiskey drinker, and what better place to start than at the local watering hole. *Someone may remember seeing him that night, maybe even saw someone talking to him. Perhaps someone who frightened him,* Flynn thought.

***

"He never talked much but, yeah, I served him a few times," a young busty girl in her twenties told Flynn when he showed her a picture of James Moreland. "He seemed nice enough. Tipped well."

"Did he flash his money around? Buy drinks for anyone else? Play pool with the boys?" Flynn asked.

"No, no. Always sat alone in a booth, by the window. He seemed sort of private, and almost shy in a way."

"Were you working July 13th? That was Thursday of last week."

The girl tilted her head to one side, trying to remember. "Mmmm . . . the 13th. I usually only work the weekend shifts, but yeah, just so happened I worked it. Took Jen's shift. Her kid came down with the flu, so I covered."

"Was Captain Moreland here that night? Do you recall?"

"I don't think so. He usually stood out simply because he was always alone, so I'd remember. Sorry."

Officer Flynn nodded and let her get on with her shift.

After leaving the bar, Flynn dejectedly drove back to the station house, Kathleen's words at the forefront of his mind: "Find what scared him and you'll find James."

Eventually, just about everyone in the town had been questioned, and the police were no further ahead in their investigation.

As the days followed, things took a turn. The search had to be called off for a couple of consecutive evenings around half past eight due to inclement weather. As time went on and relatives pinned their hope on that one last flight by the Coast Guard, hearts grew sad as the chances diminished that James would make it back alive. Knowing that he had both a life raft and a lifeboat greatly increased his chances for survival at sea, but as the days went forward, the hearts of searchers were breaking. One week later, the search became a recovery mission. The tears of relatives turned to confusion and anger. The *Whiskey Lee* case became a lower priority—was moved to the back burner, as some would put it—when William Irving, the caretaker of the lighthouse for the last twenty plus years, and Flynn's friend—was found dead. He'd been shot to death. Three days later, fishermen found a young woman drowned, wedged deep in the rocks below the very same lighthouse, known as Sixteen Fathom Hill.

Flynn found himself knee-deep in an emotional investigation that was not only close to home but made no sense whatsoever.

By early fall, the police were forced to issue a press release wherein they confirmed all searches for *The Whiskey Lee* had been halted. No new information had come to light, and Captain James Moreland was considered lost at sea, along with his fishing vessel. The community and all those involved in the search were thanked and the file was placed on a shelf.

Officer Flynn, as he was known then, reluctantly gathered his notes and filed them away. One more drive by the Moreland's home left him feeling deflated and inadequate—a *For Rent* sign was stuck unceremoniously on the front lawn. Kathleen Moreland and her kids had moved on. There was nothing here for them anymore.

4

REWIND – BEFORE THE DISAPPEARANCE – 1989

Ann Marie remembered the first time she had seen James Moreland. She was covering a co-worker's shift, tying an apron around her waist, when the bell above the café's front door jingled. She looked up and there he was. It wasn't his rugged good looks or deeply tanned skin that caught her attention, though both were extremely attractive. No—it was the air of confidence that he exuded, like he owned the room the second he entered it. He had an easy, straight-backed stride that made him appear even taller than he was. He wore dark sunglasses, which he removed as he made his way to a two-seater in the smoking section, near the window. He glanced toward the lunch counter, caught Ann Marie's eye and smiled. Ann Marie felt frozen in time, like the entire room disappeared and it was just her and this stranger. She was captivated by his mere presence, a feeling that would only grow with time.

Ann Marie discovered that James ate breakfast alone at the café every Saturday and Sunday morning. Afterwards, he'd light up a cigarette. He looked content whenever she made eye contact with him. Ann Marie normally preferred to have weekends off but she was so inexplicably drawn to this man that she traded shifts with one of the other waitresses just so she could see him. It made no sense to her at all. But there it was.

In time, she and James were chatting regularly. She found herself blushing each time he smiled at her. She hung on his every word, though to anyone eavesdropping, the conversation was anything but interesting. Light chitchat, a few teasing jokes, and an easy banter between two people who clearly enjoyed each other's company.

After a couple of visits, they exchanged names. Ann Marie felt comfortable confiding in James about her recently failed relationships. She didn't understand if it was her, or the guys that she had chosen to date. At first, she just wanted a friend to talk to. He was a good listener. Their polite back-and-forth soon turned familiar as they learned more about one another.

***

Normally James would immerse himself in the newspaper while eating breakfast at the café, but these days he found himself more interested in the young woman who served him. He was intrigued by this girl. She was intelligent, creative, and hard working, but she lacked self-confidence. A string of bad choices in men had broken down her self-esteem and he felt compelled to build it back up again with heartfelt compliments. In turn, she made him feel like a blushing, bumbling teenager with her unabashed admiration of him and her naive belief that his "words of wisdom" were gold. He basked in her attention and the feeling was obviously mutual, from what he could tell.

The fact that he was married didn't appear to be an issue for either of them. He was honest with Ann Marie, or at least as honest as he could be with himself—he was no longer happy in his marriage, and he felt empty and dead inside as a result. Sharing such a personal part of himself with a virtual stranger both confused and excited him. Ann Marie was so easy to talk to, so attentive, so understanding. Before long he found himself crossing a line he had thus far avoided like the plague.

He asked Ann Marie if she'd join him for a drink after a Saturday shift; they agreed on an out-of-the-way roadhouse on Coastal Route #1.

They met at the side of the café after closing, taking only one vehicle out to the roadhouse. Out of her element, Ann Marie was particularly shy and fidgety. James, knowing what he felt, remained calm and confident, and he delicately came to the point.

"You know I adore you," he told her, leaning across the table and touching her hand.

Ann Marie blushed deeply; her eyes were riveted on his.

"I know what I want," he continued, stroking her hand with a finger. "If you want out, just say so. I'll understand and no hard feelings."

Ann Marie stared into his eyes long and hard. Her gut told her to run. Her heart answered for her. "No. I don't want out."

Just then a burst of loud, high-pitched laughter filled the room and heads turned to look.

Ann Marie's heart sank when she recognized one of the café's waitresses making her way to the bar, with an entourage of giggling, intoxicated young women. Before Ann Marie could shield her face, her co-worker spotted her and James together, squealing an "Oh my god!" before stumbling over to their table.

"Why, Ann Marie, you little devil! I always took you for playing on the other team!" She wrapped her arm around James's shoulders and put her face close to his. "When it's time for baby girl here to go home to Mommy, you come see me . . . I'll be at the bar." Winking at Ann Marie, the woman turned and swaggered back toward her friends. Ann Marie was fuming inside. When she glanced at James, she noticed he was smiling; it was obvious he was enjoying the attention. Before Ann Marie could utter a word, he turned and made eye contact with her. The smile immediately faded from his face. It was as if he could read the boiling emotions rising from deep within her. He stood up, grabbing his truck keys in one sweeping motion. "Come on," he said. "We'll continue our conversation where it's more private."

Once back in town, James turned onto a gravel road, which Ann Marie knew led to the docks where the fishing boats were moored. Her heart was racing. After a few moments, the wharf came into sight, lit by a string of hanging metal fixtures and in the distance, a beam of light from the lighthouse beacon cast its glow across the mouth of the harbor. James parked the truck, and they walked in silence down the wharf to the docks, until he stopped in front of a fishing trawler named *The Whiskey Lee*. "This is me," he said, climbing aboard. He reached for her hand and helped her onto the deck.

The galley was typical of a working fisherman—worn, messy, and utilitarian. On the right side was a full-sized fridge, a toaster oven, and a collapsible galley table which had fishing gear strewn across it. In front of that was the cockpit, with a fancy wooden ship's wheel. Big windows surrounded the cabin. "Sorry about the mess," James said, ducking his head as he moved around. He fired up a couple kerosene lanterns and motioned for Ann Marie to sit down on the cushioned bench that ran the length of the small space. "Watch your head on the television," he warned. A small television-VCR combo was attached to an extendable bracket which could be swiveled 180 degrees. Placing a hand on it, he guided it backward into the corner and locked it into place.

"I'll see if I can find some good music for us to listen to," he said, as he reached for the tuning dial on the AM/FM radio. Eventually strains of classic 50s music filled the air.

James chuckled an apology. "Not much else comes in down here, I'm afraid." He sat beside Ann Marie on the bench seat.

It didn't take long before James was stroking her hair and kissing her softly. Ann Marie felt completely out of control and unable to determine just what exactly was expected of her. The word *affair* flung itself into her mind, and it frightened her. As she became more aroused by his touch, she ignored the little voice that told her it was wrong to be with him, a married man. She dropped her guard completely and let her heart take charge. She pulled her T-shirt up and over her head, letting it fall to the deck.

"No, no, no, Ann Marie," James whispered, picking it up and handing it back to her. "Put it back on. That's not what this is."

Confused and embarrassed, Ann Marie did as he said and slumped against the cushions. James took her hand in his and kissed her fingers gently.

"I thought you wanted—" she began.

James shook his head. "Not yet. I want to, really bad, but not yet." He pulled her close to his chest and wrapped his arms around her. "I like *this*. I like just talking and I love being with you. I want that all the time. It's so easy to be with you. I feel so comfortable around you."

Ann Marie may not have realized it until much later, but that's when she fell in love with James Moreland.

They spent the next hour embraced in each other's arms, talking and laughing, lost in the solitude of their togetherness, totally at ease with one another.

Reluctantly, Ann Marie announced that she had to get home.

James nodded. Before Ann Marie could ascend to the deck, James took her by the hands and looked deeply into her eyes. "I don't want to get hurt," he told her with intense seriousness.

Ann Marie was taken aback. *She* was the one who could get hurt. His raw, emotional statement was almost a plea. Her heart melted completely. Shaking her head, Ann Marie promised that he would never have to worry about that from her. "Complete honesty," she said. "That's what I want. Complete honesty, always."

***

As the weeks passed, Ann Marie and James spent every spare moment together. He thought of her constantly. He'd be out on his boat, fully engaged in the job at hand, and thoughts of Ann Marie would pop into his head. Something she'd said, or the silly face she'd make when he shared something goofy. A big grin would appear on his face and he couldn't help but feel on top of the world. She brought out the best in him and he couldn't help but try to do the same for her. James didn't go to the bar as much, after meeting Ann Marie. His weekly consumption of alcohol had lowered significantly.

***

For Ann Marie, her world instantly became huge and full of possibilities. James pushed her to come out of her shell and stand strong and confident in a world that was too eager to hold a person down. One afternoon, she had nervously shown him a few watercolor paintings she had done. In a burst of excitement, she explained the different techniques that could produce dazzling moonlight on the water, and she talked so fast and so intently that James had to pull her into him and kiss her hard to stop the chatter. He loved everything about her and told her so at every chance. She felt there was nothing she couldn't do as long as James was in her life.

When a nasty rainstorm had blown in from the north, producing gale winds at fifty knots, forcing all vessels to remain ashore, James and Ann Marie took full advantage. They spent the day on his boat, their bodies entwined under the blankets, the boat heaving beneath them as the stormy waves beat the shoreline. "I am so in love with you," James whispered, his fingers stroking Ann Marie's hair. She sighed, snuggling her face against his.

"We have such a connection," he continued, kissing her nose. "You're my best friend, you know that?"

Ann Marie sat up, the blanket falling from her bare body. She stroked his face as he rested his head on the pillow, looking up at her. Her fingertips caressed his forehead, followed the line of his jaw, and lingered on his half open lips. She wanted to remember everything about him—every line and curve. His eyes closed, and he smiled. Ann Marie couldn't find the words to express how she felt. Her tender touch on his body was all she could do to convey her immense love for him.

5

MAINE – PRESENT DAY – 2008

Brandon maneuvered cautiously along the seabed, careful not to disturb too much of the marine life on and around the sunken ferry. Despite the numerous dives he had embarked upon over the years, he was so deeply moved by this subterranean world, that every time felt like the first time. It boggled his mind to know that over 3000 species of marine life, from Nova Scotia to Cape Cod, Massachusetts, call this home—from sea lettuce, brittle stars, and kelp, to flounder, lobster, and thresher sharks. Though danger lurked in every corner of this murky darkness, one could not help but appreciate the absolute tranquility of this remote and seldom explored habitat. Brandon glanced over at Lou and saw that he was being given the thumbs-up—time to return to the surface. He shot a few hurried photos before the two ascended topside.

"That was fucking fantastic!" Brandon exclaimed with a huge smile, after he and Lou had resurfaced. Lou smiled back, pulling his oxygen tank off and handing it up to the captain who was waiting to assist them back onboard.

"Just another form of high my friend," Lou replied, his index finger and thumb held up to his lips in parody.

"I could stay down there forever," Brandon admitted, as he clambered up the ladder and fell onto the deck, exhausted but exhilarated.

"Me too," Lou grinned. He checked the air gauge on his tank. "Just under 500 PSI left. God, I'm good!" He laughed, leaning back in the sun.

The captain shook his head at the two men as if they were crazy. "Never understood how anyone can strap a metal canister to their back, suck on a hose, and throw themselves down there." He nodded toward the water. "I wouldn't trust that contraption in the bathtub, let alone the sea."

"Science, my good man," Lou answered as he peeled off his wetsuit. "Oxygen, nitrogen, and a small amount of trace gases—all that fun stuff." Lou held up his arm and pointed to his wrist. "This baby is a good toy to have."

"A watch?" The captain asked.

"It's a dive computer," Lou corrected him. "It provides the diver with real-time dive information, and continuously informs them how much dive time they have left."

Captain Anderson shook his head. "Nuts." He turned and walked back to the helm while Brandon and Lou smirked at one another.

Lou organized their gear as Brandon double checked his video camera to make sure it was working okay.

A sudden piercing sound of an alarm drew their attention toward the control panel. "What the hell is that?" Brandon asked, startled.

Captain Anderson was looking at a device on the boat's instrument panel, beckoning to his passengers to join him. When they did, the captain pointed to a digital barometer. "Sudden drop in the barometric air pressure," he said.

"What does that mean?" Brandon asked.

The captain dialed his radio to the marine weather channel. The report wasn't good; a bad storm was brewing east of their position.

"Severe thunderstorms and strong winds in effect for this afternoon and evening," the automated voice broadcasted. Several areas were noted as being in the path of the storm, theirs included.

"We'll have to head inland," the captain said. "Sorry guys. The wind's changed direction and the storm is headed our way. We're done for today."

The words were barely out of his mouth when they noticed a sudden shift in the wind and a gray sky moving in. The boat's flags lifted, dropped, lifted again and then changed direction several times. The captain pointed to the east. "Here she comes!"

Brandon and Lou looked out to where the captain was pointing. Just above the horizon, the clouds were orange and puffy in the middle of a dark gray backdrop. They were turning slowly, as if being cranked by the devil himself. Thin bolts of lightning danced through the center of the mass, in a spectacular light show. The flashing streaks jumped back and forth, threatening to escape and wreak havoc upon anything in their way. Deep rumbles of thunder sounded as the sky continued to darken.

"I've marked our location on my GPS if you want to pick up tomorrow where we've left off," offered Captain Anderson.

The three men looked out at the increasingly volatile expanse of sky, as the storm crept in. Bolts of lightening were coming faster and thicker, before unleashing a stellar and powerful show. Thunder barreled its way across the sky, the sound not much different from that of Taiko drummers.

Though disappointed that they had to cut the dive short, Brandon and Lou nodded in unison. They secured their gear, pulled up the anchor, and Captain Anderson set a course to get them back to the harbor as quickly as possible.

They were only back on land a short time when the storm hit with a fury. Trees and power lines were downed, and moored vessels thrashed against docks, heaving and pulling violently on the cleats to which they were tied. Ten-foot waves crashed ashore, dragging debris into the sea's clutches, only to angrily toss broken pieces back again.

Brandon had made it to his motel room just as the sky burst forth a cold pelting rain. He pushed his room door hard against the howling wind, and as a precaution, shoved the wooden desk chair beneath the doorknob. A few flicks of the light switch on the wall proved the storm had already taken out the motel's power. Brandon stood in front of the picture window, but it was fruitless trying to see anything outside, for the amount of water slamming against the glass. He threw himself down on the bed, folded his arms beneath his head, and listened to the wrath of Mother Nature outside. It was spiteful. Storms on the coast were known to be a bitch, but boredom and a growling stomach nudged Brandon into action. He remembered that there was a tavern down the road, and though he might only get deli sandwiches for supper, no electricity was necessary to fill a glass of spirits. He had a better shot at getting in there than anywhere along the shoreline. Most of the businesses along the coast were receiving a thrashing and had already closed their storm shutters.

When he arrived at the tavern's parking lot, he noticed it was dotted with half a dozen vehicles, mostly pickup trucks that had seen better days. The edges of the faded green fabric awning over the entrance were flapping precariously in the wind, the center of the awning dipping dangerously low from the weight of the rain that had accumulated within it. Above that, the faded old sign had a painting of a sandpiper in one corner and a pelican on the opposite side. Below it was a themed entrance with what looked like a boat dock leading its way up to the front door. To the right, was a thick, twisted manila rope linked from the building to part of a tree trunk meticulously carved into a pelican; it sat atop a dock post to give the entrance an appealing nautical theme.

Brandon parked the SUV close to the entrance, counted to three, and made a hasty—if not embarrassingly—rapid dash toward it. He had barely stepped inside the darkened establishment before the large wooden door slammed against his back from the force of the wind. Brandon was thrown forward a few steps, and someone inside chuckled. A few men were seated together at the bar, illuminated by two kerosene lamps and a tray of candles. An attractive young woman with long strawberry-blonde hair was busy behind the bar, washing up glasses while good-naturedly bantering with the men. She glanced up at Brandon as he took a stool at the end. Their eyes met and she dried her hands and walked toward him.

"Hello" she greeted him pleasantly. "I've never seen you in here before. Storm blow you in?" she teased.

Brandon smiled. "Vacation," he answered.

"Bet this wasn't in the brochure." She laughed, her head tilting toward the window where the rain was beating hard. "I'm Gloria. I'd shake your hand but . . ." She nodded toward the sink full of glasses. "Beer. Kind of up to my elbows in stickiness."

"So, if you were a 'gangsta,' your name would be Sticky Fingers." He grinned.

Gloria laughed. "Gloria 'Sticky Fingers' McEwan. Huh. I like that." Her eyes sparkled in the glowing candlelight.

"Brandon Summers," he said, pointing to his chest. "It's nice to meet you, Gloria."

"And you, Brandon. Might be a challenge coming up with a 'gangsta' name for you. Not enough info—yet." She winked. "Where are you staying?"

"At the Rocky Ridge Motel," Brandon replied.

"You on a break, Glo? I'm dying of thirst!" one of the men at the other side of the bar called out, causing the others to chuckle.

"Keep your hip waders on, Bob! I'll be with you in a minute," Gloria called out over her shoulder. She rolled her eyes at Brandon. "So, what's your poison, stranger? Keep in mind, I have nothing with umbrellas or fancy fruit."

The Whiskey Lee

A deafening crack of thunder filled the air. "That was a good one." Gloria shuddered.

"Yeah, this storm is pretty nasty," Brandon answered, glancing back at the window. "You have any amber ale on tap?"

"Pint?" Gloria asked. "Yes, thanks," he answered, reaching for his wallet.

Gloria reached across and put her hand on his arm. "No worries. I'll start a tab for you. You won't be going anywhere anytime soon." With another wink, she walked away to get his and Bob's drinks.

Typical of a tavern, the main fare was hot wings and fries. With no power to cook them, Gloria could only offer bowls of pretzels and nuts. "So, where you from, sailor?" Gloria asked Brandon when she returned with his pint.

"Canada," he replied, taking a sip. "Ontario, specifically, but I'm on the road a lot."

Gloria raised an eyebrow. "Sales?"

Brandon laughed. "You could say that. I'm a journalist. The goal is to sell, yes."

"And you needed an exotic vacation in the sun and sand and ended up here?" She shook her head. "Boy, did you make a wrong turn."

Brandon chuckled. "Actually, I'm into muck, rotting wood, and shriveled fingertips. I dive for fun."

It was Gloria's turn to laugh. "I guess that beats an igloo in the Great White North."

Brandon winced, good naturedly. "I'll pretend I didn't hear that."

Gloria snapped her bar towel against his arm. "I couldn't resist. Actually, I've been all over the world." She leaned on the bar and rested her chin on her hand.

Brandon raised his eyebrows. "Really? Wow, I'm impressed."

Gloria winked. "Only in my dreams, but I would love to travel the world one day."

Gloria excused herself and then disappeared into the back for a few minutes. As it turned out, she hadn't been anywhere except for a family vacation in Florida when she was a kid, and a camping trip in upstate New York as a Girl Guide. Gloria was born and raised near Ridgetown, and tough times in her family forced her to start working right out of high school. She was tired of seeing the same people day in and day out, and also had the sea in her blood. Living anywhere else hadn't crossed her mind, though traveling the world was most definitely a dream she held on to tightly.

"Can I tell you something embarrassing?" Gloria asked, after returning from the back room. She leaned over the counter toward Brandon, her voice low.

He could smell her perfume—light and floral. The candles on the bar were burning low and in their soft, yellow glow, her eyes were dark and sultry.

He nodded clumsily.

"I'm Brandy," she whispered.

Brandon blinked. "What?"

"I'm Brandy" she repeated. "You know—like in the song."

Brandon stared into her eyes, at a loss. He shook his head and shrugged. "Bob!" she fondly called out. "What's D11 on the juke?"

From the other end of the bar, Bob snickered. "A goddamned pain in my ass that, by Jesus, if I hear it again, I'll puke!" Everyone burst out laughing at Bob's retort, including Gloria.

"If you warm a stool in here again before you head home," she said to Brandon, "I'll play it for you. Kind of hard right now, being as there's no electricity."

Brandon finished his pint, paid Gloria, and promised to come back again to hear D11. Not wanting to leave the warmth and company of the tavern, he reluctantly stepped out into the storm, which was beginning to lose strength. Brandon's room was stuffy and humid without the air conditioning working. He splashed cold water on his face and, grabbing the complimentary bottle of mouthwash, rinsed his mouth out. He found himself smiling into the mirror as he thought of Gloria.

By early evening the storm had subsided, but some gusting wind still remained. It had turned to a cooler breeze. Brandon opened the door to his room, allowing in the fresh coolness. He dropped down on the bed and closed his eyes.

"***Baby's crying***," a hollow, deep voice drifted in from outside. Brandon's eyes flew open. He sat up, startled from sleep, feeling the hair on the back of his neck standing on end. A bolt of lightening sliced through the sky, illuminating the motel room just long enough for him to see the dark silhouette of a man standing in the open threshold.

"Who are you?" he stammered, not sure if he was awake or dreaming.

"***Baby's crying***," the voice repeated into the darkness. Another flash of light filled the sky, followed by a far-away rumble of thunder. As quickly as the figure had appeared, it was gone. Brandon leaped from the bed and ran outside. He looked left and right along the soaked wooden porch that ran the length of the motel. No one was in sight. He shivered and closed the door, latching the deadbolt. His heart was pounding in his chest. *Was I dreaming?* he asked himself. As the quiet of the room enveloped him, Brandon thought for a moment that he heard the faint sound of a baby crying. He held his breath, ears tuned in, focusing. It had stopped. The only thing he heard was the pouring and dripping rain water in the eaves trough, and the gusting wind howling its way through the gap in the door.

6

The next morning, the town was in full clean-up mode, picking up tree branches and debris strewn over properties, vehicles, and the main road. The local electric company had dispatched line crews in the night, once the storm had passed, to secure and repair downed wires. One house at a time, power was being restored. The Rocky Ridge was back up and running by dawn and Brandon woke to a sunny, cloudless morning.

Unfortunately, the phone service would take longer to repair and Brandon had no way of contacting Chad or Lou to find out if their scheduled splash time for that morning was still a go. It was only after he'd reached for his mobile phone that he realized his battery was critically low. *Great!* he thought, shaking his head.

He decided to take a drive down to the wharf where Captain Anderson had moored the day before. If he couldn't find him, he'd drive over to the dive shop to visit Chad. Brandon maneuvered the SUV carefully down the slight incline leading to the docks, dodging broken lobster traps, tossed buoys, and torn netting. He had had no idea the storm had been this destructive—along the shoreline he saw seaweed, half a foot thick, resting in sausage-shaped mounds, slowly drying under the warm sun. Smaller boats, whether moored along the length of the wharf or anchored offshore, had succumbed to the violent waves and lay on their sides, helplessly bobbing in the surf. Debris floated everywhere and Brandon could only shake his head at what was just yesterday a beautiful little bay. As he parked, a gray minivan with dark tinted windows pulled up along side of him, and Chad stepped out. "Thought you'd be here. Change of plans," Chad said as he gazed out over the bay.

"I figured as much," Brandon replied. "This is crazy." Chad nodded, looking around.

"It's going to take everyone some time to get back on track. Captain Anderson included."

"So, what's your plan?" Brandon asked.

"If you're into a wall dive today, we can go out to that sunken lifeboat I told you about. It's a little north of here, at Hanlon Cove."

"Count me in!"

"Okay. Well, it's only accessible by boat," Chad explained. "We've got an eighteen-foot RIB sitting back at the shop. It only has a 25 hp, but it will get us up the coastline and onto the rock ledge without damaging anything, including us."

Brandon looked confused. "RIB?"

"Zodiac, sorry. RIB is short for Rigid Inflatable Boat," Chad informed him. "It's pretty calm today, but to be on the safe side, we can anchor near the shoreline and swim out to the wall."

"What about the gear? Lou and I left it all with Anderson yesterday," Brandon asked.

Chad grinned. "Picked it up when I saw him earlier. Good to go. Just have to head back to the shop for the Zodiac. Meet you back here in about an hour?"

"If you've got a spare car phone adapter lying around, could you bring it?" Brandon asked. "My phone's dead—I wasn't able to charge it last night."

Chad inspected his friend's phone.

"Roger that. I think we have one at the house that'll fit."

They headed in opposite directions, Brandon to a little family-run place called the Saucy Egg Café, where he hoped to get a bite to eat and some strong coffee to wake him up.

As he walked through the door, his taste buds were aroused by the aroma of various breakfast smells. Brandon ordered coffee, bacon, eggs, and toast. Only a handful of customers sat in the booths near the windows, most of the town still working on the clean up. A small television in the corner was broadcasting the Boston news. Brandon kept one ear on it as he dove into his breakfast.

"Anything else?" the matronly waitress asked as she took away his plate.

"No thanks, that was great. Can't dive on a full belly," said Brandon, patting his stomach.

"Diving for your boat?" she asked, a sympathetic smile on her wrinkled face. "We haven't had a storm like that in some time."

"I'm visiting" he explained. "I came down to dive shipwrecks." The woman's inquisitiveness was evident, so he decided to throw it out there. "Going to a site today that may help lead to solving the *Whiskey Lee* disappearance."

Brandon heard the sharp clanging of cutlery dropping on china behind him. The waitress jumped, startled. A burly man with red hair brushed past her, his eyes meeting Brandon's just long enough to convey unspoken menace. He pushed the door open angrily and let it slam behind him. "Something I said?" Brandon asked, genuinely confused.

"Appears that way," she replied, writing up his check. "He's one of the salvage yard goons over at Scully's. Every town needs a bad element." She winked.

Brandon stepped out into the sunlight and surveyed the parking lot, half expecting the man to be waiting for him. It was an unnerving encounter, however brief. Since no one in town knew Brandon, other than Chad, he could only chalk up the man's behavior to hearing Brandon mention the *Whiskey Lee*.

Back at the wharf, Brandon and Chad got busy right away getting the Zodiac into the water and loading up their gear. The strange encounter at the café was momentarily put aside as the two men focused on the day ahead.

Chad paused and reached into his pocket. "See if this one works." He handed Brandon a phone charger which could be plugged into the SUV's cigarette lighter.

"Thanks." Brandon plugged it into his phone. "This'll work. Perfect!"

The weather couldn't have been better, considering the havoc wreaked on the coast the day before. It took them thirty-five minutes to follow the coastline to the site. Multiple rocky islands with windblown pines and wild brush dotted the area. Chad anchored the Zodiac as near to the underwater cliff face as possible. Once submerged, Brandon was able to get a good view of the physical features of the area.

The ledge was just below the surface and once beyond it, the rock wall dropped off to a depth of about forty-five feet. It ran the width of the inlet. Danger buoys ran across the inlet, and markers at each end warned of the hidden rock shelf below. Chad led the way, slowly and smoothly descending the face of the wall.

In the sandy murkiness of the sea bottom, a dark shape came into view and Chad motioned to Brandon that they had reached the sunken lifeboat. It appeared to be intact, lying peacefully at the foot of the wall. Barnacles clung to the hull, sharing space with small perch and sculpins that scattered as the men approached. Chad pointed to inside the boat—a mound of large rocks and broken cinder blocks filled the bottom of it, clearly weighing it down and preventing any movement from the current. Brandon stared at the pile of rubble. It most certainly looked suspicious, as Chad had said. Something inside the lifeboat caught his eye and curiously he reached in for it. He picked out a small rectangular object. It looked like a corroded piece of metal, indiscernible in its present state; he placed the object in his mesh bag for further scrutiny topside.

Chad led Brandon to the stern and again pointed. Faded and peeling red paint stood out in the gray murky water, peeking through a thin coating of green algae. The men looked at each other and nodded. They could clearly see enough of the letters to know what they spelled—*WHISKEY LEE*.

7

With the Zodiac loaded back on its trailer and their gear packed in Chad's minivan, the two friends examined the item Brandon had found on the lifeboat.

"It's definitely metal," Brandon concluded as he turned it over in his hands. "Looks like it's been down there a long time. You think it might have belonged to Moreland?"

Chad shrugged. "Maybe. Or . . . whoever filled the boat with rocks may have lost it." He winked at his friend. "A clue, my good Watson."

Brandon laughed. "Well, like Dr. Watson, I'll have to use science on this one. Vinegar and a brass wire brush might clean this up just enough to determine what it is. But that might be all we figure out."

Chad clapped his friend on the shoulder and turned toward his vehicle. "Happy cleaning, bud. I have to get back to the shop. Let me know how that works out."

By the time Brandon had showered and changed back at the motel, the phone lines and Wi-Fi were back in service. He took a quick trip to the small grocery and hardware store and bought what he needed to clean up the indiscernible lump of corrosion sitting on the dresser back in his room. He stopped in at the tavern, hoping to see Gloria there, but it was her day off. Disappointed, he returned to his room and got down to business.

Brandon started by gently wiping off all the corrosion he could with a soft bristle brush. After that, he removed the cover from the upper toilet tank and dropped the hunk of metal inside to soak overnight in fresh water. He replaced the tank cover and then took out his laptop and connected to the motel's Wi-Fi.

In Brandon's experience as a journalist, he knew that gathering background information was the first step to getting to the truth of a story, especially one that's decades old. Names, dates, and facts were his ammunition when talking face-to-face with the parties involved. Knowledge was power, and if his interviewees tried to lie or simply "forget" the details, he'd know. He also found that the element of surprise worked exceptionally well—feign ignorance, play on their emotions, then throw a curve ball and confront them with whatever dirty little secret he knew they were hiding. Being a stranger in town, it was going to be very difficult trying to delve into the mystery without having doors slam in his face. And the reaction of the man at the café, at the mere mention of *The Whiskey Lee*, had rattled Brandon more than he cared to admit.

The first thing Brandon needed was information on the disappearance itself. A Google search led him to the National Transportation Safety Board (NTSB) website. The NTSB, based in Washington, D.C., was responsible for civil transportation accident reports, which included marine. On the home page, under the investigations tab, he discovered what he was looking for. A click of a button put the information into order by date, and he scrolled down to 1989. And there it was: *Loss of the U.S. fishing vessel WHISKEY LEE, Barney's Cove, Maine, about July 14th, 1989.* He opened a PDF version of the file and began to read.

The abstract explained that *The Whiskey Lee* was a fifty-foot fishing trawler suspected of having sunk while on a fishing trip for herring. No crew was on record other than the captain, James Moreland. A week-long search by the U.S. Coast Guard resulted in nothing being found. Moreland was presumed dead and no cause for the disappearance of his vessel could be determined.

Brandon scanned through the details of the investigation, jotting down notes as he went. A few details raised his eyebrows—leads he was curious to follow up. One was that the local police had received three calls reporting Moreland missing: from his wife Kathleen, from his sister Audrey Montgomery, and the third gave no name. The second was that *The Betsea*, a salvage ship, had been reported in the area on the day *The Whiskey Lee* was last seen. *The Betsea* had ties to Scully's Salvage. Both the salvage ship and Scully's denied seeing *The Whiskey Lee*.

Brandon stared off into the distance as he pondered this twist in Chad's pet project. A search for news on *The Whiskey Lee* proved fruitless; most newspapers didn't begin digitally archiving their articles until the 1990s, which meant public libraries would be his only source. He found email addresses for those in Portland and Bangor, and sent off his query. A quick check in the phone book in the motel's lobby was a dead end—no Moreland or Montgomery listed anywhere in the vicinity. Tired, Brandon lay on the bed and mulled over a plan of attack. After a few minutes, an idea occurred to him. He grabbed his car keys and headed to Barney's Cove.

His first stop was at the local library. It was a small brick building just on the north side of the main road. After he parked, he checked his watch—it was almost 4:30 p.m. Chances were, in such a small community, every government agency would close early. He ran to the front door, found it unlocked, and hurried inside.

"I'm just locking up. You'll have to come back tomorrow," he heard a voice say.

Brandon looked around the dimly lit room for the source of the voice. Coming toward him, shutting off light switches as she went, was a tall, thin woman in an ankle length floral dress. Her dark hair was braided and hanging forward over one shoulder. Brandon thought she was attractive, in a plain and simple way; she looked to be in her early fifties, and her deep frown told him she was a no-nonsense woman.

"I'm so sorry to trouble you," he began, flashing a quick apologetic smile. "I just need a little help and I was told that you are *the* one I should talk to."

The woman's frown softened slightly. She gave him one short, curt nod of her head. "I consider myself a valuable resource of information, yes." She brushed past him and locked the glass entrance door. "I only have a few minutes," she called over her shoulder. "My ride is on his way."

"I don't suppose you keep old newspapers on hand, do you?" he asked her.

She walked around a wooden counter, assuming her position of librarian. "Local only. What do you need?"

"I need something from 1989, a—"

She shook her head, cutting him off with a wave of her hand.

"You'd have to contact the papers themselves for something that old."

"Oh," he replied, genuinely disappointed but not surprised. She stared intently at his expression. "What are you looking for, exactly?"

Brandon's mind worked quickly to find the words that would appeal to this woman. "You were probably too young to remember," he said, watching her blush. "Thanks anyway." He half turned, pretending to walk away.

"My memory is what landed me this job," she said quickly. "I remember 1989 very well, as it turns out."

Inwardly Brandon was grinning from ear to ear, though what she saw on his face was shock and gratitude. "You are a lifesaver!" he told her and she blushed again. "I'm actually here because of my uncle. He's very ill back home in Portland and he's asked me to find an old friend of his." He lowered his eyes sheepishly. "An old girlfriend, actually. Sort of a goodbye message to her from him. I suspect she was the one that got away, so to speak. His memory isn't what it used to be, so I only have a first name."

The woman nodded. "Sorry to hear about your uncle. What's the woman's name?"

"Audrey. She apparently had a brother from around here that died in 1989. Or disappeared? He can't remember exactly, and that upsets him greatly. That's why I wanted to see a newspaper."

Emotion flooded the woman's face as she whirred through the frames in her memory vault. Tears welled up in her eyes and she quickly blinked them away. "It was a terrible summer. One most of us would like to forget."

"Can you tell me about it?" Brandon asked gently. "My uncle would be forever in your debt."

She cleared her throat, gaining back her composure. "A lot happened that summer—all at once, it seemed. Audrey Montgomery is who you're asking about. She lives in a nursing home now. Suffers from dementia. I'm afraid it will be useless to contact her—she won't know your uncle anymore."

Brandon nodded his understanding. "I'm sorry. So, Montgomery? Is she married?"

"She was, but her husband developed cancer about five years after they were married and sadly, he passed away. I met him, but I was a child and don't remember too much about him. Audrey never remarried."

Brandon shook his head slowly. "That's terrible. Audrey's been through so much."

"Yes. My mother and Audrey were friends. Audrey used to babysit my younger brother and I back in the day while my Mom worked part-time. I do remember her taking us into her darkroom. She'd turn on the red light and show us how to develop photographs from her rolls of 35 mm film. I remember thinking that it was some kind of magic trick. It's odd, the things that we remember from our childhood."

Brandon nodded, letting her finish reminiscing about the past, before smoothly directing the conversation back to the subject matter.

"So, in the summer of '89 . . . what happened?"

"I was in my early thirties," she began, her voice softer now. "One day that summer—July 14th to be exact—Audrey's brother, James Moreland, mysteriously vanished, along with his boat. He was a fisherman. They never found him, or his boat either. Audrey was beside herself," she paused, remembering. "She came by to see my mother once, during the search. She wasn't herself at all. She seemed edgy and distracted, which I took for her worry over James. Mother was quite upset after the visit, too."

Brandon waited patiently for her to continue. She looked lost in her memories and he felt badly for deceiving her.

"In the weeks during the search, a young woman's body was found in the water, right below the Sixteen Fathom Hill Lighthouse. I didn't know her well—she had gone to school with my brother and served at a café here in town. Ann Marie, her name was. And that same week, William Irving, the lighthouse keeper, was killed. Shot one afternoon when he was on duty." She shook her head sadly.

"Incredible," Brandon commented quietly. "Did they arrest anyone for the shooting?"

She shook her head, confirming what he already knew. "It was a really, really bad time. There didn't seem to be an explanation for any of it; none that made sense, anyway."

Brandon sensed that there wouldn't be much more information to be gained from her recollections, so he thanked her and she unlocked the door for him.

"Audrey told my mother something that day she visited," the librarian said as Brandon stepped out into the sunshine. His eyes squinted as he glanced at her.

"I was in the kitchen at the time, so I only caught a few words."

"What did Audrey say?"

"She said James seemed troubled about something before he disappeared. He asked her if he could use her darkroom and wouldn't tell her why. That's really all I got from the conversation. It's hard when you only get bits and pieces. Neither of them shared anything with me at the time, but my mom told me later that he'd been having an affair around the time he disappeared, which Audrey knew about. That could explain his secrecy in wanting to use her darkroom. I guess, but who knows?"

Interesting, Brandon thought. He thanked her again before turning and walking down the steps.

"Audrey lived just up past the lighthouse, on Coastal Route #1 South," she called out. "Take Beacon Hill Road. Look for a little white place with blue shutters. Her grandson looks after the house now." She smiled before stepping back inside and locking the door on him.

8

Brandon sat in the SUV for a few minutes, staring up at the lighthouse from Barney's Cove. He considered what the librarian had told him, which wasn't much more than what Chad and Lou knew. With Audrey suffering from dementia, he was left with the grandson. The chances that he knew anything were slim to none. Sitting in the parking lot wouldn't get Brandon anywhere either. He headed back to Ridgetown.

***

"Can I help you with something?" An older, heavyset man approached Brandon, who was standing at the front desk of the police station. The office was empty save for a tawny bloodhound that lay dead asleep on the floor in the corner.

"I hope so. I'm looking for Officer Flynn."

The man nodded, "*Chief* Flynn now. You found him."

Brandon put his hand out. "I'm Brandon Summers. I'm hoping you can help me. I have some questions about James Moreland."

Flynn looked over the rims of his reading glasses, his eyebrows raised high. He didn't shake Brandon's hand. "No comment," he barked, before retreating into one of the offices down the hall. Brandon wasn't expecting that reaction and it caught him off guard. "I'm not a reporter, sir!" he called down the hall. The bloodhound raised his head, glanced at Brandon, and dropped it back down again. There were shuffling noises down the hall and Flynn reappeared. He stood at the desk, legs apart, with both hands resting on his hips. "Who you with?" he demanded.

Brandon kept his voice level, hoping his strategy didn't backfire. "I'm here on behalf of Audrey Montgomery, Mr. Moreland's sister." Flynn's lips pressed tight. "In what capacity?"

"She's not well, as you may know, sir. Her brother's disappearance has weighed heavily on her and she's hoping for some answers before she passes. A dying woman's wish, so to speak." His eyes didn't waver from Flynn's. A few seconds passed and finally Flynn's body relaxed. His arms dropped to his sides and he shook his head. "Come on in."

"I was the lead on that case," Flynn stated once they were settled in his office. "The Coast Guard handled the search for his trawler, *The Whiskey Lee*, but I was the feet on the ground." He pointed to a tattered cardboard box on the floor near a filing cabinet. It was marked *Moreland, James – 7/89*. "I bring it out every summer, hoping I might find something I missed. Never have."

"I read the accident report put out by the NTSB," said Brandon. "The Coast Guard had no place to start. There hadn't been any radio communication, no distress signals, and no Mayday. No one saw it, and nothing from the boat was ever found. It just disappeared into thin air."

Flynn leaned back in his chair and laced his fingers over his belly. "I was of the opinion at the time, that he did a midnight run from his family. Removed or changed the name of the boat, started a new life somewhere else."

"At the time?" Brandon asked. "Something reversed that opinion?"

"Have you been in this area long, Mr. Summers?"

Brandon blinked. "Not too long. I'm staying at the Rocky Ridge Motel, but I've explored the area a little. Why?"

Flynn sighed. "We have only a few police officers here, and I'm one of them. We cover a large area which is the only reason the taxpayers pay us. With the exception of a few drunken brawls, an occasional domestic, and kids racing their cars down the main drag, this is a babysitting job. Nothing happens here. Ever! Then ten years ago, a young man drove his car off a cliff, and in the summer of '89, I had a disappearance, a suicide, and a murder within two weeks of one another," Chief Flynn paused, as he recollected the past. "I don't believe the one was a suicide though," he said, leaning forward on his desk.

The last comment got Brandon's attention. "Why do you say that?"

"There are 110 foot sheer cliffs just down the highway—no streetlights, no traffic, and easy access. Guaranteed success if you're a jumper." He shook his head. "The young lady picked the craggy cliff up at the lighthouse instead. I just haven't been able to figure that one out. Walking all the way up there, just to . . . ?" The words seemed to get caught in his throat. "Personally, I think something else happened. Maybe she witnessed something. Who knows?" Flynn sighed.

Brandon saw his reasoning. "Do you think that maybe James Moreland committed the murders and took off?"

"Nah." Flynn dismissed the idea with a wave of his hand. "Moreland knew Will his whole life. That's William Irving. He was the lighthouse keeper back then; never had a beef with anyone. He was a kind old soul who kept to himself. That's a photograph of him and me, standing in front of the Sixteen Fathom Hill Lighthouse." He pointed to a faded framed picture on the wall. "William was an old friend of mine. Found him with one bullet in his back and one in his head just days before we discovered the girl. Now she, on the other hand . . ." His voice trailed off. Brandon was still staring at the picture, then turned his gaze back to Flynn.

"What?"

"It could be possible that Moreland was somehow connected with *her* death. Coroner established she was pregnant when she died. I had to really dig around and twist a few arms but I managed to find out they had been seen together on his boat, and they looked cozy. Married man, having some fun with a younger woman, and out of the blue she tells him she's pregnant. It couldn't have been a pretty sight."

"Would certainly account for his leaving town," Brandon admitted.

Flynn nodded. "It would, but his wife said something that just keeps pulling me away from that theory. She said he was scared—terrified—of something just before he disappeared. And that was weeks before the girl died." He stood up, looking at his watch. "Without evidence, I can't reopen Moreland's case. Without the gun that killed Will, I'm stuck, and the girl was ruled a suicide. I can't move a muscle without leads."

Brandon stood and shook Flynn's hand. "I appreciate you sharing what you did. Is there anything else that may be helpful to me?"

"Maybe, Audrey may have already told you that she had a trunk of Moreland's belongings at her place," Flynn offered as they walked out to the front desk. "We didn't find anything useful at the time but you should find out if she still has it. Sometimes a new set of eyes make all the difference. If you come across anything, make sure you contact me, pronto."

Heading out of town, Brandon ran through what he had learned. To have Chief Flynn's perspective on what Brandon had originally thought to be three separate incidents was valuable. His vacation was quickly turning into something more than just recreational diving.

Seeing the lighthouse up ahead, he pulled off Beacon Hill Road, just before it merged into Coastal Route #1 South. He parked in the dirt driveway which led to the lighthouse keeper's quarters. The battered white and red structure towered about seventy-five feet above him; it was planted in solid bedrock, overlooking the mouth of the harbor. He stepped over a chain that was strung between two metal posts at the opening to the laneway, ignoring the KEEP OUT sign. A similar warning was nailed to the doorjamb of the rusting metal entrance of the building. He walked to the edge of the cliff and looked down. Chief Flynn was right; the drop was craggy and looked to be extremely tortuous. *Hmm, not somewhere that a suicidal person would likely choose to jump from*, Brandon thought, noting that only some sections of it were sheer drops. If the plunge didn't kill you instantly, you'd probably die of internal injuries from bouncing off the rocks. It looked to be close to one hundred feet down to the ocean, and the base of the cliff was fringed with huge boulders battered smooth by the constant movement of the waves. As far as the eye could see, there were islands of majestic and completely isolated rocky cliffs. Gulls and other shore birds were nestled in the cliffs, every now and then taking flight and seeming to float on the air which pushed upwards from the ocean. Down below, the waves crashed into rocks, which didn't interrupt a few seals trying to catch up on their late afternoon sleep. Relaxed and content, they knew they were out of reach of any predators lurking in the nearby sea.

A faint sound caught Brandon's attention, and he turned, listening. He thought it sounded like a mewing cat, or a baby crying. The sound seemed to come and go on the breeze. As he neared the lighthouse, it started up again, in earnest. Now, he was sure that it was the unmistakable sound of a baby crying. It seemed to be coming from inside the lighthouse. Clouds gathered overhead, and almost instantly the area grew darker.

Brandon got to the door and pulled hard on the latch. Surprisingly the brass padlock broke apart and fell to the ground. He carefully pulled the heavy door open. The hinges creaked, as they were old and rusty. He feared they were going to fall apart too. It hadn't appeared that anyone had entered the lighthouse in years. The metal squealed as Brandon entered the darkness. He felt his way along the inside wall for a light switch. The wall was cold, clammy, and full of spider webs. As Brandon's hand inched along the wall, he could feel small pockets of missing concrete where the deterioration process had already begun. His hand touched what felt like a light switch. He tried it, but it didn't work.

After searching the dimly lit lighthouse, he was satisfied that there weren't any traces of a cat, baby, or anything else for that matter. The crying had stopped, and it appeared that the lighthouse was completely abandoned, but for some reason his senses were telling him that he wasn't alone. The smell of dampness and earthen mildew filled his nostrils. It was an eerie place and he really didn't want to spend any more time inside.

As he retreated to the entrance, the massive door slammed shut. Unable to see in the pitch blackness, he threw himself against the door shouting "Hey! HEY! Let me out of here!" A terrible wailing sound filled his ears and the hair stood up on the back of his neck. He frantically rammed at the door with his shoulder, his shaking hands grabbing for the latch. Without warning, it sprang open and he stumbled out into the fresh air. He ran toward his vehicle, hopped over the chain fence, and didn't look back.

Trembling, Brandon threw the SUV in reverse and tore out of the driveway, taking one final glance at the towering structure before merging onto Coastal Route #1, where it ran along the cliffside.

At the first lookout, reserved for camera-wielding tourists, Brandon pulled over to regain his composure. The fear that had engulfed him when the wailing started was something he had never experienced before. Grabbing his shades, he stepped out of the SUV, took a few deep breaths and looked around. Sea grass and some wild local flowers lined the other side of the road, beyond that was a forest of old pines. Looking out over the ocean, he could see islands for a few miles.

A little further along the cliffside he could make out a weathered picket fence and a white house with blue shutters. It took him a few seconds to realize that he had found Audrey Montgomery's home. Shaking off his uneasiness, he decided to try his luck. Foot-high weeds dotted the gravel drive; the lawn was overgrown. What was once a quaint bungalow with an ocean view, now appeared dilapidated and forgotten. Brandon doubted anyone had been caring for it for a while. He could see that it needed a lot of work before someone could call it home.

He parked and ascended a rotten set of stairs to the entrance. His knocking sounded hollow on the wooden door. No one answered, which he expected. He cupped his hands around his face and peeked into the dirty picture window into what appeared to be a living room. An old plaid sofa was pushed up against the far wall and a table lamp lay on its side on the floor. Other than that, the room was bare. Returning to his vehicle, he spotted a battered metal garbage can leaning against the side of the house. He peeked inside. It was empty, save for a balled-up paper bag that, after yesterday's storm, should have been water soaked and unrecognizable. Pulling it apart, Brandon recognized the logo on the outside of it as that of the grocery store in Ridgetown. Someone had been here just today. He tossed it back into the can and drove away.

9

Back at the motel, Brandon checked his email. Other than a handful from business associates, there were no replies to his earlier query. He phoned Chad and updated him on the latest events. "Wow," was all Brandon heard from the other end of the phone. "Wow," Chad repeated. Brandon chuckled. "Yeah, that's about all I've got too."

"They're all connected. That's crazy!" Chad was utterly stupefied.

"Possibly. Flynn has no proof without the missing link, and who knows what that might be."

"Maybe you've got it already, my friend," Chad said. "Get that hunk of metal cleaned up yet, that we found on our last dive?"

"Oh crap, I forgot!" Brandon exclaimed, jumping up from the chair. "I'm on it," he said into the phone. "Call you later."

Brandon removed the toilet tank cover and reached his arm into the frigid water, fishing for the small chunk of metal sitting at the bottom.

Tiny pieces of the outer layers of corrosion already started to fall away into his hands.

Brandon checked it over, carefully and gently brushing away the loose particles, piece by piece. He placed the plug in the bathroom sink, lined it with aluminum foil and then filled it with water before sprinkling in two tablespoons of table salt and two tablespoons of baking soda. He then dropped the silver piece into the water.

Each process offered a bigger sneak peek beneath the formidable exterior. After a few hours of soaking, he let the water go from the sink and poured a bottle of vinegar over the small chunk of metal to let it soak for a few more hours. Later, the vinegar in the bathroom sink was a thick, ruddy orange.

Brandon popped open the drain and waited. He placed the lump of metal in the middle of a facecloth on the bathroom vanity. Carefully, he began scrubbing it with the brass brush, occasionally shaking the cloth out into the garbage as it filled with rusty shavings. It was tough going—the item was too small to get a decent stroke with the brush—but little by little, it was becoming identifiable. Close to an hour later he had done all he could. Smiling, he held the silver Zippo lighter up to the ceiling where the yellow light illuminated the letters *JKM* engraved on the side. Motivated, he continued to work until the rest of the letters revealed something he had suspected all along.

The words seemed to jump right out at him as he stared at the front of the sterling silver lighter. Astonished, he sat back in the chair. "Wow!"

To James,
With love,
Ann Marie

Brandon's hard work had paid off. This proved to be the lighter of Captain James Karl Moreland.

Wanting to share the news with Chad immediately, he reached for his phone. Chad was ecstatic. "Good work my friend!" he exclaimed. "Beers are on me next time we go out."

"Are you doing anything tonight?" Brandon asked.

"Ballet lessons," Chad replied.

Brandon chuckled. "Okay, I'll catch you next time. Say hi to everyone for me."

After speaking to Chad, Brandon decided to go for a drink on his own to celebrate. Thinking about Gloria and his promise to play D11 on the "juke" as she called it, he headed for the Piper & Pelican.

The place was nearly packed, and everyone was talking over one another. Gloria was busy at the far end of the bar and didn't notice him enter. Grinning, he strolled over to the jukebox, inserted some change, and pressed D11. As it began to play, he leaned against the machine, watching her.

She didn't let him down. Her head immediately turned and when she spotted him, she broke into a wide smile. She waved him over and as he plopped down on an empty bar stool, she placed a glass mug of amber ale in front of him. Dropping his keys on the bar, he picked it up. The thin layer of froth caressed his lips as he indulged in his favorite beverage.

"To Brandy," he greeted, raising the glass to her and taking a long drink.

Gloria laughed. "What's up, sailor?"

He wiped the foam from the top of his lip and grinned. "I'm a Starvin' Marvin, Brandy. Tough day on the high seas. I need sustenance!"

By the time he had put down a pound of barbecued wings and a basket of fries, the crowd had begun to thin out. The sounds of a lively billiard game could be heard wafting in from a back room. The TV suspended above the bar broadcast the evening news, on low volume. It was a pleasant atmosphere and Brandon was in no hurry to leave.

"Taking a break, Mack," Gloria said to an older man in a dirty white apron. He waved a hand and began sorting through the night's receipts. Gloria came around from behind the bar and joined Brandon. "Thank God it isn't a weekend," she moaned, rubbing her shoulder. "Food okay?"

Brandon nodded. "Hit the spot perfectly."

"And how's the vacation going so far, Brandon? Putting aside the torrential rain and less-than-stimulating nightlife?" she laughed.

"Actually, it's going pretty well. Went on a couple of dives already. Can't wait to go again," he replied.

"Very exciting!" she exclaimed. "Is it risking your life that attracts you or the buried treasure you might find?" she winked.

"Aye, matey!" he snarled, doing his best pirate imitation. "What tickles me lass's fancy? Pearls? Silver? Gold coins, perhaps?"

They both burst out laughing, earning them an irritated glare from Mack.

"Actually, I love it all. Finding a treasure, mind you, would certainly be the ultimate thrill. Gold and jewel-laden shipwrecks aren't exactly a dime a dozen, I'm afraid."

Gloria nodded in agreement. "Is that your thing, though? Wrecks?"

"They're more interesting, sure. Hard to find though." He looked at her questioningly. "There is one I'd like to find. It's supposed to be around these parts. Ever hear of *The Whiskey Lee*?"

Gloria stared at him a few seconds before replying. "Well, shiver me timbers. That's a blast from the past. Um, I was very young when it disappeared. There was a lot of talk around here, especially after they found . . ." She stopped short, her eyes misting. "Break's over, I'm afraid." She quickly got up and disappeared into the kitchen, leaving him utterly speechless.

Brandon was about to call after her when he felt a presence behind him. He turned abruptly and saw the red-haired man from the café standing there, a pool cue in his right hand and a scowl on his face. "Can I help you?" Brandon asked.

The man continued to scowl, then walked confidently around the bar to where Mack was working on the receipts. He placed his pool cue against the bar and leaned into the older man, saying something to him. His narrowed eyes were glaring at Brandon.

Mack followed the man's gaze and nodded. He slapped the pile of receipts down on the bar and approached. "Closing soon," Mack growled at Brandon. "Time to go."

Brandon's body stiffened. "Something wrong?" he said, scooping his keys up from the bar.

"You've had enough. Not serving you anymore. Don't want any trouble so just pay up and head out." He stared hard at Brandon, daring an argument.

"I've only had one drink!" Brandon protested in a raised voice. A few of the customers across the room turned to look. The man with the red hair rounded the bar and stood, arms crossed, a few feet away.

"Problem here, Mack?" he asked.

"Yeah," Mack grumbled. He spotted Gloria from the corner of his eye and he waved her back into the kitchen. "Man's had enough. I want him out."

"Whoa!" Brandon stood and held his hands up as the red-haired man stepped closer. "What the hell is going on here?"

"You're disturbing my other customers," Mack continued, his stubby hands resting firmly on the bar. "Red will see you out. Don't make me call the cops."

Red moved a little closer to Brandon. He was over six feet tall with broad shoulders and thick arms. He had a look of evil in his eyes and it was all directed at Brandon. "I know you," Brandon ventured. "From the café. You gave me that same look when I mentioned *The Whiskey Lee*. Just like tonight."

Red bristled. "You've overstayed your welcome, buddy." He violently reached out and gripped Brandon's arm.

"I've got news for you; I'm not your budd—"

Without getting the rest of the words out, Brandon realized he was no match for Red's brute force. Before he could get Red's huge paws off of him, he was half dragged, half pushed around the bar and past the gawking customers. Brandon felt a hard shove from behind and he went flying down the front steps, landing in a heap on the asphalt. He jumped up in time to see Red coming at him, fists up. Brandon offered a fake left, followed by a quick right punch to the face. Nonplussed, Red retaliated with both fists which Brandon expertly blocked, then he nailed the bully square in the nose. Blood sprayed through the air. Brandon geared up for another round, his right arm cocked for a final blow. As Red put up both his hands, blocking his face, a woman screamed. Brandon turned and saw Gloria standing in the doorway, surrounded by the other customers, her hands covering her mouth, her eyes wide with fright. The sound of a siren pierced the night air. Bright headlights bobbed up and down on the coastal road and in seconds a police car roared into the parking lot. "Great," Brandon muttered under his breath.

Brandon was too tired and frustrated to argue when the officer put him in the back of the cruiser. He watched as another police officer spoke to Mack, said a few words to Red and then turned away. Brandon chuckled. He wasn't surprised. The officer got into the cruiser, and headed back to town. Brandon got one last look at Gloria's ashen face before the tavern disappeared out of sight.

***

Brandon had been in the holding cell for two hours when he heard the outer door open and footsteps approach. He looked up and saw Chief Flynn standing beneath the fluorescent light, his mouth twitching. "First off, good punch," Flynn said.

Brandon chuckled, feeling elated that he'd landed the lucky shot at all. "He deserved it."

"Red usually does," Flynn replied, unlocking the cell door. He sat down beside Brandon. "Care to explain?"

Brandon shrugged and leaned back against the cool cinderblock wall. "I had a beer, wings, then some Red guy for dessert."

"Mmmm." Flynn looked down at his hands, inspecting his fingernails. "Mack said you were drunk, caused a scene."

Brandon sighed. "I had one beer. Ask Gloria, the waitress. She served me."

"Red is a badass," Flynn continued. "Doesn't usually take much to get him started. Any idea what might have set him off?"

Brandon nodded. "Yeah, I do. *The Whiskey Lee.*"

Flynn's head turned sharply. "*The Whiskey Lee?*"

Brandon stood and stretched. "He was in the café the other day when I mentioned it to the waitress. He gave me a look like I had insulted his mother or something. I was talking to Gloria tonight at the tavern about looking for *The Whiskey Lee* and there he was again. Next thing I knew, I found myself here."

Flynn frowned but said nothing. He stood and walked out of the cell. "You can leave once I sign the paperwork. No charges are being laid. Come upstairs when they release you." He walked away, leaving the cell door open. It was after midnight when Brandon was led to Chief Flynn's office. He bowed in appreciation when he saw a pizza box and two paper plates on Flynn's desk.

"Why do I get the impression you're not here on an angel of mercy mission?" Flynn asked later, reaching for his third piece of pizza.

Brandon wiped his mouth with a paper napkin. "Well, since you were kind enough to ensure I get to sleep in my own bed tonight, I'll level with you. I don't know Audrey Montgomery. She doesn't know me. I'm on vacation, visiting a friend. I'm from Canada and I'm a journalist."

Flynn sat back hard in his chair. "Jesus Christ," he muttered. "I thought you said you aren't a reporter?" He threw his half-eaten slice back into the box.

"I'm not," Brandon assured him. "I am honestly here on vacation; my job just happens to be journalism. My friend is interested in *The Whiskey Lee* disappearance and we're both scuba divers. My investigative instincts just kicked in, I guess."

"I don't want your 'investigative instincts' getting in my way," Flynn said in a warning tone. "Understand me?"

"I went up to the lighthouse today," said Brandon, ignoring the warning.

"So?"

"So . . . I heard something inside. A baby crying. Or a cat. I don't know. I had to check it out."

"You went inside?" Flynn asked. "No one's supposed to go in there. It's locked up tight."

"Not anymore," said Brandon. "The lock kind of fell apart in my hands. You might want to get that fixed."

Chief Flynn frowned. "And?"

"And nothing. No baby, no cat. Creepy place though," he added, shivering. "I felt—well, like I wasn't alone." He told Flynn the whole story, including his visit to Audrey Montgomery's.

"Her grandson is in town," Flynn confirmed. "He's staying at a B&B south of here. Stopped in the other day to let us know he'd be in and out of the house." Flynn threw his paper plate in the garbage can. "Anyone see you go in the lighthouse?"

Brandon shook his head. "No one was around. What exactly happened to William?" Brandon asked.

"No idea," Flynn answered sadly. "Local mail carrier was passing the lighthouse and saw his body just laying there. I couldn't believe it when I saw him. Shot in the back and head like it was some sort of execution! Of all things." Flynn was visibly upset, and Brandon gave him a moment before asking his next question.

"This is a little off topic, but I heard that the beacon lights at Sixteen Fathom Hill Lighthouse go off once in a while, despite it being shut down . . . and now the baby crying up there today. Any thoughts?"

Flynn ran a hand through his gray hair. "Not the first time I've heard of that. But thoughts? No. Maybe you can put your 'investigative journalist instincts' to good use on that one too."

10

Agent Tom Rogan had been told numerous times to check in with the Bureau. He often went off by himself. He liked it that way. When he needed the Bureau's help, he would call them. Sometimes he would just turn off his phone and go incognito. He wished that was the case now because he was bored out of his mind waiting around the office for a lead on his latest case. The words on the monitor in front of him seemed to blur, and a fly caught his attention. It walked tauntingly from one side of the computer screen to the other. That was it, Rogan had enough of the office environment. He'd spent way too long researching cases online, instead of being out in the field where he belonged. He signed out and closed his laptop. It was only two flights of stairs down to the parking area. As he stepped outside, he noticed a couple of his team members standing in the smoking area. "You need a break from the Salvage Op too, Brady?" Agent Rogan flippantly asked one of them.

An overweight, gray-haired man turned toward Rogan and grinned.

"Has Rory reported in yet? Any new developments?" Rogan asked.

"Nothing yet. Dead in the water, it seems," Brady said.

"Well, I'm tired of sitting around here, so I'm taking a drive," Rogan said, pulling his car keys from his pocket.

Brady nodded, tossing his cigarette away. "Keep your phone on this time," he grumbled. "I'm not covering for you again."

"Yeah, yeah," Rogan agreed dismissively as he walked away.

His car was hot inside. He quickly lowered all the windows and opened the sunroof. Along with the smell of scorching leather seats, the fragrance of new-car scented air freshener hung in the air. The ashtray had never been used. The car was obsessively clean for a stake-out vehicle. Few would have guessed what he did for a living.

Once Rogan turned onto the main road, he appreciated the fresh salty breeze that drifted through the vehicle.

He turned off the road and into a rest stop to look out over the ocean. As he adjusted the visor, he caught his reflection in the mirror. His aging features reminded him just how much he missed his youth. He took off his sunglasses and ran his fingers through his dried-out golden-brown hair. He remembered how perfect it was when he was in his twenties. He had a full head of military-short, thick, healthy hair then. If it weren't for the crow's feet deeply burrowed into the sides of his eyes, a person would likely guess he was much younger than his forty-four years. Rogan kept himself lean, physically fit, and active but wasn't able to establish a serious relationship. The women were first attracted by what he did for a living, but they didn't stick around, as he was continuously called into work without warning. They would often be abandoned halfway through dinner, or left alone at the movie theater. This was an agent's life, but unfortunately not an ideal one for the women he dated. They didn't return his phone calls after that.

Rogan put his mirrored sunglasses back on and drove south along the winding coastal road, watching the sun disappear behind the trees, as dusk crept in. The sky turned a hazy orange. To Rogan this wasn't just a pleasure drive along the coast without a destination. It was more than that. He always had a reason for everything he did. This time he wanted to revisit a small town with a certain mystique. Not any town though. No. Not many towns could pull off the "creepy" as this one did. There was something going on with this place. Ridgetown and its seventy-five foot lighthouse, known as Phantom Hill, would always be on his radar.

This time Rogan's interest stemmed from having learned that a few of the vessels owned and operated by Scully's Salvage had been paying special interest in the coastal waters surrounding Ridgetown and Barney's Cove. It was a small and quiet area, an out-of-the-way kind of place. He liked the quaint atmosphere of the town, even though its past still loomed over it like a stinky smog cloud. Ridgetown kind of reminded him of the small coastal village he'd grown up in back in New Hampshire. Not only did Rogan admire this area, but he was eager to learn why this small town was so interesting to a big-time player like Scully's

Salvage. Something was going down here. He could almost taste it. Lately, it seemed that Phantom Hill's claws were gripping him tighter. He couldn't stay away. If he was the mongoose, Scully's would undisputedly be the snake.

He selected a little tavern off the beaten path. Rogan had been here before and still wasn't sure if the pelican sitting on a dock post out front was cute, or just a cheesy marketing attempt to draw visitors away from the main strip. Whatever, it worked for him. This little juke joint wasn't usually as busy, or expensive like the popular establishments huddled around the wharf. There was an old song playing on the jukebox when he walked in. It didn't take Rogan long to settle into a well-worn bar stool near the back of the bar. He ordered a drink and while waiting for it, his eyes shifted around the room and then back to the TV. It was a lot busier than he remembered. He hoped that none of the other patrons had paid any attention to him when he'd walked into the bar. For anyone with an untrained eye, Rogan just looked like a regular guy sitting there looking trim, minding his own business, and enjoying his drink. No one would have suspected that he was an ex-Navy SEAL, well trained in covert operations. He liked the idea of playing the role of a chameleon, one who blended in with his surroundings.

An older bartender placed Rogan's drink on a coaster in front of him. Rogan lifted the glass up. As soon as it touched his lips, his nose caught the scent of that smooth Kentucky bourbon which he'd so longed for. It went down well, but he knew that he would have to make this drink last a while. Technically he was still on duty. If he got a call, he had to respond to it. That or someone else would be given the assignment and go in his place. He couldn't let that happen. *One quick drink, and then I'm leaving*, Rogan thought.

He didn't know anyone in the bar, except that he'd seen the woman sitting a few stools down, engaged in a conversation with a man. Rogan didn't know her name, but he knew that she was a barmaid here. She'd served him on his first visit here a couple of months earlier.

The man she was sitting beside looked to be close to her age, good looking, nicely cropped brown hair, and seemed friendly enough. The strawberry-blonde barmaid appeared smitten. Her voice was extra sultry when she said his name: Brandon. The duo engaged in silly pirate wordplay but it was the man's mention of *dive* and *wreck* that were enough to hold Rogan's attention for a while. He reached for a newspaper that was sitting on the bar, unfolded it, and pretended to read, all the while his ears were now tuned in to everything that Brandon and the barmaid were talking about.

When Rogan heard Brandon mention the name *Whiskey Lee*, a flood of old memories entered his head. He had just returned from a tour in Panama when he'd first heard the bizarre story. It was five months after the incidents happened and people were still talking about it as if it had been the day before. A missing trawler, a murdered lighthouse keeper, and a female jumper, all within a short period of time. It was a lot for a relatively small and quiet community to take in, and then talk of a murderer living amid the townsfolk circulated. People had a right to be scared.

"Can I help you?" Rogan heard Brandon say.

A red-haired man was hovering over Brandon and the tension in the bar began to rise.

What's that guy's problem? Rogan thought.

Rogan had enough experience with conflict to know how fast a situation can escalate into a battle, but what really surprised him was that the older man behind the bar seemed to team up with the bully. Instead of de-escalating the situation, the old man added more fuel to the fire.

This was neither Rogan's battle nor his business, but he was trained to always be ready and remain alert. For now, he avoided eye contact with anyone, turning his head toward the big television screen in front of him. Rogan was more than ready to get off his bar stool and practice his take-down moves, but ideally, whatever aggression was building, he hoped would dissipate on its own. He didn't want to draw attention to himself. Not with the Salvage Op front and center.

"Here we go!" Rogan thought, as he watched the bully with the broad shoulders move menacingly closer to Brandon.

"I know you," Rogan heard Brandon state, "from the café. You gave me that same look when I mentioned *The Whiskey Lee*. Just like tonight."

"You've overstayed your welcome, buddy," the red-haired man growled, gripping Brandon's arm.

Next thing Rogan saw was the bully half dragging Brandon toward the front door.

The fact that they were going outside to duke out their differences didn't faze Rogan in the least, but what did bother him was the way everything went south right after Brandon mentioned *The Whiskey Lee*. That made him curious enough to want to learn more.

Rogan remained on his barstool until everyone else's attention was focused on the altercation. He got up, walked over to a side window and peeked outside. He saw that Brandon was holding his ground, so Rogan slid into the nearest vacant booth to watch. He decided to stay close to the one person who may know something—the strawberry blond barmaid who was now looking out the window, anxiously watching the fight. Bar staff were usually full of information and a local pair of ears in this town could be useful. The agent suspected the barmaid knew much more than even *she* realized.

At first when she was talking to Brandon, she appeared comfortable, relaxed, even flirtatious. But after he'd mentioned *The Whiskey Lee*, Rogan noticed that she became distant, showing nervousness, and then abruptly shut the conversation down. *The question is why?* Rogan thought. He returned to his stool at the bar and took one more sip from his glass. Reaching into his pocket he pulled out his wallet, placed a ten-dollar bill on the bar and left unnoticed.

Outside, the police were taking Brandon away in handcuffs. The bully was dusting himself off and nursing a bloody nose.

It looks like Brandon won that one. Good for him, Rogan thought. He was pretty sure that it wasn't the first time or the last time this place would have a dust up.

While all eyes were glued to the spectacle outside, Rogan slipped undetected through the crowd in the parking lot and made a hasty exit.

11

Chief Nathan Flynn hadn't been inside the lighthouse in years. The mere thought of it was unsettling. His conversation with Brandon had affected him more than he had let on. It was one thing for the local kids to spread stories of ghosts and phantom lights, but quite another for a professional, well-spoken man to share actual experiences.

Once Brandon had left his office, Flynn pulled a padlock from inventory at the station and headed straight for the lighthouse. He could have assigned the task to someone else, but to him this place was still William's. He still couldn't grasp the fact that his friend was gone, even after all the years that had passed by. It seemed like only yesterday that he was drinking coffee with him.

Flynn stood on the edge of the cliff overlooking the harbor. He could hear the waves pounding the rocks below. It was a peaceful sound on a calm summer night. He turned to walk back and was startled by a shadowy image of a man standing between him and the lighthouse. The man was half lit by the small pool of light the moon offered. Flynn squinted as he focused his eyes. He couldn't see the man's features, but the image left him feeling somewhat uneasy and chilled.

"Identify yourself," he called out.

All he heard were waves crashing into the rocks below. Just as Flynn took a step, the figure slowly raised his hand in a friendly salute, turned, and then vanished into thin air. Flynn ran forward, his eyes darting left and right. The lighthouse door swung open without warning. Cautiously Flynn moved toward it, clutching the handle of his holstered sidearm with his right hand. He thought he heard what sounded like heavy footfalls coming from inside

The Whiskey Lee

the lighthouse. He stepped closer to take a look. Pulse still racing, his senses heightened, Flynn widened his eyes in surprised as he learned it was dead silent and black as midnight inside. He took out his flashlight and aimed it up the spiral metal staircase. "Hello? Is anyone up there? This is the police!" His voice echoed in the tubular space. He held his breath, waiting for a response, but none came. The silence was deafening. Heart still pounding, Flynn took a deep breath before slowly ascending the stairs. He brushed cobwebs from his face as he went, his flashlight bobbing and weaving around the space. The only sounds were his own footfalls on the metal stairs, and his labored breathing.

He reached the top where the stairs met the lantern room. Cautiously, he stuck his head up, his right hand poised again on his sidearm. He shone his flashlight around the room but saw no one. His eyes narrowed in disbelief. Confused but relieved, Flynn climbed the last steps and took a quick walk around the massive lamp that dominated the room. He walked in slow, small circles while he continued his search. The hairs on the back of his neck stood up. There didn't appear to be anywhere for anyone to hide in the lantern room. His eyes were telling him no one was there, but his sixth sense was telling him otherwise.

He leaned against one of the windows and gazed out toward the town's lights that twinkled like fireflies along the shore. He thought of William and all the years his friend had taken in the exact same view. Flynn said a silent prayer for his school chum and turned back toward the stairs. Like an atomic explosion, the room filled with a bright, blinding white light. Flynn shielded his eyes, falling to his knees on the floor. The fear he faced now pushed a steady chill along his nerves. Heart racing, and breathing deeply, Flynn struggled to his feet, feeling his way along the wall of windows, to the staircase. The air turned colder. His shaking fingers grasped the metal railing, and he heard a low, deep murmuring coming from below. Frozen with fear, he listened, hoping it was the wind moving through the decrepit building. It grew in tempo until he had no choice but to drop his flashlight and cover his ears. It was painful. Behind him, the pulsating white light moved around and around the room, casting intermittent shadows on the wall of the staircase. "Stop!" he screamed, completely terrified now. He tried to descend the stairs, but lost his footing, sliding instead on his ass, his arms flailing in the air. Panting, he gripped the railing with both hands, pulled himself up, and forced his feet to move down,

down. A sudden gust of cold air cut through him like a knife. Flynn shivered, seeing his own breath as he exhaled.

Shakily, he made his way down the stairs and then heard what sounded like heavy footsteps pursuing him. He recoiled at the sound. Drawing his sidearm and aiming it above, he searched frantically for movement on the vacant stairway, using the available light which spilled down from the lantern room. His eyes darted side to side. It confirmed what he already knew. No one was there. A shiver ran through him again and he quickened his pace downwards, not looking back.

Soon afterwards, a wailing voice echoed off the brick wall of the spiral staircase. Terrified and confused, Flynn covered his ears again.

When he finally touched the concrete floor, he threw himself through the open door. Slamming it closed behind him, he grappled for the padlock in his pocket and plunged it through the hasp. With trembling hands, he latched it and backed away, breathless. He looked up at the glowing lantern room at the top of the lighthouse. Without warning the lamp light went out and the harbor was thrown into darkness once again. Flynn's legs threatened to buckle under him as he searched for some explanation for what he had just witnessed. His hair was matted with sweat. The wind kicked up and it brought with it the hollow sound of a crying baby. Flynn ran to the safety of his cruiser. Once inside the vehicle, one hand firmly gripped the dirty leather steering wheel of the Ford Crown Victoria, while his other hand was busy shoving the key into the ignition. After throwing it into drive and stomping hard on the gas pedal, the tires spun wildly on loose dirt before finding the asphalt of Beacon Hill Road.

12

The water was darker this time. Brandon couldn't see much in front of him. Movement to his right caught his attention. It was his dive buddy Lou and he was pointing down to something on the seabed. Brandon thought for a moment that he saw an outline of a boat, perhaps *The Whiskey Lee*. He felt like he'd been in this strange place before. It all seemed eerie yet familiar.

Brandon's legs felt bound. It was like something was preventing freedom of movement, but it wasn't the case. Brandon's fins moved freely but heavily against the weight of the water.

Instead of swimming toward the wreck, Lou swam off in a reckless manner.

As Lou disappeared, Brandon was both disturbed and confused by the divers sudden change of demeanor and apparent lack of rational thinking. Feeling apprehensive, Brandon looked toward where Lou had pointed. There wasn't a shipwreck sitting on the seabed now. It had disappeared. Troubled by the vanishing shipwreck and Lou's unusual behavior, Brandon was forced to surface. As he ascended, he couldn't understand why he couldn't see any sunlight near the surface. Usually, he'd follow the sunlight's multiple streams of light to the surface, but it seemed so dark this time. Instead, a single bright light shone down, but it was weak.

Upon surfacing, he realized that it was moonlight. Brandon realized that Lou hadn't surfaced with him. Brandon could see a beam of white light that rotated back and forth, splashing light across the harbor from the cliff above. It was the lighthouse beacon.

Nothing made sense. He couldn't understand why it was nighttime already. Was it possible that he'd stayed down too long? Why didn't his dive computer warn him? He had too many questions. At that moment, he realized something else—the charter boat was gone. He was out here alone, bobbing around in the ocean. He wondered whether he should start swimming in the direction of the mainland, but also knew he couldn't leave another diver out here.

Wondering where Lou was, Brandon felt his right fin hit something. Normally, he'd be worried, but knowing Lou was still down there, he brushed off any fearful thoughts. *Perhaps he's disoriented or horsing around?* Brandon thought. It wasn't until an arm reached out of the water and grabbed him from behind, that Brandon began to sense the seriousness of it. He didn't have a chance to put the regulator back into his mouth before being dragged beneath the waves. *What the . . .*, he thought. His heartbeat quickened as he struggled to free himself. Now, he was fuming. He was able to surface just long enough to see Lou's masked face appear beside him. "What the fu—" Brandon tried to ask, but Lou lashed out at him before he got the words out. Brandon felt his mask being ripped from his head, so he fought back, giving him a sharp blow into the side of the head with his elbow, which left Lou temporarily dazed.

Brandon swam away, desperately trying to put some distance between them. It wasn't long before he saw a boat cruising in his direction. *Oh good, the charter captain's coming back for me*, Brandon thought. He waved his arms frantically to capture the captain's attention. As the boat got nearer to him, it veered to the right. "No wait, over here!" he shouted to no avail, as the boat turned away. No one could hear him. His arms waved frantically, trying to get the attention of a woman standing on the back deck. The glimmer of light from the lighthouse made it possible to see her outline. She was holding something in her arms—*a baby?* he wondered. Brandon couldn't understand why they weren't stopping to rescue him. As the trawler passed through the lighthouse beacon's ray of light, he was shocked to read the name sprawled across the stern of the boat:

WHISKEY LEE

He struggled to make sense of it all. Helplessly, he felt himself being grabbed in a headlock from behind. Brandon struggled, as he was dragged beneath the waves. It seemed that the ocean had just opened and swallowed him. He tried to take one final gasp for air, but couldn't. All he could draw into his lungs was salt water.

The Whiskey Lee

***

Brandon jerked awake, his hands gripping the bed sheets. He stared at the white popcorn ceiling, momentarily disoriented. His body was soaked with sweat and his heart was beating fast. He closed his eyes and breathed deeply until his body relaxed. It was a dream. *Just a dream.* He let the images float in and out until the fragments came together and the dream presented itself in full. "The heck was that all about?" he said aloud, throwing off the sheet. He could see daylight peeking around the edges of his curtains. Noticing the time was a little after eleven o'clock, he shuffled to the bathroom and threw cold water on his face. Staring at his reflection in the mirror, his fingers moved toward his face, gently brushing the stubble that had grown dark on his chin. He rarely remembered his dreams, and he almost never had nightmares. The whole *Whiskey Lee* mystery was freaking him out. *I feel like I'm in a Stephen King novel*, he thought. *Any second, a long skinny finger is going to protrude from the sink drain and I'll run like a little girl, screaming for dear life.* He laughed at himself and went to check his email.

While skimming through the second one, he heard a soft knock on his door. He pulled on his jeans and peered out the window. It was Gloria.

"Gloria?" he said, surprised. He threw the door open wide.

Gloria blushed, clutching her purse in front of her. "I knew where to find you because I noticed your room number on the key tag when you dropped your keys on the bar. I couldn't help being nosy. There aren't many motels here. Sorry, I hope that doesn't come across as too weird, but I feel really bad about what happened to you last night. Are you okay?"

Brandon nodded, smiling. "All good, come on in, Detective. Thanks for checking up on me."

Gloria giggled as she sat down on a chair.

Brandon pulled on a T-shirt.

"I hope I didn't wake you up," she said

He shook his head. "Rough night—nightmares." He noticed that she seemed a little tense. "Everything okay?"

"You asked about *The Whiskey Lee*. I do know something about it. Or at least I think I do." Gloria nervously played with the strap of her purse. "You threw me off when you mentioned it at the bar. I haven't heard that name in years."

Brandon nodded and sat on the edge of the bed, facing her. "You looked like you had seen a ghost."

"Kind of. My aunt knew the captain. Quite well, apparently." She rolled her eyes and smiled.

Brandon's raised his eyebrows. "As in a romantic kind of way?"

Gloria nodded. "Something happened to me back then, and I haven't told a soul about it. Since you're looking for *The Whiskey Lee*, you should know."

Brandon frowned. "Okay."

"My friends and I were kids at the time, playing hide and seek beside the library. I noticed my aunt walking up the street, toward the library. I knew I wasn't supposed to be that far away from my house, but I wanted to jump out from my hiding place beneath the stairs and surprise her. Just as I was about to move, a car pulled into a parking spot in front of the library and my aunt got into the passenger side. There was a much older man sitting in the driver's seat—James Moreland. They embraced and kissed each other. Neither of them noticed me, but then I saw another car pull into a parking spot two cars away from them and I realized the man was spying on them."

"Had you ever seen the man before?" Brandon asked.

"No, but he looked scary. He'd probably followed James Moreland to the library. The man turned his head in my direction and glared straight at me. So many years have gone by that his facial features are a bit of a blur to me now, but I will never forget the look in his eyes. I was terrified, so I jumped out of my hiding spot and ran home as fast as I could. I'm still blaming myself for my aunt's death. I should have warned them about the strange man in the car, but I was terrified."

"I'm sorry for your family's loss. How did she pass away?" Brandon asked.

"They found her at the bottom of the cliff, near the lighthouse," she explained.

"Wow" Brandon whispered. "I heard something about that. She was *your* aunt? I'm . . . sorry."

"Thank you."

"James Moreland went missing, the lighthouse keeper was murdered, and your aunt died. You must have been terrified."

Gloria shuddered. "I was pretty freaked out. I've felt guilty ever since. Maybe if I had said something right away . . ." Her voice trailed off and she shook her head. "I know she didn't take her own life. She was pregnant. Yes, she was distraught about James's disappearance, but she'd never do a thing like that."

Brandon patted her hand. "You were a kid. And scared. No way that you could have known what was going to happen."

"Thank you. I keep trying to convince myself of that; if only I hadn't been so scared, I feel that my aunt would still be alive today," she replied. "That's why I want to warn you. We lost her, and then Ben," Gloria added.

"Ben?" Brandon asked.

"My best friend. I'll explain later." Gloria got up and reached for the door. "I have to get to work. Already running late."

Brandon grabbed one of his business cards out of his wallet and handed it to her. "Call me when you're free to chat. I really want to hear all about it."

13

After parking her rental car and checking into the Rocky Ridge Motel, thirty-two-year-old Rosie Spencer placed her black Nikon camera bag on the small wooden table in the corner of the room. She pulled out her DSLR camera, removed the battery and connected it to the charger. She did the same with her laptop. She couldn't wait to see the photographs she'd taken, but needed to fully charge all of her devices first.

With time to waste, she looked in the mirror, applied her favorite pink lip gloss, then used a pink comb to gently detangle her dark auburn, shoulder-length hair which had gotten windswept as she'd stopped to take photographs along the coastline. Dressed in cropped, torn jean leggings and an open-shouldered top, she paused at the door to slip on a pair of beige loafers before venturing outside for a walk.

The town was already buzzing with tourists looking forward to starting their annual 4th of July celebrations. On her drive into town earlier, Rosie had noticed the banners and flags lining the streets to honor the upcoming Independence Day. Already loving the great vibe of the area, she found a cozy little place within walking distance, named Brewster's. She reckoned that a little pub grub and a good stiff drink wouldn't hurt after a busy day of research for her international ghost story novels.

Rosie had been drawn to Maine due to the many abandoned lighthouses which dotted the coastline. Knowing that they would make for some interesting stories, Rosie pinned the points on her map and then booked her flight to the USA. She had noted that some of the mysterious lighthouses, like the Boon Island Lighthouse for instance, weren't accessible without a boat. Sitting on the small barren island, Boon's the tallest lighthouse in New England, at 133 feet.

Legend goes that in 1710 the ship *Nottingham Galley* ran aground on the barren island. Unable to make the six miles back to land, the last few remaining crew members resorted to cannibalism while struggling through the harsh winter.

It was the mere ambiance surrounding these abandoned and isolated structures which fascinated Rosie, and she couldn't wait to visit every one of them. Evidence of torrid days gone by, the once-proud lighthouses had seen better days as their unique paint became faded and battered. For some of them, folklore-filled stories of alleged ghosts and the unexplained remained deep dark secrets. Convinced that all lighthouses are worth visiting, Rosie believed that a ghostly presence or a creepy aura only adds to their charm and mystery. This is what motivated her to dig deeper into the realms of paranormal activity.

Rosie was glad that she had followed her passion and chosen a career as a ghost story writer. She couldn't imagine doing anything else.

"I'll have a white wine please. A chardonnay," Rosie ordered after finding a stool at the bar. She paused and then added, "Make it a large."

"Good choice to kick off the big weekend. Comin' right at cha, darlin'!" the bartender said, placing the wineglass on a coaster near her hand. "You from England?"

Rosie smiled. "Yes, as a matter of fact, I'm from a small town on the South West coast called Falmouth. It's in Cornwall. Have you heard of it?"

"No, I haven't. Never been to England. My ancestors are from there though. Excuse me just for a minute, luv. I just have to change the channel." The bartender turned away to reach for the remote. He pointed it toward the television above the bar. The channel switched to the news.

He turned back to Rosie. "We've got the best fish and chips around. Would you like to try some?"

"That sounds lovely. I'm famished. Lots of driving today. I got so carried away taking photographs that I forgot to stop and eat something," Rosie explained.

"Are you over here on vacation or business?" the bartender asked.

"A little bit of both actually. I have relatives I've been visiting in Boston, but I'm also out this way to do some research. I write a series of ghost novels. My main areas of concentration at the moment are lighthouses and ships."

"Really?" he asked, impressed. "My great-grandfather was a lighthouse keeper for over thirty years."

He pointed to a wall of black and white photographs near the door.

"That's the lighthouse where he worked. Sixteen Fathom Hill Lighthouse."

"Really? That's one of the lighthouses that I'll be visiting. Any ghost stories floating around the family?"

The man nodded and rested his elbows on the bar. "There are stories about that place, but they're rather recent. Last keeper was murdered, and since then, after they shut it down, lots of unexplained lights and sounds come from up there."

Rosie raised her eyebrows as she sipped her wine. "That's interesting."

He shrugged. "I don't believe in all that stuff, but that's the story that's been going around. Good luck with your research though, luv. I've got to warn you that folks are tight-lipped about that place. Lots of scar tissue left after the old guy was killed."

Rosie raised her glass. "Thanks for the tip."

He winked. "So, you famous or something?"

Rosie laughed. "A little, I guess. I'm published in the United Kingdom. I'm not sure if anyone in North America is familiar with my work yet."

"Rosie Spencer." She held out her hand.

The bartender took it in both of his. "It's a pleasure, darlin'. I'm Len," he offered.

"Nice to meet you." She smiled brightly. "My work includes a series of short stories set in England, about haunted lighthouses, ships, castles, restaurants, hotels . . . you name it."

"Have you visited any of the other haunted lighthouses in Maine yet?" Len asked.

"So far I've been to the Pemaquid Point, Boon Island, and Seguin Island lighthouses." Rosie beamed.

"Great choices; I haven't even been out to see them. I think Barney's Cove is the best place to view the Sixteen Fathom Hill Lighthouse. It's tall enough that you can get a nice shot of it across the bay. Can't really see it from this side unless you walk or drive up there. Too many trees in the way. Just curious, what are some of the names of your books?" Len asked.

"I don't know what this one will be named yet. Perhaps *Haunted Lighthouses of the Eastern USA*, under the main title of *North American Ghost Stories*, or something like that. I may do another one just focusing on ghost ships. There appear to be a lot of those."

"Speaking of ghost ships, have you heard of the USS *Midhurst*?"

Rosie shook her head.

"It's a former Navy destroyer that's been decommissioned. Served in World War II, the Korean, and the Cold War. The ship is permanently docked now, up at Port Bradley. It was turned into a museum. I've heard stories of a ghost floating around that place too."

"Oh, that's a new one for me. Really surprised I didn't see anything pop up about it while I was doing my ghost sightings research."

"Well, I suppose there are some things that happen around here that don't become world news." Len smiled.

Rosie nodded slowly. "I appreciate the tip about the Navy ship, I'll make sure it goes on my list of places to visit."

"Sure, not a problem. Glad to help," he replied, and then shook his head appreciatively. "You know what, Rosie? I'm jealous. What a life! Traveling the world and listening to people talk!" He chuckled. "I listen to folks too, but it's all jibber-jabber after they've had a few!"

They both laughed. "Is it okay if I use some of your old photographs of the lighthouse for my novel? I will pay you for using them and give you a credit."

"Anything you need, luv. On the house." Len winked. "Food should be ready now. Be right back."

When Len returned from the kitchen with Rosie's food, a man on the television was standing on a podium, making a speech about the environment. He was a well-groomed and polished politician, around fifty years old, wearing a custom-fitted navy blue suit.

"Handsome," Rosie admired out loud.

"Shady low-life piece of shit is what he is," Len said out loud to the television. He then turned back toward Rosie. "Sorry you had to hear that, luv. Sometimes I can't contain it. Make sure you don't get sucked in by the halo effect."

"Right, I think I know what you're getting at," said Rosie.

"That man is about as crooked as they come. I don't even know why anyone would re-elect him. I'm sure he'd sell his own family if he could. Just look at those shifty eyes."

"Who is he?" Rosie asked.

"Senator Aiden Dalton," Len said. "He's a lying, cheating scumbag. I wouldn't even trust him with my dog."

Rosie couldn't stop herself from laughing. She had already decided that she liked Len, because he spoke from his heart. "We have a few of those in England too," she replied.

14

Brandon steered his SUV onto Coastal Route #1, which would take him to Barney's Cove. He was to meet up with a few of the guys and their spouses. The restaurant was already busy and it wasn't even half past four. Chad was lucky to score a table on the patio where they'd have an unobstructed view of the fireworks, which were set to go off just after dark from an old dredging scow anchored in the cove.

"I'm glad everyone could make it." Chad raised his glass. "Happy Independence Day, everyone!"

Brandon and the others raised their glasses to honor the occasion. "Hear, hear," Brandon replied.

"Eat, drink, and enjoy. We ordered lots of food," Chad's wife announced. "We also have three pounds of chicken wings coming to our table as an appetizer."

"I hope they're diet chicken wings," Lou's wife replied jokingly.

"Yes, they are babe. I heard they'll be serving their famous diet beer tonight too," Lou teased.

"Yessah!" Chad bellowed, raising his beer mug.

They all chuckled. The evening was filled with jokes, laughter, and some reminiscing of old times.

Soon, the sound of fireworks resonated across the harbor. It was a spectacular show which lit up the sky and was choreographed perfectly with the music blasting out of four large speakers. The organizers didn't disappoint anyone with their astounding display.

After the fireworks, the crowd on the patio started to thin out.

"We should head out soon," Lou's wife said, looking at her watch anxiously. "The kids are at home with a sitter," she explained to the group. "Our kids are like night and day. One falls asleep anywhere, but Jake? He'll wait up all night for us to walk in the door. The sitter can never get him to sleep."

Lou leaned in closer to her. "I'll just finish my beer first, is that okay, Hun?" Lou smiled and kissed her gently on the cheek.

Brandon noticed her display a subtle eye roll to Chad's wife, and then both of them smiled.

At the end of the evening, Brandon paid his part of the tab, got in his SUV, and drove back to his motel in Ridgetown. Shortly after leaving the town of Barney's Cove, the streetlights disappeared, and Brandon had to switch on his high beams to maneuver the winding coastal road. As the road turned away from the coastline, it passed through many acres of hardwood bush. He was enjoying the quiet ride, lost in thought, when he felt the first hint that something was wrong. The first sign of a problem was when he couldn't maintain control of the vehicle. The steering wheel felt loose beneath his hands. As he approached a sharp curve in the road, the SUV threatened to continue straight despite his efforts to steer left. The vehicle was pulling to one side for some reason. The SUV jerked as he hit the brakes and he struggled to stay on the road. Somehow, he made it around the turn, and the wheels crunched on the gravel shoulder as he brought the SUV to a rough stop. After the dust had cleared, he searched for his flashlight. "Oh, man, I don't need this tonight. Shit!" he cursed.

After getting out and checking around his vehicle with his flashlight in hand, he realized that he'd run into some double unfortunate luck; not one, but *two* flat tires. *What are the chances of that happening?* he thought. As he searched for Chad's number on his phone, he saw a vehicle approaching. Its indicator came on and it pulled in behind Brandon.

Brandon approached the driver's side of the gray 4x4 pickup truck and the window rolled down. An unshaven man in his mid-forties, elbow resting on the door, stuck his head out the window. Brandon could see part of a tattoo on his forearm, but the rest of it was covered up by the sleeve of a plaid shirt. The man's eyes were partially concealed in the shadow created by the peak of his baseball cap. He removed a wooden toothpick from his mouth before speaking. "Hey, you having some trouble there?"

"Two flats" Brandon replied, staring with frustration at his rented SUV.

The Whiskey Lee

"Aw, that hurts," the man commented. "I can give you a lift into town if you want. You'll be here all night waiting for a tow." The man put the toothpick back in his mouth.

Brandon accepted, wanting to get back to his room. "Thanks. I really appreciate this. Let me lock it up first," he said, pressing the door lock button on the key fob.

As they drove down the road, the man was strangely quiet. It wasn't until they made a right turn off the main road that Brandon grew suspicious. "Why are we turning?" he asked.

"Shortcut," the man said bluntly.

Something didn't feel right. Brandon knew there was no shortcut back to town this way. Only one main road connected the two coastal towns. He became anxious and tried to think of a way out. His mind was racing. They were getting further away from the main road. Brandon's instincts were telling him that something wasn't right about this guy. From out of the darkness, a deer bounded across the road in front of them, almost landing on the hood of the truck. The surprised driver slammed on his brakes. This was Brandon's chance to make a break for it. When the dust cloud settled, the passenger door was wide open and Brandon was making a dash for the tree line. By the time the first gunshot rang out, he'd already bolted up an incline and was racing desperately toward the safety of the trees. The second shot narrowly missed his right ear. *Shit!* Brandon thought. *He's trying to kill me. What the...? Keep running. Don't fall!* Brandon managed to make it to the forest just before hearing another shot ring out. *Which way do I go? God, I don't want to die tonight. Not out here*, he thought. It was dark, and he couldn't see very well with the only illumination being the moonlight.

The force of the blow came fast and hard. It jolted him backward and darkness followed shortly thereafter. After a little while, things slowly started to come back into focus. His eyes were open, but everything around him was dark. The ground was cold and damp. He blinked a few times to try to clear his blurred vision. There was a buzzing in his ears. Shapes started to appear. He could hear crickets singing. Giant hands loomed above him. He chose a white circle of light to focus on. His head was pounding. Moments later, other smaller white objects started to appear in the darkness. It wasn't long before he realized that he was lying on his back, staring up at the moon and the stars. What he'd originally thought to be giant hands had now transformed into a large canopy of ferns, which seemed to be shielding him from harm. Brandon remembered the road, his SUV getting two flat tires and then—the man with the gun. He realized that he must have hit his head on a low-hanging tree branch, because it was throbbing. He also had a bit of a sore neck from the impact, but other than that he felt okay. He jerked up onto his feet and began searching for his phone. He hoped it hadn't fallen out of his pocket inside the gunman's truck. He tried to retrace his steps, moving cautiously because he wasn't sure if the gunman was still lurking out there somewhere. Brandon didn't see the truck, but that didn't mean the psycho wasn't hiding, waiting for him to come out. After Brandon's blackout, it seemed that he'd lost all track of time. He wasn't sure if he'd been lying on the ground for five minutes, or five hours. Not being able to see much in the dark, he decided to abandon the search for his phone.

Once he was sure the coast was clear, he sprinted back across the same road where he'd escaped the gray 4x4. It was the only way he could get himself back on track without getting lost. It was a long trek back to Ridgetown, so he wanted to cover as much ground as possible. After walking about twenty minutes, he saw the lights of an on-coming vehicle. Brandon wasn't sure if it was the gray 4x4 or not, so he hid behind a tree. Seeing it pass by, he slowly exhaled. It wasn't the gunman's vehicle. After ten more minutes of walking, a noise up ahead made him freeze in his tracks. It was the unmistakable sound of someone stepping on a twig. Brandon could just make out the familiar outline of a person, standing there in the moonlight. As his eyes adjusted, a truck's headlight and chrome rim also came into view. There was a muzzle flash accompanied by a loud bang. Tree bark splintered beside him, making Brandon spin and take cover. *The asshole had been waiting for me to show myself*, Brandon thought. He counted to three in his head before bolting from his position and running deeper into the forest. Another shot rang out. Brandon knew where the gunman was from the muzzle flash, but the guy had no idea where Brandon was now. He was just wasting his bullets trying to find a lucky target. Brandon wondered how many bullets the gunman had left. But while the question had entered his mind, he sure as hell wasn't going to stick around and find out. He carefully made his way through the woods in the dark, knowing that if he failed this time, it may be his last chance to get out of there alive. His eyes were starting to adjust to the darkness. The mosquitoes were thick. He could hear them buzzing around his ears. *God, I want to get out of this forest so bad*, Brandon thought. He figured that if he stayed hidden and remained calm, perhaps the psychopath will give up and go away. He wasn't sure exactly what time it was. He usually had no need for a wristwatch because he had always carried his mobile phone with him. Now, after losing his phone in the woods, Brandon wished that he'd invested in one. He tried to think of what he had in his pockets that could help him: *wallet, credit cards, keys, a small folding knife.* The knife would have to do. He was in survival mode now, as he walked several yards, then ducked behind a fallen tree and listened for movement. He had a bad feeling. The forest was eerily quiet, aside from the annoying mosquitoes and the singing crickets.

Brandon was about to stand up, when he was temporarily blinded by a bright light. The intense beam shone directly in his face. He closed his eyes, threw his arms up in front of him, and waited for the barrage of bullets. *This is it!* He expected to be shot to death right there, in cold blood. "Please don't shoot!" Brandon begged.

"What the hell is going on here?" a raspy old voice demanded. Brandon realized it wasn't the voice of the man from the truck.

"Get down!" Brandon hissed. "Turn that light off!"

The man crouched down, aiming the light away from Brandon but he didn't switch it off. It was dark in the forest and this man had just messed up all hope of Brandon's night vision being restored anytime soon.

"What the hell's going on?" The man repeated.

"Turn off your—"

But Brandon's words where instantly cut off when a shot rang out, ricocheting off a nearby tree. As the man dove for cover behind Brandon, the flashlight dropped to the ground, spilling light across the dead wood and vegetation on the forest floor. The singing crickets fell silent.

"Holy smokes, someone just took a shot at me!" the man whispered. "I thought someone was shooting off fireworks out here, so I came out to see what was going on. My ears aren't as good as they used to be." The man raised his shotgun and cocked it, aiming the barrel toward the forest. "Where is the bastard now?"

"I'm not sure. Look for the muzzle flashes. Cover me." Brandon leaped out to retrieve the flashlight and turned if off. As he felt his way back to the cover of the fallen tree, he had to blink a couple of times to re-establish his night vision.

"Who is that out there?" the man asked, while still scanning the forest. The crickets started singing again.

"It's some crazy nutjob with a gun," said Brandon.

The older man took whatever aim he had and fired blindly into the dark forest. There was no return gunfire. Each of them stayed quiet and listened for snapping branches or the rustling of leaves. There was silence in the forest.

"I'm not sure where he is now. We'll have to wait for him to make another move. Who is he?" the man whispered again.

"I don't know," Brandon whispered back. "My car got two flats and he offered to drive me into town. Next thing I knew, he was driving into the bush and that's when I jumped out. Now he's trying to kill me," he said, handing the man's flashlight back to him.

"It sounds like he targeted you. He probably gave you those flats. I think my gunshots may have scared him away though. If he's smart, he's hightailed it," the man said. "Okay, we've got to get out of here. I'm not interested in a gun fight. This is the one time I'd wished I'd listened to my wife. She suggested I watch a movie with her tonight, but instead, I'm running around the woods, being shot at by some asshole." He motioned for Brandon to follow him. "Let's go," the man whispered. The tree cover was dense. Instead of using the bright flashlight, the man pulled out a tiny penlight to help illuminate their way.

Arriving at a fence, the man stopped. "My place. Climb over, but watch for the holes when we're cuttin' across the field."

Brandon hesitated.

"Groundhogs," the man explained.

They moved as fast as the uneven terrain would allow, and soon the lights of a house penetrated the darkness. As they got closer, dogs began to bark. The door to the farmhouse swung open. The silhouette of a woman appeared, holding a long-barreled gun in her hands.

"Who's out there?" She called shakily.

"It's just me, honey," the man called back.

"Who's with you?" the woman demanded. "Was someone shooting out there?"

"This guy's car broke down and then some crazy guy out there was firing off a gun," he answered. "Everyone into the house!"

The three of them went inside. The dogs stayed outside, curiously sniffing the ground. "Come on in you two, in the house, now!" the woman called. "Hurry up!" The dogs entered the house with their tails wagging. Once they were all safely inside, she bolted the door.

"Lock all the doors," the man ordered as he walked around closing curtains and turning off lights.

"What's going on?" the woman asked, clearly frightened.

"Just trust me on this. I hope that trouble doesn't come to our door, but if it does, be ready. We should call the police."

The older woman turned and looked questioningly at Brandon.

"Your husband saved my life," he said quickly, and explained what had transpired after his tires went flat.

"Hello, police?" came the man's voice from the kitchen. "Someone's shooting out in my back woods. Nearly got me. Get someone over here, pronto." He gave his name and address. "Yes—Arthur," he confirmed with the person at the other end of the phone.

Arthur's wife anxiously approached him when he returned to the living room. "How long before the police get here?" she asked, holding onto his arm.

"They didn't say," Arthur replied.

"I'm really sorry about all this, Mrs. . . . ?" Brandon began.

"Please, call me Claire," she said.

"I'm Brandon," he introduced himself.

She smiled weakly in return.

"You might want to get yourself a gun," Arthur advised Brandon, half in jest.

Brandon ran a shaky hand through his hair. "I don't know how to thank you for getting me out of there, Arthur."

"Never heard of such a thing happening in these parts," Arthur replied, shaking his head. His wife was still gripping his arm, and he patted her hand comfortingly.

"Brandon, would you like a drink?" she asked. "I'd rather not drink alone, and I need one right about now!"

"The wife likes her wine," Arthur said. "I stay away from the hard stuff, myself. Got some good old Canadian beer, though, if that suits you."

Brandon smiled. "That suits me just fine."

Two police officers arrived shortly after, took statements from Arthur and Brandon, and then left to conduct a search of the area. They returned in short order, unable to find anything. They informed the trio that they would search again at first light with the bloodhound from the station. A description of the man and the gray 4x4 would be dispatched immediately to officers in and around the area. Brandon asked about his SUV.

"We'll get it towed to the station and hold it there for you," one of the officers stated. "Chief will probably want to take a look at those tires anyway. We'll get the bloodhound on that too to see if he can pick up a scent."

Arthur offered to drive Brandon back to his motel, but Claire was too nervous to be home alone. "What if he's out there, watching and waiting for the police to leave, Arthur?"

Brandon knew that he was the reason for the situation to begin with and sympathized with Claire's fear. He turned to the police officer. "Think I can get a ride back with you? I don't want to put these folks out any more than I already have. Besides, I need to get some ice on this bump and lay down for a while."

The officer agreed. Brandon thanked the couple for all they had done and promised to make it up to them.

Back at the Rocky Ridge Motel, the officer walked Brandon to his door. "We'll drive by a few times tonight, Mr. Summers, but the chief will want to see you in the morning."

15

Before dragging her tired heels across the threshold of her room at the Rocky Ridge Motel, Rosie glanced over at her vehicle. Double checking that it was locked, she pressed the remote key lock once. Satisfied after the horn beep, she entered her room and locked it.

It didn't take her long to crawl under the covers and fall asleep. There wasn't a sound coming from the rooms on either side of hers. Rosie appreciated the silence as she drifted off to sleep.

It was a little after ten the next morning when Rosie left her motel room. Her sunglasses were on the table beside the bed, so she scooped them up as she passed by. After finding the song she wanted to listen to on her ipod, Rosie raised the volume slightly before heading outside, but not before double checking that she had her room key. Satisfied that it was in her pocket, she left the room, closed the door and quickly turned, nearly bumping into a man, who was on his way to the adjacent room. She jumped, startled. "Oh my god!" Rosie gasped. "You scared me!"

The man stepped back. "I'm sorry," he apologized. "I thought you heard me."

She took her earbuds out. "I guess it's my fault; sorry. I had my music too loud," said Rosie.

***

Brandon sighed to himself. He wasn't really in the meeting-people mood. He had only a few hours sleep last night, and the only thing he really wanted to do was go into his room for some desperately needed shut-eye, but now there was a woman who barely reached the height of the dimple on his chin, standing between him and his bed. She had hazel eyes, dark auburn hair, and was dressed in running wear.

"My name is Rosie." She reached her hand out her hand in a casual, friendly greeting.

"Brandon." He shook her hand. "You sound like you're from England?"

"It's nice to meet you, Brandon." She said smiling. "Yes, I'm from England, just going out for my run. Hope to chat with you later, neighbor," Rosie added. Her eyes were bright and she tilted her head slightly, smiling at him.

"It was nice meeting you too Rosie," said Brandon, as he entered his room.

With squinty, sleepless eyes, he locked the door and then, before pulling the drapes closed, he peered out the window and watched Rosie walk toward the edge of Coastal Route #1. She looked north, hesitated for a moment, and then started her southward run toward the more populated part of Ridgetown.

Brandon caught a glimpse of a police cruiser slowing down as it drove by. Seeing the cruiser seemed to restore his peace of mind. He closed the drapes and kicked off his shoes. *That's good, at least I'll be able to sleep now*, he thought, as he threw the bed covers aside.

***

It was about two o'clock in the afternoon when Brandon awoke. He was dressed and showered in no time. As he opened the drapes and window, it took a moment for his eyes to adjust to the sunlight. He could hear seagulls calling from the nearby wharf. Putting his sunglasses on, he draped a light jacket over his shoulder and grabbed his room key.

As he stepped out into the sunlight, Rosie's door also opened.

"Oh, hello again neighbor," she said pleasantly, stepping outside. "We really should stop meeting like this."

Brandon smiled. "How was your run?"

"It was great. I'm feeling terrific now. It's amazing how a bit of exercise can make a person feel," Rosie said.

"Yes, exercise is good, but all I can think about right now is getting some food into my grumbling stomach. Do you know of any good places to eat around here?" Brandon asked her.

"What's your hankering? Breakfast or lunch?"

"Breakfast," said Brandon.

"I know just the right place. Would it be okay if I joined you?" Rosie asked.

"Sure, it would be nice to have some company," said Brandon, gently massaging the back of his neck. He'd woken up with a headache and muscle stiffness from the mighty blow he endured when the tree branch had clotheslined him.

"Did you have a rough night last night?" Rosie asked teasingly, and then added quickly. "Oh sorry! If you don't want to answer that, it's okay. It really isn't any of my business."

"It's okay. I just have a bit of a headache, and yes, I did have a rough night last night, actually," he said. "But not in a fun kind of way."

"Oh, that's not good," Rosie said. "I have some aspirin in my room if you'd like some," she offered.

"Uh, yeah, that would be great, thanks, he said.

"Be right back," she said, stepping inside her room, but leaving the door slightly ajar.

Brandon gingerly caressed the bump on his forehead. It felt extremely tender.

That was the moment everything changed. Brandon heard the sound of a vehicle approaching fast and he glanced toward the road. He could hear Rosie's voice through the open door of her room, but it sounded a million miles away as his attention focused on a pickup truck barreling into the motel parking lot. It made a quick turn, kicking up dust. The truck roared toward Brandon, veered, and then stopped abruptly. The passenger side window was open. As the dust cleared, Brandon saw a man's face just before he saw the muzzle of a gun come up.

Rosie's words got louder as she approached the doorway. "I know of a little breakfast place called the Saucy—" She didn't get a chance to finish. Brandon's jacket fell to the floor as he grabbed Rosie by her shoulders, spun her around, and pushed her back inside. Rosie was sent sprawling, with an "oomph" as she hit the floor with a thud. The open aspirin bottle flew out of her hand and pills scattered wildly in all directions.

"Hey! What the—" Rosie shouted.

There was a bang and then a loud crack as a bullet splintered the door frame, but Brandon was already diving for cover behind Rosie.

"Someone's shooting at us," Brandon whispered. "Stay down!" he commanded.

"Oh my god! Who is it?" she asked in a hoarse whisper.

"I don't know," he said breathlessly. He was able to reach the door with his foot, so he kicked it before another barrage of bullets came at them. "Quick, get in the bathroom. Take cover!" he commanded, as the motel door slammed shut.

Rosie crawled into the bathroom and closed the door. There was a squealing of tires out on the road, and then it became eerily quiet.

Minutes later, the silence was broken by panicked voices outside the door. On his hands and knees, heart pounding at the sudden pandemonium, Brandon scurried to the window and peeked out. The gray pickup truck was gone. There was a small crowd of people forming in the parking lot. A hysterical woman was screaming for someone to call the police.

He heard the bathroom door creak open behind him. "Is the coast clear?" Rosie whispered.

"I'm not sure," Brandon replied in a whisper. "Stay low, just in case."

"What the *hell* is going on here?" Rosie cried out in a shaky voice.

Ignoring her, Brandon peeked out the window again. *Never a cop when you need one*, he thought grimly.

"All your first dates like this? Remind me to research you later and check," she whispered back and closed the door again.

Brandon chuckled despite his intense fear. He glanced up at the door and counted the bullet holes, where streams of sunlight now passed through. He shivered, realizing how close they had come to being hit. Sirens in the distance reassured him that help was on the way. A short time later, two police cars came ripping into the parking lot. The spectators scattered just before the front doors of both cars swung open. Officers dropped to their knees and drew their pistols, aiming toward the motel. Brandon didn't like the look of this. He slid away from the window, joining Rosie in the bathroom.

"I heard sirens. Is everything okay?" she asked.

"The police have their guns drawn. We'll just stay in here for a minute until things cool down," Brandon said, leaving the bathroom door slightly ajar, so he could peer out.

A commanding voice summoned them, using a bullhorn. "This is the police! Come out with your hands up!"

Rosie and Brandon did as they were instructed.

They stepped outside with their hands in the air. Other motel patrons did the same. Brandon spoke first. "We're unarmed innocent victims here. The shooter left in a gray 4x4 pickup truck," he quickly informed the officers.

***

At the Police station, Chief Flynn folded his arms. "Why doesn't it surprise me that whenever there's trouble, you are right smack in the middle of it, Summers?"

"It's nice to see you again too, Chief," said Brandon. "For a small town, it sure has lots of action."

"Funny, it was quiet for a long time before you arrived," Flynn answered, smirking.

Chief Flynn unfolded his arms and moved a folder on his desk to reveal something underneath it. "By the way, here's your phone back." He passed Brandon his cellular phone.

"Wow! Where did you find it?" said Brandon, inspecting it for damage.

"Officer Nolan found it near the road. It must have dropped out of your pocket while you were running for the trees."

"Thanks! I didn't think I was ever going to see it again." Brandon's said.

"So, what happened at the motel?" Flynn asked patiently.

"I'll do my best at describing what happened. Any idea yet who owns that gray 4x4?" asked Brandon. "I'm almost one hundred percent it was the same guy from last night."

"We don't really have anything yet, but it sounds like you've really pissed him off! Did you get a look at him, plate number, any other details?" Flynn asked while he eased back in his swivel chair, clasping his hands across his stomach.

Brandon shook his head. "It all happened so fast. All I saw was the truck and a quick glimpse of his face under the baseball cap before the gun barrel come up. That was when I shoved Rosie back into her motel room and dove in behind her. That's pretty much the story on how I ended up in her room. I'm sure he was the same guy who was shooting at me in the forest. Same gray pickup truck too."

Flynn nodded without expression.

"That's okay. I'm glad you two are okay. I'll need you to tell me everything again from the start of when you got to this town. This may take a while. I just want to make sure we haven't missed any details." Flynn offered Brandon some water.

After an hour of questioning, Brandon finally got to ask his own. "Hey, what happened to the police officer that was going to watch over my motel room?"

"We did have a cruiser come by, but it is the 4th of July and an extremely busy weekend. I honestly didn't think anyone was going to try anything in the middle of the day, you know, with so many witnesses around."

"Yes, I guess that makes sense." Brandon eased off.

"We have Rosie in the other room. She's also being questioned. How long did you say you've known each other?" This caught Brandon off guard. His surprised reaction showed Flynn exactly what he wanted to know.

"Rosie and I just met each other today at the motel. The only thing we have in common is that her room is beside mine. Nothing more," Brandon assured him.

Flynn nodded. "That's what she said too. Just confirming it."

"Okay, so you're saying it's likely the same guy that tried to kill you out in the forest. Correct?"

Brandon nodded. "I'm pretty damned sure of it."

Flynn nodded while jotting something down in his notebook. He took a deep breath and then looked up at Brandon.

"Okay, the first thing that I suggest is that you move to another motel. Stay clear of this area for a while," Flynn added. "It looks like you've overstayed your welcome at the Rocky Ridge Motel. I could probably suggest a couple of locations, fairly secluded and out-of-the-way."

"Sure, I'll take a look at some of your recommendations," Brandon replied. "What about Rosie?"

"I'll suggest the same for Rosie. She's pretty shaken up. She doesn't want to stay at that motel anymore either. Don't say as I blame her. I'll go get those listings for you right now. It may not be easy to find something, with the holiday long weekend. Do you want some coffee or anything?" Flynn got up to leave the room.

"Sure; black, one sugar. Hey, uh, before you leave, could you let me know when my SUV will be released?"

Flynn turned. "You'll probably be good to go in within the hour. Do you have a tow truck to pick up your vehicle?"

"No," said Brandon.

"Well, you may consider getting one because your tires are still flat. Our officers only comb it for evidence, nothing more."

"I guess I'll be phoning roadside assistance then," said Brandon.

"Sure. You can use that phone on the desk to call them if you want. I'll be right back," Flynn said, leaving Brandon in the room alone. While Brandon waited, he tried powering up his cell phone. He had a weak battery signal and two messages showing on the screen. One call was from Chad and the other one from a number he didn't recognize.

Not long after he'd phoned roadside assistance, Brandon received the first text message from them. The driver would be arriving to pick up the SUV within the hour.

When Chief Flynn returned, he gave Brandon the list of accommodations as promised, as well as the directions for a service garage that he knew would be open on the long weekend. Shortly after that, Brandon's vehicle was released.

***

Unfortunately, the nearest service garage open for business was about eight miles away. After Brandon's rented SUV was safely secured on the back of the tow truck, Officer Nolan led them to the edge of town. Before reaching a white stone church, the police officer pulled to the side of the road to let them pass. Brandon looked in the mirror, catching a glimpse of the cruiser pulling a U-turn before it sped back to Ridgetown. Brandon and the tow truck driver were on their own now.

16

After settling up with the mechanic, Brandon scanned through Flynn's recommended list of places to stay. He was elated to have his truck back. Glancing nervously into his rearview mirror, just in case he was being followed, he pulled off the road into the parking lot behind the white stone church to contact a few of them. The words *no vacancy* seemed to repeat themselves. Getting desperate for a place to stay, his next call was to Chad. He quickly updated Chad on his run-ins with the gunman, and asked him if he had any leads on any out-of-the-way accommodation in either Ridgetown or Barney's Cove.

"What the hell man! Are you okay? Now I feel bad. I was the one that invited you down here for a vacation," Chad said apologetically. "Some friend I am, huh?"

"It's all good. I just wanted to tell you that I'm still alive and kicking."

"The offer's still open if you want to stay here man, otherwise just give me five minutes and I'll call you back. I know a place just outside of town that rents out small cottages along the Herring River. My friend does all the maintenance over there. He drives around on an ATV all day and calls it work. Ha!"

Chad called him back within five minutes, as promised. "You're in luck, Brandon. My buddy Hans said there's a small one-bedroom cottage available, overlooking the river. It's got a small kitchen with a microwave, coffee maker, and a toaster. By some fortunate luck the guest checked out early this morning. Only thing is, the fridge quit yesterday. New one isn't being delivered until Tuesday. That may explain why it's available."

"Sounds good," said Brandon.

"I've got a large cooler in the garage that you can borrow. Just stop by and pick it up anytime. All you need is a bag of ice and a case of beer."

"Okay thanks bud. What's the phone number for the cottages?" Brandon was stoked to hear that Chad found a place so quickly. He jotted down the information. After that he placed a call to the outpost which ran the cottages.

A woman answered. Brandon asked her to put the vacant cottage on hold for him.

"The fridge is broken in that one. Do you mind? I could give you a bit of a discount, but not much."

"That's perfect. I'll be over to check in within the hour." Feeling satisfied, he ended the call and raced back to Ridgetown to collect his belongings from the motel.

Once arriving, he saw a couple of police cruisers in the parking lot. Rosie was chatting with a couple of the officers in front of the motel. He parked his SUV and approached the group.

"Hi," he said, strolling up behind them.

Rosie turned. "Hi, Brandon."

"Is it okay if I collect my stuff from my room now?" he asked the one of the police officers.

"Yes, go ahead," a young officer replied. "We had to search your room, so things may not be where you left them."

"Okay." Brandon lifted the police tape in order to enter his room. He briefly paused to examine the damage done to Rosie's door and frame. It finally dawned on him how close they came to being filled with lead. He shivered at the thought before entering his room.

While gathering up his stuff, a soft knock at the door snapped him out of his thoughts. Brandon pulled open the door with anticipation. He had a strong feeling it wasn't the police.

"Are you leaving town?" Rosie asked curiously.

"Uh, no I'm not. I found another place to stay nearby," he replied.

"Okay, good." She smiled. "Me too. Chief Flynn found me a place to stay near the wharf. Maybe I'll see you around here again then," she said, tilting her head, and running her fingers through her hair.

"Yeah, that would be nice." He grinned back at her warmly. "Hopefully, our next encounter won't be as bad as the first one. I really hope you forgive me for pushing you to the ground. I am truly sorry."

She smiled as she walked slowly backward in the direction of her room. "You didn't hurt me. I'm okay. You saved my life. Thank you." She turned toward her room, while still keeping eye contact with him. Offering a little wave, she disappeared into her room.

***

The cottage site was off the beaten path, in a wooded area. There was nothing but trees and a winding gravel road in front of him.

Brandon had picked up the cooler from Chad before stopping to check in at the Herring River Outpost, just off Coastal Route #1. After receiving the key for his cottage, he couldn't wait to get settled in. When the middle-aged woman with the long, braided gray hair had given him his cottage key, she said there would be a small sign at the end of the lane, which indicated the cottage by name. All five cottages were named after types of trees. Brandon's was fondly named *The White Pine*.

He had taken the first left, as instructed, but started to think that he'd passed the laneway to his cottage as the road was longer than he thought it would be. He slammed his foot on the brake, grinding his wheels to a halt and stirring up dust as he passed the hidden laneway on his left. The gravel crunched beneath his tires as he backed up and turned into the laneway. Brandon tapped the brakes once, as a chipmunk scurried across the road in front of him. Songbirds lined the trees beside him, and he heard a distant tapping of a woodpecker which echoed through the trees.

He smiled, impressed by the remoteness of the area. He eyed the rustic but quaint little cottage up ahead. It was perched up on a small hill, surrounded by tall trees. Brandon could see the other four cottages, but they were well spaced among the trees for the privacy of the guests. Each had their own laneways, barbecues, horseshoe and fire pits, along with a mesmerizing view of the Herring River.

Once settled into his private little hideaway, Brandon called Chad to tell him that he'd checked in okay.

"This is a sweet little place, Chad. Thanks for finding it. The only problem that I can see is that it doesn't have Wi-Fi. Also, remind me to pick up some bug repellent. The mosquitoes have laid out the welcome mat for me already."

Chad laughed. "Don't complain; at least they don't carry guns. Hey, let's meet up for another dive soon, so I can keep your ass out of trouble," said Chad.

"Ha! *You* keep *me* out of trouble? That's a good one." Brandon chuckled and then became serious. "You know what? I wouldn't be surprised if this 'Let's kill Brandon' shit is related to the *Whiskey Lee*. I'm getting strange reactions every time I mention the name."

"What kind of reactions?" The tone in Chad's voice was an indication of his growing concern.

"I'll tell you when I see you. I've been keeping in close contact with Chief Flynn. I'm learning something new every day."

"Okay, just keep me updated. Are you saying the beer is going to be on me?" Chad asked.

"Maybe," Brandon laughed.

"You keep yourself safe, man. I mean that. Maybe it's time to step back and let Chief Flynn handle things."

"I'm in too deep to turn back now," Brandon admitted.

"I get that. Well, if you need help at anytime, I'm just a phone call away," said Chad.

"Sure, thanks."

After hanging up with Chad, Brandon hesitated before calling the unknown number on his call history.

A female voice answered after the second ring. "Hello?"

"Hi, this is Brandon Summers. Did you phone me earlier?"

"Yes. It went to voicemail earlier, so I hung up. How's the search going?"

He smiled when he recognized her voice.

"Gloria, sorry. I didn't recognize your number. I lost my phone last night and didn't get it back until about an hour ago. Police Chief Flynn returned it to me."

"Police chief? What happened? Is everything okay?"

"It's all good, other than the fact that I got shot at twice in under twenty-four hours and knocked myself out while trying to escape a shooter in the woods," he explained. "My head still hurts."

"Oh my gosh! That's awful!" she shrieked.

Brandon explained everything to Gloria, including the engraved Zippo lighter he and Chad had found on the wall dive. She was shocked to learn all that he had gone through and feared for his safety.

"Sorry to cut this short, but I need to get ready to go to work soon," she said.

"Okay, I've got a few things I need to do too. Maybe we can get together later and catch up some more."

After that, Brandon went out to grab a few things: A bag of ice, take-out fish and chips, and a case of beer.

***

Exhausted, Brandon slept late into the next morning. After coffee and a bowl of cereal, he went for a light jog along the bank of the river to clear his head.

He drove into Barney's Cove to visit Chad at the dive shop and deliver some coffee and donuts, in thanks for loaning him the cooler. The gesture was much appreciated.

After the two friends caught up, Brandon headed down to the wharf. The area was alive with tourists meandering along the shore, and recreational boats cruising out on the water. His thoughts somehow got around to Rosie as he enjoyed the midafternoon atmosphere, and he found himself smiling. The sound of her voice wafting across the breeze behind him didn't come as any surprise.

"Might have known I'd find *you* down here," he heard Rosie say.

He turned, and the first thing he noticed was how her yellow lacy blouse brought out the depth of her dark auburn hair. Her white capris showcased sculptured, tanned legs, and he instantly felt a stirring in his jeans.

"Hi again!" Brandon replied, with a sheepish grin. "It's a small world, isn't it?"

"Small town, actually," Rosie corrected him as she leaned on the railing next to him. "Is it safe for me to be this close?"

His eyes took in her curves with a deep appreciation, but before he could utter a flirtatious comeback, he caught the flash of indignation in her eyes.

"Look, I'm really sorry for what happened yesterday. It's been a really, really bizarre couple of days and I'm sorry you got in the middle of it all," he said honestly.

Rosie stared hard at him for a long time. Eventually her eyes softened and a tiny smile appeared on her face. "I'll have to admit, I've never had that much drama when meeting someone for the first time. Talk about sweeping a girl off her feet, literally."

Brandon smiled, embarrassed. "Are you sure you still want to hang out with me?"

"Try me. After all, I did come here for an adventure." Rosie placed a foot up on the bottom railing and deeply inhaled the fresh sea air. "Of course, being shot at wasn't exactly what I had in mind."

"What kind of adventure are you looking for?" Brandon asked, with a teasing smile.

"I'm a writer," Rosie replied. "I'm open to anything."

"Really? I'm a writer too, but on vacation right now. Came down here from Canada for my own adventure."

Rosie raised her eyebrows.

Brandon put his hands up in defense. "Uh, I know what you're thinking. I didn't plan on being shot at either. I came down here to dive old shipwrecks with my buddy, Chad."

"You know what's funny?" Rosie asked. "When I told my best friend Marian that I was going to the United States for a big adventure, you know what she said? Be careful what you wish for; that's what she said. Well, I guess we have three things in common then—we're both writers and we're both here for an adventure," said Rosie.

Brandon smiled. "What's the other thing? That's only two."

"We were both shot at yesterday. That's three. Boy, you must have hit your head really hard. Have you forgotten already?" She smiled teasingly.

Brandon rolled his eyes.

She winked good naturedly. "How's your head today anyway? I never did get a chance to give you the aspirin."

He placed his hand on his head. "Feels better now, but it will take some time for this bump to go down. Thanks for asking. So, what do you write about?"

"I write mostly ghost stories," said Rosie.

"Interesting," said Brandon. "And creepy."

Rosie chuckled. "Well, I guess now you now know a little about me. How about you?"

"I'm a journalist. One day I'd like to try my hand at writing a mystery novel," he admitted.

"Murder mysteries?"

"I'm hoping," he smiled.

"How did I guess?" She laughed. "Was that you getting into one of your character's yesterday? I guess I'm going to be in your book now too. Just make sure you change my name," Rosie teased.

Brandon grinned at her witty sense of humor.

"Do you feel like going for a walk?" Brandon asked.

"Where?" Rosie asked.

"I don't know. Maybe just along the waterfront here. I thought about going into Danny's for a drink. Care to join me?"

"Sure, I'll join you," said Rosie, without hesitation.

In the harbor, seagulls screamed jubilantly as they swooped and soared behind the departing and arriving fishing vessels. Along the way, Brandon's phone buzzed. He pulled it from his pocket and read a text message.

Hi Brandon, it's Gloria. Where are you right now? I have something for you.

"Sorry Rosie, I don't mean to be rude, but I need to reply to this."

Rosie dismissed it with a wave of her hand. "Go ahead. It's okay." Brandon sent a quick text to Gloria.

I'm in Ridgetown, heading to Danny's Restaurant by the wharf.

Great, I'll meet you there. This can't wait.

Ok, see you there, Brandon messaged back and then put the phone back in his pocket.

He turned to Rosie. "That was my friend Gloria, from the Piper & Pelican. She wants to meet me at Danny's to give me something."

Puzzled, he wondered what could be so important.

17

The horn blared loudly, announcing the Dodge Challenger's arrival. Gloria had just locked her door and was about to descend the front steps when she heard the powerful rumble of the Hemi engine as the vehicle rolled up and stopped in front of the house. It was her friend Sasha. Gloria opened the passenger side door and stuck her head inside. "Did you bring it, Sash?" she asked.

"Yes, I have it," Sasha replied. She pointed to a carefully folded towel protruding from a plastic bag on the seat beside her.

"Perfect," said Gloria, placing it on her lap after she got in and shut the door.

They headed in the direction of Danny's Restaurant. "If we get pulled over, stash that bag behind the seat," Sasha cautioned.

"Okay," Gloria replied. "I really appreciate this."

"He must be a real hottie."

"Sasha!" Gloria replied, blushing. "Well, yes, he is handsome, but he seems like a really nice guy."

"I knew it! You have the hots for him! You go, girl!"

Gloria didn't want to admit that she liked Brandon in that sort of way. "We're just friends."

"Sure, for now." Sasha winked, smiling.

***

"There's a table free over there." Brandon directed Rosie to the far corner of the patio.

Four chairs encircled the glass tabletop, with flowers in a small vase decorating the center. A floral umbrella gently flapped in the breeze above them. Brandon was mindful to choose the chair in the corner so that he had full view of everyone on the patio. He couldn't be too careful after the latest chain of events.

"I like my view better," Rosie said, grinning as she sat down.

Brandon wasn't sure if she was referring to him, or the spectacular view of the harbor behind him.

Their server immediately brought them menus and poured them each a glass of water.

"So, you mentioned that Gloria is your friend? Not your girlfriend?" Rosie asked curiously.

"That's right. We're just friends," Brandon replied.

"What about your other half? Doesn't she like scuba diving?" Rosie pressed inquisitively.

"There's no other half." He smiled inwardly at the way she carried that out.

"You?" He tilted his head inquisitively.

"Same." She held up her left hand. "No ring yet."

He grinned.

"Where are you staying now, Brandon?" Rosie asked, leaning an elbow on the armrest, running her fingers through her hair.

"Police suggested I don't tell anyone," Brandon replied matter-of-factly. Inwardly, he squirmed at the question and directed his attention to the menu.

The server returned with their drinks and left them to look over the menus. To Brandon's dismay, Rosie continued the conversation where they'd left off.

"So, how's that working for you, Brandon? Not telling anyone where you're staying." She gave him an impish grin.

He glanced at her then turned his attention back to the menu. "So far, so good. I'm still alive."

"It sounds like you don't trust me, either," she said with an accusing tone. "It's not like you're too hard to find. I found you today without even trying."

Brandon looked up, realizing that he'd offended her. A gust of wind from the ocean blew her hair across her face, and he was reminded how pretty she was.

"Don't take it personally, Rosie. I'm not supposed to tell anyone where I am staying, and at this point, I don't know who I can trust."

Their server raised an umbrella at a nearby table and seated an elderly couple. Rosie leaned in toward Brandon and said in a quiet voice, "Really? If I remember

The Whiskey Lee

correctly, both you *and* I were getting shot at, in *my* motel room. Did I plan that?" She continued in a mocking voice, pretending to speak to someone not there, "Oh, crazy man with a gun! Remember, you're not supposed to shoot *me*! I'm hiding in the bathtub, so make sure you miss me, but get him!"

Brandon couldn't help but break out into a huge smile when he tried to picture it in his head. He tried not to laugh, taking a sip of beer instead.

Rosie looked annoyed. "Oh, it's funny now, is it?"

The look on her face made him almost spit his beer out as he tried desperately to hold in his laughter.

Rosie began laughing too. "Oh, this beer is going down well," she said with a captivating smile.

He finally swallowed the mouthful of beer, and offered his outstretched hand out to her. "I'm sorry. Are we still friends?"

She slid her chair closer to him, accepting his hand. Her voice softened. "Oh, I guess so, but only because you're the only friend I've got here, besides Len the bartender."

Brandon continued to smile.

In a natural reflex, he pulled his hand from Rosie's when he saw Gloria approaching their table.

"Hello. I hope I am not interrupting anything?" Gloria asked, her eyes resting briefly on the pretty woman sitting comfortably close to Brandon.

"Gloria! Hi! Um...no, you're not. This is Rosie. The one I told you about—my neighbor from the Rocky Ridge Motel. We were playing dodge-the-bullets together yesterday."

"I can't imagine what you two went through." Gloria gently laid a hand on Rosie's shoulder. "I hear you had quite the dramatic experience. Are you okay, Rosie?"

"Physically, I'm alright, but I don't know about mentally. I'm still a little shaken up by the entire ordeal," said Rosie.

"That's understandable. Well, I'm glad to see that no one got hurt. It must have been so scary for you both." Without hesitation, she turned to Brandon. "That's sort of why I'm here. I'm glad you were nearby because I don't want to be dragging this thing all over town." Gloria drew their attention to the bag she held in front of her.

"Please, take a seat." Brandon gestured toward a chair.

"No—not here. Do you think we could go out to the parking lot and talk privately for a few minutes?" Gloria turned to apologize to Rosie. "I'm sorry, Rosie. This is rather important. It won't take long."

"That's okay. I don't have anywhere else to be right now. I'll wait here," Rosie said.

"Thanks, Rosie," said Brandon as he rose from his chair. "Order an appetizer for us if you want to. I'll be right back."

He followed Gloria out to the parking lot. Gloria turned. "This is something to keep you safe," she said, handing Brandon the plastic bag.

Brandon frowned. He peered into the bag and reached for the folded towel inside.

"No, no!" Gloria hissed, slapping his hand away. "Not out here in the open," She whispered, "It's a gun. Keep it concealed."

Brandon's mouth fell open in shock, and his heart started to race.

"If you have any questions or concerns about it, you can ask my friend Sasha. She's the one who provided it. Her car's over there." She pointed. Brandon followed Gloria over to the shiny red Challenger, where a young woman stared into her rearview mirror, applying lipstick.

"Nice car," Brandon said to Sasha through the open passenger side window. He noticed with admiration the fancy-stitched, two-tone red and black leather bucket seats, which complimented the rest of the car.

"Well, it's nice to finally meet you, Brandon. Gloria's been speaking highly of you." Sasha lowered her voice to a mere whisper. "Said you needed something for your protection." She nodded toward the bag in Brandon's hands and then put the cap back on her lipstick. "I'm sure the Beretta Tomcat will do the job for you. My dad used it as a backup weapon. He was a police detective in Brooklyn for twenty-five years."

"I don't know what to say, other than thanks. Could you tell me about it? What caliber?" Brandon asked, leaning his arm on the passenger door.

Sasha leaned over the seat to get nearer to him. "Have you ever used a handgun before, Brandon?" she asked.

"Yes," he admitted. "My friend was a handgun instructor. I went with him a few times."

"So, you know how to handle yourself. That's good," she said, nodding admiringly. "The Tomcat is smaller and lighter than the standard semi-automatic

The Whiskey Lee

pistols. It's a great conceal weapon. No one will see it. The bullets are .32 ACP, in a detachable magazine. They are inside the bag. And don't worry, the gun is clean. It has never been used."

"I'm not sure what else to say. This is a game changer for sure, but why are you giving it to me?" Brandon asked. "Not that I don't appreciate it. This has just caught me completely by surprise."

"Let's just say that I know everything about what Gloria and her family have gone through. If you can bring some good luck back to this town, I'm sure the locals will be eternally grateful. I just want to help any way I can."

"Okay." Brandon accepted her answer. "What if your dad wants it back?"

"He's not going to need it back. My dad passed away five years ago and Mom doesn't want any more guns in the house," Sasha explained.

"Oh, I'm sorry for your loss," Brandon muttered sincerely.

"Thanks. Just do the right thing, okay? Use it for your protection. If you do something illegal with it, make sure it doesn't come back on either me or my mom," Sasha warned. "Give it back to Gloria when you're done with it."

"I will. You have my word," Brandon assured her. "Thank you, both of you." Brandon stepped aside to allow Gloria to enter the car.

"Just promise me that you'll stay alive," Gloria said to Brandon, as she pulled the car door closed. They continued to chat through the open window.

"I will, and I'll also keep you updated on what I find out," Brandon promised.

"Okay, thanks," Gloria said. "Oh, by the way—I thought of a 'gangsta' name for you."

"What is it?" Brandon asked smiling.

"*Lucky.*" Gloria gave a little wave as the red Dodge Challenger rumbled to life and pulled away. Brandon waved back. He paused for a moment, listening to the deep purr of the engine as the vehicle turned left and roared off down the road.

Still smiling, he walked a short distance to the side street, where he'd left his SUV. "Brandon *Lucky* Summers?" He chuckled, as he entered the vehicle. Once inside, he scanned his surroundings before locking all the doors. He carefully unraveled the towel enough to see a black pistol grip, and then revealed the rest of the Beretta. "Hmmm." He nodded in appreciation at the short barrel. Sasha was right, it was going to be a good conceal weapon. He checked to make sure the thumb safety was on. It was. *It's been a while since I've held a gun*, he thought as he examined it. He checked the detachable box magazine and then lifted the gun up just enough to inspect the alignment of the sights. Satisfied with it, he rewrapped it in the towel and stashed it under the seat, out of sight. He reached back and placed the bag with the bullets behind the seat, got out, locked the vehicle and walked back to Danny's.

As he approached their table, Rosie glanced up. She waited until he sat down before she spoke.

"What was that all about? Or should I even ask?" she questioned, taking a sip of her beer.

"That was Gloria giving us a little home-field advantage."

Rosie gave him a curious look.

"She gave me a gun," he whispered.

Rosie's mouth dropped open. "Why?"

"For my protection."

Rosie frowned and shook her head. "I don't get it. That seems so random, for a friend just to turn up out of the blue and give you a gun. How long have you two known each other?"

"I met Gloria just after I arrived here, about two weeks ago. She works at the Piper & Pelican Tavern."

Rosie took a quick sip of her beer. Brandon blinked and then shifted in his chair. "Okay, I'm going to be completely straight up with you. I've been looking into the disappearance of a fishing trawler and its captain that vanished from this area in 1989. There were two strange deaths a short time after the disappearance. One was a young woman and the other was a lighthouse keeper." He took a gulp of beer.

"Would this be William Irving you're talking about? The murdered lighthouse keeper of Sixteen Fathom Hill?"

Brandon nodded, impressed. "I see you've done your homework."

"That's the reason I'm here. I researched that lighthouse before traveling out here. Some of the locals call it Phantom Hill because it's haunted," said Rosie.

"Correct. I've been asking a few questions around town. The woman who plunged off the cliff and died was pregnant. Her name was Ann Marie. She was Gloria's aunt."

"Oh . . . no!" Rosie said solemnly, putting her hand up to her mouth.

The Whiskey Lee

He nodded. "Someone in this town may not like the fact that I'm here asking questions. I know that because I already received a not-so-warm welcome when I mentioned *The Whiskey Lee*."

"*The Whiskey Lee*?" She looked confused.

"That's the name of the fishing trawler that vanished. It belonged to Captain James Karl Moreland. Ann Marie was his lover. I'm thinking their cases could be connected," Brandon considered.

"Oh, I see now. You know, that's a really interesting revelation you have there. Connected? Hmmm, so that may explain why someone would want to kill you, because you're sticking your nose in the case?"

"Exactly. That's the only thing that makes sense to me too."

"Aren't you scared?" asked Rosie, "I mean, you could be onto something big here and things could get really dangerous. I understand why Gloria gave you the gun now. Have you ever used one before?"

"Yes, about ten years ago," he said. "What about you?"

"Never. Why were you using a gun ten years ago?" She queried. "You don't have to answer if you don't want to."

"I had a friend that was a handgun instructor. We went out to the shooting range quite often. He . . . uh . . . joined the military, got sent to Afghanistan six years ago, drove over a . . ." Brandon winced as he felt the emotional pain surface from deep within him.

"I'm sorry," Rosie said. She touched Brandon's arm compassionately, seeing he was still struggling with it. "You don't have to go on. Let's change the subject. Have you been to any of the marine museums here?"

"No, actually I haven't had a chance yet."

"Well, I definitely recommend the Maine Lighthouse Museum in Rockland."

"I'll have to put that on my list," he said, smiling.

They chatted for a while about museums, treasures, sightseeing and travel. Brandon felt more comfortable with Rosie with each minute that passed. They definitely had some chemistry. Gentle flirtation and teasing back and forth made for a relaxing evening. After receiving their food, they couldn't wait to dig in. Not much needed to be said while they ate. Brandon had a fresh Maine lobster, steamed and served with drawn butter, while Rosie indulged in scallops with lemon and garlic butter.

"The food was bloody delicious." Rosie stated after the meal.

The sun was partially hidden by big fluffy clouds, and a gentle breeze caressed their faces as they enjoyed their meal. Eventually, their server returned.

"Could we have another order of drinks please?" Rosie asked their server, noticing that Brandon had finished his beer.

"Same as you had before?" their server asked.

Brandon nodded. He wasn't sure for what reason Rosie was sent to him, but he did know this—she was making his life better by being here.

"Are you going to be okay driving after having the beer?" Rosie asked.

"Yes, I'm okay," he reassured her.

They concluded their dinner, sharing a parfait for dessert and chatting flirtatiously beneath the setting sun.

"Would you like to do something after dinner?" Brandon asked. He wasn't quite ready to call it a night.

"Sure! What did you have in mind?"

"Do you bowl? I saw a bowling alley down the street," he said.

"Absolutely! That sounds like fun!" she replied enthusiastically.

Brandon took out his wallet and paid the server. He left a generous tip. They walked down the wooden steps and onto the street. "We can walk. It's not far from here," he suggested.

"Yes, good idea."

After two hours of bowling, they reached the front of Rosie's motel, which was conveniently located across from Danny's Restaurant.

"I had a really nice time with you tonight. I hope we can do this again soon," Brandon suggested. He felt immediately warmed by her smile as she turned to face him.

"Yes, me too. I had a lovely time. Almost don't want it to end."

The sun had partially dipped below the horizon, which painted everything a warm orange. It was a beautiful sunset and Rosie's face radiated its soft glow.

It doesn't have to, Brandon thought. "It's handy having your motel right across the street from Danny's," Brandon observed suggestively.

"Yes, it's the best—close to everything. They serve breakfast over at Danny's too," Rosie hinted. She ran her fingers through her hair, playfully sweeping a loose strand behind her ear.

Sensing he wouldn't get an invitation tonight, Brandon reined himself in. "How about having breakfast there with me tomorrow morning?" he asked.

"I'd like that. What time were you thinking?" Rosie asked, unlocking her room door.

"Would ten o' clock work for you?" he asked.

"Yes, that sounds perfect. I'll bring a few snippets of my writing for you to see. I have it all on my laptop," Rosie said enthusiastically. "Bring yours too," she suggested. With a wink, she went inside and closed the door on him.

Brandon's drive back to his rented hideaway in the woods was peaceful. He couldn't stop thinking about his time spent with Rosie. They seemed unusually comfortable in each other's company, given the peculiar and somewhat unprecedented introduction.

The approach to the cottage was eerily silent, other than the gravel crunching underneath the tires. Since leaving Rosie's motel, Brandon found himself continuously checking his rearview mirror to see if anyone was following him. He felt relieved at not seeing any menacing headlights behind him, but kept his guard up. He would ensure the Beretta was loaded and ready by his side all night, just in case.

18

REWIND – 1989

Winding her way up the grassy slope, Ann Marie rested a hand beneath her belly button to support the little round bump, which had grown noticeably bigger in the last few weeks. Now, feeling desperate and alone, she vowed to make every effort possible to find answers regarding the strange disappearance of the man she truly adored. As she rounded the cluster of tall pine trees and stepped into the clearing, the towering Sixteen Fathom Hill Lighthouse appeared in front of her. Seeing it was an indication that she wouldn't have to walk much further to get to Audrey's house. She had lots of questions, and the fact that she didn't have any answers weighed heavily on her mind.

It just so happened that on the day James Moreland had disappeared, Ann Marie decided to walk down to his boat to see what he was up to. To her surprise, both *The Whiskey Lee* and the old lifeboat were missing. She remembered him mentioning that he never took that old lifeboat with him anymore. He'd invested in a newer inflatable two-person emergency life raft. James explained that, "Yes, it's a pricey addition, but it takes up less space than a regular lifeboat and it's better to pay the price now, than pay later, if the vessel should go down in a storm."

Ann Marie looked at her watch. It was late in the afternoon. She thought it was strange because he never fished that late in the day and it was getting close to dinnertime.

Not sure where to turn next, she found herself pacing back and forth along the wharf, wondering who she should ask for help. Ann Marie didn't know anyone at the wharf other than James. Everyone usually kept to themselves.

Seeing another boat captain unloading his daily catch gave her an idea and she quickly approached him.

"Hi, I'm trying to find Captain James Moreland. I'm a little worried that he hasn't come back in yet. Could you please do me a big favor and call him on the radio for me?" She asked.

"Sure. I'll do that for you, sweetheart. But just so you know, James is one of the best mariners around here. He's probably into a big catch. None of us heard a Mayday today. If we did, we'd be out there. We all monitor our radios and wouldn't hesitate to go and help someone in trouble, especially one of our own. We fishermen stick together."

After calling a few times on the radio and coming up empty, the boat captain frowned, looking confused. There was no response from *The Whiskey Lee*. "That's strange. He always answers. Maybe something's wrong with his radio." The concerned look on the man's face crushed Ann Marie's heart. Now she felt both anxious and helpless, growing more concerned by the minute. *Did something happen out there? This is unlike him. He always answers. Where is he?* Her eyes welled up, and a small teardrop escaped, slowly sliding down her cheek. She thanked the captain and walked toward the main shed. Wiping her tears away, she regained her composure and checked her watch again. Seeing a pay phone near the corner of the boat shed, she hurried over to it. *OUT OF ORDER*, a sign taped to the front of it read. Distraught, she frantically looked around for another pay phone.

"That phone's been out of order for a while. There's another one around the corner," a man's voice behind her said. She spun around to see who was talking. "Go around that way," a friendly older man with a full gray beard and mustache said. He was carrying a small, rickety step ladder and gestured toward the corner of the shed.

"Thank you," she replied, taking his advice and sprinting in that direction. Turning the corner, Ann Marie saw the pay phone and ran toward it. She quickly fumbled with the coins in her pocket, while scanning the phone book for the number of James Moreland's sister, Audrey Montgomery. Once finding it, she placed the handset to her ear and inserted her coins.

"Hello?" She heard Audrey answer.

"Hi Audrey. This is Ann Marie."

"Hi, Ann Marie. How are you dear?"

"I haven't been able to get in touch with James. *The Whiskey Lee* isn't here at the dock and I'm worried that something's happened to him out there. He's never out this late. Do you think you could call his wife and see if you can find anything out for me?"

"Kathleen called me about half an hour ago, dear. She was looking for him too."

"Could you call her again please to see if she's heard from him? I'll call you back in about fifteen minutes from this pay phone."

"I'm sure he's okay. He probably got into some fish and time may have escaped him. Just hang tight. I'll phone her right now."

Audrey's words had done nothing to ease her worry. After hanging up the phone Ann Marie paced anxiously. All she could do now was go back to the dock and gaze at the empty abyss where *The Whiskey Lee* was supposed to be moored. Tauntingly, it offered no answers.

Audrey regretfully informed her that James's wife hadn't seen him since the day before. "He often sleeps aboard his boat after going to the bar, that's why Kathleen didn't worry that he hadn't come home last night," Audrey reminded her.

Ann Marie was absolutely beside herself. She was frantic, as she knew that every minute mattered when someone was lost at sea. She lifted the handset and called the police to report him missing. When they'd asked for her name, she hung up the phone.

Ann Marie tried to ready herself for the gut-wrenching news of his demise. *No. No!* she told herself. *Don't think like that! I'm sure he's okay, like Audrey said.*

James Moreland's wife had filed a missing person report with the police the same day.

Over a week went by and there wasn't a day that Ann Marie didn't utter a silent, teary-eyed prayer for the safe return of her love. Away from her parents and coworkers, she silently mourned for him, desperate for answers, all the while keeping in touch with Audrey for any updates on the search. No one could have prepared her for the reality that her unborn baby's father was gone and there wasn't anything that she or anyone else could do to bring him back. Sadness had consumed her, until one day she lifted her head off her pillow. The wheels inside her head were in motion once again as her senses returned. Her sadness changed to confusion, determination, and anger. Ann Marie took a deep breath and exhaled slowly. She sat upright on her bed, swinging both legs onto the floor. *It's time for some answers*, she thought. She became obsessed with knowing why James had been taken from her so suddenly. She stood, reaching for the ivory phone perched atop her blue painted dresser.

"Hello?" Ann Marie heard the once vivacious, exuberant woman answer on the third ring. Audrey Montgomery's voice now sounded spiritless and tired. The fact that James had been missing for more than a week now had taken a toll on her. The initial shock had faded and things would have cooled down over at Audrey's house now. Police investigators would likely have come and gone, focusing on their search out on the water. Most of Audrey's family would be back to their normal routine by now.

"Hi Audrey, it's Ann Marie."

"Are you okay dear? How are you holding up?" she asked.

"I've been going through so many emotions, but otherwise I'm okay; is it safe for me to come over and see you yet?" Ann Marie asked.

"Yes, no one's here. I'm alone. I'd love to see you," Audrey replied weakly.

"Okay, I'll see you soon," Ann Marie said, before hanging up the phone.

19

"Where are you, James?" Ann Marie whispered as she peered out over the ocean. She had just stopped at the lighthouse to catch her breath after walking up the seemingly endless trail. A few deep breaths later, she moved closer to the edge of the cliff. She could feel a nice gentle breeze blowing through her hair. Closing her eyes, she felt the warmth from the sun caressing her face. Now she understood why Audrey had chosen to live up here. It was peaceful.

Before proceeding onwards to Audrey Montgomery's house, Ann Marie squinted and then raised a hand up to shield her eyes from the blazing sun. She scanned the sea again for any sign of the red fishing trawler before moving on. She clung to the last bit of hope that she'd see his bright red trawler returning from some big fishing adventure, casually impressing everyone with a big fish story as to why he's been missing for over a week without contact. Feeling both somber and helpless, Ann Marie closed her eyes and said another silent prayer for James in hopes that he would somehow be found alive.

A shuffling noise behind her caused her to spin and instinctively glance in that direction. She gasped when she saw a strange man coming at her, fast approaching. His venomous face wore an evil scowl. She stiffened as she tried to focus on the item gripped tightly in his hand; it was something dark gray, but his hand was moving too fast for Ann Marie to get a clear look at the object. As the intruder closed the gap between them, there was a mere fifteen feet between him, her, and the edge of the cliff. Knowing he had her successfully cornered, he slowed his sprint to a walk. The tall stranger, who looked to be in his mid-twenties, raised the dark gray object in his right hand and Ann Marie found herself looking down a gun barrel.

It appeared to be aimed directly at her mid-torso. Now, trapped on the edge of a cliff, which only a few moments ago had brought her peace and comfort, she dreaded what was going to happen next.

"Where's the roll of film?" the brash, thin young man barked.

"What?" she asked nervously. "I . . . I don't understand," she stuttered.

"The roll of film, you idiot! The one your boyfriend used in his camera. Don't play stupid with me. I haven't got time for this. Tell me where it is, and I'll let you live," he threatened.

She could only try to de-escalate the situation as he took a step closer. Raising her hands in defense, she spoke softly. "I'm sorry, I don't know what this is all about." Her body started shaking uncontrollably. "Maybe you have me confused with someone else . . . I don't . . ."

"No, I have the right person alright. You are Ann Marie, James Moreland's little whore. I've been following you. The roll of film with your face on it was hidden in the boat. I want the other one. A fair trade and no one else need to get hurt."

Ann Marie couldn't stop herself from trembling. "Please don't hurt me. My baby!" she pleaded as she looked down, placing both hands protectively across her belly.

"Aww. Am I supposed to care about that?" the young man asked coldly. "Frankly, I care very little for you *or* what's inside of you."

He took another step toward her.

Ann Marie stepped backward.

"Just give me what I want, and you and your precious cargo won't get hurt," he threatened again.

The lanky man moved forward again, forcing Ann Marie to back away from him once more. She was inching closer to the edge of the cliff.

"Please, I wish I could give you what you want, but I don't honestly know anything," Ann Marie pleaded.

"You're as bad as your boyfriend. Both of you disgust me," he spat, stepping toward her again.

Ann Marie stepped backward again but this time she was trying to calculate the steps she'd made; it dawned on her that she was dangerously close to the edge of the cliff. Her eyes were wide with fear, all the while searching the stranger's face for any sign of compassion.

"Please, I . . ." she pleaded, terrified.

"Goodbye," he said, as he gave her a hard shove with both hands.

The killer recoiled, leaving her desperate, flailing arms free to wave around. Her hands grappled the air for anything to stop her from plunging backward over the cliff. The last thing she saw was the callous smirk smeared from one side of his face to the other.

***

William Irving was in the lantern room at the top of the seventy-five foot lighthouse when he spotted a young woman walking on the grass below. She seemed to be enthralled by the sunshine and solitude. He watched as she ventured nearer to the edge of the cliff to take in the magnificent view.

Off to the left, William saw a movement as a lanky looking fellow darted across the grass. He grew suspicious at the man's menacing body language as he stalked cautiously toward the woman. William tried to see what was in the man's hand before he disappeared below the lighthouse. William's gut told him it was a weapon and feared the woman was in trouble.

As the man bolted from his cover toward the young woman, William only hoped he could get down the metal steps of the lighthouse quickly enough to help. He grabbed a hammer and took to the spiral staircase. Feeling light-headed from the rapid descent, William put his hand up to shield his eyes from the sunlight as he lunged toward the heavy door to push it open. Now, outside and out of breath, he pivoted toward the young woman and her assailant. It was too late, William watched in horror as she was pushed over the edge of the cliff, plunging to certain death.

With the hammer in his hand, William instinctively made a move toward the stranger, but before he could act, the killer spun around to face him. When he saw the gun in the man's hand, William froze. The hammer released from his grip and fell to the ground. He staggered backward and then tried to make a hasty retreat toward his house. The sound of a gunshot made William skip a stride; it was at that same moment he felt a white-hot pain rip through his lower back. Falling to one knee, injured and bleeding, he summoned the strength to stand and flee. Shuffling along, holding his back, he managed to crawl up the front steps of his porch—but he didn't make it to the faded red door. Exhausted, and unable to go any further, he collapsed on the deck. William listened as the killer's footsteps ascended the wooden steps behind him. He silently prayed that this would end quickly without any more pain. The next bullet pierced the back of his skull.

The gunman ripped William's wallet out of his back pocket to make it look like a robbery, before leaving the horrific, crimson-soaked scene behind him.

20

PRESENT DAY – 2008

Brandon parked at the back of Rosie's motel, out of view from the road, before crossing the street to meet her at Danny's.

He searched for her on the patio as he hiked up the steps. A hand waved at him, directing his attention to a table in the corner where they'd sat previously. Rosie already looked like she belonged there, sitting comfortably underneath the brightly colored umbrella, sipping her morning coffee.

"Hi," Brandon said.

"Alright?" Rosie asked.

"Yes, I'm good. Have you been here long?" Brandon asked, as he strode up to the table. He noticed that she'd saved the chair for him in the corner, facing the entrance.

"I just got here a few minutes ago," said Rosie. Brandon took a seat. "I haven't ordered yet, only coffee for us both. I asked the server to bring yours out when you got here."

"Thanks! I'm starved!" said Brandon, picking up the menu and scanning it. "Everything looks good in these pictures."

"I'm going to have at least two eggs for protein, so I'll have that extra bit of energy to dive for cover if that horrible man comes around shooting at us again," Rosie announced, grinning.

Brandon chuckled at that. "Be careful. You may get what you wish for."

The server brought Brandon his coffee, refilled Rosie's, and took their order.

"So, what kind of adventure do you have planned for us today then?" Rosie asked curiously, leaning an elbow on the table, her chin resting on her knuckles.

"I didn't really have anything planned so far," Brandon replied. "What are *your* plans? You mentioned yesterday that you're a writer. Did you bring your laptop?"

"Yes, I have it right here." She picked it up off the floor and removed it from a padded case. "I'm glad these things are getting more compact," she added, placing the laptop in front of her on the table.

Brandon chuckled knowingly. "Mine's a relic. I need to upgrade to a new one soon."

"Is your novel going to be fiction or nonfiction, Brandon?" Rosie asked, as she powered up the laptop.

"A little bit of both."

"Have you published anything yet?"

"No; I haven't even started writing the first one," he grimaced.

She reacted with a smile. "I may be able to give you some helpful tips. I have a series published already. Do you believe in ghosts?"

"That's a tough one to answer. I'll have to say no."

"Would you like to read a couple of pages of what I've written?" she asked.

"Sure, I'll read it." Brandon waited while Rosie turned the laptop around for him. As he scanned the screen, he could feel her eyes on him, waiting for his reaction. "*Haunted Lighthouses*. I like it," he nodded his head. "I went up to Sixteen Fathom Hill Lighthouse."

Rosie raised her eyebrows. "Really? Did you have any strange encounters?"

"Let's just say I had an odd feeling and an unusual experience."

"Unusual how?" she asked.

He told her about the door slamming closed while he was inside the lighthouse and the sound of the baby crying. He added that it was the second time he'd heard the baby, the first time being at the Rocky Ridge Motel after the mysterious man had showed up outside his door. "Lou—a guy I dive with—mentioned something about the lighthouse's beacon turning itself on at night, too."

"How creepy! I can't wait to visit. What evening did you hear the baby crying at the motel? I'm just curious. I didn't hear or see anything and my room was right beside yours."

Brandon explained that it was the night of the big thunderstorm.

"Oh, I hadn't checked into the motel until after that storm passed through," said Rosie. "That explains it." She frowned. "So, you said you went inside the lighthouse? It's open?"

"It is now," Brandon replied sheepishly. "I broke the lock by accident."

Rosie broke out in laughter. "You broke in by accident? Now, that's funny!"

"What can I say?" Brandon shrugged, smiling.

"Rebellious. I like that," she said admiringly, tilting her head sideways. She continued, "You know what? There's a World War II battleship that is said to be haunted. It's been decommissioned and it's now docked in Port Bradley, up the coast. Is there any chance that you could break into the ship?" she winked. "I'd really like to go for a tour of it."

"You're kidding, right?" He asked, unsure.

"Of course, I am, silly," she replied, grinning. "Actually, they provide public tours, for an entry fee, of course. It's the only way they can afford to keep the ship maintained. Otherwise, it would be rotting away in a scrap yard right now, waiting to be cut up. It was moved there two years ago from South Carolina for restoration."

"Port Bradley is to the north of us, correct?" Brandon asked.

"Yes," Rosie confirmed.

"I wouldn't mind seeing that too." Brandon nodded.

"I've already mapped out all my routes of the places I want to visit. GPS helps tremendously."

"What's the name of the ship?" Brandon asked.

"The USS *Midhurst*," Rosie told him. "I would be more than happy if you'd accompany me on a tour of it tomorrow. I'm sure there won't be a big crowd because of the weather. It's supposed to rain, but should clear up later in the afternoon," Rosie said. "Who knows, maybe we'll even see the ghost that's said to be haunting it," she added.

Brandon rolled his eyes, revealing his doubt.

"Why are you making a face?" Rosie asked.

"Let's just say, I'll believe it when I actually see one, but yes, I'll be happy to take a tour of the ship with you tomorrow," said Brandon.

"You won't be disappointed. It'll be fun, I promise," said Rosie, in a joyful tone.

***

The Whiskey Lee

Brandon offered to drive, so that Rosie could spend her time taking photographs of some of the small villages and landscape along the way.

The ship was well hidden in the inner harbor. They drove until the paved road ended. Brandon wasn't sure if this was the right place because all he could see was an expanse of seawater as the bay met the end of the road. Seeing no ship in sight made him question the GPS's accuracy. The ship was about 380 feet in length and thirty feet wide, so it would be hard to miss.

As they neared the water, a gap in the middle of the trees revealed massive white numbers on a gray steel background. It was unmistakable. The ship seemed to appear out of nowhere. As they got closer, they could see the gigantic hull emerging, followed by the big twin guns on the deck as the rest of the ship came into view. It looked massive. Brandon immediately felt a sense of excitement, respect, and gratitude for this majestic ship. Miraculously, it managed to make its way back home safely in one piece after at least two wars.

Brandon and Rosie eagerly purchased their tickets and fell in line with the small crowd ascending the gangway which led to the ship.

"Welcome aboard!" a uniformed young man addressed the crowd. We hope you enjoy your visit."

Another attendant handed out maps and gave everyone a basic rundown of some of the safety rules to abide by. One rule was that they had to face all ladders when climbing up or down, and hang on tightly. Another two were not to run, and to watch for trip hazards. Regardless of being informed of all the safety rules, a visitor in front of Rosie and Brandon walked through a door and still managed to bump his head on the upper part of the steel doorframe when he tried to step through it. Rosie heard a "thud" as his head connected.

"Ouch . . ." Rosie whispered to Brandon. "That's going to leave a nice bump."

Halfway through the tour, Rosie's camera was still clicking away as she moved about the ship, trying to gather all the reference material that she could relating to the ship's history.

While Brandon focused on the mechanics of the ship, Rosie made it her business to find out where the captain's quarters were located. It didn't take her long to find it. She imagined Brandon would already be scaling down the single steep ladder into the belly of the ship, while she lingered curiously near the door of the captain's day cabin. Craning her neck to take a sneak peek inside, she could already see that there was a substantial amount of information and pictures in the room. A captain's uniform sat in the corner with shiny brass buttons on it.

"It's okay—you're allowed to go inside," one of the ship's volunteers urged, as he removed a yellow plastic chain from across the doorway to allow her through. Rosie stepped in, slowly moving around the room, examining and admiring all the old pictures on the wall. Some were in the form of re-created prints of the heroic ship at war on the high seas. Track lighting in the room caused a glare and cast an annoying reflection on the glass protecting the pictures. It was a challenge for Rosie to read the captions or take a decent photograph. She moved a little to the left, and what she saw next frightened the heck out of her: There it was, a reflection of a man's face with deep hollow eyes and it was staring hauntingly back at her.

Instantly, the blood drained from her face. Gasping, her reflexes kicked in, causing her to jolt away as she spun to face the invader. No one was there. She was completely alone in the room. When Rosie turned back to take another look at the framed picture, the image of the man's face had vanished.

What the hell was that? She wondered.

After meeting back up, Rosie and Brandon strolled through the main deck of the ship; excitedly she recounted the mysterious appearance of the strange face in the glass.

"I wish I'd been there to see it," he said. "Maybe it was the lights playing tricks on your eyes?"

"I wished you'd seen it too," Rosie agreed. "It was clearly a man's face. I'm sure something was in there! I could feel a presence," she insisted.

"Maybe you found your ghost after all," Brandon offered.

At each passageway, their steps echoed off the bulkheads, reflecting the fact that they were alone as they stepped through different doors. The bulkheads and overhead areas were painted a dull battleship gray, while most of the decks were brought alive by a retro red and white checkerboard pattern.

"We could seriously play a good game of checkers on these floors," Rosie mused. "It really breaks up all the dull gray of the rest of the ship." She moved toward a shiny red telephone attached to the wall and touched the receiver. "I doubt they had this phone onboard during the war. Could you take a photo of me pretending to ring my parents in England?" she asked jokingly.

Brandon lifted the camera up to take a photo, but a man standing behind Rosie diverted his attention. Looking as if he belonged on the ship, the man wore a navy blue wool sweater and a denim peaked cap. "Hey Rosie, there's a man standing behind you. Do you mind if he's in your shot?" Brandon asked.

Rosie half turned her head, using her peripheral vision to see how far the man was away from her. "No, I don't mind. He can be in the background," she said, quickly turning her head back to offer her photographer a glamorous pose.

"Nice smile," Brandon complimented her, checking the image briefly before the two of them moved on.

A video playing in a loop, portraying the history of the ship, was playing on a television in the crew's living quarters. Rosie wanted to sit down and watch it for a few minutes, so Brandon continued exploring the room. He glanced down the passageway and caught another glimpse of the man in the navy blue sweater and peaked hat. The strange man dominated the middle of the passageway, blocking it, and staring in Brandon's direction. His stance was steadfast as he continued to stare with his dark, hollow eyes, releasing an unsettling vibe. Brandon nervously shifted his weight to the other foot. Something familiar, yet creepy, loomed around the mysterious man. Brandon turned his eyes away briefly, glancing over at Rosie who was still completely absorbed by the video. When he turned his eyes back to the passageway, the man had disappeared.

Brandon quickly grabbed the camera out of his pocket, switching it over to the browse mode in order to take another look at the man who had shared Rosie's photo. He was surprised when he saw the man's image wasn't there.

Dismissing it as some kind of camera-light-refraction trickery, an exasperated Brandon marched along the passageway in search of the man. Not seeing him anywhere, Brandon crossed through the breezeway to the port side where he'd taken the photo of Rosie beside the red phone. The man wasn't there either.

He turned and moved through the passageway in the opposite direction, slowing just before reaching the radio room. Brandon could smell a musty "old" smell coming from the room as he walked closer. He stopped, took a deep breath and then moved toward the door to carefully peer inside. Even though he'd half expected to see him, the man's presence still startled him.

The man in the peaked hat and wool sweater seemed almost zombie-like as he stood inside the roped off radio room, staring at the instrument panel. He slowly turned to face Brandon so that his facial features were revealed. His eye sockets looked deep and shadowy. Perhaps a good-looking man earlier in his years, his face now appeared to be drawn and lifeless. While the man continued to stare at Brandon, he voiced a desperate plea. "I can't rest. The baby's still crying." He gritted his teeth and clenched his fists in anger.

Brandon had to avert his eyes from the man's disturbingly chilling stare. *Wait a minute... I know that voice*, he thought, and he turned his attention back to the man in the peaked cap. There was no question that he'd heard that soul-stirring voice before. "**Baby's crying**," the hollow, deep voice had announced outside Brandon's motel room. It was the night on which the harrowing thunderstorm had cast its wrath upon Ridgetown and Barney's Cove.

The musty smell in the room was stronger. It was mixed with a chill in the air, and now Brandon noticed the four faded green military seats which sat before the radios. The zombie-like man standing before him didn't move at all. It was as though the stranger, like this room, was from another era, an old illusion somehow thrown into the future.

"Who are you?" Brandon demanded. "What baby? What do you want with me?"

The man's eyes and their sockets seemed to grow darker. Brandon stepped back as he felt more cold air rushing from the small enclosure. It encompassed him now. He could see his own breath as he exhaled.

The man turned his back on Brandon, as if to walk away. *Walk away.* There was no other way out, unless he walked through the wall. The man would have to walk directly past Brandon to exit the radio room.

Brandon heard Rosie calling out his name from further down the passageway.

The man turned back and spoke again. "Hallam," he uttered in his hollow voice, "Find Bet... Sea."

"Bet Sea?" Brandon asked the daunting figure.

"You're close. Search the..."

"Brandon!" The sound of Rosie's voice interrupted the man.

"Search the what?" Brandon asked, turning his head to shoot a warning look at Rosie as she neared the radio room. "Wait!" he whispered to her, raising a hand to signal her to stop. He turned back to the radio room but the mysterious man had vanished again. "Gone again! Really? Damn!" Brandon cursed in a slightly raised voice. "Search the what?" he asked the empty room.

Rosie moved close to him. "Is everything okay? Who are you shouting at?"

"It was the guy in the wool sweater and cap that was standing behind you by the red phone when I took the photograph."

"In here? What did he say?" Rosie asked, peering past him into the room. "It's bloody cold in here." She shivered.

"He said something about a baby crying and then he said "Hallam," "Bet Sea," and "Search the..." Brandon gestured with both palms up, "something." He dropped his hands in frustration. "But that's when you came along and he simply vanished into thin air."

Rosie stared at him before breaking into a smile. "That's rubbish! You really had me going for a minute. It's not funny to make up stories about ghosts. You're just doing this because I told you about the man's reflection that I saw in the captain's day cabin." She gently tapped his arm with her fingers. "Got me, didn't you?"

"I think you'd better take a look at the photograph on my camera, Rosie," he said in a serious tone. "Tell me if you notice anything."

She studied the image in silence. After a moment, her expression changed when she'd realized what she was looking at, or rather *not* looking at. Her eyes grew wide.

"No way! There was a man standing behind me! We both saw him." Rosie exclaimed as she stared at the photo, trying to comprehend what her eyes weren't seeing now. "His image isn't in the photo at all," Rosie whispered. "Ghost!"

"It was the same guy that I saw in here just a minute ago—I'm sure of it! And his voice... same one I heard when I was in my motel room during the storm." Brandon scratched his head, at a loss. "I think he's trying to tell us something."

"Do you believe in ghosts now?" she asked.

"I don't know. Maybe I'm starting to," Brandon admitted.

"That may explain why the air is so cold in here. I've learned from my research that if there are spirits in a room, the air will suddenly turn cold."

"Should we be scared?" Brandon asked.

"Not sure. You'll know the answer if things start flying off the wall in our direction. Maybe he's just looking for our help," Rosie suggested.

They finished up their tour of the ship, though now their interest lay in what—or who—might be inhabiting the numerous rooms. There were no more sightings of the man in the peaked denim cap but he dominated their conversation on the return home.

"I still haven't got a clue what *Hallam* means," Rosie said, her frustration evident.

"Me neither," Brandon sighed as he steered the SUV down the highway. "What's Bet Sea? It sounds like someone's name, doesn't it? Betsy." Something was gnawing at his brain but he couldn't put his finger on it.

"Maybe we should search it on the internet once we're back," Rosie said.

21

At a small internet café, Rosie browsed the web on her laptop to see if she could make heads or tails of the names. "*Hallam*: Means *at the rocks*, or *the nook*," said Rosie.

"Okay, now look up *nook*," Brandon suggested.

"*A corner of a place which is sheltered or hidden*?" read Rosie.

"I'm afraid it's too vague to mean anything. We'll need more. Look up the words *Bet Sea* or *Betsy* to see if anything pops up," Brandon suggested.

Rosie keyed in both names. She tried the name *Betsy* first.

Many names came up, but nothing which drew any interest in relation to their quest.

"Try *Bet Sea*," said Brandon.

A few names appeared on the screen. Rosie scrolled down.

"Wait, what's that?" Brandon pointed to the screen.

Rosie stopped scrolling to read it. "It's a salvage ship," she replied, continuing to read. "This is a news article about a salvage company that recovered artifacts from an old famous shipwreck in August of 2001. It's called Scully's Salvage. Oh, look at this . . ."

"What?" Brandon asked enthusiastically, as he leaned in closer to her.

"Well, it's saying that the salvage boat in the photograph is named *Betsea*," said Rosie.

"That's it!" Brandon said excitedly, smacking the top of his leg. "That's what's been gnawing at my brain. *Betsea*'s a ship—a salvage ship. Jeez, it took me long enough. The NTSB report I read, said *The Betsea* was reported as being in this area the time *The Whiskey Lee* disappeared in 1989."

"A connection or clue perhaps?" said Rosie, raising her eyebrows.

"It's worth looking into. What else? Does it mention where Scully's Salvage is located?" Brandon asked, peering at the screen.

"Yes, there's a map here. I'll just . . ." She double clicked the mouse. "Well, how about that then!" Rosie noted. "Are you ready for this? It's at the same shipyards as the USS *Midhurst*."

"We were right there," said Brandon.

"Yes, so close to it that we could have thrown a stone and hit it from the bow of the USS *Midhurst*," Rosie agreed.

"The um . . . *ghost* said, "You're close. Search the . . ."

Rosie's mind was working faster than she could muster the words to end Brandon's sentence. "Shipyards? Ship? Betsea? Salvage company? Scully's?"

"At first I thought the stranger meant that I was close when I asked if the name of the baby is Betsy, but he meant close as in my physical proximity to *The Betsea* or the salvage company, Scully's."

"There's only one way to find out. We need to get back on board the USS *Midhurst* and find our ghost again. I have a feeling that he has more to tell us," said Rosie.

"If what we are dealing with here *is* an actual a ghost, then it seems that he's more comfortable appearing when there are no other witnesses around. You said yourself that you saw a man's face appear in the captain's day cabin, while you were *alone*. I'm betting that's the same guy," said Brandon.

"Yes, and now I wish I'd taken more than a quick glance at the bloke who was standing behind me while I posed for the photo by the red phone. Unfortunately, it wasn't a long enough look to register the details of his face. What did he look like?" she asked.

Brandon described the man's facial features.

"Yep, sounds like the same bloke alright," said Rosie, convinced.

"That settles it. I'm going back aboard when it's quiet. Later in the evening would be a good time to go. I also want to take a look at Scully's Salvage and see what they are up to." Brandon waited while Rosie looked it up again.

"I don't think the *Midhurst* is open in the evening, and I seriously doubt the salvage company would be giving tours to the public at all. My guess is we'd probably need an access card to get through the security gate," said Rosie.

"Hmm, yeah you're right, so I'll have to try and sneak in," said Brandon. "It's my only option."

"*What?* Have you completely gone *mad*?" asked Rosie. "First you don't believe in ghosts, and now you want to break into a well secured area at night, to go and look for one?"

"That's right, but you'd be lying if you told me that you weren't even a little curious and somewhat excited up by this, correct?" Brandon questioned, raising an eyebrow.

"Damn!" She shook her head disapprovingly. "You really got me; after all, you are talking to someone who writes ghost stories for a living. It seems like you know me already. This has to be a well-thought-out plan," she said. "I can see it now, *me* writing my next ghost story from an American prison. Imagine what my Mum would say if I rang her up from jail."

Brandon laughed.

"It's not funny," she replied, glaring at him.

"So, are you in or out?" Brandon asked her.

"Hmm, well I guess one could say that I'm in already because I've been shot at?"

"True, but you still *do* have a chance to walk away."

She gave Brandon a questionable look, while pondering the idea.

"I'll let you think about it," said Brandon.

"Okay, I thought about it. I'm in, dammit!" Rosie retorted quickly. "Let's do this! But just so you know—I really hate you right now."

Brandon smiled brashly, clapping his hands once. "Atta girl. Okay, it's time to think of a plan."

"While you're thinking of one . . . What about the crying baby? You said it's the second time that ghost mentioned the baby crying. What does it have to do with anything? How does it fit in?" Rosie asked inquisitively.

"That's a good question—it's got me completely baffled."

"Maybe all this has got something to do with the lighthouse too," said Rosie.

Brandon pondered that idea for a moment. *Phantom Hill* . . . He nodded. "I've got to go back up there as well."

"Correction, *we've* got to go up there, together. That lighthouse is on my list of places to visit for my research anyway. I'm not going to sit idly by while you have all the fun."

"Okay, deal," said Brandon, closing his hand to offer a fist bump with Rosie. "Let's go tomorrow morning."

She accepted. "It will be my pleasure to join you," said Rosie. "How much do you think we can stir this town up?" A mischievous smile appeared on her face.

***

The next day, they parked near the entrance of the trail and followed a blazed path into the woods. It was a damp morning, extremely misty, but a great day for hike up to the lighthouse. They could've easily driven up Beacon Hill Road, but Brandon suggested they walk. Everything was green and fresh in the forest.

They could smell pine in the air. Rosie inhaled deeply, feeling a soothing sensation as the oxygen seemed to reach every part of her.

"This was a great idea," said Rosie. "It's so relaxing out here."

"I'm glad you could join me," said Brandon.

"I wouldn't miss it."

"This trail leads up to the cliff—goes right past the lighthouse. That's where we'll be stopping first," said Brandon.

"Are we going somewhere else after the lighthouse?" Rosie asked.

"Yes, we're going to look for a little white house with blue shutters," Brandon informed her.

"Is it a haunted house?" Rosie asked.

"Uh, no I don't think so. It belonged to Audrey Montgomery. Captain Moreland's sister. I'm hoping her grandson will be there," Brandon replied. "I thought we could mix a little investigative journalism in with our hike."

"Brilliant idea!" Rosie replied.

As they emerged from the shaded forest into the intense sunlight, Brandon had his sunglasses in his hand already. He put them on and pointed. "It looks like they beat us to it."

Rosie was in awe, as she squinted keenly at the tall red-and-white candy-cane striped structure before her. Brandon remembered the lighthouse appearing dull and menacing the last time he'd visited. Now the structure seemed vibrant and inviting as a few tourists gathered near the foot of it, for photo opportunities.

"It doesn't look very scary to me. Can we go inside?" Rosie asked, as they approached the door.

"It looks like the lock's been replaced," said Brandon.

"Can you break it again?"

Brandon gave her a dubious look. "Sure . . . I'll just take the bolt cutters out of my back pocket," he said sarcastically.

Rosie shook her head slowly, chuckling. "Seriously, I'd really like to see inside. Is there another way to get in?"

Brandon scanned the area. "Even if I wanted to . . . Not happening today. Too many witnesses around."

"Okay, maybe we could drive back here later. We could always replace the lock with one exactly the same. Who would know?" She shrugged.

He smiled. "The key holder would."

"What I'm figuring is that the key holder won't be opening it for a while. Yes, they may come by to see if the lock is still on the latch, but may not try to open it if they think it hasn't been tampered with. Remember the state that last lock was in. No one had touched it for years," said Rosie.

"Hmm . . . valid point," he agreed.

"See, I'm not just a pretty face, am I?" she winked.

Brandon's eyes softened. "One thing I really want to do is see what makes this lighthouse tick."

They walked over to the electrical shed.

"It's locked too." Rosie touched the metal lock with her hand.

"Careful, you could get zapped."

Rosie pulled her hand away quickly. "For real?"

"Well, if there's a short in the wires it could arc out, and the lock is metal. You'd be the grounding for the current. I'm wondering if that's why the lights keep going on and off mysteriously at night."

"Well, thanks for warning me *after* I touched it. Good thing I didn't get zapped . . . Otherwise, you'd be phoning the ambulance right now."

"I'm glad you didn't too, because I'd have to hold your hand while we were waiting for them to arrive."

"And what would be so wrong with that?" Rosie frowned.

"Nothing, but I'd rather be holding hands *this* way and not with you going to the hospital." He held his hand out for hers.

Rosie lips formed a smile, accepting it.

"Wow! That was incredibly smooth," she complimented.

"I know. Thank you," he replied with grin.

Before leaving the lighthouse, Brandon made a mental note of the type of lock used on the electrical building's door.

"We'll bring the SUV next time, and a pair of bolt cutters."

"Yes, *now* you're talking," said Rosie.

Brandon squeezed her hand lightly before they continued along the grassy plateau toward Audrey's house.

The little white house with the blue shutters was almost unidentifiable from the back of the property. It was amid the haggard, unkempt garden. The paint was cracked and peeling from the side of the house. A blue window shutter was hanging off its hinges and there were spaces where a few of the wooden slats were missing.

"Just go along with anything I say." Brandon readied Rosie, before he knocked on the door.

The first time he knocked there was no answer. Brandon tried again. He knocked harder the second time.

The door swung open. A young man stood in the doorway. He had earbuds in his ears, and was wearing disposable painter's coveralls. His hands, untied work boots, and forehead were all covered in dust. The sandpaper in his hand looked well used. Brandon could see it was a bad time to be dropping by unannounced.

"Yeah?" The young man asked impatiently, while pulling his dust mask down to rest it across his chin.

"Um, sorry if this is a bad time; we can come back," said Brandon.

"Well, I'm off the ladder now. You selling something?"

"Uh, no, no we're not. We're here to ask Audrey Montgomery some questions. Are you her grandson?" Brandon asked.

"Yes, I am, but you won't get anything out of my grandmother. She doesn't live here anymore. She lives in a long-term care home and suffers from dementia. What's this about?"

"I'm sorry to hear that. I'm Brandon, this is Rosie. We're here representing the families of missing fishermen. Maine's Missing Seafarers & Vessels—MMSV."

Rosie raised her eyebrows slightly, but then masked her surprised reaction by following it with a quick nod in agreement.

"Never heard of it, but then again I'm not up on the latest community groups," the young man said, while casually giving Rosie a leering once-over.

The Whiskey Lee

Brandon noticed the young man's wandering eyes and intervened to turn his attention back to focus on him. "Rosie and I are starting to get lots of supporters and funding for this project. We're also working with a team of divers out of Barney's Cove."

"And I'm guessing you're here looking for donations?" The young man frowned. "You got the wrong house for that. This fixer-upper was donated to me by my parents. I'm a starving student. I've got no money."

"Oh. No, no. That's not why we're here at all," Brandon assured him.

"We're only here because we're interested in finding your Great-Uncle James Moreland and the missing *Whiskey Lee*."

The young man raised his eyebrows in surprise.

"Would there be any photos, letters, or anything else of James Moreland's that we could submit to the group to help them locate him?" Brandon asked.

"Well, I have some stuff here of his," the young man said, while gently rubbing the small amount of stubble on his chin. "I saved it because I was going to try to find out what happened to him myself, but then got too busy with school and my job."

"And now you're busy fixing up the house," Brandon added.

"Yep . . . My mom and dad told me about what happened to my great-uncle when I got a bit older. I was really young when he disappeared, only about three or four years old. I don't really remember him at all, except for the stories about his disappearance, and also from his old photographs."

"Would you mind if we look through them?"

He shrugged. "I usually wouldn't care, but it's stored away in the back of the bedroom closet in a big wooden chest. I'll have to bring it out for you, but I can't today. I'd really like to finish this room before the sun goes down. I don't have any other light source in here. The electricity's been shut off for a while now."

"Okay, sure. I totally understand. Is there a better time for us to come back?" asked Brandon.

"Give me a day or two to catch up here. I'll give you my cell number. The name's Cody."

Brandon entered his contact information into his phone.

"Thanks Cody. I really appreciate it."

"No probs." Leaving the door open, Cody walked back to his ladder in the hallway. He placed the dust mask back over his nose and mouth before climbing the ladder to continue sanding the top of a door.

"Would you like us to close the door or leave it open?" Rosie asked him.

"You can leave it open for ventilation," said Cody. "Thanks Rosie. It was really nice meeting you," he added sincerely.

"Likewise. Bye for now," Rosie uttered quickly, before catching up with Brandon on the path.

"So, what's our next move, Sherlock?" Rosie asked, as they walked back down the hill together. "I'm feeling a little unsatisfied at the moment."

"Me too." Brandon was deep in thought. "Okay, are you ready for this? We're doing it tonight."

"I beg your pardon?" Rosie asked defensively, but still managed to produce a smile at his candid approach.

"The USS *Midhurst*." Brandon smiled. "We're going back aboard tonight."

"Oh. I thought you meant . . ." She shook her head, "Never mind. What's your plan?"

"We'll have to improvise when we get there."

"Lovely," Rosie muttered sarcastically.

Brandon felt a couple of rain droplets hit his face and arms.

"Now it's starting to rain."

"Wonderful," Rosie said, rolling her eyes.

"No, that's a good thing . . . we can use the cloud cover to our advantage tonight. The darker it is the better."

22

THE USS *MIDHURST*

The Nissan Rogue's headlights reflected off the mist in the air, which made for even poorer visibility in the dark. It almost looked like a mini sandstorm in front of them. The battleship and museum had long since closed for the day. A security guardhouse was stationed near the gate for access control. Brandon thought it would be best to enter at the side, out of sight. Rosie climbed over the metal rung fence first, with a boost from Brandon. She then waited for the sound of an alarm to be raised. Nothing happened. Brandon kept watch on the other side, waiting for Rosie's signal to join her. After he did, they didn't waste a second making their way over to the ship.

"Hopefully we don't get nabbed boarding the ship. Better make it quick. We'll go on three." Brandon held her hand and counted as they bolted from their position and darted up the gangway. Once on the deck they took cover behind an exhaust vent.

"We made it. I don't think anyone saw us," Brandon whispered. The earlier rain had subsided; now all that remained over the inner harbor were clouds which partially covered a skeleton moon and the light cool mist which seemed to be lingering about the ship. Brandon and Rosie made their way through the narrow gray passageways. After not finding a ghost in the crew's quarters and the radio rooms, Brandon suggested to Rosie that they search the lower decks.

"You're not claustrophobic, are you?" he asked Rosie, pulling open the hatch, which led to down to the engine room. "This is a bit of a confined space to descend into."

"I'm okay with that. Not one of my fears," Rosie whispered.

"That's good to know. You'll make a good scuba diver then," he whispered back.

"Um, I can't say the same about sharks," she whispered back. "They terrify me."

He grinned as he pulled a black headlamp from his pocket. "That's usually the common fear for anyone who has never been scuba diving." After securing the headlamp on his head, he positioned himself to face the ladder to descend.

"Someone's prepared," Rosie acknowledged.

"Always, like a Boy Scout. Stay close to me, Rosie, but watch my fingers when you step down. I'll switch on my headlamp once I'm clear of the hatch."

Brandon disappeared down the ladder into the darkness.

"Leave the hatch door open," Brandon whispered up to Rosie, as he stopped on the ladder to switch on his headlamp. "I'd hate for us to be trapped down here."

"Okay, I'm coming down! Watch out, fingers!" she announced, clambering down the ladder.

"Fingers clear," he replied.

The engine room was one of the darkest places on the ship, but also the most interesting. Loud sounds were heard here, more than anywhere else. As there was nothing but hard surfaces in the engine room, the groans and creaking noises continued to reverberate throughout the space, adding extra mystique to the room. It seemed like the ship was angrily protesting being tied up.

"This sounds like my neck of the woods." Rosie rubbed her hands on her jeans to wipe them clean them after letting go of the final ladder rung.

"Yeah, it's kinda creepy down here," said Brandon. "Not exactly a place I'd like to spend the night."

After investigating every corner and coming up empty, they climbed back up to the main deck after about ten minutes.

"That was really something, although I'm a bit disappointed we haven't seen our ghost yet."

Brandon closed the hatch door. "It's a big ship. We still have a lot of area to cover. Let's go before we're spotted by security."

It wasn't until they reached the center of the ship that they both heard some strange noises coming from the ship's intercom system. It was loudest in the passageway and the mess area. With Brandon in the lead, they slowly crept closer to where the sound was coming from. As they approached, he could hear the most irritating static chatter discharging from the loudspeakers on the wall, and following that, a piercing whistle cut through the noise. Rosie covered her ears.

Brandon recognized the sound as a boatswain's call of "All hands on deck!"—which was something that a naval officer would use to indicate that someone important was boarding the ship. Brandon peered around the corner of the passageway.

"I'll be down below with *The Whiskey*!" a hollow voice bellowed as it rose up from a lower deck. Startled, Brandon and Rosie both jumped involuntarily. After regaining his composure, Brandon felt a chill go up his spine, which caused the hairs on the back of his neck to rise.

"It's him. Stay here Rosie," he said. "I'm gonna check it out."

"But . . ." she started to protest.

"Just stay put for a minute. Please," he begged. "I'll be right back." He squeezed her hand gingerly as his blue eyes locked onto hers.

She nodded. "Be careful," she whispered, letting go of his hand as he moved away cautiously along the passageway. He stopped at an open hatch near the center of the ship where a ladder joined the upper and lower decks.

He swallowed hard. "Hello? Is anyone down there?" He whispered. Again, he heard the boatswain's call, as the piercing sound of a whistle carried its way throughout the intercom system. He jumped, taking a step backward.

The apparition appeared in front of him. It was the same man he had seen before, the one wearing the navy wool sweater and peaked denim cap.

"Look for the false bottom," the man instructed as he walked closer.

"What? Where?" Brandon questioned nervously, as he took another step backward. He felt his body involuntarily start to shake.

The man stopped walking, uttering a deep sigh.

"It holds secrets!" Appearing agitated, the ghost turned, retreated, and then dropped down the ladder to the lower deck.

"Wait! Come back!" Brandon said.

Rosie bolted toward Brandon. "I saw him too." They both sprinted over to where they last saw the ghost. They peered down through the hatch. The stranger had disappeared.

"Hello? Are you still there? Who are you?" Brandon said in a raised whisper.

He didn't hear a sound.

***

A day later, Cody met Brandon and Rosie at the door of his little white house with the blue shutters and led them inside. They entered a narrow hallway to a modest living room where a medium sized wooden chest awaited them. A couple of apple crates had been placed on either side of it for them to sit on.

"Sorry for putting you two on apple crates. I got rid of most of the furniture. It was old and musty. The good dining room chairs and table are covered up in the other room. I've been doing some painting in there," said Cody.

"Apple crates will work. We won't be here that long," said Brandon.

"I believe the police already went through this chest nineteen years ago and didn't find anything. I think everything in here belonged to Uncle James," said Cody.

"So, you don't mind if we . . . ?" Rosie asked.

"Go ahead, knock yourself out. Take whatever you want. I'm getting rid of it soon anyways. I'm only keeping a few photos and throwing the rest out," said Cody.

"Okay, just wanted to make sure you're okay with this," said Rosie.

"Yep, I'll just be in the other room painting if you need me for anything else," he said, excusing himself.

"Sure. We don't want to stop you from working," said Brandon.

Cody disappeared through a doorway, leaving them alone to shuffle through the old photos.

With the first photograph that Brandon picked up, he paused while studying it. "Whoa, it's him."

"Who?" Rosie asked.

"Our ghost." He handed the photograph to her.

She accepted it, staring disbelievingly. "Oh my . . ." She didn't finish her sentence. "Wow!"

"It may explain why the ghost mentioned a baby crying too. Could be his and Ann Marie's ghost baby he's been talking about," said Brandon.

"Yes," she said blinking. "That would make sense."

After carefully sifting through the old photographs and other items, they finally reached the bottom of the cedar chest. Brandon paused, frowning. He folded his arms, deep in thought, and then turned to Rosie, with an odd look on his face. "Well shit!" he said, staring at the now empty cedar chest in front of them, as if a light bulb in his head had just clicked on. He peered at the outside of the chest wall and then back at the inside of the chest.

"What is it?" Rosie asked.

"Help me find a way to pull the floor of this chest up." He gestured toward it. "Feel around the edges for holes or a pull string."

"*Look for the false bottom. It holds secrets,*" Brandon whispered, trying his best not to let Cody hear him in the next room. "That's what Moreland's ghost said. I think this is what he was talking about."

They both searched for an entry point where they could grasp the floor and pull it up. Brandon tapped on it lightly to listen for hollow areas.

"Found it! There's a finger hole on this side," Rosie whispered enthusiastically, as she stuck her finger in the hole and pulled up the false floor.

"Yes!" Brandon whispered victoriously. "Way to go Rosie!"

Brandon shone his flashlight into the area. Light splashed across a white plastic bag which had been carefully stored underneath the false floor. He reached down and picked it up. Opening the bag, he found more photographs.

"I think we found something important here, maybe even a clue," he whispered to Rosie. "I doubt that Flynn saw this when he searched this trunk before."

Rosie produced an ear-to-ear grin. "Sherlock Holmes would be so proud of us right now."

"We can't just take them," he whispered.

"Cody did say take whatever you want. Remember?" Rosie whispered back. She cleared her throat and then called out to Cody in the other room. "Hey Cody?"

"Yeah?" Brandon heard him reply.

"Are you sure we can take whatever photographs we want?"

"Yeah, it's fine. I have all the pictures I want to keep. Take 'em all if you want."

"Well, you heard him," Rosie whispered to Brandon.

"Right. Let's put all the stuff we don't want back in this chest and get out of here before he changes his mind," Brandon urged in a whisper.

***

The following day, Brandon picked Rosie up and they drove over to meet Chad at his dive shop to examine the photographs.

Chad was dumbfounded when Brandon explained the connection between the mysterious figure, the crying baby, and Captain Moreland.

"Ghosts? Holy crap!" Chad explained. "That's unbelievable."

"It's all we have so far. We've got nothing else that would explain what's been going on," said Brandon. "Here, look at the rest of these photographs. These are the images we pulled out of the bottom of the chest," he pointed.

Chad stood over the photographs that Brandon had carefully laid out across his desk. He leaned in for a closer look, examining them. "Shit . . . can't see too much in these photos. Whoever took them was too far away," Chad examined each of the photographs in front of him.

"Have you got a magnifying glass or anything like that?" Rosie asked, as she strained to see the details in the photographs closest to her.

"Not here, but I think my wife has one," said Chad.

Brandon tried to organize the photographs in sequence for Chad. "I think James Moreland took these and I also think he could have seen something he wasn't supposed to," said Brandon as he showed him the large vessel and a smaller vessel moored up against it. A group of men were standing on the portside. "I tried to interpret what they were doing according to the sequence. It looks like four guys are standing there and then it appears that one of them drops to the deck in this next photo."

"Maybe he fainted?" Chad suggested.

"Or, he was killed by the other guys. Too bad there aren't any other photographs to show what exactly happened to the guy. If they killed him, that could be a reason to go after Captain Moreland. Another angle would be nice and maybe a close-up?"

"Now, you're asking for the impossible. This is definitely something worth looking into though. You know what, bud? I'll grab the magnifying glass from home and when I have some spare time, we can try and figure out what these guys were up to and where exactly this is. The rocky outcrop looks familiar along the shoreline here," he pointed to the photograph. "But I just can't pinpoint where exactly it is right now off the top of my head. Inventory has clouded my brain today. I'll lock these away in my safe for us to look at later," Chad added.

"Okay, but I'm going to keep a couple of them with me, just so we're not putting all our apples in the same basket."

"Yeah . . . Good idea," Chad agreed.

"In the meantime, may I borrow your Zodiac and motor?" Brandon asked.
"Sure. Gonna do some exploring on your own?" Chad asked.
"Sort of . . . Rosie and I are going on a little mission."

23

THE MISSION

Rosie and Brandon had prepared their gear, along with the eighteen-foot Zodiac and motor, which Chad had loaned them. After securing the trailer to the bumper hitch on the SUV, they were ready. Brandon only brought what was necessary for their overnight mission: a few essentials, including snacks, bottled water, his scuba gear, and a phone equipped with a camera which would be sealed in a watertight storage bag.

"I'm so thrilled! I feel like I'm a Navy SEAL going on a secret mission," Rosie said, climbing into the passenger seat.

"Rosie, are you sure you want to do this? It could get dangerous you know."

"Oh, hell yes! Of course, I want to. This is exciting!"

Brandon nodded and started the vehicle. "It's your last chance to back out. You have to be prepared to go all in."

"I'm all in!" she announced enthusiastically.

They arrived at a public launch dock, which had a beach with a sandy bottom. Brandon decided to drop off the Zodiac and load it with their lifejackets and other gear after tying it to the dock cleats. He then left Rosie to watch over it while he parked his vehicle and small black trailer in the parking lot near a natural area of shrubs and trees. The important thing was that it was out of sight if anyone happened to be driving by.

"Have you ever operated an outboard motor?" Brandon asked Rosie after returning to the launch ramp.

"I've steered a boat, but not like this one," said Rosie. "It had a steering wheel."

"Okay, this one's a bit different, but it doesn't take long to get used to," said Brandon.

A quick demonstration on how to operate it was all Rosie needed. She caught on fast. "This is neutral, forward, and reverse. Remember, neutral can be your best friend. It will stop the propeller from turning without you having to cut power to the motor." He reached for the tiller. "Turn this handle for faster or slower. It's also your steering lever." He moved the tiller side to side. "Move it in the opposite direction of where you want the bow to go. Turn it the same direction if it's in reverse." Brandon added.

"Got it!" Rosie said.

"Now, I'll show you how to start it."

Once on their way, they switched seats so Rosie could get comfortable with the outboard motor. Keeping the Zodiac on course required more patience than Rosie cared to admit. She had a tendency to keep over steering.

"Oh, give me a break! Why does it keep drifting like that?"

Brandon could sense she was getting frustrated as she continued to fight a losing battle against the wind gusts and choppy water.

"This isn't as easy as it looks," she remarked.

"Give it a little more gas. It'll be easier to steer," said Brandon.

As she cranked the throttle, Brandon lost his balance, almost falling backward off the front bench seat.

"Easy on the throttle!" Brandon hollered back to her, as he scrambled to steady himself.

"Sorry," she replied sheepishly.

While cruising toward the shipyards, Brandon used the time to suit up in his diving gear, finding what he needed using a small waterproof flashlight. To remain unseen, they had strategically planned to run the inflatable boat without lights, only using the existing glow from the moon to navigate.

"Okay, cut the engine now," Brandon advised Rosie.

"But, we're not even close to the shipyards yet," Rosie argued, but followed his instructions and the motor fell silent.

"You're not going to like this, but we're going to have to row the last leg of the journey," said Brandon.

"What?" Rosie asked.

"Row... otherwise they'll hear us coming. It's a stealth operation, remember?" Brandon reminded her. "I've got to get suited up."

"I didn't sign up for this part," Rosie sighed.

She muttered something under her breath.

"What?" Brandon asked.

"Nothing!" Rosie replied.

Within fifty feet of their destination, Rosie dug the oars in with all her strength against the fierceness of the waves, and wind gusts. Brandon could only see the back of her, but imagined Rosie's face wincing as she heaved the oars, leaning back into every pull. He knew it wasn't easy, and tried offering some encouragement.

"Rosie, you're doing great, we're almost there."

"Oh, sod off!" she replied, glancing over her right shoulder.

Brandon smiled at her strength and perseverance. Turning his attention forward, he directed her to their mooring spot.

They arrived at an isolated area behind a big yacht, where they weren't likely to be spotted by anyone. It was a perfect hiding spot in the shadows, which concealed them from the illumination of the moon and the dock lamps. A few waves bounced off the wall, making the Zodiac pitch and sway. Grabbing the bow line, Brandon tied it off to the seawall, and then climbed over some gear and seats to secure the stern line.

"That's better," said Brandon. "Good job Rosie."

"Thanks. I think my arms are going to feel it tomorrow," she said.

"Don't worry, I'll massage them for you," he grinned.

Rosie grinned too, but then her look turned serious. "Please be careful out there okay Brandon?"

"I will," said Brandon, reaching for his fins and mini scuba tank. It was a stealth mission, requiring compact gear. He put on his mask and snorkel.

"If you're in any danger, or I don't make it back here before sunrise, get out of here. It will mean that either I got caught or had to find another way out."

"Okay," she nodded reluctantly.

He strapped a sheath to his leg. Inside of it was a dive knife. Brandon had a basic idea of the layout of the shipyards because of his previous visits to the *Midhurst*. The only question would be whether there was any electronic security on the windows or doors in Scully's warehouse. The security guards that patrolled the shipyards might also be a bit of a concern. He guessed it would take them approximately an hour or more to patrol the entire area.

Once ready to go, Brandon gave Rosie the thumbs-up and uttered a quiet "Hooyah," before he put the respirator in his mouth and slipped over the side and into the water. Convinced that he hadn't made a splash, he looked up at Rosie and waved before submerging.

"Be careful," she whispered as Brandon disappeared beneath the waves.

Brandon swam toward the lower docks of the shipyards. As he surfaced, he felt dwarfed by the massive ships lining the wharf. Once reaching a ladder he grasped it and ascended using one hand over the other. At the top, he made sure it was clear before making a quick dash over to a shadowy area behind a shipping container where he could stow his scuba gear. Making sure that his gear was all out of sight, he took a shortcut through one of the large boat sheds to get closer to Scully's main building and yard. Hiding behind the forklifts, yard vehicles, and boats, he slithered his way through the warehouse until reaching the other side.

Trailers and empty pallets lined the other side, where he cautiously walked through an overhead door to get a view of the rest of the shipyard. There were several pot lights on around the shipyard for security and safety. Brandon stayed in the shadows. He looked around, making a mental note of where some of the other dimly lit areas were, just in case he got caught out in the open and needed to take cover fast.

He made sure that all his movements were done covertly, as he maneuvered his way through the shipyards, stopping occasionally to check his surroundings from the shadows.

Brandon didn't see any cameras mounted on the buildings other than the ones he saw at the security gatehouse. Now, standing across from Scully's main building, he took a moment to examine the exterior. He searched for security weak points, looking for any doors propped open or windows unsecured. It didn't take him long to notice a window open on the upper floor.

A noise to his right startled him. Someone had stepped into the clearing after rounding the corner of the building. The man in the white shirt was close to Brandon's position, but fortunately hadn't seen him. The uniformed security guard was now preoccupied, trying to light a cigarette.

Brandon moved surreptitiously into the shadows, staying just beyond view behind an empty recycling bin. The hefty middle-aged security guard took a deep drag off his cigarette and then grabbed both sides of his black leather belt and hiked his uniform trousers further up his waist. Brandon saw a long flashlight dangling down off his belt and tried not to make a sound. He didn't need to give the man a reason to shine the beam of his light Brandon's way, or club him in the head with it.

His eyes caught movement to his left, as a smaller figure crossed the pool of light. It was a ginger cat moving toward him. Brandon held his breath as it crept closer, not wanting to startle it. The cat was obviously searching for rodents around the yard. It looked up, surprised by the sight of Brandon, and bolted off across the pavement in front of the security guard.

"Skippy! Here boy!" Brandon heard the man say in a pleasant greeting. The cat trotted over to him, and butted its head up against the security guard's leg, waiting for the man to lower his hand to pat it. Brandon stayed well out of sight, continuing to keep his breathing regulated until the cat ran off and the security guard left the area. He watched the man turn the corner in the direction of the docks. Once the coast was clear, Brandon exhaled and bolted across the road, not wasting any time getting back to his mission.

Reaching the back of Scully's warehouse, he scampered up some stacked pallets along the wall, then grabbed hold of the piping affixed to the building. Hoping the stuff wouldn't fall apart and send him hurling to the ground, he was careful to secure himself with another grab hold. It was dusty as hell too, but he was glad that his gloves offered a little bit of reinforced grip at the thumbs and fingertips. He peered through the dirty, partially open upper window.

He couldn't see too much, but there didn't appear to be any security devices on the window or motion detectors inside the room which would set off alarms once he stepped inside. Satisfied that he didn't see any, Brandon climbed in through the window.

He had no idea what he was searching for, but anything would be helpful. Panning his flashlight around the loft and then down over the railing to the main floor of the warehouse below, he could see that the warehouse was full of stuff recovered from shipwrecks. He saw some old anchors, ship's wheels, brass this-and-that, cannon balls and guns from old warships, propellers, pottery, and other treasures. He noticed what looked like three offices located on a second-level mezzanine, with an overlooking balcony view of the warehouse.

Brandon walked to the far side of the loft, careful not to trip over anything as he went. This was mainly a storage area for materials. He found a ladder and descended to the second level. At the first office he came to he tried turning the door handle. It was locked. That was no surprise. After trying the other two doors and finding them all locked, he pulled out his knife and carefully used it to jimmy the first door. He was in. *That was too easy*, he thought.

Searching with his flashlight, the beam fell onto a couple of gray filing cabinets across the room. He pulled on the top-drawer handle but was disappointed to find it was locked. He tried the other cabinet. It was the same. Now, searching the room without much time to spare, he tried to think of a good spot to hide keys.

He focused his small waterproof flashlight into the gaps at each side of the cabinets. Seeing nothing but cobwebs and dust, he tipped each cabinet back to see if the keys were underneath. More dust. His eyes were moving around the room until he focused his attention on the desk. He opened the center drawer, feeling around; he'd remembered that sometimes people tape keys to the top, side, or underside of a drawer. The keys weren't there. As his eyes scanned the top of the desk, he noticed a dark green plastic cup filled with pens and pencils.

He turned it upside down, dumping all the pens out onto the desk. Not only did pens fall onto the desk, but two small silver keys on a key ring appeared too.

Yes! he whispered victoriously, as he tried a key in the cabinet lock, turning it slowly until he heard the lock pop open. He pulled open the top drawer, closed it, and then decided to start from the bottom and work his way backward from Z to A.

A couple of the files were the subject of strange names: *Viper, Osprey?*

After examining the contents of the files, Brandon realized that these were the names of some of Scully's Salvage vessels. In each file were photographs of a different vessel, so he snapped a shot of each of them with his phone and then emailed them to himself in case he lost his phone, or had it taken away. Finally, Brandon got to the top drawer. He pulled it open and discovered other salvage vessel files inside. One named *Chameleon* and a familiar name which seemed to jump right out at him, *Betsea*. His eyes went wide after seeing it.

He carefully removed the files. Inside, he found some information pertaining to the vessels, along with some more photographs.

He picked up one of the photographs. Studying it, he believed it was the same ship as in the photo he'd collected from Audrey Montgomery's cedar chest, only the ship looked different in this photograph. The *Betsea* appeared as though she had received more than her share of upgrades and new paint since the days of her faded navy blue look in the 80s. The ship's color had been changed to a vibrant white, with blue and red stripes. It was undoubtedly the same ship.

Nice makeover Betsea; looks like someone's raking in the dough, Brandon thought as he flipped it over to read the back. The date read *June 1993*.

He continued to rummage through the file until he discovered a hidden pocket. Sliding his fingers carefully inside, he found two glossy photographs, one of which he recognized as being the original photograph used for the newspaper article in 2001. This one included a group of men standing beside the *Betsea*, posing proudly for the camera.

It was the last photo that caught his attention. It showed the ship in its faded navy blue paint, as it looked in the 80s photograph. This was the kind of evidence he needed for proof it was the same ship.

Snapping images of everything with his phone, he returned all the photographs as they had been. He flipped swiftly through the rest of the files, stopping at another folder, this one marked *Private*.

Inside was a photo of a fishing trawler. As he slid the photograph out of its sleeve to reveal the name of the vessel, he hadn't yet realized that he'd stumbled on something important. There it was in bold white lettering on a red vessel: WHISKEY LEE. *Holy smokes!* he thought, as he clicked away with his camera phone.

Afterwards, he returned everything back to the way he'd found it, and closed the drawers. While searching the second filing cabinet, he discovered another file named *Private*. Brandon opened it and found another key. Wondering what it was for, he scanned the room with his flashlight. There was a small storage closet in the corner. The door was unlocked, so he opened it and peeked inside. Shining his light up on the shelf he saw a gray box, about the size of a shoe box. He reached up and pulled it down. Blowing the dust off it, he tried the key in the keyhole. It opened.

Inside the box were more photos: close-ups, of a man with a clean-cut designer beard, and smartly clad in a polo shirt, khaki trousers, and deck shoes. He was standing with some other men, pointing a pistol with a long barrel at

The Whiskey Lee

another man standing before him. Brandon guessed it was the *Betsea* they were standing on. He wondered if it was the same group of men that he'd seen in the photos he and Rosie had taken from the wooden chest at Audrey's. The difference was, these photographs were snapped from somewhere aboard the *Betsea*, possibly the bridge.

Brandon knew he had to get out of Scully's immediately or he could face the same fate as the young man in the photograph—Brandon would never forget that look of horror in the young man's eyes as he stared down the gun barrel. These guys were hard core thugs and they weren't to be messed with. Two attempts on Brandon's life had already given him a clear message that he was butting his nose in where it didn't belong. Again, his camera phone snapped images of the evidence before he put all the photos back where he'd found them. He dropped the keys back exactly where he'd found them. Scanning the room, he felt satisfied it looked undisturbed. He was ready to leave.

An unexpected noise from the warehouse downstairs made him freeze in his tracks.

It was the sound of a door closing. Brandon remained still and listened. Someone had entered the warehouse. He instantly took cover behind the door just in case they wandered upstairs.

His heart rate elevating, he tried to take slow, deep breaths, while listening to muffled voices rising from the main level. He couldn't make heads or tails of what they were saying. The rumble of what he assumed to be the big overhead door opening and then the noisy thrust of an engine was indication that a truck was backing up to the door. He heard the rear bumper of the truck connect hard against the dock cushions, and the engine was turned off.

He waited silently, still listening.

After more clanging and banging, mostly from the dock plate being lifted and lowered, the men finally powered up the truck and left.

Brandon stayed put long enough to make sure they had gone before moving downstairs to the warehouse. He scanned the crates and oil drums, reading the labels to try to figure out what they were up to. He took some more photos before leaving. He was about to peer into one of the crates, when he heard the main door swing open, thwarting his plan.

A panicked Brandon made a dash toward the side door, pressing the push-bar to open it. Unfortunately, he didn't realize it was alarmed until he heard a high-pitched squeal pierce the air. It was too late to reconsider his actions.

Shit! He stumbled out into the laneway. Hearing startled voices coming from inside the warehouse, he broke into a sprint.

"Someone was in here! Get him!" The words were followed by the sounds of running footsteps. Three men followed. One of the men caught up quickly. Brandon could hear the footfalls getting closer.

The sound of the running feet behind him stopped all of a sudden.

"Hey!" the man yelled. "Stop, or I'll shoot!"

Oh dang! Brandon dreaded what would come next, but kept running. He zigzagged to try to avoid being hit by a bullet. The gunshot sounded muffled. At the same time, he heard the sound of something ripping past his right ear. The projectile ricocheted off something metallic ahead of him, making a loud clanging sound.

Brandon ducked left through an open overhead door.

"Are you crazy, Mugs?" he heard another man's voice scold. "Put that thing that away! You forgetting about the security guards here?"

Brandon used the opportunity to escape. The thought of giving Mugs another chance to use him for target practice was undisputedly off the table. He realized he hadn't thought this part of the plan through very well and was certain that he wouldn't be very convincing as a Navy SEAL. Yes, he managed to elude the gunman, but he was sure they'd alerted their friends already. Time was critical as he rounded another corner and found himself face to face with one of the patrolling guards. *Damn, can't a guy catch a break!*

This security guard, much younger than the first, had his eyes down, completely consumed by the illuminated screen before him. His fingers were busy moving back and forth across the device.

Luckily for Brandon, the guard hadn't noticed him, so he quickly took cover behind a recycling container. *Thank god for electronic distractions*, Brandon thought, while the security guard passed by him. After checking that the coast was clear, Brandon made another dash in the direction of the docks.

He retrieved his hidden scuba gear from behind the shipping container. Quietly gearing up, he slipped his phone back into its waterproof case and then peered out to see if anyone was around. With the coast still clear, he made a hasty sprint across the driveway toward the ladder. Now, on the second rung from the water, Brandon quickly pulled on his scuba fins and eased into the water.

By the time he was halfway back to the Zodiac, he could see a few men along the seawall with flashlights. He slipped beneath the water and didn't resurface until he was out of their view. He popped his head up at the side of the Zodiac but couldn't see Rosie. He reached his hand up and grabbed the rope which ran along the tube. "Rosie!" he whispered, holding onto the side of the boat. There was no response.

"*Rosie!*" he whispered again, this time a little louder. She peered slowly over the side, rubbing her eyes.

"Were you *sleeping*?" he asked.

"Ah, I'm sorry. I couldn't keep my eyes open and must have drifted off," she whispered. "What's going on? What time is it?"

"Shhhhh! Not now—I'll explain later. Right now, we're in deep shit. We've got to get out of here and fast!" he said.

"What did you do?" she asked. "What happened?"

"Let's just say I've stirred up the beehive and the bees have guns," he explained. "Help me into the boat."

"Oh my god!" Rosie exclaimed. "Get in, quick!" She grabbed his arm, helping to pull him up out of the water just enough so that he could swing a leg over the side of the boat and roll in.

As soon as Brandon was in, Rosie untied the boat and jumped into the rower's seat. She pulled hard on the oars.

"Shhhh, quietly," Brandon reminded her. "They may hear the splashing."

"Okay," Rosie whispered and slowed down her pace.

Once they were out far enough, Rosie started heaving on the oars again. "I don't know if I can do this. I'm knackered."

"Let's switch," said Brandon. Rosie didn't object to that. She seemed relieved to switch places with him, taking her position on the smaller bench seat at the front of the boat.

As Brandon sat down, he grabbed the oars in both his hands and was facing the area where the Zodiac had been moored behind the yacht moments ago. The bow of the yacht was getting further and further away.

Now, they were completely out of sight of the men who were searching for them on shore. A new movement caught Brandon's attention, causing him to stop rowing as he curiously observed something black stirring in the water near the yacht. He blinked several times as he tried to focus on the moving object in the dark.

For a moment he thought it was a fish or seal that had broken the surface of the water, but as Brandon watched, it was clear what had popped its head up above the surface. It was another scuba diver.

"Who the hell is that?" Brandon asked out loud.

By the time Rosie's eyes turned to follow in the direction of Brandon's pointing finger, the other diver had disappeared below the waterline, leaving only a swirl of water and a few bubbles as evidence anyone had been there.

Once they were far enough from the docks, Brandon fired up the outboard motor and they gunned it full throttle back to the launch ramp.

As they approached the ramp, Brandon cut the power to the motor, placed his hand in the groove at the top of the engine case and heaved the propeller out of the water. He placed the locking pin in place to prevent it from falling back down.

The Zodiac's momentum and the surf carried them the rest of the way, making for a perfect docking. Brandon tied it up to the cleats.

"Good job! You docked that like a pro," said Rosie.

"Thanks," said Brandon. "The great thing about these boats is they tend to just bounce off the dock if you hit it."

"What happened back there anyway?" Rosie finally asked.

"Do you mean before or after you fell asleep?" Brandon asked.

"Well, I was bored and it was the rocking of the boat that did it—Hey! I asked a question first! Why didn't I hear any gunshots?"

"He must've been using a silencer," said Brandon, as he disconnected the hose from the gas tank.

Rosie helped him remove everything from the inflatable boat.

"I'll save us some time and go and get your SUV and the trailer. Toss me the keys," Rosie said.

He hesitated. "Make sure you remember to drive on the right side of the road, not the left. We're in America," he teased.

"Oh, bugger off! I'll drive on whichever bloody side I want to. We're in an empty parking lot," Rosie said.

He chuckled as he watched her walk away.

While Brandon was trying to pack up the rest of the gear in the dark, he heard the faint sound of a boat motor out on the water. He crouched low behind the bushes to remain unseen by anyone in the approaching boat. At first, he thought it could be someone looking for them, but he didn't hear it slowing down, or attempting to turn in toward the boat ramp. The boat was clipping along rapidly from left to right across the horizon. The interesting part was that they were also in stealth mode, just like Rosie and Brandon were. No lights could be seen on the watercraft. He thought that was odd.

Once the boat had passed by, Brandon relaxed and stood as he heard the SUV approach the boat ramp. Brandon opened up the SUV's back door, grabbing a duffle bag in which he kept a towel and some dry clothes. He slipped out of his wetsuit, down to his skin-tight shorts, and dried himself the best he could.

"Let's pull this boat out and get the hell out of here," he said, pulling a dry T-shirt over his head.

Rosie proceeded to untie the boat and waited with it, while Brandon backed the trailer down the ramp.

It was a quiet drive back to town, other than a random snort from the passenger side. Rosie had fallen asleep again. *This woman can sleep through anything*, Brandon thought. He tried to remain attentive, checking his rearview mirror often for anyone following them. Fear? Paranoia? He wasn't quite sure, but he stayed alert regardless.

He rolled the window down to feel the cooler air on his face. It would help to keep him awake. While Rosie slept, Brandon had some time to think about the mission. Although it was somewhat successful, it didn't leave him with a feeling of virtue. He wanted to do things morally, but it never seemed to work out that way. The choice was clear. If he wanted answers, he had to do this *his* way.

As they traveled along the dark road, Brandon's mind was working overtime. He thought about the ghostly appearance of Captain Moreland, the crying baby, and the dreams he'd had. After that his thoughts turned to Gloria, the gunman at the cliff, and then immediately his mind jumped back to the shipyards. His thoughts came to settle on the lone mysterious diver who'd popped his head out of the water near the yacht. That seemed to disturb Brandon more than anything. *Who was that? Friend or foe?*

He dropped Rosie off at her motel before driving along the deserted road to his cottage in the woods. Once inside his hideaway and satisfied that he wasn't followed, he kicked off his shoes, grabbed a beer, and flopped down on the sofa. Barely able to keep his eyelids open, he thought about how dangerous all this was becoming; not just for him, but for Rosie too. He soon drifted off to sleep. In two hours, the sun would be making an appearance over the horizon.

24

It was around half past eight in the morning when the squawking scolds of a blue jay resonated through the thinly paned cottage window, jostling Brandon awake.

Lacking energy, he lowered both legs over the edge of the bed, stood up, yawned, and stretched. After trudging to the bathroom, Brandon stopped at the small kitchenette to make himself a coffee. Peering from beneath heavy eyelids, he selected the strongest roast, which routinely made up for his lack of sleep.

He pushed the brew button and then shuffled over to the night table, where he'd left his phone to charge. He knew Chad would be at the dive shop by now, so he selected the number from his phone's list, then pressed *Send*.

"Seas the Moment dive shop," he heard his friend answer in a hurried tone.

"Hey Chad, Brandon here."

"Hey, what's up bud?"

"I got some more photographs for you to look at if you have some time today. I think you'll be really interested in what I have here."

"Uh, yes I would. That's great Brandon, but to be honest I'm running off my feet here today. I'm short-staffed again. I probably won't be able to look at them till later on this afternoon. Could you send them over?"

"Sure, I'll text them to you right now. Just confirm that you got them, okay?" said Brandon.

"Yup, I'll do that."

After sending the photographs, the aroma of freshly brewed coffee tantalized Brandon's taste buds. He slowly inhaled, savoring the smell as he watched the last few droplets enter his coffee mug. He picked up the phone to call Rosie, but then realized it was way too early and she may not appreciate being woken up.

What am I doing up so early? he thought to himself. Still feeling tired, he drank his coffee and then crawled back underneath the covers. Soon, his eyes closed and he drifted back to sleep.

It was early in the afternoon when he awoke. He wasted no time dialing Rosie's number.

"Hey sleepy head," Rosie's voice filled the phone.

"I could say the same thing to you. I almost phoned you around half past eight."

"Glad you didn't. I really enjoyed my beauty sleep after our all-night adventure," she said.

"What are your plans today?" he asked.

"Well after last night, I think I'm just going to take it easy and catch up on some of my writing. My arms are still throbbing from all that rowing," she said.

"Sorry about that. I guess I'll have to make that up to you later on. I owe you a massage, remember?" He reminded her.

"Yes, you do and I will collect on that," Rosie replied. "In the meantime, could you fill me in on what happened at Scully's shipyards last night?" said Rosie.

"Sure." Brandon caught her up on everything that happened at the shipyards. After that, the conversation turned to some flirtatious banter back and forth.

"Even though I'm enjoying talking to you, I really need to take a shower and let you get back to your writing. How about I phone you later on? Maybe we can meet for a drink in the evening if you're up to it."

"Yes, that will be perfect. Ring me later. I'm looking forward to it," she replied.

"Me too," he admitted, before ending the call.

***

That evening brought with it an overcast sky. Brandon was pounding away at the keys on his laptop while sitting at an old card table out on the screened-in porch. The only sounds were crickets and the occasional muffled voices from the nearby cottagers. The peace and solitude offered him a chance to catch up on some of his latest creative writing ideas. That was, until he received a text notification. Reaching for his phone, he saw there was a message from Gloria. She was asking him to meet up with her at the lighthouse. Brandon checked the time. He thought it was strange that Gloria was asking to meet up with him at this hour, because usually she worked at the Piper & Pelican most evenings.

It must be important, he thought.

Sending a quick text back to Gloria, he curiously asked why she wanted to meet up.

Gloria replied, mentioning that she had something important to show him.

Another text popped up almost immediately. This time it was Rosie. She was asking if he was still meeting up with her for a drink.

Brandon sent Rosie a quick message explaining that he had to meet up with Gloria first, for something important.

Okay, I'll be at Brewsters, meet you there, said Rosie.

Sure thing, he replied.

He then replied to Gloria's last message, agreeing to meet with her at the lighthouse. Before he dashed out the door, he saved his work on his laptop, grabbed his jacket—and then hesitated when noticing the Beretta sitting on the counter beside his keys. *I probably won't need it, but I'll take it anyway.*

He scooped it up along with his keys before darting outside.

Brandon arrived earlier than their scheduled meeting time. It was dusk. The evening was filled with a slightly cooler breeze. Reaching for his phone, he wanted to let Gloria know that he'd arrived.

A voice from behind him made him freeze.

"You've been a big fuckin' problem to us lately," the lanky man said as he strode toward him. Brandon squinted toward the approaching figure. As the man approached, Brandon could make out some of his features in the dim light. He guessed his age to be in the mid-forty range. The man was thin, tall, and more than six feet in height. He was holding a weapon, tightly gripped in his right hand and it was aimed directly at Brandon.

"Hey wait," Brandon questioned, raising his hands. "Who are you? What's this all about?"

"None of your fuckin' business," The man snarled.

"You're going to shoot me, and I don't get to know why? Do you want my wallet or something?" Brandon asked nervously. "You can have it. No problem." He attempted to reach for it.

"Keep your hands where I can see them!" the man growled. "I think you know why I'm here, so stop playing games."

Brandon's thoughts kept drifting back to Gloria. *I hope she doesn't show up right now.*

"It's become my responsibility to rid the company of any loose threads," the man said.

Brandon cursed himself for leaving the Beretta under the driver's seat of the SUV.

"And what company is that?" Brandon asked, trying to buy himself more time.

"Again, it's none of your fucking business! You're going to die today. That's all you need to know!" the man barked angrily.

"I don't even get to know why I'm dying. That's not fair. Please . . . I think you have the wrong man," Brandon pleaded.

"Let me jog your memory. The shipyards! I wish I'd let the kid shoot you back there and then all I would have needed to do was tie an anchor to your feet and drop you in the sea," the man scowled.

Mugs—*that's what he'd called him.* "*Are you crazy, Mugs? Put that thing away,*" Brandon remembered.

"Wouldn't I have left a blood trail?" Brandon didn't want to reveal how scared he actually was, but as long as the man was still talking to him, he figured he may have some time to think of a way out of this.

"*SHUT UP!*" The man yelled. Brandon could tell he was clearly annoyed. He sensed that he'd just escalated the situation and braced for the bullet that could soon be coming his way.

"Take your phone out slowly; toss it to me," the man ordered.

With trembling hands, Brandon did as the tall man instructed, only, instead of tossing it to the man, he hurled it way over the man's head. He figured he'd have an opportunity to make a run for it as the man turned to fetch it.

It landed with a thud in two separate pieces behind the gunman.

"That was a stupid thing to do."

Brandon shrugged. "I never excelled at team sports. Sorry."

"You think you're funny, but actually you're pissing me off," the man with the gun said in a low, calmer tone. He moved in closer, which caused Brandon to instinctively move backward. Glancing over his shoulder, he made a mental note of how far away the edge of the cliff was.

Brandon thought he was going to feel a hot bullet rip through his body any moment.

"Here's how it's going to go down," The gunman said. "You're going to turn around and voluntarily jump off this cliff."

"And if I don't?" Brandon asked warily.

"What do *you* think?" the man asked, flicking the end of the gun barrel up and down as an evil smirk appeared on his face. Brandon's mind raced. *If this guy was going to shoot, wouldn't he have done it already?*

"You have a chance of living, if you jump far enough out into the water," the man said, "but if I shoot you, you'll die for sure."

"So, you want to make it look like a suicide instead of murder," Brandon guessed.

"Tsk, Tsk. *Murder* is such a harsh word Mr. Summers," the lanky stranger mocked, shaking his head. "Why don't you just make it easy for all of us?"

How does he know my last name? Brandon thought.

"I don't even know *your* name. Why I should make it easy for you Mr. . . . ?" Brandon queried.

"You don't need to know my name," the man responded, moving closer.

Brandon instinctively backed up. His mind raced for ideas as the gunman pushed him closer to the edge of the cliff. He was almost out of time when an idea popped into his head.

"Have you met William?" he asked with a serious face, trying to distract him. He had averted his gaze to the towering structure behind the man.

"Who?" the man snapped, taking a nervous glance behind him.

"William, the lighthouse keeper. He's probably watching us right now," said Brandon.

"There's *no* lighthouse keeper," he laughed. "I made sure of that. He's been dead for a long time, just like you are going to be soon," The man said menacingly, while still pointing the gun at Brandon.

"Did *you* kill him? . . . Ann Marie? Did you kill her too? The same way you're going to kill me now?" Brandon pressed. "Did you force her over this cliff nineteen years ago?"

"You'll never live that long to know. I see you've done your homework though. Congratulations. Not that it will do you any good when you're six feet under—or, I should say, a hundred feet down," the man scoffed, still smiling.

A familiar hum broke the silence and light filled the lantern room.

"If there's no one looking after the lighthouse, then who just turned the light on?" Brandon said, scanning his eyes upward to the lantern room.

"What?" The gunman glanced quickly over his shoulder again, to see the bright beam of light coming from the inside the lantern room. Brandon wasn't lying.

Looking uneasy, the gunman looked around nervously. "What's going on here? Who's up there?"

A commanding voice from the darkness startled both of them. "*DROP THE GUN, NOW!*" The voice bellowed from the base of the lighthouse.

The gunman spun wildly and blindly fired a shot toward the lighthouse, then dropped down into a crouched position. Brandon used this opportunity to tackle the man. He grabbed the man's right hand, trying desperately to pry the gun from his grip. As they wrestled on the ground, Brandon felt sudden pain as his head collided with something solid—perhaps a rock. He fought to regain focus, while still maintaining a death grip on the gun.

The gunman used Brandon's disadvantage to hurl the two of them closer to the edge of the cliff. Brandon was aware of their position and managed to guide them back to a safe distance, but the gunman was slightly stronger. The struggle for control of the gun finally ended when Brandon was able to release it from the man's long, bony fingers. It dropped to the ground with a thud. Now, the two men continued to wrestle, perilously near the crest of the cliff once again.

Brandon came to the shocking realization that he was in trouble when the ground disappeared below his feet. At the last moment he instinctively reached out and grabbed some tree roots jutting out from the cliff, saving himself from falling down to the jagged rocks below. The gunman made a last-ditch attempt to save himself by reaching out to grab Brandon's leg with both hands. Brandon could feel the man's hands sliding down his leg as he fought to get a good grip. Now, the man was holding on with both hands around Brandon's ankle, refusing to let go. Scared, and feeling the weight of the tall man pulling him down, Brandon had no choice but to use his free foot to kick the gunman's hands. He wasn't sure how much longer the tree roots would hold both of them. A couple of kicks had little effect, so Brandon gave one final hard kick to the man's hands. The weight of the gunman was no longer a concern. Screams of terror could be heard as the gunman fell downward to the rocks below.

Seconds later, all Brandon could hear was the sound of waves crashing against the rocks. He took a deep breath and then summoned all of his strength to scramble back up the edge of the bluff. Loose dirt and sagging jeans, now sitting well below his waist, had him struggling to find a secure foothold. He was terrified that he would soon meet the same fate as the gunman. Tired, he started to feel light-headed and feared he would pass out. Just before exhaustion forced him into unconsciousness, someone from above grabbed both of his wrists and heaved him upwards. Brandon's mind was hazy, as was his vision. *Am I going to heaven now?* He wasn't sure if he was hallucinating because of his semi-conscious state.

After a few moments, he jerked awake. All he knew was that he was lying on his stomach and his nose was pressed into the ground. It was cold and smelled like a mixture of earth and grass. He lifted his head to look around. Now, he remembered where he was and what had happened. He winced from the pain in his head and arm as he sat up. There wasn't anyone in sight now. He was alone near the edge of the cliff.

Quickly, he scanned the ground for the gun, but couldn't locate it. He'd remembered the general area in which it had fallen but it wasn't there now. He got to his feet, pulled his jeans up, and felt his head. A sharp pain made him wince. Quickly withdrawing his hand, he looked at it. *Blood?*

Brandon stumbled in the direction where he'd remembered tossing his phone. The phone's screen had a colossal crack across the face of it. He picked up the two separate pieces, snapping the back cover in place. He hurried back to his vehicle, walking in a similar fashion to someone in a drunken state. Trying to catch his breath, he fumbled in his pockets for his keys. His hands were still shaking. As he pulled the keys out of his pocket, movement near the roadway caught his eye. Brandon managed to just catch a glimpse of a man in dark clothing darting toward Beacon Hill Road before he disappeared out of sight.

Adrenaline kicked in and now Brandon was alert. He grabbed the gun out from under the seat. His eyes darted back and forth, searching for any movement. He wondered how many thugs were out there. Up on the roadway, a white van caught his attention as it tore out from behind some bushes. The van appeared to be heading for Beacon Hill Road, or it could turn and head along Coastal Route #1 South. Brandon wasn't sure what lay up ahead for him.

With the gun in his lap, head still throbbing with pain, and what felt like a torn muscle in his arm, Brandon waited to make sure the coast was clear before pulling out. He powered up his phone and was amazed that it still worked.

Placing the Beretta in the console, he shifted into drive and stomped on the accelerator, leaving behind a huge dust cloud before turning onto Beacon Hill Road.

***

The white GMC van was difficult to spot in a partially hidden driveway, just down the hill on Beacon Hill Road. The driver knew that Brandon would probably be taking this road back to town. Well concealed, the man sat idly waiting for Brandon's rented SUV to drive by. As soon as he saw the black SUV go by, he pulled out to follow.

***

Seeing the white van pull out behind him, Brandon stepped on the gas.

The van caught up quickly and was gaining on him. Brandon could see the van's bumper was closing in and now merely inches away from the back of his vehicle.

He gave the accelerator some more gas, but the white van wouldn't let up. Brandon felt a bump as the van nudged his rear bumper. *Asshole! He's trying to run me off the road!* Brandon thought, as he floored the gas pedal. Grasping the steering wheel firmly in a white-knuckle hold, he fought to keep control as the road twisted and curved down the hillside in front of him. Still groggy from hitting his head, he noticed the pursuing vehicle's front bumper gaining on him again. A little way down the road he noticed a small hidden side road, which forked sharply off to the left. *This will screw him up*, Brandon thought, putting just enough distance between the SUV and the van. *Come on—closer, closer*, Brandon was thinking. *Half a car length*—and then without warning, he cranked the steering in a hard turn, jarring the tires and making them squeal as he veered left onto to the side road.

"Goodbye asshole!" Brandon shouted, after completing the turn. He eased his foot on the accelerator as the side road took him past a few century-old homes and farms. He knew that his pursuer would be descending the hill, with absolutely no room to turn around, but just in case he backtracked and tried to follow, Brandon didn't leave him any bread crumbs. He made a few evasive left and right turns along the gravel back roads to throw the driver off. It was unlikely his pursuer, or anyone for that matter, was going to find him now. Mr. 'Lucky' Summers was lost.

Brandon turned right at the next intersection and as soon as he felt safe, he stopped the vehicle. Grabbing the phone, he called Chad for directions. He got right to the point. "Hey Chad, someone's chasing me. I just need the quickest route back to town, avoiding Beacon Hill Road."

"Where are you right now?" Chad asked.

"I'm on a dirt road, at an intersection. There aren't any signs. I made a bunch of turns and got myself lost after taking an unmarked side road off Beacon Hill Road."

"Okay, at least you're still alive dude. That's a good thing. Now, take a good look around you . . . What do you see?"

"A big red barn—*Abbie Farm* is written across it. I also see a rusty tractor in the field and a few horses. There's a blue school bus in a driveway across the street from the barn," said Brandon.

"Good, I know exactly where you are," said Chad, giving him the directions. "Call me when you're safely back here."

"Thanks bud. I will. Got to find Gloria first," said Brandon.

The next call he placed was to Gloria's phone. It went straight to voice mail. "Don't go to the lighthouse," He warned.

Once back on the road, he did a random check of his mirrors to make sure he wasn't being followed. The road looked clear, so he headed back to town.

25

When Brandon approached the bar, the first thing he noticed was a half-eaten meal in front of an unoccupied bar stool. Next to the food was an open photo album full of images.

"It looks like you had a rough day. What can I get for you?" he heard Len say.

Brandon didn't have the chance to check himself over before walking into Brewster's, and realized that he must look appallingly disheveled. In plain view were a series of fresh scrapes and cuts on his face and arms. His tattered clothing had some ground-in dirt and grass stains, revealing that he'd either just participated in a game of rugby or was in another type of scuffle.

Brandon shifted uneasily from one leg to the other, as he felt Len's eyes studying him. "Have you seen the British woman that usually comes in here, sometimes with me?"

"You mean Rosie?" Len asked.

"Yes," said Brandon.

"I think she's in the ladies' room right now," Len said. "That's where she's sitting." He pointed to the half-eaten meal and unoccupied bar stool. "She's been looking through my family photo album for pictures of the lighthouse."

"Oh, look what the cat dragged in!" Brandon heard Rosie's mocking voice as she walked up behind him.

As he spun to face her, a look of regret spread across Rosie's face. Unable to retract her words, she placed a hand up to her mouth.

"Oh my . . . What happened to you? I was just kidding about the cat dragging you in. Actually, it looks like the cat dragged you across a field. What happened? I should clean up those cuts for you."

"There's no time Rosie," he whispered, as he noticed Len walk to the other side of the bar. "Two men tried to kill me tonight; one went over the cliff and another one is driving a white van and he's still out there looking for me."

"Oh, my goodness, I thought you were meeting Gloria."

"I did too," said Brandon. "I received a text from her phone to meet her at the lighthouse, but when I arrived someone ambushed me. Gloria may be in danger and I need you to help me find her."

"Oh jeez! Of course, I will do whatever you need me to do," she replied without hesitation. "I'll just pay Len and we'll go find her."

Brandon slapped some bills down on the bar. "Is that going to cover Rosie's tab Len?"

"That'll more than cover it and a tip too," Len smiled. "Thanks."

"Yes, thank you Brandon," Rosie echoed, affectionately placing her hand on his arm. "Did you try phoning Gloria yet?"

"I did, but the call went straight to voicemail. The guy that tried to kill me must've had her phone in his pocket. It doesn't make sense that Gloria would set me up for an ambush."

"Why would she do that?" Rosie asked.

"Exactly—she wouldn't. Gloria's the one who asked for my help in the first place. I hope nothing's happened to her. We need to find her fast," said Brandon.

"We will, don't you worry," Rosie encouraged. "I'll look up the number for the Piper & Pelican and see if she's there."

"Question: did you ring the police yet?" Rosie asked, while searching the internet.

"No. I'll do that later," said Brandon. "Wait here, I'm just going go to clean myself up." He walked toward the washrooms.

"Good idea. I'd like to help you with that, but I'm not allowed in the men's room," Rosie teased fondly.

Brandon just smiled, shaking his head slowly. "Okay, I'll be back in a minute."

***

Rosie found the phone number for the Piper & Pelican. Three rings later, there was still no answer; Rosie started tapping her index finger nervously on the bar. She silently pleaded for someone to pick up the phone at the other end.

"Piper & Pelican," she finally heard a man say in an unwelcoming tone.

"Hello, may I speak to Gloria please?"

"Who's calling?" the man snarled.

"Her cousin," Rosie lied.

"Gloria can't come to the phone right now. She's busy serving tables."

"I'll try her later. Thanks. Bye." Rosie hung up quickly, frowning.

"Did you get a hold of Gloria?" Brandon asked, emerging from the men's room.

"No, but I found out from the not-so-friendly man on the other end of the phone that she *is* working tonight. He said she's too busy to come to the phone."

"That was probably her boss, Mack. At least we know she's okay," Brandon said. "Come on, let's head over there."

"See you later Len," Rosie said, following Brandon toward the front entrance.

"Take care luv," said Len.

***

As they attempted to exit, Brandon glanced out the window. He shuddered when he saw a familiar set of headlights pulling into a parking spot near the front of the pub. It was the white GMC van. The driver's door opened and a man with a shaved head stepped down from it. As the man approached the front entrance of Brewster's, he paused briefly to give the black SUV a once over.

"Rosie, change of plans. That's the other guy from the cliff outside," he said grabbing her hand. "We have to go out the back door, right now!"

Rosie turned back in the direction of the bar, yelling to Len, "Len! Quick, show us the way out the back door. Someone's after us! I'll explain later," Rosie said. The urgency of her voice galvanized Len into action, and a few patrons turned to see what all the fuss was about.

"Quick! This way!" Len pointed, shuffling them through the double swinging doors which led to the kitchen and out the back.

"I'll try and stall him for you. Good luck Rosie!" Len said, as he turned to resume his position behind the bar.

***

"Nothing to see here, go back to what you were doing," Len waved off the curious customers.

Brandon's pursuer stormed into the pub three seconds after that.

Len tried to remain calm and appear casual as the man with the shaved head, tight jeans, and black motorcycle boots stomped toward the bar. Len noticed he had a pock-marked face and a scar which split his left eyebrow in two. He could see the intense look in the man's eyes as he scanned the room.

Len knew exactly who the man was looking for, but maintained his ruse. He nodded his head in friendly greeting. "Lovely evening tonight, what can I get for you?" Len asked cheerfully.

The man with the shaved head didn't answer. Only a scowl as he continued to study faces in the room.

His fierce eyes settled momentarily on the vacant bar stool, half glass of beer, and unfinished meal sitting at the end of the bar. He glanced at Len before storming into to the men's restroom to search for the owner of the food. He not only checked the men's washroom, but the ladies' washroom too.

Before Len could react, he heard an angry woman's voice scolding the man from inside the washroom.

"*Get out pervert!*" she yelled.

The man with the shaved head made a hasty retreat.

***

The brief distraction allowed Brandon and Rosie a few extra minutes to escape. Rosie climbed into the passenger side of the SUV, while Brandon's shaky hands fumbled with the ignition key.

"*Quick!*" Rosie shrieked. "Start the engine! Gosh, this is starting to feel like a bad horror film."

Brandon anticipated the man with the shaved head would emerge any second.

By the time the man emerged, Brandon's SUV had left the parking lot and had absolutely no intention of returning to Brewster's anytime soon. They were safely out of sight for now.

"Hey, we're going to get a speeding ticket in a minute. Slow down," Rosie uttered.

Brandon eased his foot off the accelerator, bringing the needle back down to where it should be.

"Oh well, that's another bar we can't go to anymore. We're seriously running out of places to drink in this town," said Brandon, checking his rearview mirror nervously.

"Speak for yourself. I can still go in them. No one knows I exist," Rosie winked.

"Where's your car, Rosie?" he asked, as an afterthought.

"It's still at Brewster's. No worries, I'll pick it up later. No one's looking for *my* little rental car."

"Once we put those assholes in jail, I promise the two of us will go back to Brewster's together and celebrate with Len, deal?" He removed his hand from the steering wheel, enticing Rosie to accept it.

"That's a deal," Rosie agreed, gracefully accepting his outstretched hand.

Rosie looked strangely at him. "Why does your hair look wet on this side?"

Brandon ran his fingers through his hair, only to feel the same sharp pain that he'd felt earlier at the cliff. It felt wet and sticky. In the minimal light of streetlamps, he could see that his fingers were crimson coated.

"Blood," he replied.

"How did you do that?"

"I hit my head on a rock during the struggle," he said.

"Jeez, what are you down to now, four lives?" she asked.

"Mmm," he said, as he checked himself in the rearview mirror.

"Please keep your eyes on the road. Here, let me check that cut for you."

As Rosie leaned over to examine his wound, Brandon couldn't help but smell the sweet aroma of her perfume.

"It doesn't look too bad. Do you have a first aid—" Rosie didn't get a chance to finish what she was saying because Brandon jammed his foot on the brake, slowing the vehicle. He made a quick right turn into an industrial parking lot and drove behind the building to park.

"What are we doing in here?" she asked.

"I've wanted to do this for a while." He switched off the ignition, which killed the headlights. Turning his head toward her, he looked deeply into her eyes, searching for some kind of reciprocal response. Rosie returned his sustained gaze, with partially open lips. He leaned in, closing his eyes as his lips made contact with hers. She accepted him with urgency as they came together in a prolonged kiss. When their tongues met, they engaged in a swirling, teasing dance. Brandon felt a gratifying tingling sensation from deep within him when he heard Rosie let out a small groan of pleasure. They parted slowly, with each of them inhaling deeply to catch their breath.

"Wow," Brandon whispered.

"Likewise," Rosie admitted, smiling timidly.

"Uh, we really should go," said Brandon, still trying to catch his breath.

"Are you sure you're feeling alright?" She asked. "Should we go to a hospital and get those injuries looked at?"

"I'll be okay." He held out his hand again for hers.

She accepted it.

"Here's the deal, if I pass out from the bump on the head, you can drive. We can do more of this later too if you want to," he said, leaning over to give her another kiss.

"Yes, you still owe me a massage too." She couldn't help but smile as noticed the rise in his jeans. "Um, do you need to wait a few minutes before we go anywhere?"

He looked down with an embarrassed grin. "Uh, sorry. I'll be okay. It's going to take a few minutes to drive there anyway."

26

It was business as usual for the Piper & Pelican. Vehicles crammed the lot, making it a challenge to find a desirable, yet inconspicuous place to park. Blaring music sounded more like a muffled continuous thumping as it resonated out through the walls and windows.

Brandon saw a vehicle leaving a parking spot near the front of the tavern, giving him an unobstructed view of the entrance. He backed into the empty spot.

"That was lucky. Now that we're here, where do you keep your first aid kit?" Rosie asked.

"I didn't bring one. This is a rental remember?"

"Oh. Well, there must be one inside. I'll go in and ask Gloria for one."

"See if you can get her to come outside to talk to me. Stay on the lookout for anything strange."

"Um, you want me to stay on the lookout for something strange happening in a *tavern*?" she smirked.

"Well put," he responded fondly. "You know what I meant, if the driver of the white van shows up here. They've seen me talking to Gloria, but I don't think they've seen you with me yet. If I remember correctly, you were still inside the motel room when the guy in the gray 4x4 stopped to take a shot at me. I pushed you to the floor."

"Yes, thanks for reminding me," she displayed a playful frown. "So, it's best that I pretend not to know you. Play it low key. Got it!"

"If Gloria can't come outside right now, ask her what time her break is. We'll wait for her."

"Okay. Be right back," Rosie said eagerly.

Brandon waited while Rosie entered the bar. She returned a short time later.

"Gloria's taking a break in about five minutes. She's running around in a panic now because her phone is gone," Rosie announced. "She'll bring the first aid kit out for you."

"Good job! Thanks," said Brandon.

Five minutes later, Gloria exited the Piper & Pelican with a first aid kit in hand. Rosie promptly exited the vehicle, waving in order to draw Gloria's attention to the black SUV.

Gloria approached the vehicle. "Brandon, what's going on? Are you okay?" She asked through the half-open window, passing him the first aid kit.

"I'm okay," he said.

"I didn't notice my phone was missing until Rosie mentioned it. When I went to get it from the bar, it wasn't there. I remember leaving it plugged in to charge my battery. Why would someone take my phone?" She asked in a panic-stricken voice.

"Hop in. I'll explain." As she opened the rear passenger door of the vehicle to enter, Brandon passed the first aid kit over to Rosie.

Brandon explained everything to Gloria about what had happened to him, starting with when he'd received the first text from her phone.

"Oh my god!" She gasped. "I feel so bad." Gloria was horrified at the thought of Brandon almost being killed. "I'm sorry. I feel like it was my fault for leaving my phone out in the open for someone to take it. I should have been more careful, especially since what happened to my friend Ben. You've got to keep that Beretta with you always."

"What happened to Ben?" Brandon asked.

"Maybe when I tell you, then you'll understand why I'm so insistent on you carrying the gun," she explained.

"Ten years ago, my friend Ben was helping me try to solve the case of what had happened to my aunt, and he was also looking into the disappearance of Captain Moreland. We were only twenty years old and full of curiosity and determination. Benny was a smart kid. He was responsible, kind, and a good driver. Never once did I see him drinking and driving, or racing his car with anyone. He dreamed of becoming a police officer. Well, to make a long story short, Ben's car was found in the sea at the bottom of the cliff. Somehow, it went off the road and plunged over eighty feet, killing him." She sighed deeply with regret and sorrow and then shook her head. "I was devastated. I still don't understand it. I think there was foul play involved. I think someone murdered my sweet Ben, and probably my aunt too. Do you think it could've been the same guy that tried to push you off the cliff this evening?"

"It may have been the same guy. He was determined to make it look like a suicide," said Brandon.

"What did he look like?" she asked.

"Tall, lanky guy in his mid-forties. Brown hair, and a bad attitude," he said.

"It doesn't sound like anyone I know. I guess he got what he deserved though. Thank you, Brandon," Gloria said.

"You're welcome. It would be nice to know why he did it. Not sure if we'll ever find out now," said Brandon.

Gloria nodded. "After Ben's car went off the cliff, I was terrified for myself and my family. I vowed never to bring up my aunt's death or *The Whiskey Lee* again. At the time it was as if someone had slapped me in the face. I felt like someone was sending me a message—a warning to forget about what happened in 1989. My mind kept flashing back to the scary man I saw at the library. Most of the people in this town were afraid to talk about it . . . still are. I guess you understand a bit more about me now?"

"Yes, I do . . . and I'm so sorry for what you have gone through. You should've told me about this earlier."

"Yes, I should have. Sorry. As much as I'd like you to visit me here at work, it's really a bad idea to come here until things cool down—too risky."

"I totally get that, but this is the last place anyone is going to think of looking for me because I'm banned from here, remember?" He winced from the throbbing pain in his head.

Gloria nodded. "Yes, but hopefully we can sort that out later too."

"My concern is that there's another guy still looking for me. He may have been the one that took your phone and may have been at the bar the night I came in asking about *The Whiskey Lee*. The guy who's after me drives a white van. He probably assumes we've been in contact since then." She took a moment to recollect. "Red's been here all night. I don't think it was him."

"No. It definitely wasn't him. The guy may have been sitting at the bar that night though," Brandon said. "Try and remember who was in here and we may have our guy."

The Whiskey Lee

"I know most of the regulars, but there were a few faces I didn't recognize that night, but usually I try to talk to everyone. I'll need some time to think about it. Maybe it will jog my memory."

Gloria glanced at her watch, uttering a sigh.

"I'd better get back to work. My break is over in three minutes and someone's bound to come out here looking for me if I don't go back inside," Gloria said, as she leaped out of the vehicle, stopping to talk to Brandon through the open window. "Oh, by the way, did you happen to get my phone back from that guy before he fell?"

"No, I'm sorry," Brandon said regretfully. "I was more concerned about staying alive, and I wanted to make sure you were okay too."

"Thanks for trying. I may have been overdue for a new one anyway. Just wish I'd backed up all my phone numbers first."

"We'll wait here for you to finish your shift if you want," he added.

"Are you sure? I'm done in two hours. That's a long time to wait," Gloria said, checking her watch again. "You know what—I'll arrange for some takeout for you. Just let me know what you want."

"I know what I want: a burger and fries," said Brandon.

"Well, that was quick. Okay, I'll prepare the order when I go back inside. Rosie, could you bring it out for him when it's ready?"

"Yes," said Rosie. "I'll be in in a little while."

"Brandon, if you need to use the washroom anytime, Rosie can open the side door for you. I'll show her where it is. That way Red and Mack won't see you," said Gloria.

"Okay, I appreciate that. You should go back inside before they send out the search party," said Brandon.

"Yes. See you later," Gloria hurried back inside the tavern.

"Flipping heck, what are we going to do for two hours?" Rosie voiced.

"I can think of something," Brandon said, grinning flirtatiously.

"Hold still," Rosie said as she nonchalantly doused a cotton ball in hydrogen peroxide, reached over and gently began swabbing the gash on his head with it.

"Ow! That stings!" he exclaimed, flinching.

"Oh, just sit still, you big baby. I have to clean it properly or it'll get infected." She leaned in closer, now securing his head with her hand.

After cleaning the cut the best she could, Rosie leaned back, catching Brandon intensely staring at her. She stopped what she was doing. "What now?" she asked. "Are you okay?"

Something inside of him melted when she looked into his eyes. He felt completely spellbound by her caring nature. "Thank you," he whispered.

"You're welcome," she whispered back.

Brandon stared longingly at her, his gaze eventually settling on her lips, which parted in anticipation. Captivated by the way her lips glistened in the soft light, he couldn't help but feel they were beckoning him. He slipped one hand around the back of her neck, pulling her closer. His other hand came to settle on her thigh. She leaned toward him. Their breathing sped up as eager lips pressed together. Brandon's tongue met hers as a familiar sensation travelled down through his stomach, and into his groin.

"I have butterflies in my stomach," Rosie admitted.

"I think I have more than that. My god, you've got to get out of here before . . . Maybe you should go inside the Piper & Pelican . . . I'm pretty sure I won't be able to keep my hands off you," Brandon admitted.

Rosie turned to look at him with a glint of passion in her eyes, before slowly opening the passenger door to exit. She blinked once, smiled and then came around the vehicle to the driver's side. "I'll keep checking on you to make sure you don't pass out from that nasty bump on your head. I'm really concerned you know."

"I know," he said, gazing into her eyes.

She smiled. "Has anyone ever told you that you have the most gorgeous blue eyes?" she asked, tilting her head in a flirtatious manner.

"I swear, I'm either going to introduce you to the back seat or drive away if you don't go inside that tavern right now," he joked.

"Ha, ha, ha. No, you won't," She mocked. "I'll be back soon." He watched as she sauntered back to the bar, her hips swaying side to side.

Brandon smiled, feeling content that she was going inside. It was probably safer for her. He looked at his watch. *Two hours with absolutely nothing to do.* He hoped the time would go by quickly.

With Rosie safely inside, Brandon moved the SUV to a less conspicuous parking spot. At this point he even considered trading it in for a different rental vehicle.

Twenty minutes later, Brandon saw Rosie emerging from the Piper & Pelican, so he flicked the headlights to get her attention.

"You bugger, I thought you'd left," she fretted, walking toward the vehicle.

"Nope, still here. Did you bring me a beer?" Brandon asked jokingly.

She handed him a bottle of ginger ale. "It's inside the tavern, why don't you come inside and get it?" Rosie teased.

"You're too funny," he said with sarcasm.

"Okay, suit yourself," she said, entering the vehicle and passing him the take-out container full of hot food. "Here, you can wolf this down while I check that wound again. Don't let your chips get cold."

"What about you?" he asked.

"I'll have mine when I go back inside."

After Rosie wrapped Brandon's head wound and was satisfied that he had everything he needed, she strolled back inside the tavern to have her meal.

Fifteen minutes later, Brandon ducked low in his seat, gripping the gun tightly, as he carefully avoided being noticed by the man with the shaved head. Accompanied by a young woman, the man walked toward the entrance of the Piper & Pelican. She was scantily dressed in a slinky, low cut black mini-dress and high heels. Brandon hadn't seen the white van pull into the parking lot, but it didn't mean the guy couldn't have switched vehicles. He had ample time to do that and pick up the young lady. Brandon was certain it was his pursuer as he studied them walking underneath the tattered green awning. The man strode confidently, protectively looking around as he rested his hand on the small of the woman's back as they entered the juke joint.

Maybe this is his alibi. He must've had this evening planned all along, Brandon thought.

The original plot had undoubtedly been derailed because it was Brandon's body that was supposed be found at the bottom of the cliff.

I wonder if he knows his buddy went over the cliff, he thought.

He felt an undeniable sense of satisfaction when he thought about that. A twisted grin nudged his lips, but it was short lived. *I need to get inside that tavern, now! That guy is dangerous . . . Dammit! Rosie and Gloria are in there.*

Brandon bolted across the parking lot and peered through the window, arriving just in time to see his pursuer and the young woman strolling toward the back of the Piper & Pelican. They took a seat at a small table in the back corner.

After slipping inside, Brandon scanned the tavern. It was busy inside. Rosie was where he thought she'd be, sitting at the bar. He was hoping to make eye contact with her, but she hadn't seen him enter. He noticed Red standing on the other side of Rosie, but he was watching the baseball game on TV. Brandon slid in behind some guys standing near the bar, while he searched for Gloria.

***

"There's that fucking guy again. What the hell is he doing in here? I'm going to throw his ass out," Rosie overheard the hulking man with the cropped red hair saying to the older man working behind the bar. Rosie wasn't sure who he was referring to, so she casually glanced toward the door.

Uh oh, she thought, when she realized who it was. Brandon was making a horrid example of trying to blend into the crowd. The bandage on his head didn't help matters.

She watched as he pulled Gloria aside to talk to her, after she'd finished serving a customer.

Rosie could see that Red's anger was steadily increasing as he fixated on Brandon. He grunted while trying to get around a few of the patrons gathered near the far end of the bar. Rosie casually got off her barstool in order to block him, as he proceeded toward Brandon. "Oh, I'm really sorry," she said, getting in his way purposely, only moving in the same direction as him while he tried desperately to dodge her. "Oops, sorry again. It seems as if we're dancing," Rosie chuckled innocently.

"Get out of my way!" Red snorted, as he tried to get a visual on Brandon. He placed his hands on each of her shoulders to move her aside. That was a big mistake. Rosie planted her knee so hard into Red's groin that he dropped like a bowling pin. "Never, *ever* put your hands on me again," she scolded, waving her index finger.

Knowing Red would be furious and soon back on his feet to pursue her, she turned and made a hasty dash for the front entrance. She paused long enough to make eye contact with Brandon, and made a quick sweeping action of her left arm. "It's time to go!" Rosie hollered over the music.

It didn't take Red long to get up off the floor to engage in a pursuit, but he was stalled by a group of bar patrons who'd stepped into his path. As he stumbled around them, it gave Gloria enough time to usher Brandon toward the side

The Whiskey Lee

exit. Once outside, Brandon joined Rosie in the parking lot, grabbing her by the hand as the two of them sprinted over to the SUV.

Rosie ducked down in the passenger seat to try and hide as they zoomed past the front entrance. Brandon caught a glimpse of a very unhappy Red emerging from the tavern. He had a scowl on his face, and was shaking a fist at the SUV.

As they raced away from the front entrance, Brandon glanced in his rearview mirror again, just in time to see another man emerge from the tavern. As the man stepped into the pool of light in front of the Piper & Pelican, Brandon knew who it was by his profile. It was his pursuer—the man with the shaved head who had been driving the white GMC van.

Brandon didn't relax until he saw the two images in the mirror step back inside the tavern. He exhaled a sigh of relief that they weren't pursuing him.

As they drove back toward Barney's Cove, Brandon kept a close eye on his mirrors for any vehicles following them.

"So much for playing it low key," said Brandon.

"What about Gloria? Do you think she'll be okay?" Rosie asked with a concerned tone.

"She'll be fine. I'm the target, not her. I didn't have time to tell her where the guy was sitting though. Everything happened so fast. I would have felt better if I could have pointed him out to her," said Brandon.

"Do you think Red and the bloke with the shaved head are working together?" Rosie asked.

"I don't know, it's possible," said Brandon.

"I guess *I'm* never allowed in the Piper & Pelican again either now. When I saw Red coming for you, I dropped him like a hot potato. I'm surprised he got back up off the floor so fast," said Rosie.

Brandon laughed. "Me too, but I'm sure it was pure adrenaline that got him up. He's going to be hurtin'—that's for sure, and cranky too. Thanks for watching my back Rosie," said Brandon.

"We're a team, remember?" She replied.

"Yes, we are," he smiled, as they pulled up, out of sight at the back of Rosie's motel.

"We'll pick up your car tomorrow," Brandon offered.

"Yes, that would be wonderful, thanks," she replied. "Will you be okay?"

"I'll be fine. I just have a bit of a headache," said Brandon.

"Isn't that supposed to be *my* line?" she said, smirking. "Okay, just let me check that bandage once more before I go. You've got to stop hitting your head, you know," she said, as she examined him with care.

"I know."

"It looks a bit better now. I think you just need some rest." Rosie leaned over to give him a good-night kiss before getting out of the vehicle.

27

"Are you joining me today to check out the haunted pub and hotel in Portland?" she asked with an elated tone.

Brandon glanced over at Rosie sitting in the "shot gun" seat of his SUV. He vaguely remembered that she wanted to do that. "Was that today?" he replied groggily, still feeling pain in his head. A lump had formed underneath the bandage.

"Yes, but if you're not up to it, I understand. You've been through a fair bit," she said compassionately.

He wanted to go, but Brandon had to be honest with himself; he didn't really feel like doing much of anything, especially if it involved creepy places, bright sunlight, or talking to *anyone*. He was glad that he'd grabbed his sunglasses before driving Rosie over to Brewster's to pick up her car.

"How's the ole noggin' doing, anyway?" she asked.

"Hurts."

"Are you taking any meds for the pain and swelling?"

"Yes, I've got some over-the-counter stuff."

He saw Rosie's car parked in front of Brewster's and pulled into the parking lot beside it.

"Thanks for driving me to pick up my car. I wouldn't have minded walking if I was still at the Rocky Ridge Motel."

"It's the least I could do. I'm the one that dragged you out of the bar last night."

"Oh yes, and I was kicking and screaming too. Do you remember?" She winked.

He attempted his best grin, which appeared more like a wince.

"Oh, you're in rough shape." She placed a gentle hand on his thigh. "Do you want me to stay and take care of you Brandon? I don't have to go sightseeing today."

"No, you go. I insist. Something tells me I'm not going to be great company today."

It worked out well. Rosie went to her haunted sites, while Brandon got some much-needed R&R. He grabbed a bag of ice from the gas station and returned to his cottage to fill his cooler. Sitting on the sofa with his feet up, he propped the pillows up behind his head to make himself a bit more comfortable. The thought of getting rid of the black Nissan Rogue entered his mind again. He could trade it in for another color. That was his last thought before drifting off to sleep.

***

Later that evening, he drove down to the wharf, opting for a casual stroll along the docks to clear his head. He hid the SUV from view, as usual. It was a damp evening, with hardly any wind. There was a cool mist rolling in off the ocean. Brandon's thoughts drifted back to James Moreland.

As the dock creaked beneath him, he stood still. A cold chill encircled him as the fog crept closer. It moved across the docks, now surrounding him. Off in the distance, he could hear the unmistakable sound of a baby crying. It was echoing across the bay. Consumed by his thoughts, Brandon couldn't help but feel like he wasn't alone. Fear flowed through his veins as he slowly scanned his surroundings. He felt for his Beretta and realized that he'd left it in his vehicle again. *Why do I keep doing that?* he thought.

Brandon considered returning to the parking lot, just before movement up ahead caught his attention. A lone shadowy figure stepped out from the fog on the main dock in front of him. Brandon's eyes were now locked on the mysterious man, who was staring back at him. The man wore the familiar navy wool sweater and peaked denim captain's cap.

"Hello again," said Brandon. "Nice night, i-isn't it?" he stuttered, while trying to stop himself from shivering.

There was no answer.

"May I help you?" Brandon asked.

The fading form turned away from him.

"Wait! Are you Captain James Moreland?" Brandon asked.

Brandon's words seemed to have an immediate effect, as the mysterious figure stopped in dead his tracks. He half turned to look at Brandon; on his slightly translucent face, a faint smile appeared, just before he was consumed by the dense fog.

"Wait!" Brandon shouted again, while running along the dock toward the man's fading image.

"Please wait, maybe I can help youuuu!" was all he was able to utter, after entering the fog.

As Brandon's feet left the dock, a short silence was followed by the sound of a heavy SPLASH! The sudden clap of the water separating underneath him echoed inland afterwards.

He managed to surface, reaching his arm out to grab hold of the dock. His clothes were heavy and waterlogged. He heard hinges creaking loudly as the metal gate at the foot of the dock swung closed.

Brandon searched for a ladder or something to climb up. Hand over hand, he moved along the dock until he located a boat with a swim platform and a ladder attached to it. He hauled himself out of the water. Once up on the dock, he kicked off his shoes and emptied the seawater out of them. He couldn't see much in front of him. *This fog is so thick I could cut it with a knife*, he thought, as he listened to the gate hinges creaking for a second time. Sound traveled well in these conditions. Brandon wished he could see the dock ahead of him.

"Hello? Is everyone okay?" He heard a familiar voice call out from the direction of the gate. The English accent was too familiar to be confused with anyone else.

"Did someone fall in the water?"

"Rosie?" Brandon called out. "It's me. I'm over here!"

"Brandon?" she asked.

"Yes," he said, emerging from the fog.

"Late-night swim hun?" Rosie mocked.

"Uh, ya," Brandon said, feeling embarrassed.

"I just sent you a text to see how you were doing. No wonder you didn't answer me," said Rosie.

"My phone is a little waterlogged right now," he said.

"What happened? I was just walking over to Danny's Restaurant and heard a loud splash so thought I'd come down here to investigate. I had no idea I'd see *you* out here taking a swim in your clothes," said Rosie.

"Yeah, it was a surprise to me too," said Brandon.

"Where's your SUV?" she inquired.

"It's hidden. You must have walked right by it." He turned his head so that his right ear was facing the ground; using the palm of his hand, he gave a couple of light taps to his head to try to clear the water which had accumulated in his ear canal.

"That's just going to aggravate your head injury. What on earth were you doing out here anyway?" Rosie asked.

"Chasing ghosts." He straightened his head to look directly into her eyes.

"Of course, why did I ask?"

"It was Captain James Moreland again. The same ghost we saw at the USS *Midhurst*. I followed him into the fog, but it seems that someone made the dock too short," said Brandon.

Rosie broke into a fit of laughter.

"I didn't think it was that funny."

"I'm sorry, it was just the way you said it," she eventually stopped giggling and wiped the tears from the corner of her eyes.

"Some rescuer you are. I was already on the dock by the time I heard you opening the gate," he retorted.

"I didn't open the gate. It was already open," said Rosie. "I heard it swing as well; that was before I got to it."

"I heard it twice. I think it closed and then opened again," said Brandon.

"You do realize there's very little wind tonight?" Rosie asked, as they both stared curiously at the gate. "It's not moving at all now," said Brandon.

"Spooky. I don't know what to tell you, but I must say that I'm getting goose bumps right now." She shivered. "How are you feeling today, anyway?"

"I feel much better, thanks. I came down here to do some thinking—to clear my head."

"Now your head's full of seawater?" she smiled.

"Yeah."

Now that Rosie mentioned it, he could still feel water lodged in his right ear. *The secret to that is clear it out right away*. He shook his head more aggressively.

"Heeeey!" Rosie said, stepping back from him. "You're getting me wet and you smell like a wet barnacle."

"Okay, whatever that smells like." He chuckled. "I could seriously go for a beer right now."

"*You* have a *beer*? You've already fallen into the sea once tonight... Oh, I'm just getting started," she giggled flirtatiously.

"I can see you're having fun with this. Would *you* like to go for a late-night swim?"

"Nooo, no. Don't you dare!" She warned, backing away.

He smiled. "Well, if you don't mind the smell of wet barnacle, maybe you could join me while I drive back to my cottage to change my clothes. I may need a shower while I'm there too."

"Thought you'd never ask," said Rosie, stepping closer.

"Maybe we can sit outside on my deck afterwards. I have some cold beer in my cooler." He held out his hands for her.

"Okay, I'll come closer, but don't push me in, okay. My watch isn't waterproof and neither is my phone," she pleaded warily.

"I won't. You can trust me."

As she reached for his hands, he pulled her in, wrapped both arms around her, and pressed his body tightly up against hers.

"Oh, you're so cold and wet," she said breathlessly. "Bugger."

They exchanged a passionate kiss.

"You'll warm up soon. I promise. Will you to stay with me tonight?" he asked softly.

"Okay, I just need to pack an overnight bag," she replied.

28

THE NEXT DAY

After a night to remember, Brandon dropped Rosie off at her motel. He gave her one more kiss, before driving over to Barney's Cove to meet Chad. Splash time was scheduled for 12:30 p.m. It's the earliest time that Chad could leave the dive shop. Mornings were generally busy, but it gave Brandon and Rosie more quality time to spend with each other before parting ways.

"I had an amazing night with you," Brandon said to Rosie.

"Me too," she said. "Stay safe out there."

"I will," Brandon reassured her. "It's probably safer for me to be underwater than it is out on these streets right now."

She nodded. "I believe you."

"What are you going to do today?" he asked.

"I'm going to visit the local graveyard."

"Sounds like fun," he said sarcastically. "There's still so much I don't know about you."

"I like to try and remain a little mysterious. I can't tell you all my secrets yet; you may get bored of me."

"Oh, I don't think that will ever happen," he said.

They parted ways with an embrace and a kiss.

"See you later," said Rosie.

"You bet," he replied, grinning flirtatiously.

***

Shortly after walking into Brewster's, Rosie noticed how surprisingly busy the place was. There was one empty bar stool on the other end of the bar, so she hurried over to it.

"Alright then, Len?" Rosie asked as she pulled the worn-out bar stool closer to the bar.

"I'm doing okay thanks, my luv. It's just a bit crazy in here today. What can I get for you?" He moved closer to her.

She ordered a glass of red wine, and then listened contentedly to several hipsters playing their ukuleles up on the small stage, while she scanned the menu. Len didn't stick around for the usual chitchat. He was now at the other end of the bar. The crowd was made up of mostly families, seniors, and businesspeople who had stopped by for Len's famous lunch specials. Finally, he came over and took her food order. "Sorry luv, would you like to order something to eat?"

"I think I'll have the classic Philly cheesesteak."

"Excellent choice, my dear! Make sure you try some of our lobster ice cream for dessert," he said, shifting his eyes past Rosie, toward the front entrance—seeming somewhat distracted.

"Sorry, I don't mean to offend you, Len but that sounds absolutely disgusting."

Len wasn't even listening to her now. She turned her head in the direction he was looking. His eyes were fixed on the smartly dressed trio of men who'd just entered the pub.

"Oh no, look who just walked in here," said Len.

The first thing Rosie noticed was the overconfident swagger in the leading man's step. She noticed it was the handsome man whom she'd seen on the television at Brewster's few days earlier. The man was striding toward a booth in the corner with his entourage.

Don't get caught up in the halo effect, Len had warned. She couldn't help but notice that the man looked even more handsome in person.

"This should be an interesting day," Len said sarcastically.

"Isn't he the one you don't like?" Rosie asked.

"Yes, but just because I don't like him doesn't mean I can't take his money," Len said with a devilish grin. "He comes in here now and then for his afternoon meetings."

The hipsters played an uplifting tune, which seemed to mask the negative vibes which now seemed to be lingering in the air.

"When you're in this business, you learn to tolerate a lot of shit. I still have to put food on my table and pay my mortgage. As long as no one causes any trouble in here, then it's all good," Len growled, as he took out a clean beer glass and filled it up for a customer.

"Okay, I'll try not to cause any trouble," said Rosie, winking.

Len smiled back at her. "You're no trouble luv, except I'm not sure about that character that followed you in here the other night."

"Brandon?" Rosie said surprised.

"No, no, that other shady character with the stone-cold face that came in here after Brandon arrived. The one you said was after you. It's none of my business, but I'd prefer not seeing those types around here. I don't want to have to show him where the door is, if you know what I mean."

"Absolutely," she said.

"So, how come you're alone today? What's Brandon up to?" he asked her.

"He went scuba diving today."

"That sounds both interesting and dangerous. Never catch me doing something like that." Len placed a cardboard coaster on the bar and set the beer down for the customer beside her.

"I don't know if I would try it or not. I'm always open to new adventures though," said Rosie.

Len looked at his watch. "I'll go and see if your order's ready now, luv. Let me know if you need anything else. I'll be back in a minute." He disappeared through the double doors which led to the kitchen.

After lunch, Rosie had some time to relax, so she stayed for another half hour or so, to listen to the hipsters finish their set.

The businesspeople, as well as the rest of the lunch crowd, had vastly thinned out after three o'clock. The ukulele players had packed up all their equipment and were placing it into a minivan.

Len had some time on his hands once again. He came back to where Rosie was sitting.

"It's quiet in here now," she said.

"Yes, it's a nice little break before the dinner crowd starts to roll in."

Rosie's phone rang. It was from a number she didn't recognize. "Sorry Len, I just need to get this."

Len nodded and then left her alone for a few minutes.

"Hello."

"Hi Rosie, it's Brandon."

"Hi, I didn't recognize the number. Are you finished your dive?" Rosie asked.

"Yes, actually we just got back. I'm using Chad's phone. Mine's still sitting in rice, in a plastic bag," said Brandon.

Rosie remembered why and chuckled. "I'm sorry for laughing."

"I thought about you all day," he said.

"You did?" She smiled. "I thought about you too."

"Do you want to sleep over again tonight?" Brandon asked.

"Of course," Rosie replied.

"How about joining me for surf and turf with wine later? Chad recommended a place."

"Oh, that sounds lovely," she said in an elated tone.

"Let's say around six-thirty. Does that work for you?"

"Perfect!" Rosie replied.

"I could pick you up at your motel, first I'll need to go back to my cabin to shower, and then after that I'm taking the Nissan Rogue back to the rental agency to trade it in for different one."

***

Brandon couldn't wait to rid himself of the black SUV. In his request he made a point of asking for a lighter color because the black one was too hot. It wasn't a lie.

"Ah, yes, the darker colors do tend attract the sunlight more. I'll see what I've got out back for you," the rental agent said, while tapping his fingers across the computer keys, searching his inventory. The agent was mainly concerned about how much fuel Brandon used in the Rogue. He did a quick walk around and then signed off on the paperwork. Brandon hoped he wouldn't notice the slight indentation and small scuff on the bumper, where the GMC van had tried to force him off the road. The scuff was hardly noticeable after Brandon had buffed it out with some car polish and a soft cloth. He was issued a new contract and the car keys were handed over without any further questions.

Brandon was now driving a white Ford Explorer. It came custom with beige leather seats and tinted windows. His phone was dried out and working again, so he phoned Rosie and let her know that he was on his way. She was waiting outside the motel for him.

"This is really nice. I could see myself driving one of these. Maybe I should trade mine in too," Rosie remarked as she climbed into the vehicle.

Brandon nodded, but his mind was elsewhere. He really wanted to get something off his chest.

"We're probably getting way too close to finding out what happened to Captain Moreland. I still didn't get a chance to show you the photographs I took at the shipyards. They're in my duffle bag on the floor in the backseat . . . if anything happens to me. Chad has the rest of them."

"Oh, please don't . . ." said Rosie, holding up a hand to stop him.

"Sorry, I have to let you know where they are."

Brandon leaned over and gingerly kissed her before starting the Explorer. He backed carefully out of the parking space. "There's a photograph I took of something I'd found at Scully's Salvage. It was a photo of a guy holding a gun on someone. I think he may have murdered someone. I'd hate to think how many people those guys have killed. We don't even know how many or who we are dealing with. That's the scary part," Brandon said, while checking his mirrors to see if anyone was tailing them as he pulled out onto the main road.

"Shouldn't we give the evidence to the police?" Rosie asked.

Brandon's head tilted to one side, as if the continuous turning of wheels in his mind had already been developing an answer.

"I don't really have the feeling that they're going to do anything with the evidence at this point. Without bodies, what do we have? A hunch? It's not enough. Trying to get them to reopen the case is like trying to squeeze blood out of a stone. I've come too far to back out now, but if you want to, I'll totally understand," he said, as he pulled into a parking space close to the back of Lizzie's Seafront Restaurant.

Placing the vehicle in park, he pulled out the Beretta Tomcat.

"Whoa!" Rosie exclaimed, as she leaned back, raising her hands.

"Relax Rosie. Listen, I'm supposed to keep this with me, but I have no way of concealing this weapon. It's too hot for me to wear a jacket, and I'm sure someone will see it if I carry it in my waistband. I'll look like a gangster. I need you to do me a favor and keep it in your handbag for me. Don't worry, I made sure the safety's on."

Rosie considered her answer for a moment before replying. Her mind drifted to everything that's happened to them lately.

"Okay, I don't like guns, but I'll do it for you, Brandon. It's better than leaving it in the SUV," she said.

Brandon nodded. "Thank you." He leaned over and kissed her again.

As they strolled into the restaurant, Brandon immediately noticed two TVs facing each other, mounted on opposite walls. The same news channel showed on both televisions. It wasn't a fancy place. The square tables were painted green, with a light wood border. The curtains looked like they hadn't been washed in a while. Their outdated orange-and-white checked pattern didn't hide the fact that this small family restaurant hadn't spent anything lately on upgrading the place. He wasn't sure why Chad had suggested it, but had faith in his friend's food recommendations. The fact that Lizzie's was packed, also re-assured him that it was a good place to eat. The couple selected a booth along the wall.

On the television, a news anchor was reading the live daily newscast.

"Be right back," Rosie said.

"Okay," Brandon said, watching her hips sway as she walked toward the lady's room.

The distraction caused him to miss the man in the dark suit and mirrored sunglasses entering the restaurant. Brandon turned to watch what was happening on the television. With the TV's volume turned down low, Brandon read the caption above the news anchor. It seemed that a story was unfolding about the body of a man found floating in the sea, not far from the lighthouse.

Brandon didn't see much after the man approached his table, blocking his view. "Excuse me. I was watching that," Brandon said, eyeing the man. He was vaguely aware that he'd seen this guy somewhere before. He just couldn't place him.

"Interesting story on the news, wouldn't you agree?" the man said. "You know, if you were my target, you would have been dead already? You didn't even see me approach your table."

Brandon wasn't sure how to reply to that.

Thank you for not killing me in the middle of a seafood restaurant, in broad daylight, Brandon thought.

"What do you want?" Brandon asked frankly. "Who are you?"

"No Brandon, the question is, what are *you* doing here?" The man deflected.

"I asked first," said Brandon. "What exactly do you want with me? Get to the point."

The man sat down directly across from Brandon, showing him some identification before removing his sunglasses.

"I'm Federal Agent Tom Rogan. What I *want* is to talk to you in private, not here. This isn't a secure location."

"Am I under arrest?" Brandon questioned.

"No, I just want about half an hour of your time to talk and then we'll both understand a little more about what the hell is going on here. Are you armed, Brandon?"

"No," Brandon replied honestly. He was damned certain that Agent Rogan would have confiscated the gun from him if he hadn't left it in Rosie's care.

"Good," Rogan said.

Rosie had walked out of the ladies' room in time to notice the man in the dark suit showing his identification to Brandon. She stayed hidden while her fingers scrambled to send a text message to Brandon. His phone was sitting on the table in front of him.

***

He heard the alert as the message popped up on the screen. Brandon's eyes shifted to his phone and then to Rogan.

"Is it okay if I get this? I'm supposed to be meeting a friend here?" he asked.

"Sure, but I already know that you're here with one of your lady friends. Is she the one that's sending you a text message right now?" Rogan asked, looking around the restaurant and then settling his eyes upon the dark auburn–haired woman staring at her phone near the washroom. "Aw, there she is," he smiled, gesturing. "She's a cutie. Well done."

Brandon frowned, turning to see Rosie staring down at her phone. "Leave her out of this."

Is everything ok? Rosie's text message popped up on the screen.

Yes, stay put. I'll be back.

Okay, be careful. Call me if you need help, she wrote.

"Okay, let's go outside and talk," Brandon said urgently.

"This won't take too much of your time, I promise," Rogan assured him, as he put his sunglasses back on before going outside.

As they got closer to the agent's car, Rogan stopped him.

"You probably don't trust too many people at this point, I get that. You have every right to feel that way. I'd feel the same way if I was in your shoes, but I assure you this is legit. Please turn your phone off, Brandon," said Rogan.

Brandon turned the volume down but left the phone on. As he walked toward Rogan's car, he casually observed a man lurking near his newly acquired Explorer.

Rogan opened the rear door of his sedan for Brandon to enter. "Please take a seat in the back and we'll chat some more."

"Are you sure I'm not under arrest?" Brandon asked.

"Trust me. You're not. We're only going to talk."

Rogan closed the door and then entered the car via the driver's door. Once inside the car, Brandon began fielding the agent's questions almost immediately.

"First off, I want to ask you about the man at the cliff," Agent Rogan informed him.

"Okay," said Brandon. He was a bit surprised the agent knew about that.

"Did you know the man?"

"No, I did not."

"How about the driver of the white van? Have you ever seen him before?"

Brandon was dumbfounded that he knew so much. "No, I didn't know either of them, or have I any idea why they were trying to kill me."

"You know what? That seems odd to me. Not many people go out of their way to kill someone for no reason. I usually know why my enemies are pissed at me," said Rogan.

"I don't know. I swear," said Brandon. He wasn't sure how much he should reveal to the agent.

"What did the guy at the cliff say to you?"

"He said he wanted me to walk to the edge of the cliff. He wouldn't tell me why. I stalled as much as I could until a voice yelled, 'Drop the gun,' or something like that. So, I took the opportunity to attack the guy and knock the gun out of his hand. It all happened so fast and the next thing I knew I was dangling over the edge of the cliff, trying to find a foothold. That's when someone pulled me up."

"Someone helped you. Who?" Rogan asked, removing his sunglasses. Brandon could now see his eyes in the driver's rearview mirror.

"I don't know, but I'd like to thank him," said Brandon.

"Fair enough," Rogan nodded. "Okay, let's go back to the guy that tumbled over the cliff."

Now, Brandon remembered where he'd seen the agent before. He was in the Piper & Pelican the day that he and Red got into the dustup.

Rogan continued. "Why would he go to all that trouble to want to kill you if you've never met? It doesn't make any sense to me at all."

"Me neither, but when you figure it all out maybe could you fill in some of the blanks for me," said Brandon.

"Honestly, I'm still trying to piece it together. You may have something of theirs, or you witnessed something? Anything ring a bell? Does the woman who works at the bar know those men?" Rogan asked. Brandon raised his eyebrows at the reference to Gloria.

"I don't know. You'll have to ask Gloria. Could you open up a window? It's getting really stuffy back here." He grasped at his shirt collar to pull it away from his neck.

Rogan opened the windows to allow some fresh air to flow through the car. "Better?"

"Yeah, thanks," said Brandon.

Rogan continued. "Why do you think that guy took Gloria's phone?"

"Because they wanted to trick me into thinking that he was Gloria, so they could lure me up to the cliff."

"And now we're back to why," Rogan sighed. "I'm sorry, but I need more. I still don't think you're telling me everything. Feel free to offer more information. I'm only trying to help you here."

"Sure," said Brandon, still wary.

"Okay, how long have you known Gloria?"

"I just met her two weeks ago, why?"

"If you don't mind, I'm asking the questions. You'll have your turn later," Rogan replied, studying him in the rearview mirror.

"Alright," Brandon did the hand gesture for zipping his mouth closed and then folded his arms.

"So, how did you and Gloria meet, anyway?" Rogan continued.

"I met her at the Piper & Pelican. I came down here to Maine for my vacation. Gloria served me the first time I went in there."

The Whiskey Lee

"Nice little joint, but could use a little fixing up. By the way, where do you live? I'm guessing you're not from around here," said Agent Rogan.

"Ontario, Canada," Brandon said proudly.

"That explains a lot," the agent smirked. What about the other lady that's waiting inside Lizzie's for you? How does she fit into all this? What's her name?"

Brandon didn't offer her name. He stayed silent.

"That's okay. It's easy enough to find out."

"We just met. Keep her out of this."

Rogan smiled. "Hmm . . . It sounds to me that she's more than just a friend . . . Look Brandon, I'd like to work with you, but I will need your full cooperation."

Brandon wondered who this Agent Tom Rogan was and why he was so interested. He didn't know if he could trust him yet, let alone offer up any of the evidence he'd found so far. *Rogan could just be fishing for information or maybe he already knows and wanted to see how much I know. Is he a real agent?* Brandon wasn't quite sure how this hand was to be played, but he was no amateur when it came to holding a poker face when the chips were down.

"You're a tough egg to crack, Brandon. I admire that," the agent acknowledged, "but, I'm pretty sure that it won't be long before you'll be needing my help. You know that news story you were watching when you failed to see me approaching your table?" Rogan asked.

"Yeah, what about it?" Brandon questioned defensively.

"That was *your* man they found in the sea," said Rogan. "The one from the cliff."

Brandon felt the blood drain from his face, as he realized he could face jail time. "I-I didn't . . ." he stammered.

"You can relax," Rogan squinted, studying Brandon's face in the mirror before putting his sunglasses back on.

"It didn't look like you did it intentionally, but I do need your full cooperation in this investigation. So, if you're thinking of holding anything back, that may not be a smart choice. Like I said before, I'm just here to help you."

"Were you there?"

"No comment. Look, just try to be straight with me, okay Brandon? I don't like games. I like honesty. Your life will be much easier that way. If you don't waste my time, I won't waste yours," said Rogan.

"Sure. You got it; whatever you need," Brandon replied cooperatively. Just then his phone sounded an alert.

"See, that's exactly what I'm talking about. I thought I asked you to turn your phone off. Well, you may as well go ahead and answer it," Rogan huffed.

"Sorry, it's my uh ... friend, Rosie. She sent me a text, wondering if I'm okay," said Brandon.

"I figured as much. Go ahead and reply to her," the agent said, gesturing with a wave of his hand.

Brandon sent Rosie a text back. *I'm just outside in a dark blue sedan. All is ok.*

Rosie messaged back to him: *If you need me just text 32 and I will come to save you.*

Brandon grinned inwardly at the reference to *32*. It was the caliber of bullet that the Tomcat used. It was code for *Bring the gun.*

No need, just stay inside, Brandon replied.

"Look, whenever you're finished talking your girlfriend, here's my card in case you remember anything else that you forgot to tell me today," Agent Rogan handed Brandon his business card.

"Oh, my mobile number has changed. You can write my new number on the back of the card," Rogan offered.

"Sure, but do you have a pen that I can borrow? I don't have one," said Brandon.

"No problem," Rogan replied, reaching into his shirt pocket and removing a stainless-steel ballpoint pen.

After writing the number down, Brandon eyed the pen before handing it back to the agent. "Nice pen."

"You can keep it if you want. I have lots," said Rogan.

"Are you sure?"

"Yeah," the agent replied. "They're a dime a dozen."

"Thanks," Brandon said, placing it in his own shirt pocket.

Rosie was waiting near the window at the back of the restaurant when Brandon returned. He assumed she'd been watching them the entire time.

She bolted over to him as soon as he walked through the door. "Tell me what happened. Who was that bloke? I was so scared for you," Rosie uttered anxiously.

"Let's get out of here. All of a sudden I don't have much of an appetite," he muttered.

Rosie followed him out the door.

He drove across town to the nearest garage which specialized in oil, lube, and filter changes.

"You need an oil change? Isn't this a rental?" Rosie raised an eyebrow inquisitively.

"It wouldn't hurt to get one while I'm here," said Brandon.

"While you're here? It's an oil change garage. Enlighten me. Why else would you be here?" said Rosie.

"I need it swept," said Brandon.

Rosie shrugged. "Okay."

The service technician guided Brandon's vehicle over the gap in the floor.

After turning off the ignition, Brandon got out to talk to the tech. Rosie noticed him slipping the young man a handful of cash.

"What was that all about?" Rosie looked confused as hell as he entered the vehicle.

"I'm getting the technician to sweep underneath the vehicle for anything that shouldn't be there, for instance, a location tracking device that maybe the agent planted."

"Well, aren't you the genius! And here I was thinking you've gone completely nuts."

"Thanks for having so much faith in me," he laughed.

"So, you think someone put something underneath your vehicle?" Rosie asked.

"I'm not sure, but it won't hurt to have it checked. How much do you want to bet he finds something?" Brandon challenged.

"Well, I'm not really the gambling type, but you can give me a massage tonight if he doesn't."

"You're on!" Brandon replied delightfully.

The service technician had found two location tracking devices. He handed them to Brandon through the open driver's window. "Here you go, sir. I'm not even going to ask how they got there."

"Are you sure there aren't anymore?" Brandon asked.

"Yes, I went back and forth a few times just to make sure I got them all. That's it," the tech replied.

"Thanks!"

"You're welcome. Thanks very much for the generous tip," the tech said, and then walked away to open the overhead door for them. Brandon turned to look at Rosie. "So, I guess I'm the one getting a massage tonight," he smiled deviously, as he drove the vehicle out of the garage.

She shook her head slowly at him, smiling. "You are *so* naughty. How did you know they were there?"

"I suspected something when I saw a guy hovering around the vehicle," he admitted.

A few minutes after leaving the service garage, Brandon stopped in a parking lot at the back of a hardware store and dropped the two location trackers into a dumpster.

29

Matt Riker selected the M42 bolt-action sniper rifle for the job. *This is going to be too easy*, he thought, as he saw his target partially emerge from behind a dumpster. He spied through the powerful scope and took aim.

Just before taking the shot, Matt heard some movement near his position. His finger hovered anxiously over the trigger.

"I thought you were working the graveyard shift tonight," a voice from behind him said.

"I am," said Matt, as he tried to concentrate on the task at hand.

His friend Chris moved in closer, appearing on Matt's right side.

"Then, dude, why aren't you sleeping right now?" Chris queried.

"I just want to kill this asshole first." Matt gave a frown as he tried to focus. "Shut up for a minute, I need to concentrate."

Matt took the shot. The lifeless body dropped to the ground in front of the dumpster.

"Sick shot!" Chris congratulated.

"Thanks. Now, I'm going to bed," said Matt, as he got up from the sofa, placing the video game controller beside the console on the coffee table.

"Uh, could you leave the game on? I'm going to play after I eat my lunch," Chris said.

"Sure, keep the sound down though. I need my beauty sleep," Matt said, as he walked into his bedroom and shut the door.

***

The overnight shift at the shipyards wasn't ideal for Matt because he was only able to get three hours sleep during the day. He wasn't sure if he'd like the new job or not, but he was willing to give it a try.

Around two in the morning, Matt was taking a short break from driving the forklift, when his boss appeared in front of him.

"Hey Matt, seeing as you're not doing anything, could you go out back to the storage container and pick up the portable air compressor? Here's the keys," the foreman said, tossing them to him before receiving a reply. Matt grabbed the keys in midair, nearly spilling the can of soda he was holding. "Sure," Matt said quietly.

As he walked toward the back of the warehouse, he wiped the sweat from his forehead with his sleeve. At the back of the warehouse, two of his coworkers were idly leaning up against the pallets, contentedly socializing about their weekends. They glanced over at him, smirking as he strolled by. It angered him.

Sure, it's okay . . . the new guy will do everything, Matt thought sourly.

Outside, Matt inhaled deeply as he stood in front of the double doors of the big gray container. Searching for the right key to open the padlock, he was temporarily distracted by a voice summoning him from the shadows between the container and the back of the warehouse.

"Hey! Over here!" A man's voice said.

"What the f—" Matt said, startled. "Who is that?"

"Hide!" The man cautioned.

"Who the hell are you?" Matt responded, clenching his fists, ready to engage the intruder.

Matt stood over six feet tall, a lean young man of twenty-two years, with facial scruff and shoulder length curly blonde hair. Through the years he'd had plenty of practise throwing off the gloves while playing hockey. He wasn't the type to be messing with.

He heard a door to the neighboring warehouse open, just before the mysterious man stepped halfway into the light. Matt still couldn't see the man's face, but he could see that he was wearing a dark sweater and a peaked sailor's cap. Matt's attention was drawn to four men emerging from the warehouse next door. The first man was middle-aged. He was wearing a baseball cap, plaid shirt, baggy jeans, and exhibited a protruding beer gut. The second man was younger, approximately thirty-something, with a shaved head, and wearing jeans that seemed way too tight for him, motorcycle boots, and a long-sleeved fitted jersey. The third man looked to be in his forties. He was lanky with short-cropped hair. The last man to leave the warehouse looked a little older, was almost bald, and was extremely annoyed. He was scolding the other three men as he walked closely behind them.

"They are bad men," the mysterious man warned again, as he stepped back into the shadows. "Hide."

Matt decided to heed the advice of the stranger and quickly took cover. "Who are they?" Matt whispered to the stranger. "Bad men," the stranger repeated.

He tried to steal another glance of the stranger, but it was too difficult to get a good view of the man's features.

A raised voice cut through the air. It was the angry man from the other warehouse. "Listen you three, I don't care what you have to do, but clean this mess up before Cy finds out! I can't believe you morons let someone break into the warehouse. Who knows what he saw! We could all go to jail for a very long time if this shit gets out."

Matt could no longer see the outline of the man who had summoned him to hide in the shadows, but he could still hear him: "Bad men," he repeated in a hollow voice.

Matt tried to listen even harder to what the man in the yard was saying. Now, the angry man turned to direct his attention to the man wearing the plaid shirt and the baseball cap: "Evans, I want you to take care of Brandon once and for all. No more fuck ups. Cy's pissed already that you didn't finish him when you had the chance. That was two chances you had, by the way! Do you think you can handle it this time? If you can't, I'll get my little sister to do it. Just get him out of our way," the angry man growled, before turning to the younger man in the tight jeans and motorcycle boots.

"Mugs, you go through this place top to bottom. Make sure nothing's missing or tampered with. Check the offices too. Make sure they're locked. I have to stay and wait for the truck. We've got to start moving everything out of here soon."

"Are we moving all those fucking drums tonight Lewis?" The lanky middle-aged man asked.

"Yes, Nash, we are moving all those fucking drums tonight, because you guys *screwed up!*" His voice elevated as his temper rose, spitting each word out in a thunderous roar.

"Hey man, try to keep your voice down," Mugs suggested.

"Don't tell me to keep my voice down, Mugs," Lewis glared disapprovingly. "There's absolutely nobody out here that can hear us right now. Why couldn't you have been paranoid before?" He turned to Evans. "You remember what happened to Dennis, don't you Evans? Ace was there too. He'll remind you if you've forgotten. Do you guys want to end up like that sorry-ass deckhand? What the hell were you three thinking, anyway?"

He turned, storming back to the building and then stopped to glance in their direction.

"Why the fuck are you clowns still standing there? Are your jeans too tight, Mugs? Let's go!"

Lewis entered the building, now followed by Mugs, while Evans and Nash walked toward their vehicles. The warehouse door slammed closed after Lewis and Mugs entered.

Matt could now hear the man in the baseball cap cursing as he strode toward his gray 4x4 truck. He threw his cigarette down on the ground, angrily stomping it out before reaching for the door handle. *"Can I fuckin' handle it this time?"* Evans mimicked to Nash, pulling the door open to climb in. "As easy as I can handle bringing the hammer down on both Lewis's and Cy's heads. Mother fuckers! They don't know who they're dealing with."

Nash opened the driver's side door of his vehicle. "Don't let Lewis get to you. I'm sure he'll get over it. He's just blowing off steam like he always does. He's too chicken to do things himself. That's why we always have to do the dirty work for him."

"Yeah!" Evans slammed his truck door closed, revved his truck a couple of times, and then tore out of the parking lot, squealing the tires.

Matt stayed hidden in the shadows in order to remain out of sight. After waiting for the other vehicle to pull out, he searched the area between the container and the warehouse. Strangely, the mysterious man had vanished.

30

Matt didn't return to the warehouse job the following evening. His first graveyard shift would be his last. The next job that Matt was hired for was with a privately-owned landscaping company. One of the company's contracts included the gardens surrounding the Senate office building in Port Bradley.

About an hour and a half after his lunch break, Matt was feeling exhausted from the hard rays that the sun was casting down upon the workers. The property offered virtually no shade, with small and poorly placed trees scattered among concrete and endless grass. Matt needed to refill his water bottle and use the washroom. There wasn't very much wind that day, which didn't help.

"Is it okay if I borrow the access card to use the washroom inside the building?" He asked his supervisor.

Matt's supervisor had a good relationship with one of the building's full-time maintenance personnel, who didn't mind lending him his access card. The card allowed the landscapers to bypass security via the side door, which gave easy access to the washroom. It saved valuable time. The landscaping company was trusted and had been assigned to the Senate building for over ten years without any incidents. It was their biggest contract—their bread and butter.

"Okay, but before I give it to you, you'll have to listen and agree to my instructions," the man said, sternly.

"Sure." Matt agreed.

"It's the third door on the right. Don't draw any attention to yourself, don't go anywhere else, and don't talk to anyone. Go to the washroom and come straight back outside. If you don't follow instructions, you don't come back to work. Got it?" his supervisor warned.

"Yes, got it," Matt replied, accepting the access card.

Matt followed the supervisor's directions and walked along the small corridor until he found a water station to refill his water bottle. He found the men's washroom on the right-hand side after that.

Inside, Matt was surprised to see a man already standing in front of the mirror. He wore a peaked cap, and a navy wool sweater. Matt thought his choice of clothing was a little overboard, considering the high temperature outside. *Maybe the guy likes the feeling of being in an oven*. Matt shrugged it off, trying desperately to ignore the man, while proceeding toward an empty washroom stall.

Matt closed the door quickly. "*Don't talk to anyone. Don't draw attention to yourself.*" He kept hearing his supervisor's voice repeating in his head. He tried to concentrate on the task he came in here for. He stood in front of the toilet, trying to relax.

"*Dalton is a bad man*," the man blurted out.

There was no one else in the washroom besides Matt and this strange man. The feeling of awkwardness arose inside of him.

"W-What?" He asked shakily, now realizing that he'd heard that hollow voice before. Matt flushed the toilet and flung open the stall door, just in time to see the man vanish into the hallway.

Matt decided to follow the mysterious man.

Out in the corridor, Matt stopped walking when the stranger turned to lock eyes with him. It was the first time that he had really taken a good look at the man in the peaked cap. He was sure that he was same guy who'd spoken to him from the shadows between the container and the warehouse, at the shipyards. "*Bad men*," that's what he had said before. "*Bad men*." It was the same voice that just said, "*Dalton is a bad man*."

"Who is Dalton, and who are you?" Matt demanded.

The stranger didn't answer. He continued walking away, until he vanished around a corner.

Matt went after him, but faced only an empty hallway as he turned the corner. "Whoa!" He muttered to himself. Clearly shaken by the mysterious man's disappearing act, he hastily made his way back along the corridor toward the exit.

Soon, Matt felt the inkling that something was amiss, when the hairs on the back of his neck rose up. His eyes shifted toward the stairs. There, standing on the landing about halfway up, was the stranger in the peaked cap. As Matt watched him, the man turned his gaze away and continued slowly up the stairs toward the second floor.

Matt wanted to follow the instructions that his boss had given him. *Go to the washroom and come straight back outside.* He could hear his supervisor's words running through his head again.

It would have been so easy for him to walk a few more meters to the door which led outside. No, that would be the smart and sensible thing to do, but that wasn't like Matt at all. He knew that he would be fired if caught roaming the Senate office building without permission. *Don't be an idiot.*

Matt considered the consequences for a moment, before his curiosity got the best of him. He couldn't let this go. It was a risk he was willing to take. His foot found the first step and his hand reached for the handrail. He ascended the stairs two at a time.

Once on the second floor, Matt looked left and right. The mysterious man now stood at the end of the corridor in front of an office door, which was made out of some type of expensive hardwood. The man turned and disappeared down the corridor. Matt hurried to catch up, not wanting to lose him. When Matt peered around the corner, he wasn't surprised to see that the man had vanished once again.

Matt sighed, thinking he was wasting his time. He glanced at the mahogany office door in front of him.

The nameplate beside the door read: *Senator Aiden C. Dalton.*

Before Matt could turn away, the door swung open. A gray-haired man standing in the doorway didn't offer a very friendly greeting. "What do *you* want?" Senator Dalton snarled, "Speak!"

Matt averted his eyes. "I—uh—I just got lost. I was looking for the washroom."

"Down the hall. Now move! Or I'm calling security!" The man rudely slammed the door in Matt's face. He knew that Senator Dalton would be calling security as soon as he'd closed the door, so Matt bolted to the nearest flight of stairs. *"Dalton is a bad man."* The words kept entering his mind as he hastily made his way down the staircase. He had to leave the Senate building before being intercepted and detained by security.

Once he was within arm's reach of the exit door, he pushed on the door release bar with both hands. The door sprung open, then swung back, as it reached the limit of its hinges. It almost hit him on his way out. He heard it slam hard behind him. Feeling relieved that he didn't get caught by security, Matt went back to work.

That same evening, Matt received a phone call from his supervisor. "Don't bother coming back to work tomorrow," he said. "I don't have to tell you why."

Matt knew why. He'd broken the rules. Not just one, all of them!

"If you don't follow instructions, you don't come back to work. Got it?" It was pretty fucking clear. How could anyone possibly screw that up? Idiot, Matt thought.

31

The afternoon brought with it a breeze carrying the smell of pine.

Brandon inhaled as he reached for the SUV's door handle. "Do you smell how fresh it is out here Rosie?"

Rosie nodded. "Yes, it smells as fresh as your new vehicle," she said, after climbing into the white SUV. Did you pick up a case of beer for Arthur?" Rosie asked, changing the subject.

"It's in the back."

"We should probably pick up something for Claire too," Rosie suggested.

"I got that too; a bottle of Italy's finest vino," Brandon boasted.

"I'm impressed. I didn't know you were a connoisseur of wine."

"Stick around. You may learn what a true romantic does in his spare time," he winked.

Turning left into the long, unpaved driveway of Arthur and Claire's farm, the first thing Brandon noticed was the old red fire truck. It sat among overgrown grass and weeds, in front of the old barn. Next, he noticed the ducks and geese swimming in the quaint little pond to the right. He slowed down and waited while four ducks waddled their way across the driveway in front of them. Arthur and Claire's Labrador retriever and German shepherd ran out to greet them as they drove closer to the farmhouse. The farm looked much different in the daytime. Arthur called off the dogs and walked toward the vehicle. "Hi Arthur," said Brandon.

"Well, this is the second time that you've surprised us with a visit. Who did you bring with you this time?" He strained his neck so he could see Rosie in the passenger seat.

"This is Rosie," said Brandon.

"Hi Rosie," Arthur replied with a smile.

Rosie waved. "Hello."

Brandon and Rosie got out of the vehicle. "We brought you some beer and wine. It's in appreciation for you and Claire helping me the other night," Brandon explained.

"Ah, that's nice, but you didn't have to do that," said Arthur.

"No, but I wanted to. By the way, I like your fire truck. How did you acquire that?" asked Brandon, handing Rosie the bottle of wine, then removing the case of beer from the back.

"Oh, I've had that for a few years. It was at an auction for charity. If no one bid on it they were going to send it to the scrap yard, so my friend and I got it for next to nothing."

They strolled toward the back of the house, where Claire stood on the deck to greet them.

Arthur continued. "We had originally planned to fix it up and make it shiny new again, but it never happened. My friend and his wife bought a condo in Florida after that. We're not sure what to do with it now. Perhaps I'll sell it to a collector."

"Are you talking about restoring that old fire truck again?" Claire said.

Arthur smiled. "She doesn't like it sitting out front," he whispered to Brandon and Rosie.

"It's a bit of an eyesore," Claire added.

Brandon placed the case of beer on the picnic table.

"Claire, this is Rosie," Arthur said, ignoring her last comment.

"I used to be a volunteer firefighter in my early days; still have all my fire gear that I wore too," Arthur added. "I have another old collector item if you're interested in seeing it. It's in the barn. That baby's mine. A '68 Plymouth Duster—everything's original on it," Arthur boasted.

Brandon turned to look at Rosie for her approval before proceeding.

She smiled, "Its okay. You can go. I'm not really into cars that much," she gestured with a wave of her hand.

***

"While the boys go play with their cars, would you like to join me for a cup of tea?" Claire offered.

The Whiskey Lee

Rosie smiled. "That would be lovely. Thank you."

"I'll bring everything outside. It's a beautiful day." Claire turned and walked up the three steps to the deck, which wrapped around the back of the house. Rosie looked around, admiring the property.

The dogs stayed close to Rosie, rubbing up against her and competing for her affection. "Oh, you like that, don't you?" Rosie said, as she rubbed the Lab gently behind the ears.

"Would you like some help with that?" Rosie offered, seeing Claire emerge from the house with her tray of goodies.

"No thanks. I've got it."

After Claire had set the tray of fine china on the picnic table, Rosie noticed that she'd also laid out an assortment of biscuits and cheese.

"Here's the milk and sugar if you'd like," Claire offered.

"Thanks so much. I feel like I'm getting the royal treatment here. This is really kind of you."

"It's no bother. I needed an excuse to use my china tea set. I don't see the point of staring at it in my curio cabinet and never using it."

Rosie smiled. "I agree."

"My husband said I should save it for special occasions. Well, in my eyes it *is* a special occasion when someone visits, especially when that person has traveled all the way from England."

Rosie giggled.

"Are you on vacation, Rosie?" Claire asked.

"Yes, well, it's a mixture of business and pleasure, actually," she replied, anticipating the next question.

Rosie saved Claire the trouble of asking, by volunteering why she was here and what she did for a living.

"Oh my!" Claire couldn't hold back her excitement. "I love ghost stories. My friends and I like to share our stories around the bonfire."

Later, after spending the afternoon making small talk and sipping the wine and beer, the foursome were now sitting around a raging bonfire Arthur had started.

"Arthur, did you know that Rosie here is an international ghost story writer?" Claire asked exuberantly.

"No, I didn't." He turned to Rosie. "Wow, you two will have lots to talk about. Claire loves ghost stories."

"We're about to put some hamburgers on the barbecue. Will you two join us?" Claire asked.

Rosie looked at Brandon. "Oh, we don't want to impose."

"It's okay. No trouble at all. It would be our pleasure," Claire insisted.

"It's nothing special, just burgers," Arthur offered.

Brandon acknowledged a slight nod of the head by Rosie before answering. "Sure, that'll be great," said Brandon.

***

After they ate their burgers, they all remained seated around the bonfire. "This really is a nice place you have here," Rosie said, as her face appeared to glow orange in the light from the hot flames. Arthur continued to feed the small inferno with the last of the cut wood in the wheelbarrow. He politely excused himself so that he could gather more. Claire walked toward the house with him.

Left alone, Rosie and Brandon watched the embers rise far up to the sky. The night was calm, and the sky was cloudless. Away from the city lights and with only the light of the fire, the stars shone brightly. Rosie could just about see the entire galaxy from where she was sitting. It was a beautiful night. While the two were enthralled by the fire and feeling relaxed, they stood almost simultaneously to stretch their legs. They walked slowly until meeting on the far side of the bonfire. As they looked toward the edge of the meadow, they could see tiny flashes of light in front of them and throughout the tall grass. Fireflies were everywhere. The couple followed the specks of light up into the night sky with their eyes, until they were staring only at the twinkling stars in the night sky above them. A shooting star darted across the sky. "Make a wish, quickly," said Rosie.

"I already have," said Brandon, turning to face her. The orange glow from the fire wasn't as strong where they were standing, but it still mildly lit up one side of her face, while the other half of her face remained in shadow. He held her hand in his, pulled her closer and tried to kiss her on the cheek. She turned to meet his lips with hers. It didn't last too long, as Rosie broke away from the kiss too soon. "Aw, the bloody mosquitoes are biting me now," she said, as she slapped her calf. "How to ruin a romantic kiss in two seconds . . ."

"Hmm, they must be after your sweet English blood," said Brandon. "Let's go back to the bonfire."

"As long as I'm here, you're safe Brandon. I don't know why they are so attracted to me," she said, following Brandon back to their chairs.

"I do," Brandon replied. He stopped to give her another kiss.

"I leave for firewood and you two are off frolicking in the meadow with the birds and the bees," Arthur teased, as he sauntered back to the bonfire.

"And the mosquitoes! Don't forget the mosquitoes," Rosie added.

"Oh, you met the thirsty little blood suckers, did you?" he cackled. Come on over here and stop feeding them. Stay close to the fire. Mosquitoes hate smoke."

"I've got marshmallows!" Claire hollered, emerging from the farmhouse. "What did I miss?"

"Nothing dear, Rosie's just out here feeding the mosquitoes."

"You can feed them all you want, Rosie, as long as they leave me alone." Claire pulled her chair closer to the fire. She opened a new bag of marshmallows and passed it around for everyone to take one.

"It's so nice of you two to join us this evening for a bonfire. We don't get many visitors up here," Claire said, as she handed a stick each to Brandon, and Rosie.

"We usually do a bonfire every Guy Fawkes Day in England, but we usually have sparklers," said Rosie. "I'm not really sure what I'm supposed to do with this stick. This is a first for me."

"You've never roasted marshmallows over an open fire, Rosie?" Claire looked surprised.

"Roast marshmallows?" Rosie asked, as she watched Brandon place his on the end of the stick and hold it over the open flame.

"Oh, that's why you gave me the marshmallow. I ate mine already. May I have another one please?" Rosie asked sheepishly.

The older couple broke out in laughter.

"I can't believe you've never done this before," said Brandon, trying to refrain from laughing.

"Well, I suppose there's a first time for everything," Rosie replied, shrugging.

Rosie took another marshmallow out of the bag, placed it on the end of the stick and then held it close to the flames. It erupted in an orange blaze. "Oh, my goodness, it's on fire!" Rosie gasped and then laughed nervously. While pulling the stick back from the flames the marshmallow slid off the end and landed in the fire pit.

"Um, Claire? May I have another marshmallow please? I'm afraid I'm not very good at this," Rosie humbly announced.

Claire laughed again, passing her the bag of marshmallows. "It's okay dear. It happens to everyone."

Brandon wasn't paying attention to what he was doing, as he was focused on Rosie. That was, until his marshmallow caught on fire.

Rosie laughed. "I don't feel so bad now. It's a good thing you've got a fire truck out front."

Brandon pulled his back and tried to blow out the flame. It slid off the stick and into the fire pit as well. Rosie laughed.

"I hope you've got lots of marshmallows, Claire!" Rosie said, still giggling.

"That's why I always buy two bags," said Claire. "I'm glad you two are having fun."

"So, Claire, you mentioned earlier that you like telling ghost stories while sitting around the bonfire?" Rosie urged.

"As a matter of fact, I do," she began. "I love ghost stories. There are a few about Maine lighthouses alone, never mind some of the ghost ships that cruise along the eastern coast. North America has so many ghost stories to share. I have been reading up on some of them. I think the campfire is the best place to share them, don't you agree Rosie?"

"Yes absolutely!" Rosie agreed. "What about the USS *Midhurst*? Have you heard anything about the ghosts on that ship? I heard it's haunted."

Brandon shot a quick glance over at Rosie.

She smiled at him reassuringly. It was a clever way of dropping the bait. Rosie was using Claire to fish for information.

"I've heard some rumors that a ghost may be haunting that ship," said Claire.

"So, there could be a ghost?" Rosie asked.

"I'm curious, how did you hear about the *Midhurst* ghost?" Claire questioned.

"Oh, when I searched it on the internet it came up that an apparition had been sighted aboard the USS *Midhurst*, apparently more than once by staff working aboard the ship."

"Well, now that's interesting. I guess it's a good way for them to sell tickets," said Claire. "Now, I'd like to share a couple of my ghost stories with you, if you'd like to hear them? I promise you won't go home the same person."

Rosie looked at Brandon. "I'm sure I won't anyway," Rosie whispered.

He smiled.

"Now, sit back, relax, and look into directly into the fire. Concentrate on the fire, because this story is about a ghost ship in flames," said Claire. "Would you like some more wine before we start, Rosie?"

"Yes, please," said Rosie.

Claire poured the wine. "I'm thinking you are probably going to have nightmares tonight, after you've listened to my stories," Claire added.

"I'm sure we can handle it," said Rosie, winking at Brandon, now slightly amused.

Claire started her story.

"The ship cruises the Hog's Head Bay, between Maine's north-east shore and the Fundy Islands. To most, it looks like a sailing vessel in flames. It's a ghost ship believed to be that of Captain Oswald. He was a pirate."

"Ohhh, I like this already," said Rosie.

Claire told her ghost story while Rosie listened intently. Brandon's mind drifted in and out, as if he were being hypnotized by the fire itself. His mind zoned out to the point that he hadn't heard much of Claire's story until she had finished telling it and Rosie spoke up.

"Wow!" Rosie said. "That was quite the story, Claire. It would be interesting to see that ghost fireship," she added.

Brandon quickly snapped out of his reverie.

"Are you ready for another beer?" Arthur asked.

"Sure," said Brandon. "Thanks," he said, as Arthur handed it to him.

"I really enjoy those kinds of stories. You told it very well," Rosie said to Claire.

"Would you like to hear another one? I have lots," said Claire.

"Oh, yes, please," said Rosie.

"This next one is called Hagen's Ghost, also known as the Night Screamer," Claire informed them.

"Some people have heard the horrifying screams at night along the Duncan River. It is believed to be the ghost of a young man who worked at one of the lumber camps in the 1700s. His name was Hagen Flaherty. He decided to go for a swim in the river, but never returned. The other loggers went looking for him and found blood all along the shoreline, and to this day they've never found his body. The next day was when they started hearing the haunting screams coming from the forest near the river. Some feared that maybe an animal had killed Hagen, but what terrified them the most was a different story: that someone from the same logging camp killed the young man and then dragged his body into the forest. Terrified, the rest of the loggers didn't know what to believe, so they left the area and never returned. Since then, that area of forest has been haunted by a ghostly screamer."

Rosie and Brandon were so absorbed in Claire's ghost story, that neither of them noticed Arthur sneaking up silently behind them. Arthur waited patiently for his wife to finish her last sentence. Claire ignored her husband and continued the story: "... along the banks of the Duncan River, to this day, people can still hear the screams of Hagen's Ghost."

At that moment, Arthur let out a bellowing scream behind Rosie.

Rosie nearly jumped out of her chair. Brandon was startled too, but he didn't react the same.

"Christ!" Rosie yelled, spinning around. "You scared the hell out of me!"

"You should have seen the look on your face!" Claire said, chuckling. "My husband gets everyone with that story. I'm sorry, I should have warned you." Claire was still giggling.

"Scared me half to death. Now I see why you don't get too many visitors up here." Rosie gave Brandon an odd frown.

He was amused by the look on her face.

"Yes, we scared them all away, didn't we Arthur," Claire added proudly.

He laughed.

Rosie smiled.

"Were any of those ghost stories even real? Or, did you just make them up?" Rosie asked.

"Oh, yes, the stories are original folklore passed down through the generations," said Claire. "You must have some really fascinating stories, Rosie."

"I have so many ghost stories to tell, but I'm afraid we don't have that much time tonight. I'll give you one of my books to read. It's about haunted places in the south of England."

"That sounds wonderful. Please do. I can't wait to read it," Claire replied.

The Whiskey Lee

Rosie's mind drifted, trying to focus on their mission at hand. She only had one thought in her mind now. It would be a great time to pick Claire's brain for information, now that she was relaxed. "I thought perhaps you'd know about some local folklore, you know, that maybe someone has shared with you on bonfire night?" Rosie asked.

"Well, I'll tell you everything that I can remember. I don't have a really good story, only bits and pieces," said Claire.

"That would be okay. I find it all very interesting," said Rosie.

Claire began.

"My friend, Elizabeth, told me that her nephew, Matt, had a few encounters with the same ghost—once at the shipyards, close to where the USS *Midhurst* is docked, and then somewhere else . . . the Senate office building, I think. He only told Elizabeth because she is the spiritual aunt and he knew she would listen to him without judgment. She tells me everything. We've been close friends since public school."

Rosie listened intently as Claire recounted what she'd learned. "Elizabeth's nephew now works as a trail guide at Hog's Head National Park," she recounted.

"Is that the same area where the ghost fireship is said to be haunting? Hog's Head Bay?" Rosie asked.

"Yes, that's the same place," Claire replied.

Claire told them that Hog's Head National Park was one of the nicest parks in the State of Maine. Rosie also learned that the park offered some amazing scenic views.

They had lots of questions of their own for young Matt, but Brandon knew that it would be at least a two-hour drive to get there.

Arthur yawned.

"Uh, well." Brandon looked at his phone. "It's getting late. Looks like it's time for us to get going, Rosie."

"Anytime you want to visit, just drop by," said Claire.

Rosie nodded. "Thank you both so much for having us this evening. I'll drop one of my books off for you Claire, whenever we return."

"Okay, how much do I owe you for it?"

"Oh, don't be silly. It's my gift to you. I'll sign it for you as well."

"Thank you," said Claire, holding Rosie's hand in both of hers. "You two be careful; and if you go to the National Park, say 'Hi' to Matt for me."

"We will," said Rosie.

Once in the SUV, Brandon turned to Rosie.

"Rosie, I'm glad you didn't mention anything to Claire about our ghost sightings."

"I wouldn't do that. It would compromise our mission."

They followed the winding road back to Brandon's hideaway in the woods, just outside of Barney's Cove.

As they entered the cabin, Rosie turned to Brandon. "I'd really like to visit Hog's Head National Park now."

"I was thinking the same thing. It wouldn't be a bad idea to get out of town for a day or so. Let things cool down. I think we both could use a break. I almost forgot what it was like to relax, until I was sitting at that bonfire tonight," said Brandon.

"How about we go to Hog's Head tomorrow? Are you doing anything?" Rosie asked.

"I haven't got anything planned," Brandon replied. "Actually, I wouldn't mind talking to that Matt guy and asking him firsthand what he saw. Maybe it's the same ghost that we saw on the Midhurst."

"It doesn't sound like we're going to do much relaxing, but I'm in—let's do it. I can pick up my stuff in the morning," Rosie said with enthusiasm.

***

The next morning, Brandon waited patiently outside Rosie's motel while she picked up her hiking boots and Nikon camera. He was completely unaware of the two men watching him from the silver sedan parked across the street.

32

HOG'S HEAD NATIONAL PARK

Getting lost hadn't entered into the plans when calculating the estimated time of arrival, but it didn't take Brandon too long to learn which roads *not* to take. Their time was mostly wasted by backtracking. GPS would have been ideal for this road trip. He noticed a silver sedan had turned around too.

Okay, I'm not the only one lost, he thought.

The pothole-laden road which led to the main gate didn't help at all. It gave Brandon no choice but to slow the SUV to a mere crawl through that section. The road was in desperate need of resurfacing. The location of the park was in a forested and hilly area.

He peered into the rearview mirror again, noticing the silver sedan behind them.

"Call me paranoid, but I keep seeing the same silver sedan behind us," he said to Rosie.

She peered behind. "It's probably a coincidence. I'll bet they're going to the same park we are. No one would even know this vehicle."

"I guess you're right."

Rosie had Brandon stop at a small trading post on the way into the park. Brandon noticed the silver sedan also pulled in, stopping to fuel up at the gas bar. He didn't recognize the men inside the vehicle, and decided he was just being paranoid again. The men in the vehicle weren't even interested in him. He waited patiently outside while Rosie picked up a bird watcher's field guide, compass, and a topographic map of the area.

Once inside the park's boundaries, the road got a little better. They stopped at the gatehouse, paying their admission fees before proceeding to the staging area where they'd meet the other hikers for their guided group tour. Before reaching a curve in the road, Brandon checked his mirror again. He noticed the silver sedan pull up to the gatehouse. It's the last time he saw it.

Brandon didn't have much time to prepare for the four-hour hike, but water, comfort, and snacks were always first on the priority list. Because of their tardiness, they were aware they'd already missed the first group hike, which was guided by Matt. "Do you have a pen I can borrow Brandon? I forgot to bring one," said Rosie, before they joined the group of hikers.

Brandon reached into the SUV and handed her one.

"Thanks," she said. "Now I can tick off all the birds I see on this checklist in the book."

"I wouldn't tick off the birds if I were you," said Brandon. Rosie gave him a look. "Tut. You know what I bloody well meant."

"Yeah, just having some fun," said Brandon, smiling.

The north end of the park came to a point which overlooked the rugged landscape of Hog's Head Bay and the Fundy Islands, which Claire had mentioned.

Brandon and Rosie learned from their hiking guide, Laura, that they would be meeting Matt's group at the rendezvous point. The ridge was usually where they'd meet for lunch and take advantage of a breathtaking photo opportunity.

The hike was mostly an uphill grind, but scenic. Anyone that didn't truly appreciate nature would most likely have wished they'd stayed home.

Their group made it up to the ridge a bit earlier than planned. That's around the time that Matt's group ran into trouble. An urgent call for help on the two-way radio indicated that a hiker from Matt's group had a badly injured ankle.

"What can I do to help you, Matt?" Laura radioed back.

"Could you come down here and take the rest of my group to the ridge for me? I've got to get this hiker transported out of here by ATV."

Brandon was listening to Matt's desperate plea for help across the radio.

"10-4. Hold tight, Matt. I'll be down there in about ten to fifteen minutes to get them," Laura replied.

Brandon volunteered to go with Laura to assist with the injured hiker. She accepted his offer.

"Okay everyone, I'll need you all to stay here and wait for me please, while I bring Matt's group up to the ridge. If you have any questions, you can ask my

The Whiskey Lee

friend Stephen here." She gestured to a young man, approximately five feet, six inches tall; with a slim body, a perfectly clean-shaven face, and short blonde wispy hair.

"Hi everyone," said Stephen, giving a small wave to the group.

"Stephen knows these trails well. He used to be a guide here," Laura added, turning to Brandon. "Shall we go?"

"Just a sec." He turned to Rosie.

"Should I come too?" Rosie asked.

"No, I think we can handle it. Just hang out here, have a rest, and enjoy the view. Take some nice photographs for us," he lowered his voice to a whisper. "This will give me a good chance to speak to Matt alone."

"Okay, right," she agreed. Brandon kissed her before he joined Laura on the trail.

***

Rosie watched them walk down the path. She waited until she saw Brandon disappear through the gap in the trees before taking a seat in an unoccupied Adirondack chair. It was made of wood, featured wide armrests with a sloping seat and back, and looked inviting. The ridge overlooked some of the prettiest scenic views of the ocean and hard bluffs. Rosie appreciated the spectacular view of the natural craggy coastline. Beyond that, the seemingly endless ocean was captivating.

"Beautiful view, isn't it?" a woman sitting in the chair beside her said.

"It certainly is stunning. I could get used to this," Rosie replied, but she was already preoccupied with thoughts of the ghost fireship Claire had mentioned. She stood to gaze down at the sea. Oswald's ghost ship was said to be haunting these waters, just off the north-east shore. Rosie wondered what the people had actually seen. Was it real? Or, could it have been the sunset reflecting off a ship, creating some sort of light bending trick or mirage? Either way, she saw nothing remotely resembling a fireship down there in the glimmering ocean.

***

After Brandon introduced himself, he helped Matt move the injured hiker down to the open space where an ATV would meet them. They had some rocky areas to conquer first. The terrain was extremely uneven. It was strictly a hiking trail, and for a very good reason. There were lots of trees, rocks, roots, and steep inclines.

The National Park Service emergency medical providers were able to meet them on ATVs, so once they could reach a suitable clearing, the injured hiker was transferred to their care. Brandon started feeling a little more relaxed after that. It wasn't until after the ATVs had left and they were halfway back up the hill that Brandon noticed that his left bootlace was untied. "Aw, now my lace is undone. Hold up a minute Matt." He stopped, lifting his foot up, balancing it on one of the rocks for support; he then bent over to lace it up.

A gunshot rang out from the trees.

"Take cover!" Brandon yelled.

Confused on which way to go, Matt instinctively followed Brandon into the nearby thicket. Now, under cover of the bushes, they peeked out cautiously. Brandon quickly removed the Beretta Tomcat from his daypack.

"Whoa. Why the hell do you have a gun, man? What's all this about?" Matt whispered.

"I'll explain later. Did you happen to hear or see which direction the shot came from?" asked Brandon, scanning the surrounding area for movement.

"No, I didn't. It was echoing all over the place," Matt replied, looking back and forth.

Matt's radio crackled.

"Turn that down!" Brandon ordered in a whisper. "You'll give away our position and get us both killed."

Matt turned down the volume.

***

After Laura had brought Matt's group of hikers back to the ridge, they settled in right away, taking lots of photographs. Rosie noticed Laura doing a head count of the newly merged hiking group. Looking confused, she counted again, and then a third time.

Afterwards, the concerned hiking guide started asking people if they'd noticed two other people leave the group while she was gone.

Rosie overheard one woman say that she'd noticed two men who didn't seem to have any interest in connecting with the group. "They kept to themselves for the entire hike. I don't even think they took any photos of the amazing landscape. I don't see them anywhere now," the woman said.

Rosie thought it would have been easy for the men in question to slip away unnoticed. Ten minutes after calling out to them, Rosie heard what sounded like gunshots, not too far off in the distance.

"What's going on?" Rosie overheard Stephen ask Laura.

"I'm not sure. That sounded like gunshots," Laura replied.

"They'd better not be hunting, or someone's going to be in serious trouble," Stephen said angrily.

"I don't like it," Laura said in a shaky voice. "I'm calling it in." She grabbed her radio to report the shots fired.

The hikers were all glancing at each other with looks of confusion and worry on their faces. "Were those gunshots?" a man asked, searching the guide's face for answers.

Rosie couldn't hear what was going on over the two-way radio, so she moved closer to where Laura and Stephen were standing.

When there was no response from Matt's radio, that's when Rosie became even more worried for Brandon.

"Matt's not answering. What should we do, Stephen?" Laura asked in a trembling voice.

"I think we should get everyone out of here," Stephen suggested.

"I'm with you," Laura agreed.

Rosie had a serious look of concern on her face. "Wait, we can't leave Brandon and Matt out there!"

"We have no choice," Laura replied, with a disheartened look. She then turned her attention to the rest of the hikers. "Listen up everyone. I think we should leave this area now."

"I'm really worried," said Rosie. "I'm not leaving my boyfriend out there."

"I understand how you're feeling, but right now, our main concern is the safety of everyone in this grou—"

"The hell with safety!" Rosie interrupted gallantly. "It could be too late by then." She ran off down the trail in the direction of where she'd last seen Brandon before he'd disappeared through the gap in the trees.

"No, wait! Come back!" Laura yelled frantically.

Rosie didn't stop.

"I'll go with her. She doesn't know this park." Stephen ran off after her.

"Wait!" Laura yelled with an urgent plea. "Stephen!"

***

"Hey, wait for me!" The sound of Stephen's voice slowed Rosie's pace as he ran up behind her.

"What?" She turned defensively.

"I'm coming with you. What's your name?"

"Rosie."

"Rosie, do you have a contingency plan? You know, in case we run into some trouble," Stephen asked.

"Yeah, run for your bloody life!" Rosie replied, quickening her pace.

Stephen: "No, come on, we need to know where to meet if we get separated." Rosie slowed down again.

"Okay, we will try to meet up with the group and if that doesn't work, we will go back to base camp."

"Base camp?" Stephen asked.

"You know, where we started from—the parking lot? Staging area?" Rosie said.

"Do you have a map?" he asked.

"Yes, I do." She stopped and unfolded it.

"Good, let's look at it. I'll show you where we are, just in case. We could get separated."

She passed the map to Stephen, who turned it so that they could study it together.

"We're here," he pointed. "There's the staging area or *base camp*, as you named it."

"Okay, got it!" Rosie folded the map up and put it back in her backpack. "Let's go, we're wasting precious time. Brandon and Matt may be in trouble," Rosie urged.

That's all she needed to say to light a fire up under Stephen. There was no holding him back after that. Stephen ran ahead of Rosie. "Follow me," he said, and like a deer running through the woods, he bounded off down the trail with Rosie in hot pursuit.

Rosie heard the whumping of moving helicopter blades long before reaching the clearing. The dark gray helicopter made its final sweep of the area and then

The Whiskey Lee

hovered for a few minutes just above the clearing. Rosie and Stephen stayed well out of sight just beyond the tree line, lying low on their stomachs, so they could watch while remaining out of sight.

Stephen reached for the compact binoculars inside his pack. He raised them to his eyes and rested the soft eye cups against his eye sockets. He tweaked the focus just enough, so that the images became clear. They were still pretty far away, so he wasn't sure how much he'd see.

"What are they doing?" Rosie asked.

"Nothing, just hovering," Stephen replied.

He could see several ropes being dropped on each side of the chopper, followed by six figures, armed with military-type assault rifles and outfitted in camouflage fatigues. They were dropping down from the chopper on each side to the field below.

"Oh, shit!" Stephen exclaimed. "Sorry about my language."

"Oh, shit is right. What should we do now?" Rosie asked.

"Part of me says run, but the other part of me is still curious," said Stephen.

The tactical team spread out across the field; some ran into the trees on the other side of the clearing and brought a man out, with his hands up. They put the suspect facedown on the ground after searching him for weapons.

"Can you see if it's Brandon or Matt?" Rosie asked anxiously.

"No," said Stephen.

"No, it's not them, or no, you can't see?"

"I can't identify them from this distance. We're too far away. This isn't a telescope, you know."

"I may be able to tell you if it's Brandon or not, even from this distance. Let me see," said Rosie.

Stephen handed the binoculars over to Rosie.

Soon afterwards, another man was brought out of the woods. He was treated the same way as the first man.

"Neither of them is Brandon," Rosie concluded, feeling relieved.

The captured men were hoisted up to the hovering chopper. The helicopter remained there for a little while, and then some of the commandos were hoisted up.

On the ground remained three men who hadn't boarded yet. One turned his head, pointing to the treed area where Stephen and Rosie were hunkered down.

"Oh my gosh!" said Rosie, ducking her head down. Stephen ducked as well. "I hope he didn't see us."

Stephen motioned with a quick beckoning of his hand for her to relinquish the binoculars back to him.

"Maybe the sunlight reflected off the binoculars?" Rosie whispered.

"I doubt it. They're anti-reflective lenses," said Stephen, keeping his head down. "We should probably get out of here soon. There's not much we can do for Matt or Brandon anyway. Hopefully they're keeping their heads down."

"I wonder where they are," said Rosie.

Stephen raised his head enough to take a quick glance. "I don't know, but so far the guys in fatigues aren't headed this way. I'm hoping it was just a coincidence that the guy pointed in our direction, but we should get out of here anyway."

Once Rosie and Stephen were away from the clearing, they quickly headed back toward the hiking group. It wasn't long before they met a fork in the path.

"The trail to the right will be quicker. It bypasses the ridge." He said pointing to the Fox Run Trail. "We have a better chance of meeting up with them on the other side. Laura will be guiding the hikers back to the staging area along the Sunridge Trail."

Rosie was getting tired and having trouble keeping up. She had tripped over tree roots more than once in the last ten minutes. She looked over at Stephen, with his wispy blonde hair, just seeming to glide over and around all the obstacles. Her mind drifted to Brandon and how terrible she felt that she had to abandon him. *I hope he's okay*, she thought, as she tripped over another tree root. "Shit!" she exclaimed.

"Are you okay?" Stephen asked.

Thinking she was far enough away from the danger now, Rosie stopped running. "Wait Stephen, I'm going to try phoning Brandon. I need to rest a bit too." She sat down on a partially rotted tree trunk while Stephen joined her for a couple of minutes. She selected Brandon's number and waited. "It's no good, it went straight to his voicemail," she said.

"Come on, we should keep moving, Rosie," Stephen suggested, standing up. "I want to keep some space between us and those assault rifles."

"Damn! What a workout!" Rosie put her phone away and followed Stephen.

"You may be able to get service up on the next hill," Stephen advised.

He's either trying to save my life or trying to kill me, Rosie thought.

"Go hiking they said. It will be fun they said," she muttered under her breath.
"Did you say something?" Stephen asked.
"No, carry on!" Rosie replied. *He's got good hearing too.*

33

Brandon and Matt watched in silence as a team of commandos rappelled down from the chopper.

"Who are they?" Matt asked.

"Not my monkeys. Not my circus," said Brandon as he watched them hit the ground running. The unexpected tactical team scattered in all different directions.

"We're right on the edge of this ravine," Matt acknowledged. "FYI Brandon, we're trapped up here. There's nowhere out of here except down that steep embankment behind us, which drops down to the creek."

Brandon peered over his shoulder. "Yeah, we're kind of screwed, aren't we?" He turned his eyes back to spy on the intimidating figures dressed in full military camouflage, clutching what appeared to be fully automatic firearms. Brandon guessed US military, but there weren't any markings on the dark gray chopper. That's what was troubling him the most. He didn't know if they were good or bad. "I'm feeling really uneasy about this," he forewarned Matt.

So far, two men had been plucked from the forest, apprehended, and now were being hoisted up to the awaiting helicopter. Brandon noticed three soldiers still standing downwind from the helicopter. It seemed as if their mission wasn't over. In the hands of one man was an electronic device. It appeared that he was briefing the others while using his hand in a sweeping motion across the landscape to point out different areas. The man pointed to a position on the other side of the clearing and then turned his head back toward the hill where Brandon and Matt were hiding.

The Whiskey Lee

"Damn!" said Brandon, ducking his head even lower. "I don't like this. I think we should move now."

Both Brandon and Matt crawled backward out of sight, until there was nowhere else to go. They stopped at the edge of the embankment. Matt leaned his forehead against the palm of his hand. "I'm not looking forward to this."

"Got any other ideas? It looks like it's our only option," said Brandon, peering over the edge of the steep embankment. He noticed it was filled with dead wood, shrubs, and trees, with thick roots protruding out all over the place.

"I've got nothing," Matt sighed, with a look of deep regret. "Well, after you Brandon," he said, sweeping his hand toward the ravine.

"Gee, thanks a lot," Brandon replied sarcastically, and then jumped feet first down the embankment. He slid and tumbled in a tangle of arms and legs; he grabbed for some vines which snapped under his weight. His body bulldozed a small tree, which seemed to break his fall momentarily before he began tumbling some more. He stopped short of hitting a hollowed-out tree which rested at the bottom of the embankment. A chipmunk popped its head out, squeaked a series of scolding chirps at him, and then scurried off to find another hiding spot.

Matt tumbled down the embankment in a similar fashion.

"You okay?" Brandon asked, as Matt landed with a thud beside him.

"Yeah, I think so," he said, rubbing his hip. "I don't think anything's broken. I may have a few scrapes and bruises though. Ah man, that was literally the biggest pain in the butt," Matt griped. He had a chance to catch his breath before Brandon reached out his hand to help him to his feet. "I'm never doing that again," Matt added.

"Well, at least we didn't get shot," said Brandon.

They crossed the creek where it narrowed and climbed the embankment on the other side. It was an agonizing climb. There was no clear route other than that created by the local wildlife that cut a path down to the river.

"I think we should keep heading in this . . ." studying the GPS and pointing ahead of him, ". . . direction; eventually we will hit the main road. There are no blazed trails on this side of the river at all," Matt explained, reaching for his two-way radio. It was no longer clipped to his belt. "Damn, I lost my radio. It must've fallen off when I fell down the embankment."

"This just keeps getting better, doesn't it?" Brandon muttered sarcastically. "Let's try our phones. See if we have any service."

"No signal," said Matt.

"Nothing on mine either."

"There aren't any phone towers near here either. Not for miles," Matt added.

"Somehow that doesn't surprise me," said Brandon.

It was physically exhausting trying to track through dense forest but Brandon figured it was still better than facing a team of well-armed commandos. About fifteen minutes later the duo stumbled upon a hydro field.

"This must be where we are, right here," Matt pointed. "If I'm correct, we can cut across that stretch of the forest, right there." Matt pointed to another section on his map. "It should bring us out on the west side of the gatehouse. We can call for someone to pick us up there."

"Okay, but let's stay near the tree line for now, just in case that chopper passes overhead," said Brandon.

Matt nodded in agreement.

"How far would you estimate it is to the gatehouse?" Brandon asked.

"My guestimate is probably about five miles, but I could be off a mile or two in either direction," Matt replied.

"Perfect. Make sure you watch our six for any movement," said Brandon, as he walked on ahead.

Matt smiled at the *six* reference. He'd watched enough action movies and played enough first-person soldier games on his game console to understand what it meant. It was a word the military used when referring to *watch our back*. It refers to the six position on the face of a clock. He turned to look behind them to see if they were being followed. "Our six is clear."

When Brandon told Matt that he was here to talk to him about the ghosts and what he'd seen at the shipyards Matt looked dumbfounded.

"Is that why those guys were shooting at us? Because of ghosts?"

Brandon said, "No. I'm just here to record this for Claire. I have no idea why those guys were shooting at us."

"Record it for Claire? You mean my aunt's friend? How did you . . . ?"

"Long story. Yes, same Claire. I told her I'd record your ghost story on my phone for her. She's really into her ghost stories," said Brandon, hoping Matt would buy it.

Matt stopped walking and tilted his head with growing skepticism. "Wait, you came all the way up here for my ghost story?" Matt asked. "That's so lame. Sounds like total bullshit to me."

"Not really. I'm on vacation. I just wanted to come up here for a nice hike. That's the story I'm sticking to, anyway. If anyone questions me, I don't know anything. It's true. I actually don't know anything. For all I know that guy was shooting at *you*, not me. Anyway, that's the best I've got. We should keep moving."

Matt didn't move for a moment, as he seemed to still be absorbing what Brandon had just said.

"I'm really confused now."

"Are you coming or not?" Brandon asked as he trotted on ahead. "Quit wasting time."

Matt started walking again, faster this time, trying to match Brandon's gait.

"Did anyone else know that you were coming here?" Matt asked, as he caught up.

Brandon said, "Just Claire and Rosie."

"Rosie?" Matt asked.

"My girlfriend. I left her up at the ridge with the other hikers. Hopefully they're safe. I'm kind of worried about them right now."

As they walked along the edge of the hydro field, Brandon slowed his pace and nervously glanced back to scan the tree line. "Did you hear that?" he asked nervously, referring to a rustling in the bushes.

"It was probably a squirrel," said Matt, cautiously watching the forest.

Brandon had every right to feel jumpy. Deep fear arose from within. It wasn't a fear of the wild animals lurking in the woods. It was a fear of that one predator that could line you up in their crosshairs without blinking or flinching as they squeeze the trigger. The fear of not knowing what was about to happen until it's too late. Brandon was barely conscious that he'd quickened his pace.

"Damn! You've got me jumping at every sound now," Matt said, taking long strides to catch up with him. "I was having such a nice hike today too. Why'd you have to come here today, anyway?"

"I told you why, and it's a good thing I did because you needed help with the injured hiker. Oh, and by the way, I had absolutely nothing to do with that," Brandon said bluntly.

"Oh yeah, I guess I didn't thank you. Thanks for your help."

"No problem. Hey, while we have time on our hands, how about you tell me everything you know about the strange ghost encounters you had. It'll keep our minds from overreacting to every little noise we hear. Start from the beginning," said Brandon, reaching into his pocket for his phone to record it. "Before I start recording, you've got to promise me that if anyone at all, police or whoever questions us about anything that happened today, we know nothing. Just tell them what we witnessed and that's it. Do not offer anything more! Things can get twisted fast. I still don't know who I can trust."

"Sure," said Matt. "That's kind of why I chose to work way out here. It's better. Less trouble I can get into. How do I know I can trust you?"

"Haven't you figured it out yet that I'm on your side? You don't have to be afraid of telling me anything. It's better if you do. I want to get these assholes put behind bars quickly," Brandon explained.

"Okay, but I still don't see how my story is going to help your case. But whatever floats your boat."

Brandon raised his eyebrows. He wasn't sure if Matt's choice of idiom was intentional or not. The mere references to *float* and *boat* were enough to pique his interest.

Matt told him everything, starting from the first encounter with the mysterious man who'd been hiding in the shadows near the gray shipping container. "He wore a peaked sailor's cap. That's about all that I could see of his head and face. It was mostly just an outline." Matt then told Brandon about the three men who'd emerged from the warehouse and the heated conversation that went down. "Wait a minute," Matt's eyes narrowed in suspicion. "Are you the same Brandon that this guy Evans was supposed to take care of?"

"Yes, but I haven't done anything wrong, honest. I'm just an innocent bystander investigating the disappearance of a captain and his trawler from nineteen years ago. Maybe I'm getting closer to the truth of what happened and these guys are getting paranoid."

"That's just great," Matt said sarcastically. "Now they're trying to kill me too."

"Not necessarily. Keep going with your story, please. Tell me everything you know. It will help piece this puzzle together. I will go to the police, I promise, but I need whatever information you have right now."

"Okay but leave me out of this," Matt demanded. "It's your fight, not mine."

"No problem," said Brandon.

Next, Matt explained the sighting of the same mysterious man he followed at the Senate building; the same one who wore the peaked cap and a navy pullover sweater.

"Did you get a good look at the guy in the peaked hat before he vanished?" Brandon asked.

Matt gave him the best description he could of the man's features. Brandon thought he bore an uncanny resemblance to the ghost which he and Rosie had seen. "Did the guy happen to mention anything about a baby crying?"

"Don't believe so. Mostly he kept muttering, 'Bad men.' It was strange how he disappeared after that. The dude was creepy. I lost my landscaping job after my encounter with Dalton. It was only my second day working there."

"You were fired? When?" Brandon asked.

"Last Tuesday," said Matt. "I guess I didn't follow the rules."

"And you started here at the park this week?"

"Yeah, I put an application in months ago. Only been here a few days and then all this shit happens. Seems like bad karma following me wherever I go."

Brandon nodded, "I hear ya." His mind drifted to something else that Matt had mentioned. "I just want to jog your memory for a minute. Let's go back to the guy at the shipyards, you know, the one that took off in the gray truck—'Evans,' I think you said his name was. Could you describe him?"

Matt described the man and explained that he'd noticed *4x4* graphic across the back of the truck, behind the back wheel.

The similarities can't be a coincidence. Brandon believed it was the same man that tried to kill him in the forest on the July 4th weekend. The clothes, truck, and description of the man bore too close of a resemblance to be anyone else.

***

Brandon and Matt emerged from the dense forest on the west side of the gatehouse, as predicted.

"Gatehouse, twelve o'clock," Matt informed Brandon.

Brandon glanced up and noticed there was still quite a bit of distance to cover on the dirt road. Feeling dehydrated, he reached for the water bottle he had tucked in the side pouch of his backpack. The water was warm and had a plastic taste to it.

Matt checked his phone for service. "I've got two bars," he announced to Brandon, while placing a call for someone to pick them up.

Brandon checked his phone and then called Rosie.

"Oh my gosh! I was sick with worry," Rosie exclaimed at the other end of the phone.

***

"Are we ever happy to see *you*!" Brandon exclaimed, as the driver of the white and green parks truck pulled up beside them.

"Wow, you guys look like you've been to hell and back. Jump in!" the driver said, handing each of them a cold bottle of water as they climbed in.

"Thanks," Brandon said, removing the lid and quickly guzzling half the bottle.

"What the hell happened out there today? I heard some wild stories about gun shots and commandos from the hikers. They were terrified," said the driver.

"We don't know exactly. Someone was shooting at us and the next thing we knew, commandos were dropping out of the sky from a huge gray chopper, so we hightailed it out of there. Did you hear anything about who they were?" Brandon asked.

"No, it's like trying to solve a freakin' Rubik's Cube. I'm trying to crack it, but no solution. Hey, don't you have a radio, Matt? Laura tried calling you more than a dozen times."

"I lost it after jumping into the ravine, while we were trying to escape," Matt replied.

"Wow, you jumped down there and didn't break anything? Well, I guess you'll have a good story to tell the boss as to why no one could reach you. A few of our rangers got on their ATVs and headed out toward where the chopper was spotted, but then came back a short time after. Not sure why they returned so fast. It would be nice to know what the hell's going on out there."

When truck pulled into the staging area parking lot, Brandon's eyes anxiously searched the crowd of hikers for Rosie. As he emerged from the cab of the truck, Rosie broke from the group and came running full throttle toward him. He hardly had time to steady himself as Rosie's impact almost knocked him clean off his feet. They clung to each other in a tight embrace. "I thought I'd lost you," Rosie said, kissing him, with a tear in her eye.

"Let's get the hell out of here Rosie, before someone questions us."

"Okay," Rosie said shakily.

Brandon took her hand, leading her away from the frantic group of people.

The Whiskey Lee

About ten minutes after Rosie and Brandon had left the national park, they noticed two law enforcement cruisers speeding past in the northbound lane.

"I know where they're headed." Brandon watched as the cruisers turned at the road which led to the park.

"It's a good thing we left when we did," said Rosie.

"Yeah, we would have been stuck there answering questions all night," said Brandon.

"What exactly happened back there?" Rosie asked.

"It was unbelievable." He explained everything that happened. "I couldn't even call you. We didn't have a phone signal until Matt and I got near the gatehouse."

"Wow, I didn't have a signal either. Stephen and I came looking for you. We saw the commandos and thought we'd better get out of there too," said Rosie.

"What? You were there? Who the heck is Stephen?" Brandon asked.

"Hmmm, so many questions, but mostly concerned about who Stephen is? Interesting," Rosie answered, nodding her head slowly and smiling.

"Are you crazy, Rosie? You should have stayed with the rest of the hikers," Brandon frowned.

"Okay, maybe I am a little crazy, but that's beside the point. Now, I have a question for you. Would you have run the other way if it was me out there?" Rosie asked.

"Of course not," said Brandon.

"I guess we're both a bit crazy then, aren't we?"

He smiled. "You're something else, you know that?"

"Thank you," she replied, smiling.

"How about we stop at that roadhouse we passed on the way in," said Brandon. "I've been dreaming about a cold beer all day."

"Really? With everything that happened today you were dreaming about a cold beer?" Rosie said.

"I was dreaming about you too, of course."

Rosie smirked. "Nice catch."

As they pulled into the parking lot of the roadhouse, Brandon noticed there were a couple of motorcycles and probably less than five other vehicles outside. They parked at the side of the building, out of sight. It was only eight o'clock in the evening, but there was a sign indicating that a live blues band would be playing later.

An old stereo cranked out a classic rock song as they walked in through the double doors. The speaker above the door crackled, revealing years of abuse by cranking up the volume.

Once inside the roadhouse, they noticed the smell of greasy fried food, old spilled beer, smoke, and chicken wings.

A chalkboard sign was affixed to the wall, welcoming people and instructed everyone to seat themselves. There were a few pool tables in a big open space. A few pool players turned to see who was entering. Once they realized it wasn't anyone they knew, their attention quickly turned back to the game.

On the far side, in the corner, some of the guys from the blues band were setting up their equipment and doing sound checks for their upcoming gig. Two well-used dart boards hung on the back wall. Rosie and Brandon found a booth by the window on the far side of the pool tables. There wasn't much to see through the dirty windows, just a view of an almost empty parking lot, and Route 12.

Before Rosie excused herself to go and look for the ladies' room, she placed something down on the table. "I almost forgot, here's your pen. I'll be back in a minute." She turned with a half twirl and wandered off in the direction of the *Guys* and *Dolls* washrooms.

"Thanks." He stuffed the pen in his shirt pocket, and then pulled his phone out to update Chad.

"We had quite the adventure today, Chad. Got shot at by someone and then a team of commandos dropped in uninvited at the national park."

"What?!" Chad exclaimed. "I can't leave you alone for a minute. No wonder you didn't return my call earlier."

"I didn't have any phone service for most of the day, so I didn't see that you'd called until a few minutes ago."

"Are you and Rosie okay?" Chad asked.

"Yes, I'm fine and so is Rosie. Listen, it's been a tiring day, but I think I gathered some useful information. I'll tell you about it tomorrow. We're just sitting in a roadhouse off Route 12. Rosie will be coming back to the table soon and I still need to order a couple of beers for us."

"Sure, send me a text when you get back into town, so I know you made it back safely."

"Yup, later."

34

THE NEXT DAY

The photos were spread out across Chad's office desk. He'd removed them from his safe just prior to Brandon and Rosie's arrival.

The sunken lifeboat had already been determined to belong to *The Whiskey Lee*. There was no question about it, after Brandon added the polished silver Zippo lighter to the equation. Now, they only had to present the evidence to Flynn.

"Lou and I both studied the photographs. We agreed that this photograph was taken just off Hanlon Cove, also known as *Hallam*. That's what the local fishermen know it as, anyway."

"Did you just say *Hallam*?" Brandon asked.

"Yep, sure did."

"Why is it called *Hallam*?"

"It's a nickname given by the locals. The fishermen often give nicknames or code names to places along the coast. That way, if outsiders are listening in on the radio, they won't have a hope in hell of knowing where the good fishing spots are that day," Chad explained.

Brandon looked at Rosie, nodding his understanding.

"Well, I guess us outsiders know where Hallam is now," said Rosie.

Brandon took a thin folder out of his duffle bag, opened it, and then lifted a single glossy photograph out to place it on the desk. "Maybe you can help us with identifying some people, Chad," said Brandon. "It's from a different angle, but it's the same day and same people. Look at the clothes they're wearing."

Studying the photograph for a moment, Chad shook his head. "I don't think I know any of these guys. Is that a gun he's holding? The barrel is long. Looks like they attached a silencer? Come to think of it, that guy with the beard looks familiar. It's a profile view though. It's hard to tell. Maybe you should give it to Chief Flynn. I'm sure he'll be interested in this one."

"I'm sure he will too. Okay, so now we've got a location, the lifeboat, and an engraved Zippo that belonged to Captain James Moreland, given to him by Ann Marie." He pointed at the photographs. "I'd say these photos represent motive and probably the most important clue to the case. It's obvious to me that Moreland witnessed the shooting aboard the *Betsea*," Brandon summed up.

"Wow." Chad clapped his hands together three times. "Geez man, you should have been a detective. You're in the wrong business."

"I'll take that as a compliment, and I believe the beer tab is on you, my friend." Brandon clapped Chad on the shoulder.

Chad laughed. "You deserve it man."

"We'll need to set up a dive at Hanlon Cove," said Brandon.

"How about this afternoon? Maybe you should update Flynn on what you found, just in case he wants to organize his own dive," said Chad.

"Okay, I'll call him right now." Brandon picked up his phone and made the call.

"Flynn," he heard the chief answer at the other end.

"Hi, it's Brandon Summers."

"Hello Brandon. How's your search going?"

"I just wanted to let you know that my friends and I are planning to dive at Hanlon Cove this afternoon. There's a chance we may find something of major significance to the *Whiskey Lee* case. I have photo evidence that someone may have been shot in this bay nineteen years ago."

"Is it Moreland?" Chief Flynn asked.

"No, but it's possible that it's related to the missing *Whiskey Lee* though. I'm not sure yet, but it may be motive for why he disappeared. I also have evidence that will help to prove the sunken lifeboat belonged to *The Whiskey Lee*."

"Okay but remember, don't touch or disturb anything down there," Flynn cautioned. "You get back to me right away if you find anything out of the ordinary. In the meantime, I'll try and assemble a small dive team of officers."

"Sure, sounds good," said Brandon, as they ended their phone call. A few hours later, Brandon rang Chief Flynn's number with an update.

The Whiskey Lee

"My friends and I found something suspicious out here at Hanlon Cove, Chief Flynn. You may want to come out here and take a look for yourself."

"What is it?" Flynn implored.

"A least ten 55-gallon steel oil drums, all sealed."

"Okay, stay away from the drums. My divers and a boat are almost ready to go. We'll meet you guys topside in about thirty to forty-five minutes."

"Sure, Chief," said Brandon.

They waited for Flynn's team to arrive.

Agent Rogan showed up first, with a military-style RIB accompanied by two other guys clad in black neoprene wetsuits.

"Who called you guys?" Brandon asked Rogan, as the twenty-five-foot black inflatable boat pulled up beside Chad's smaller eighteen-foot Zodiac.

"We have our ways of finding out things," Rogan replied as he tied the watercraft off to Chad's vessel.

Brandon turned to Chad. "This is the agent I was telling you about. He has the habit of showing up unexpectedly."

"That's what they do best," Lou replied.

Chief Flynn showed up next. He pulled the police boat up along the other side of Chad's boat.

Brandon caught Flynn peering at Agent Rogan and felt he should make a formal introduction. Before he could do that, Flynn hollered over to the agent in the black RIB, "We meet again Tom!"

"Oh, you two already know each other?" Brandon noted.

"You could say that; we've crossed paths a few times over the years," Flynn revealed.

"Yes, we also had a chance to compare notes regarding the man found at the bottom of the cliff last week," Agent Rogan added, as both his and Flynn's gazes shifted in Brandon's direction.

Feeling somewhat awkward under their stares, Brandon swallowed hard before changing the subject. "Uh, I have some photographs here that I told you about on the phone, Chief Flynn. Would you like to see them now?"

"Sure, let's see them," said Flynn, moving to the side of the boat.

Brandon rummaged through his duffle bag for the envelope of photographs.

Lou looked over his shoulder. "Hey Brandon, do you have a pen I can borrow? I just need to record our last dive in my logbook."

"Sure, here you go," said Brandon, passing him one.

Before Brandon could hand off the photographs, he paused while Chief Flynn and Rogan got caught up on things. Their discussion began to heat up.

"Anything happening around here should be run by me first. This is my jurisdiction," Brandon heard Chief Flynn say, in an agitated tone. "We have an ongoing investigation here."

Brandon, Chad, and Lou were listening now as the two law enforcers argued over jurisdiction.

"Hey. Um, excuse me, gentlemen," Brandon piped up. "If I'm not interrupting, perhaps I could brief you guys on the latest in . . ." he cleared his throat, "*my* investigation." Brandon held up a photograph in each hand.

"Wise ass," Chief Flynn smirked, reaching his hand over the gap between the two boats for one of the photographs.

Brandon passed the other photograph to Agent Rogan on the starboard side.

"What have you got here, Brandon?" Flynn asked.

"These are old photographs of someone being shot and then thrown overboard. Chief Flynn, did you have any other missing persons around the time Captain Moreland disappeared?" Brandon asked.

"Not that I can recall offhand, but unfortunately, people go missing at sea all the time," said Flynn.

Flynn studied the photograph. "Do you have any more photos? How do we know he was killed? It just shows a man holding a gun on another guy in this picture."

"Yes, but all the photos aren't here," Brandon replied. "When you see them, you'll know he was killed. I have the other photos in a safe place. I don't like to keep all my apples in the same basket, just in case the evidence ends up in the wrong hands."

Chief Flynn nodded his understanding. "I feel like I've seen the young man at the wrong end of the gun before, somewhere."

"Hmm, that guy holding the gun looks familiar." Rogan removed his sunglasses to study the photo.

"Maybe I should go through some of my old case files," said Flynn.

"Does the name Cy ring a bell? That's what was handwritten on the back of the original photograph," said Brandon.

"Not to me. What do you think Rogan? Heard of him?" Flynn asked.

The Whiskey Lee

"The name doesn't ring a bell, but I do feel like I've seen this guy before. Too bad it's not a different angle. We'll have to imagine what he looks like now. He may have gray hair and be between fifty and sixty years of age." Rogan squinted, looking more closely at the image. "It looks like he's using a silencer on that gun, I can tell you that much."

"How did you figure out this location from this photograph? Flynn asked. It doesn't show anything behind them but water."

"I have some other photographs, which I believe are from Moreland's camera, at a wider angle. It shows this area, taken on the same day. It's the same bay and rock formation that this area has. See the rocks over there?" Brandon pointed. "That's how we figured it out, exactly the same as the rocks in my photographs."

"So, Moreland may have witnessed the murder of that young guy in the photo. That's motive," said Flynn.

"Exactly! And later, I'll show you the other photographs that I have stashed away, so you can see for yourselves. This could be the most important link to the missing *Whiskey Lee*," Brandon said with confidence.

"Hmm, do you happen to know the name of boat they're standing aboard in this photo?" Flynn asked.

"It's the *Betsea*, Scully's Salvage," Chad interjected.

Flynn looked shocked.

"That doesn't surprise me. I knew they were up to no good, but it sounds to me like you've been holding out on us Brandon," Rogan accused, frowning.

"I just wanted to make sure I had all the facts, first. No point in chasing a lead if it's a dead end," said Brandon.

Flynn paused before speaking again. "Okay, Tom, I think we should chat more about this later at my office. What do you say? Let's get all the divers in the water and see what else we can find down there."

"Sure, Chief," Rogan agreed, while suiting up. He handed his photograph to the operator of his RIB, and then fitted a mask and snorkel over his head. "I'll be in touch with you this afternoon."

"Absolutely Tom, give me a call at my office after we've wrapped up here." Flynn placed his photograph in an evidence bag and then turned to Brandon. "I'll need those other photographs as soon as possible. Could you meet me and Agent Rogan at my office later today, after the dive?"

"Sure can," said Brandon.

"Perfect, now where did you say those oil drums are located?"

"Right over there." Brandon pointed toward the small island. "On this side of the island, in about sixty feet of water. I placed markers over them."

"Good job!" Flynn commended.

Agent Rogan's RIB made its way out to the area Brandon had pointed to, dropped the anchor, and set out their dive flag. Shortly after that, Brandon watched the agent do a backward roll off the inflatable. Another diver from Rogan's team followed him in the exact same manner, leaving one remaining team member onboard the black RIB.

Brandon turned to Lou after Flynn's boat had departed for the marked area. "Aren't you suiting up, Lou?"

"Nah, I think I'll sit this one out. I'm going to eat a sandwich and finish logging my dives. You guys go ahead. I'll put this back in your duffle when I'm done," he said, waving the silver pen.

Chad turned to Brandon. "Okay, let's roll. Keep your eyes peeled. Try not to be too shocked if we find any skeletal remains. We'll stay far away from the oil drums. Flynn and Rogan's team have that section covered, anyway."

***

After the dive, Rogan was already sitting in Chief Flynn's office, deeply engaged in discussion before Brandon showed up.

"I have someone in interrogation. We've been tracking this guy for a while. He's already got a rap sheet for his part in an armed robbery in Connecticut," Rogan said.

"What happened in Connecticut?" Flynn asked.

"He made a deal with the prosecutor and took a lesser charge. That's why he isn't sitting in a jail cell right now. He received a shorter sentence and . . . well, I don't need to explain the rest of it to you."

Flynn nodded. "Sounds like he ratted out his buddies."

"Yeah, and if he did it once, he may do it again. Anyway, he's the guy we picked up at Hog's Head National Park. 'Ace' is the name he goes by. Not his birth name, of course. We're going to try and keep him behind bars as long as we can this time. Lots of charges coming his way: conspiracy to commit murder, accessory, attempted murder, associating with members of organized crime, along with multiple weapons charges, and that's just for starters."

"I thought there were two shooters at the park. That's what Brandon told me," Flynn reminded him.

"The other guy was Rory. He's the one that took the shot. Luckily, that guy was one of ours. We needed boots on the ground to infiltrate their little cesspool of an organization."

"That explains why he missed his target, because he was one of yours," Flynn interpreted. "It's a good thing Agent Rory was there. I'd hate to be the one to break the bad news to Brandon's parents."

"Yes, that's one of the dreaded parts of our job, isn't it? I guess someone has to do it. I always feel for the people at the receiving end," Rogan said sincerely.

"Yeah, me too." Flynn remembered how drained Kathleen Moreland looked when he'd showed up at her residence to discuss the case of her missing husband. Other cases too, where he was faced with the grim task of telling people that their loved ones weren't coming home.

"Anyway," Rogan continued, "Agent Rory was trying to gain their trust in order to get inside Scully's and find out what's been going on there. It was the only way we could get eyes and ears in there. Rory had the perfect opportunity to miss his target when Brandon bent down to tie his boot lace," Rogan explained.

"So, someone ordered a hit. They couldn't have picked a better guy for it. An undercover federal agent. Perfect! I don't think Agent Rory could have planned for a better miss," said Flynn. "Amazing that he was able to pull it off."

"Yes. Only our guys knew he was an agent. Scully's didn't have a choice but to use Ace and a new face that Brandon wouldn't recognize. They were running out of options. It worked out well for us."

"I reckon it was a test by those running the operation to see if Rory, the new guy, would actually pull the trigger on someone. It had to look real or he'd be a dead man," Rogan explained. "Anyway, after that things got kind of crazy out there at Hog's Head, so we had to move in fast. We couldn't afford to compromise Rory's cover, so we had to arrest and airlift both of them."

"Afterwards, we searched Ace's silver sedan, and found an arsenal of weapons stashed in the trunk. I think he was preparing for a war or something. Brandon's a lucky man. He should go to a casino and play some craps."

Flynn smiled. "I think I'll go with him."

A light knock interrupted them. Rogan reached over and pulled the door open.

"Sorry, I heard some of your conversation," Brandon said, standing awkwardly in the doorway.

"It's okay, come on in Brandon. Have a seat. We've been waiting for you." Flynn motioned with his hand. "Close the door."

Brandon swung the door closed and took a seat in the remaining gray swivel chair, resting his elbows on the armrests, and looked at Flynn, waiting for him to speak.

"Agent Rogan and I had a chance to review a few things before you showed up."

"And? Are we all on the same page now?" Brandon asked.

"Well, don't get too excited; there are lots of missing pieces to this case that we'll still need to iron out," Flynn said.

Flynn took a deep breath. "This is all off the record, of course. Nothing said from here on in leaves this office. Those photographs could be the key evidence we need to put the *Whiskey Lee* case to bed." He looked back and forth between Rogan and Brandon as he explained. "How we go about obtaining them has to be strictly by the book. Every little bit helps to move us closer to obtaining a search warrant. I just don't want anything to go wrong here and have the guilty bastards walk right out of court. That's happened more times in the past than I care to discuss."

"How did you obtain the evidence, anyway Brandon? That is either going to make or break this investigation," Rogan asked.

Brandon pondered the question for a moment. "I see where you're directing this. That's why the original photographs were left there."

"Where?" Rogan asked.

"Scully's," said Brandon.

"You were inside Scully's? When?" Rogan asked.

"Well, if I did go inside, which I'm not saying I did, it most likely would have been last Wednesday night," said Brandon.

Rogan shook his head slowly. "That was *you*? Of course." He slapped his own leg. "I saw you leaving the shipyards in the silver Zodiac."

"Maybe it was me, maybe it wasn't—Wait, *you* were there?" Brandon snapped his fingers, pointing at Rogan. "The mystery diver that popped up out of the water. That was *you*?"

"Yes, and let me be the first to tell you that you nearly compromised my entire investigation that night. What the hell were you doing in there anyway?

The Whiskey Lee

I couldn't get near the place after you stirred things up. Guys were running all over the place looking for you. I had to abort my mission," said Rogan.

"Oh, jeez, I'm sorry about that. Had no idea."

"I'm guessing, like me, you weren't invited in there," said Rogan.

"No comment." Brandon glanced sheepishly over at Chief Flynn.

"Can you tell us where exactly the originals are now?" Flynn inquired.

"Maybe—that is, if they haven't been moved."

Flynn folded his arms. "Now, I have a question for you Brandon. Breaking and entering is a criminal offense, as you know. Will we find any evidence inside that warehouse indicating that you entered that warehouse illegally?"

"I'm one hundred percent sure you won't find anything which suggests that I forced my way into that warehouse, or any evidence that will suggest I was even there." said Brandon, remembering that he'd been extra careful about not leaving any fingerprints or other clues. "I feel like I'm getting thrown under the bus here."

Flynn studied him carefully for a moment. "You're a smart man and you probably know that if there's the slightest possibility that you entered that warehouse illegally, you could face criminal charges. Also, whatever evidence you found in there could be deemed inadmissible by the court."

"I'm fully aware of that, sir. You won't find any trace of me inside there, not even a shoe print. It's funny though, I keep having this re-occurring dream about offices on the second floor, a cup full of pens and pencils, gray filing cabinets, and a little box up on a shelf, inside a closet."

Chief Flynn peered over at Rogan, whose grin was growing wider.

"Did you get all that Agent Rogan?" Flynn asked.

"Sure did, Chief." Rogan was already in the process of jotting everything down in his notebook.

"What about the other photographs you said you have, from Moreland's camera? How did you obtain those?" Flynn persisted, tilting his head slightly, awaiting an answer.

"Legitimately," said Brandon. "I was told I could take whatever photographs I wanted by the owner of the house."

"Would that be the little white house with the blue shutters, up on the hill, by any chance?" Flynn asked.

"Yes."

"Well done," said Flynn, looking down at the photographs on the desk in front of him. He leaned over to study the close-up of the man holding the gun.

"What I'm wondering is who could've snapped this incriminating photo, and why. It was obviously someone on board the *Betsea*; taken from the bridge by the looks of it," Flynn said.

Agent Rogan's eyes scanned the photo; he paused for a moment before speaking. "It could easily have been someone looking to profit from this, hold some leverage over the shooter, or use it for blackmail?" he surmised. "The captain of the salvage vessel? Or, it's possible they killed the photographer before they had the chance to expose the gunman."

"I must say, that's very intuitive Rogan, but if they knew about the photographs they wouldn't have had to look very far. I doubt the captain would have been careless enough to store the photos in Scully's office if he was trying to blackmail the shooter," Flynn said.

"Maybe they didn't know about the photographs," said Rogan.

"That's what I'm thinking."

Brandon placed a clear plastic bag on Chief Flynn's desk. "Here's one more thing for your evidence file. This was left behind. I'd say it's a deal-closer." Through the clear bag, the polished sterling silver Zippo lighter could be seen. "I took a bunch of photographs of it, before and after I cleaned it up."

"What's this?" Flynn asked.

"Let's just say that it's a gift from Captain Moreland," said Brandon. "It's the chunk of metal I told you about, the one I found in the sunken lifeboat when we did our wall dive the other day. After I cleaned it up, there was no doubt in my mind that it belonged to James Moreland. You can read the inscription for yourself. I believe this is the proof you were looking for to tie the lifeboat to *The Whiskey Lee*."

"Wow! Great work Brandon!" Flynn exclaimed.

"What happened with the oil drums? Did you find out what's in them?" Brandon asked.

"Not yet. So far, we've got twelve 55-gallon oil drums filled with god knows what, so I've called in the hazmat team to deal with them," said Flynn.

Agent Rogan shifted his gaze over to Brandon. "I know one thing Brandon; these guys are going to great lengths to get you off their tail. You're like the elusive fly on the wall that's bugging them. Why else would they have made all those attempts to end your life?"

"It sounds like you've been following me," Brandon said, smiling warily.

"Let's just say that I've pulled you out of the shit pile twice already," said Rogan.

"What do you mean?" Brandon asked.

"This is strictly off the record, of course." He waited for Brandon's and Flynn's reactions.

The two men nodded.

"Brandon, your ass needed saving out there at Hog's Head National Park and I wasn't going to sit idly by while someone filled you with lead. I was in a position to help and, let's just say I pulled some strings."

"Wow, those were your monkeys? Absolutely flippin' incredible!" Brandon said, astounded.

"You're welcome," Rogan replied.

"Wait, you said you got me out of the shit twice. When was the other time?"

"I was the one that saved you from the edge of that cliff, at the lighthouse."

"So, it was *you* who yelled, *Drop the gun*?"

Rogan nodded, smiling.

"Wow, well I guess that answers *that* nagging question. I thought it was William," said Brandon.

Rogan looked at Flynn in time to see him shift nervously in his chair.

"William?" Rogan asked, looking curiously at Brandon and then back to Flynn, who remained silent. "You mean . . ." He peered up at the framed photograph on the wall behind the desk and pointed inquisitively. "The lighthouse keeper?"

Flynn only shrugged.

"Never mind. Forget I said that." Brandon shook his head defensively.

"Okay," said Rogan, clenching his jaw, trying to hold back his smile. It was his eyes that revealed he was genuinely entertained by the fact that Brandon believed his savor was a ghost.

"Regardless of how funny you think that was, I still owe you a thanks because I wouldn't be sitting here right now if it weren't for you, Agent Rogan. I'm curious, though. Why were you out at the lighthouse?"

"I was following Gloria's phone."

Brandon tilted his head and raised one eyebrow.

Rogan explained. "It was merely a coincidence we were up at the cliffs at the same time. One evening, I dropped by the Piper & Pelican and saw a guy grab Gloria's phone, so I did what any good agent would do: I followed him. That's when I stumbled onto your little dance with the devil at the edge of the cliff."

"That's the day you started following me, wasn't it? It was *you* who took the gun from the cliff." Brandon shifted uncomfortably in his chair.

"Yes, I needed to dust it for fingerprints," Rogan disclosed.

"And then your guy placed the location tracking devices on my SUV, at Lizzie's Restaurant," Brandon concluded.

"Yes, guilty again, but you found them. I really hate dumpster diving by the way," said Rogan. "Next time, could you put the devices under some concrete steps or something?"

Brandon's smile grew as he imagined Agent Rogan climbing into a dirty dumpster to fetch the tracking devices.

"Obviously I didn't find all the devices you planted, because you still managed to follow us out to Hog's Head National Park," said Brandon.

Rogan didn't say anything. His lips curled into a faint grin.

"Give him time and I'm sure he'll find all of them. This guy's like James Bond." Flynn smiled.

"I'm sure he will too." Rogan looked at Brandon strangely. "The only thing that really bothers me is why the hell you made us follow you all the way up to Hog's Head National Park?"

"Oh yes, well, you probably already know that Rosie is visiting from England to do research for her next ghost story novel. Some people have claimed to have seen a ghost ship in flames out there in Hog's Head Bay," Brandon explained.

Rogan looked at him with skepticism. "I send in a military team to help you, all because your girlfriend wants to see some folklore bull shit—a ship in flames?"

"I know it's hard to believe, isn't it?"

"Okay, now the truth," Rogan said. "I've been straight with you and saved your ass twice. Let's return the favor now, huh?"

"Does the name Aiden Dalton mean anything to you? I think he may be involved in all this." Brandon looked seriously at Flynn and then Rogan.

"Well, if the sun doesn't rise in the east." Chief Flynn was aghast, looking at Rogan. "No wonder he's up to his neck in deep water."

The Whiskey Lee

Flynn turned to Brandon, pursing his lips. "Dalton's a well-known, respectable senator."

Brandon shrugged. "Hey, I didn't come up with this information on my own, and have no reason to give you a false lead."

"May I ask who you're getting this information from?" Rogan asked, while jotting some stuff down in his notebook.

"I can't say. My source doesn't want to be revealed. Besides, you're not going to believe it anyway," said Brandon.

"Try me," Rogan replied inquisitively.

Flynn intervened. "Brandon, it would help if you have some evidence to back this up."

"I'm still working on that part. All I'm saying is, now you have two names. Cut me some slack here. I'm sure Agent Rogan could pull some strings and look into it," said Brandon.

Chief Flynn and Rogan both looked at each other. Rogan nodded.

"I guess we'll just have to work backward from the names and see what turns up," Flynn agreed.

Rogan leaned in and rested his elbow on Flynn's desk. "I don't know about you, Chief, but for me, this is adding up. Brandon may have something here. For some reason I believe him; given all the attempts at trying to silence the so-called, "thorn in their side," a person in a position of power could be responsible. Anyone who may know anything mysteriously gets killed or disappears. Local people in this town are reluctant to even talk about what's been going on here. This may be orchestrated by someone with some pull, such as someone in Senator Dalton's position," Rogan concluded. "It's all circumstantial right now, but it's a start. We'll just need more solid evidence to back it up."

Flynn nodded in agreement. "Do you think your team could put surveillance on him?"

Rogan nodded. "That's what we do best."

Brandon smiled.

"We can't let any of this leave this room. As far as I'm concerned, this conversation never took place. Brandon, have you talked to anyone else about it?" Flynn asked.

Brandon nodded. "Just Rosie, Chad, and the guy that provided me with the names."

"So, that means your informant's life may be in danger too," said Rogan. "You should probably give me his name so I can provide protection for him."

"Nope, he won't talk to you," Brandon replied rapidly. "Like I said, you're not going to believe how he obtained the information, anyway. I'm having trouble believing it myself. It's best that you just roll with me on this. I've been right so far."

Chief Flynn nodded. "Okay then."

Brandon picked up a folder and placed it on the desk. "Here are the rest of the photographs. Maybe we can make something out of this." He spread them out across the desk. "I made them a bit larger. Maybe it will help with the identification of the shooter."

Rogan dropped the larger photographs beside the stack of other photos.

Flynn reached over to turn his desk lamp on and then directed it to shine on the photos. "Okay, now let's take another look at the people in these photographs." As Flynn leaned in, he scrupulously analyzed the photo in front of him.

The moment he identified the gunman, his eyes widened.

35

Evans parked his gray 4x4 truck on the street near Barney's Cove Marina. He noticed a damp chill in the air even before he'd opened the driver's door. Reaching into the back seat, he grabbed his brown leather jacket. The cooler temperatures out on the ocean were known to be somewhat relentless, especially after sunset. He pulled the jacket on and strolled through the open chain-link gate. He remained inconspicuous while casually searching for the other men that he was supposed to meet here. Lewis had a special way of telling people to be on time.

Don't be fuckin' late. Those had been his exact words. *Rude son of a bitch*, Evans thought, as he stopped to peer at his stolen Rolex. The time showed 10:15 p.m.

He sauntered his way through the parking lot, toward the wharf and docks. He knew the breeze had picked up, because Evans could hear the lines slapping against metal masts from the sailboats moored out in the harbor. Along the coast it was common for sailboats to be moored away from shore because of the vast, ever-changing tide activity. If not, a sailor could return to find his vessel stranded, and have to wait hours for high tide to release the boat from the grip of the mud.

"Over here," he heard a voice say, from the space between two recreational powerboats resting on wooden cradles in the confines of the boat storage area.

A burly man between the ages of forty-five and fifty, with a goatee, emerged from the space between the boats. He was smoking a cigarette. Mugs stepped out of the shadows behind Lewis.

"Did you bring the gun I gave you?" Lewis grunted.

"I never leave home without it," Evans replied with a rebellious tilt of his head, while he chewed a wooden toothpick.

It was an odd instruction from Lewis to tell Evans to bring his gun with him. *Does he think we're amateurs or something?* Evans thought.

After Lewis had phoned him, Evans had left his tiny apartment behind the bakery; he'd made sure that he'd packed an extra piece for good luck: a Glock 25 semi-automatic pistol. It was his pride and joy. If Lewis had taken any interest in getting to know him, he'd know about the extra piece Evans carried. He felt a surge of adrenaline as he stuffed the Glock into the back of his waistband and strode out the door to the back alley where his truck was parked.

Maybe Lewis is expecting some big trouble to go down tonight and he just wants to make sure we're prepared. Well, I'm ready. Someone's going down tonight! Evans thought.

Lewis caught him looking off in another direction and rudely snapped his fingers in a condescending way to get his attention. "Hello? Are you still with us?"

Evans frowned at him.

"I've got a powerboat lined up for this job; it's a twin-engine, thirty-footer with a cuddy cabin. We've got to be fast. I don't want anyone seeing us take it. It will be good enough for what we'll need it for tonight."

"What's going down tonight, anyway?" Mugs asked.

"You'll find out when we get there," Lewis barked.

"Where's the boat?" Evans interrupted.

"It's over there on *E* dock," he pointed. "It's close to the wharf, in slip number three." He inhaled deeply after taking another drag of his cigarette.

"Do you have anymore smokes? I'm out," Evans asked.

"No, I don't. This is my last one," Lewis snapped, before continuing with his instructions. "So far, I haven't seen anyone walking around here tonight, but there's one guy still on his boat—the fucker is right opposite the one we're going to be stealing. His car is the maroon Acura in the parking lot. He just carried some stuff out to it a little while ago. I think he's leaving soon," Lewis added. "We're moving in as soon as that asshole gets in his car and leaves. You're on lookout Evans. Can you handle that? Cy doesn't want any screwups tonight."

"Sure, I can handle it." Feeling a bad taste at the back of his throat, Evans casually removed the toothpick from his mouth, forced something up from deep within, and spitefully ejected it onto the pavement in front of Lewis's foot. It landed with a splat.

The burly man didn't say anything, but his eyes narrowed and the deep furrows on his forehead were pressed tightly into a frown. He'd obviously taken offense to the disgusting reaction.

Cy doesn't want any screwups tonight, Evans thought.

Evans had only seen Cy once. At that time, both Cy and Evans were younger men. He remembered those cold hard eyes the day Cy had killed Dennis Cain. Lewis had ordered Evans to grab the hose and clean the blood off the deck. He also had to help dispose of Cain's body before the crew returned from lunch belowdecks.

Cy, Ace, and Evans disembarked the *Betsea* after that, returning to the mainland with Lewis at the helm of the private yacht.

Evans was paid generously for the job. A few days after that, he was informed by Lewis that Cy had another special job for him. The pay wasn't something he could turn down easily and he also didn't want to disappoint the top boss. It was his moment to prove himself. Maybe it would help bump him up through the ranks.

Evans didn't mind doing what he did back then, but not so much now. Those were better days for sure. Everyone had changed, including Lewis. If Evans had a hate list, Lewis would be number one on it. It was unfortunate that Lewis was pretty much running things now. *What is Cy doing now?* Evans thought. *It's like he went totally incognito after the deckhand was killed.* The three men watched the maroon Acura leave the parking lot. They stayed hidden until it turned onto the main street.

"Okay let's go," Lewis commanded, as he and Mugs walked on ahead. Evans dropped back to keep watch. After establishing that the coast was clear, Evans joined them on the thirty-foot powerboat. The exhaust blowers were already running, and Lewis was fidgeting with some wires, trying to get it started.

During their briefing, Lewis had told them that they'd be meeting the salvage vessel, *The Osprey*, at an undisclosed location.

"Cy wants us to board *The Osprey* and inspect the cargo tonight," Lewis had said.

The request wasn't out of the ordinary. Clearing cargo was usually an easy task. Although, they didn't usually steal a boat. Something didn't feel right to Evans. "Where's Ace?"

"Don't know," Lewis replied bluntly.

After clearing the harbor, Lewis pushed the throttle down to gain some speed. The boat made an incredibly large wake as the hull plowed through the waves of Dack's Bay. Once it gathered enough momentum, the vessel's V-hull was able to cut a path through the choppy surface. About ten minutes later, as the vessel cruised northeast along the coastline, Lewis commanded Mugs to slow the boat down.

"Why are we stopping here?" Mugs asked.

"This is where we're meeting *The Osprey*," said Lewis.

Evans looked around. "Are you sure this is the right spot? I don't see it anywhere."

"Yes, it's the right spot. Cy specifically said northeast of Hanlon Cove, on the other side of the first island. Maybe they're just running late," he replied, placing a gray gun case on top of the inboard engine's cover. "I'll need you to give me the guns back that I gave to you. I'm going to replace them with two new clean ones."

They both looked at each other, and then peered at the guns inside the gun case as Lewis opened it. Evans moved in for a closer look.

"No, wait. You can see it when you've given the other one back to me," Lewis said, stopping him with his hand.

Evans reluctantly surrendered his gun to Lewis first and then Mugs handed his over.

After receiving the guns, Lewis stepped aside. Evans moved toward the gun case to pick up his new weapon. Lewis threw the two handguns overboard and then pulled out his own pistol. By then, Evans had discovered the guns in the case were pellet guns. Lewis had deceived them, and now his pistol was aimed point blank at Evans, mid-torso. In a natural reflex, Evans stepped backward, raising both hands.

"What are you doing Lewis?!" Mugs yelled.

"Now you've both proved that you're really *that* stupid," Lewis barked.

Evans had his eyes locked on Lewis, but didn't say anything.

The Whiskey Lee

Lewis shook his head in disgust. "You guys can't even tell the difference between a real pistol and a pellet gun."

"How could we tell? It was inside a case. I might have known you were up to something. *The Osprey*'s not meeting us out here, is it? You're planning to kill us," Evans realized.

"You'll die first, mostly because you have the worst attitude and you're our biggest liability."

"Hey, in all fairness, that guy who got into the salvage building wasn't my fault," Evans explained. "And the other stuff I did, Cy ordered me to do it." He slowly lowered his hands, resting them on his belt.

"Don't try anything," Lewis warned.

"How can I? You threw my gun overboard," Evans reminded him.

"Cy said he wants no loose ends, so I have to kill you. Sorry, but it will be my pleasure."

A sudden groan of an engine startled the three men. They turned to the port side to see a large trawler descending upon them. It seemed to appear out of nowhere. The trawler passed by so close that the three men felt the wake almost immediately. They were caught completely off guard, as it tossed the stolen vessel side to side.

Lewis spun to catch hold of a side rail to steady himself. With his attention diverted, Mugs didn't waste a second before pouncing on him, trying to pry the pistol from his burly fingers as the two struggled to keep their balance. The boat pitched and swayed on the waves as the two struggled. Being the heavier man, Lewis shoved Mugs off him, sending him hurtling to the deck. He lifted the pistol to take aim. As the boat rocked, Lewis found that he was unable to keep his feet planted, so was unable to take proper aim. He remembered that a slight bending of the knees allowed a person to become one with the motion of a rocking boat. This allowed Lewis to take aim at the middle of Mugs' chest.

BANG!!! A shot rang out.

Lewis slumped and dropped hard onto the deck. Blood oozed from the side of his head, dripping onto the white deck that was slowly turning crimson.

Evans stood there with the Glock still smoking in his hands. "I don't know the difference between a real pistol and a pellet gun, huh?" he mocked. "I guess you took one for the team, Lewis," he scoffed, spitting his toothpick at the lifeless body laying on the deck.

Mugs got to his feet. "Nice shot man, thanks," he praised.

"It's a good thing I packed my Glock. That son of a bitch! Who the fuck does he think he is, anyway?" Evans glared before turning Lewis over. He reached for the pack of cigarettes in Lewis's blood-spattered shirt pocket. He opened up the pack, shaking his head.

"So, you *did* have one smoke left. Liar!" he accused the dead man. He removed the cigarette, placed it between his lips and then dropped the empty cigarette pack on top of Lewis's motionless chest.

From his own pocket, he grabbed his blue butane lighter and lit the cigarette. He inhaled deeply. "A job well done. No screwups this time," he boasted with satisfaction as he exhaled the smoke.

"What about Cy?" Mugs questioned. Now Evans could see Mug's scar prominently as it split his eyebrow in two parts. He remembered the day that Mugs had taken a knife slash to the head. The blade had been intended for Evans, but Mugs had stepped in and blocked the attack with his head. *Crazy son of a bitch*, he thought. It wasn't the smartest thing to do, but at least Evans didn't owe him anything now.

"To hell with Cy!" said Evans, as his face hardened. "I'll kill him too, if I see him," he admitted coldly. "That lying, cheating piece of shit has some nerve trying to have us knocked off tonight. After all we've done for him," Evans growled. "That's some gratitude, huh?"

"I've never even seen him. Have you?" Mugs asked.

"Just once, but I probably wouldn't know him if he passed me on the street now," Evans replied honestly.

Mugs turned his head, searching for the vessel that came dangerously close to them. "Hey, what happened to that other boat that almost hit us just now?"

Evans started looking for it too.

"Just about knocked me clean off my feet. It came out of nowhere," said Mugs.

Mugs and Evans watched as the red fishing trawler returned for another pass.

Evans narrowed his eyes as it cruised by them; it was close enough that he could see the outline of the people on board, but they were dimly lit by the only available light source, the moonlight. The area suddenly became illuminated by the bright beacon from across the bay. It was coming from Sixteen Fathom Hill Lighthouse, high up on the cliff. As the trawler passed through the beam of light it also became illuminated. Evans could clearly see a woman standing on the back deck of the boat. She appeared to be holding a small bundle in her arms.

Evans gasped. The filtered cigarette came loose from his mouth and dropped to the deck. His mouth failed to close as the bold white letters came into view. There, at the trawler's stern, the words sprawled across the red-painted transom unleashed a haunting revelation . . .

WHISKEY LEE

"No way! It can't be. How is that even possible? It sank. I watched it sink!" Evans yelled.

"Start the engines Mugs, quick! Let's get 'em!"

Mugs started it and then pushed the throttle down hard, the stolen vessel now thrusting forward. It slammed its way through the unforgiving waves to catch up to the *Whiskey Lee.*

Evans, who was standing near Mugs at the helm, lost his balance and fell sideways when the deep V-hull smashed against a good-sized wave. The back of his hand hit the corner of the dashboard beside the open hatch and he dropped the gun. It fell through the opening, dropping with a thud onto the lower deck.

"Shit!" Evans cursed, getting back to his feet. "I've got to go down and get the gun."

Mugs didn't hear him. His eyes were fixated on the fleeing vessel. It was almost as if he was in a trance. Determined to catch up to the trawler, even if it meant taking a violent beating from the waves.

Evans descended the ladder into the lower cabin. As his foot tried to find the third step, the vessel hit another big wave and he lost his balance. He stumbled, falling hard to the floor. He recovered quickly, gathered himself and searched for the gun. The vessel took another direct hit by another wave, dislodging the gun from its hiding spot under the galley table. Evans scooped it up, but as he tried to retreat to the ladder, all the lights in the cabin went out. Outside, the waves surrounding the stolen vessel were growing in size and seemed to be coming at them from different directions.

In pitch blackness, he heard Mugs yell something down from the helm.

"What?" Evans replied, feeling his way in the dark as he approached the ladder. It was impossible to hear him over the roar of the engines.

"I lost them! The damned lighthouse beacon light went off, and now I can't see a thing out there!" he heard Mugs yell.

"Slow down!" Evans hollered up through the open cabin door, while fighting to stay on his feet. The raging waves continued to thrash against the side of the boat violently. He guessed Mugs didn't hear him, because he still hadn't eased up on the throttle. *Shit!* Evans thought, grabbing for the ladder with his free hand. His other hand held the gun, so it could only be used for support. Steadying himself, Evans began his climb.

What happened next changed everything; the boat's hull hit something solid that felt like a brick wall. It broke apart with a deafening crash. The back end of the boat reared up and the engines whined as the boat stopped dead in its wake. Evans flew toward the bow of the vessel, hitting his head. Everything went black for him before gallons of water poured in through the gaping hole in the hull. As the boat sank in the depths of Hanlon Cove, the twin engines died almost simultaneously.

"*I'll be down below with the Whiskey. Ha, ha, ha, ha, . . .*" the haunting voice taunted, as the words echoed across the water. It was followed by the sound of moaning as the boat pitched onto its side and submerged within minutes.

36

Early the next morning, Flynn had been sipping his morning coffee when he'd received the call regarding the stolen thirty-foot cabin cruiser. He had just opened another of his missing persons files in order to re-examine the contents. This was the case file of a young man named Dennis Cain who had been reported missing months after the *Whiskey Lee* had vanished. It was another unsolved mystery that he'd refused to give up on. Chief Flynn had all the photographs neatly laid out across his desk. He put the lid back on the file box soon after receiving the call from the panicked boat owner at Barney's Cove.

"Okay, try to remain calm, ma'am. I'll be over there in about ten minutes," Flynn assured the frantic woman at the other end of the line.

Ending the call, he rose from his desk. "What next?" he mumbled to himself. Flynn took one more sip of his steamy coffee before leaving the office.

As he arrived at Barney's Cove, Flynn already had a feeling that the missing boat would become a recovery mission. During his drive out there, a fisherman had called in reporting lifesaver rings and other debris floating at the surface near Hanlon Cove and the islands. Regardless, he couldn't assume anything at this point.

After gathering the statement from the owner of the boat, Flynn organized another marine search in the area of Hanlon Cove.

Agent Rogan didn't attend, but Brandon and Chad were invited along to help. While Chief Flynn took care of the stolen boat, Rogan was out following one of the leads that Brandon had provided.

It didn't take Flynn's team of divers long to discover the wreck of the 30-foot cabin cruiser.

A diver popped his head up out of the water, removing the regulator from his mouth. Another diver soon joined him at the surface.

"So far, we've found three bodies. One looks like he may have taken a bullet to the head. They must have slammed into something really hard. The huge hole in the boat's hull looks like it was ripped open by Jaws," the first diver said.

Flynn scratched his head. He was utterly stumped as to what the boat could have hit.

"Rock? Or whale?" Officer Coyne offered from the police boat's helm.

"I don't know. I'm sure there would be some evidence if it had hit a whale or any other marine animal. There are lots of rocks and small islands out here though," said Flynn.

The scuba diver continued to share his observations, with his mask now perched on his head.

"From the damage it appears as though it hit another boat, maybe a bigger one, but I don't see any other boats around this area with any damage, either above or below the surface."

The situation weighed heavily on Flynn. He shook his head and sighed deeply, looking at Officer Coyne. He then turned his attention back to the divers still bobbing in the waves.

"Okay Caz, good work. Keep searching. Let me know what else you guys find down there."

Caz nodded. He placed the regulator back into his mouth, set his mask in place, and then did a flip, kicking his fins as he dove beneath the surface. The other diver followed him.

Flynn turned to Officer Coyne. "Why does everything have to happen at Hanlon Cove? What is it with this place, anyway?" Flynn asked, raising both hands in the air.

Coyne shrugged. "I don't know. Why can't it ever be easy?"

"If you wanted easy you chose the wrong career, Coyne."

"I guess so, but I think I'd make a lousy fisherman," he grinned. "This area is just bad luck, Chief. It must be something to do with Phantom Hill over there. Maybe it's cursed." Officer Coyne nudged his head toward the lighthouse.

Flynn turned to look at the menacing red and white structure towering in the distance.

The Whiskey Lee

"I don't get it. It's almost as if the rocks picked themselves up and dropped into the path of the stolen boat and then moved back again." He paused for a moment with his hand resting on his chin, before turning back to Coyne, who now had a deeply concerned look on his face.

Flynn quickly extinguished Coyne's growing uneasiness. "Okay, I guess we'll have to stay alert to anyone requesting boat damage repairs in the area. That's all I've got to go on right now. We should monitor all the marinas and boat repair establishments. Sniff around—see if anyone's noticed or reported any vessel damage," Flynn ordered.

"Yes, Chief," Coyne replied, urgently picking up the radio to pass along the information to his fellow officers. Flynn couldn't help but shift his attention back to the tall structure sitting atop Sixteen Fathom Hill. The lighthouse deeply rattled him. *Phantom Hill* . . . He exhaled a lengthy sigh.

Shortly afterwards another police diver broke the surface of the water. "Chief, we also found a human skull and bones on the sea floor. Looks like they've been down there a while."

The skull found by the divers was protruding out of the sand near the wreck of the cabin cruiser. An anchor and chain lay near the remains. It looked like it had been sitting in the salt water for a number of years.

This interested Flynn more than finding the three men that were alleged to have stolen the cabin cruiser. The extra skull and bones presented a new twist which truly ignited him. His mind flashed back to the missing file case sitting on his desk. *Could this be the skeletal remains of Dennis Cain or James Moreland?* Flynn wondered. His mind was racing to make a connection. He thought back to the timeline of events. *Is he our John Doe from the photograph? The one who was shot aboard the* Betsea?

"We need you guys to search out in deeper water," Flynn instructed the team of divers. "Officer Nolan, I need you to do some crowd control. This is a crime scene. I see some nosy rubberneckers out there in their recreational boats, just cruising about, trying to catch a glimpse of whatever we bring to the surface. If they aren't helping in the search, I want them *all* gone! Clear them out! I know Moreland's fishing trawler is out there and we're going to find it. I'll contact everyone if there are any developments or changes."

***

"Let's go further north. I think we should search the other side of the small islands," Chad said to Brandon, pointing. He was getting edgy.

"Brandon nodded.

As the Zodiac passed the second island, Brandon had an unsettling feeling that they were headed in the right direction—he also had a strange feeling that they weren't alone. Chad had the Zodiac clipping along at a steady cruising speed, before slowing to check the depth.

"That's Skull Island over there," Chad pointed to a large island off their starboard side.

Brandon's phone rang, so he reached for it. He thought it may be Flynn with an update. The phone crackled as Brandon was unable to get a clear connection. All he heard was static on the other end.

"Hello?" he repeated a few times, frowning in frustration. "Damned dead zones!" He stared up at the towering cliffs surrounding them. They were beautiful, yes, but didn't offer any breaks when it came to mobile phone service.

Through the crackling on the phone, Brandon heard a faint, but recognizable voice uttering something: "I'll be down with the *Whiskey*." Fear engulfed him as realized who it was. To hear that ghostly voice over the shoddy phone service was nothing short of disturbing. As Brandon focused on the hollow voice over the static, he froze as Captain Moreland's ghost rhymed his startling words into a song:

Ohhhh, there once was a trawler named Whiskey Lee; *now it sits on the bottom of the deep blue sea.*

When the devil passed through, he never knew his fate, till the Whiskey *rose up, after years in wait.*

The bastards didn't know, for all their sins they'd pay, as the Whiskey *came a callin' for some killers that day.*

Down the ladder one went, but stumbled and fell, as the Whiskey *crashed through—she sent those killers straight to hell!"*

It was followed by haunting laughter.

Brandon's eyes were wide. He couldn't control the chills that traveled up his spine.

Chad saw the look on his face. "Who's on the phone?"

Brandon just shook his head slowly without saying a word. He was speechless.

It seemed to appear out of nowhere, right in front of them. Brandon instantly recognized it from his dream. It was the red phantom trawler: the *WHISKEY LEE*.

The two shocked men stared at it. Brandon realized that he and Chad were the only divers who were witnessing this ghostly manifestation.

"Let's follow it," said Chad.

Brandon turned to look directly at him.

"You look like you've seen a ghost," said Chad.

"Chad, you'll never guess who was on the phone." Brandon thumbed in the direction of the *Whiskey Lee*.

"*What?* Get out of here!" said Chad. "There has to be an explanation. Someone's playing some sort of trick on us. When I catch him, he's going to see just enough of my fist before his lights go out," Chad fumed, as he followed the trawler eagerly toward deeper water.

Brandon remained silent for a moment before speaking. "Okay, let's see where the trawler goes, but please try to keep your threats to yourself. We're still not sure what we're dealing with here." Brandon could feel his heart racing.

Chad made eye contact with him; that's when he realized how serious his friend was. "Okay," he agreed.

Brandon looked at the towering rock faces off their right and left sides. The craggy cliffs of the mainland were on their left. Skull Island appeared menacing on the right. It had fitting name. Brandon watched the *Whiskey Lee* plow through the waves effortlessly. Feeling apprehensive, he started to wish he'd stayed closer to the police divers. They were being drawn too far away from Hanlon Cove.

The VHF radio crackled. Both of them stared at it momentarily, before looking back to the red trawler; when they did, both were astonished to see the *Whiskey Lee* had vanished.

"What the actual f . . ." Chad said, turning his head one way and then the other, searching for the boat. He slowed his boat down to about five miles per hour, in the area where they last saw the trawler.

"Don't say I didn't warn you. We're dealing with something way bigger than both of us. I think we both just witnessed the *Whiskey Lee*'s ghost ship. I also think James Moreland is trying to tell us something." Brandon looked cautiously over the side of the Zodiac. "How deep is it here Chad?"

Chad placed the Zodiac in neutral and checked the depth.

"It's 150 feet," he replied, staring at his depth finder.

"That's fine," said Brandon. "Do you have a long enough anchor rope?"

"Sure do," Chad smiled.

"Okay, then it's splash time for us," Brandon said with a nervous, but excited edge in his voice. "Drop the anchor."

Resting in its watery grave in approximately 150 feet of water was the sunken wreck of the *Whiskey Lee*. It was half buried in the sand of the seafloor.

***

Back at Hanlon cove, a team of police searchers discovered what appeared to be two old discarded lifesaving rings, an unused two-person life raft, and two old wooden oars. All appeared to have been intentionally and forcefully wedged into a crevice way above the waterline, where they weren't likely to be pulled out to sea when the water level rose with the tide.

The police recognized the lifesaving rings to be those from the *Whiskey Lee*. The name of the vessel was still intact, printed with vinyl in bold red letters on a white background. Police officers continued to comb the area for more evidence. It didn't take them long to discover other buried items, including a red lumber jacket, and a wallet which belonged to James K. Moreland.

37

REWIND – 1989

It was shortly after eleven o'clock at night. Captain James Moreland had gone to a bar as usual, downing more than four whiskeys. The night was calm, with no storms expected over the bay in the next few days. It was quiet—almost too quiet. Moreland habitually visited the same drinking establishments time after time. It was a routine he found hard to break. Like many other nights, he put on his hat, paid his bill, pulled his red lumber jacket over his T-shirt and left the bar. Only, this night would be different. He wouldn't be returning.

He set out for the docks in a pleasant mood, humming and singing a song as he stumbled along:

Ohhhh, out on the water, that's where I'll be, fishing some Marlin in that big ole sea.

Once I'm retired, I'll do just that—head down to Florida and say, "Screw that!"

"Oh wait, I said *that* twice," he chuckled to himself, then paused to take his silver Zippo lighter and a cigarette from his pocket. After lighting the cigarette and taking a long drag, he continued on his way.

He tried the last part of his song again:

Once I'm retired, I'll throw in the hat—head down to Florida and say, "Screw that!"

He chuckled to himself again. "Yeah, that's better! Ha, ha, ha." After getting about halfway to the docks, he needed to urinate. Knowing he wasn't going to make it to the boat, James threw down what was left of the cigarette before heading to his favorite spot between two buildings. Once finished his business, he zipped up his fly, and returned to the street. That was the moment that a young man appeared in front of him, startling him. "What the ffffuck do you want?" James said, while he slowly swayed back and forth. "Run along. Go on now!" James drunkenly gestured, waving a hand at the stranger to move out of his way. "You're Captain James Moreland, right?" the younger man asked.

"Who wants to know?" Moreland stopped and looked the man square in the face while narrowing his eyes. "I don't know you. Can't a guy even take a piss around here? Did you get a good look sunshine?"

"I know what's going on between you and Ann Marie," the younger man said, chewing on a toothpick.

"Mind your own fuckin' business and get out of my face." James reached out with his arm to push the younger man out of his way, but the man was quicker. He took a step to the side, causing Moreland to lose his balance and take three running steps toward the curb near the road. "You're a tricky one. If you stand still long enough, I may hit you," Moreland threatened.

"Where's your camera?" the young man asked.

"Oh, so now you want to steal my camera? Well, fuck you!" James staggered off down the street.

As James walked away, the young man gave him one final warning.

"I think you've made a big mistake, Moreland. You saw something and my boss isn't happy."

"What part of *fuck off* don't you understand?" James shouted, turning to raise his middle finger at him. "And here's one for your boss too." He raised the middle finger of his other hand before turning back around and continuing on his way. "That's your double salute, sonny boy!"

* * *

Before going to bed, Captain Moreland had felt warm, so he'd taken off his favorite red lumber jacket and draped it over the bench in the main cabin before descending the ladder to enter the *Whiskey Lee*'s V-berth. Seconds after flopping down on one of the beds, Moreland had passed out before he'd even had the chance to remove his second boot.

The Whiskey Lee

About an hour and a half later, he stirred to a sound in the cabin. He slid his other boot onto his bare foot and climbed a few of the ladder's steps. "Who's there?" He demanded, but didn't hear a reply. He climbed a little higher, now nearing the top step. "Who's—?" He was about to repeat his question, but was met by a mighty blow to his head, knocking him backward and causing him to fall into the dimly lit V-berth below. His body landed with enough force to send a jarring pain through his tailbone. The back of his head followed through, making a loud crack as it connected with the unforgiving lower deck. With blurred vision, Moreland tried to get back on his feet, but before he was able to fully recover, he was met by several more blows to his head. Blurred vision soon turned to darkness.

***

Once he was certain that Moreland was dead, Evans grabbed the nearest item of clothing, a hand-knitted navy blue pullover. He covered Captain Moreland's blood-stained head with it before making some quick preparations to ensure that James Moreland and his trawler would never be seen again. He grabbed all the life jackets and threw them on top of Moreland and then searched for anything else that might float up to the surface after the boat sank. He placed Moreland's wallet in his own back pocket, stuffed everything else into the V-berth and latched the door. He then pulled Moreland's red lumber jacket on over his own T-shirt and found the captain's peaked hat sitting on the dash near the helm.

***

It was around half past four in the morning, when retired pilot Russell Grey awoke on his boat the next morning. The sun hadn't yet risen on the horizon. He wasted no time in getting ready for his fishing charter, which was scheduled for 6:00 a.m. Some movement on the *Whiskey Lee* at the other end of the dock caught his eye. The first thing he noticed was the familiar red lumber jacket and denim peaked hat, which Captain Moreland regularly wore. Grey waved a friendly hello to him.

***

While standing onboard the *Whiskey Lee*, Evans was momentarily frozen as someone at the docks noticed him and waved, thinking he was Moreland. He nervously glanced over to see who it was, trying not to make eye contact. He acknowledged the man with a short casual wave back and hoped he wouldn't come over and talk to him. *It worked*, Evans thought. *The guy thinks I'm James Moreland*. After the brief exchange, he turned his back to carry on with his duties. Evans couldn't waste anymore time. He had to get out of here fast before someone grew suspicious. While he was pondering what to do next, the *Whiskey Lee*'s V-berth, bulkheads, and buckets were already being filled with water through a hose, fed in through the front hatch. It would help the speed up the process when it was time to scuttle the vessel. He hoped the man hadn't noticed the vessel sitting too low in the water. The waterline sat unusually high on the trawler's deep V-hull. Evans went over and cut the ropes to the three inner tubes which rested alongside the dockside of the trawler. He re-tied them all to the dock. Only three orange teardrop fenders remained on the port side of the trawler. He decided to leave them there for now. Time was against him. He tied the old wooden lifeboat to the back of the vessel and got underway. Captain Moreland had now been dead for about an hour, and other fishermen would soon be arriving to the docks. It was a good thing the sea was calm, or the boat might not have cleared the marina with all that water inside the bulkheads.

***

Once at his destination, Evans unlatched the hatch to the V-berth. Satisfied that there was enough water down there, he took off the peaked hat he was wearing and threw it down on top of the floating lifejackets and body of Captain Moreland. The water was already trickling though the main cabin, reaching the helm and the galley. Out on deck, he removed the orange teardrop fenders which were dangling from the port side of the vessel. He slashed them all with a knife before cutting them loose and tossing them down into the V-berth. He closed the hatch and then made his way toward the vessel's stern, to the engine room. Above the bulkhead door was a note: *TO BE CLOSED AT SEA*. Evans smirked rebelliously, stepping through the door. It didn't take him long to disconnect the bilge pump and scuttle the vessel. On the way back out he left the door open.

Standing on the back deck, Evans glanced at the crimson-soaked hammer in his hand. It was the weapon with which he'd delivered the fateful blows. "I won't need this anymore." He threw it far out to sea. It landed with a splash, disappearing immediately as the ocean devoured it. He turned and noticed two lifesaving rings that he'd overlooked. Scanning around the outside of the vessel, he checked to make sure he hadn't forgotten anything else. Something yellow caught his eye; it was a rectangular box attached the outside wall of the cabin. He pulled the door open, and noticed there was an orange two-person life raft inside. He suspected it would likely be designed to inflate automatically when it hit the water or when it reached a certain depth. He couldn't risk that. Evans grabbed it, along with the two lifesaving rings before departing the *Whiskey Lee*.

Climbing into the safety of the wooden lifeboat, Evans paddled to a safe distance. He watched for about forty-five minutes while the *Whiskey Lee* sank. Finally, the tip of the bow disappeared beneath the waves. With satisfaction, he rowed back to shore, pausing briefly to see if anything from the vessel surfaced. Nothing came up. *Good*, he thought.

The only sounds he heard were rolling thunder off in the distance and the small waves lashing at the side of the lifeboat.

As daylight crept in, the sky didn't appear to be getting any lighter as dark gray clouds moved in over the area. The massive Skull Island, beside him, conveniently provided cover from any prying eyes from fisherman out on the sea, and the remote shoreline made sure that no one witnessed this horrific crime from shore. *The plan's going perfectly. Moreland went out fishing and never came back*, Evans thought.

Once reaching the safety of Hanlon's Cove, Evans quickly secured the lifeboat and then climbed the rocks, stashing the lifesaving rings, orange life raft, and the two oars deep into a crevice in the rock. He stuffed it with moss and loose pine branches. Evans then pulled out Moreland's wallet, grabbed the cash, and proceeded up an incline to softer ground. He took his shovel, dug a hole, and threw Moreland's wallet in, along with the red lumber jacket. A lighter fell out of one of the lumber jacket's pockets. Evans picked it up, admiring the polished silver Zippo. It had an inscription on it. Smiling, and acting against his better judgment, he dropped it into his pocket as a souvenir.

With sweat beading on his forehead, Evans walked down to the water's edge with the shovel. He placed it on the front seat of the lifeboat and then loaded the bottom of the lifeboat with as many rocks as he could lift. As he leaned over to distribute the rocks evenly throughout the lifeboat, he didn't notice the silver lighter drop out of his pocket. It made a small plop as it hit the water. Evans didn't hear it. He was too busy trying to rid himself of the lifeboat. The silver lighter had managed to wedge itself in a small groove between the rocks and the bench seat. After Evans was satisfied there was enough well-distributed weight in the boat, he guided the lifeboat out as far as he could, towing it by its rope. Turning it around, he made sure the bow faced the shore before coming to the deep rocky ledge drop-off just underneath the water. It prevented him from walking any. He looked out beyond the drop-off, into the deep area of the ocean. The water looked black. It was the perfect place to sink it.

Evans reached into the front of the boat to pick up the shovel. He threw it as hard as he could toward the deep water. In front of him lay a seemingly endless ocean. The wall that dropped off below his feet was about forty-five feet deep. One more step and he'd be swimming for sure. He turned the boat around in order to pull the plug out of the bottom and then steadily pushed the boat outward over the drop-off. Watching the weighted lifeboat fill with seawater, Evans felt it pulling away from him as it submerged. Down it went, and fast. He released the rope from his grasp just in time before he was pulled down with it. He watched the bow of the boat slip below the waves quickly. In its final moments the lifeboat sank in a fury of small bubbles.

As Evans stood there, he realized the seawater was getting cold around his waist. He shivered as a cool breeze swept across his back and neck. It was eerily quiet, except for the waves caressing the shoreline and the sound of birds in the forest.

A light rain had started. He could see multiple droplets starting to hit the surface of the water and knew he had to get going. He still had to climb his way up to higher ground, and then hike through the woods to find Coastal Route #1.

It was the only road back to Barney's Cove, and his return was the only thing he hadn't planned very well. Evans removed the toothpick from his mouth before attempting his ascent. At this point, nothing would ruin his day more than being stabbed in the back of the throat by his own toothpick.

He used vines and roots to steady himself while he climbed the embankment. The inclines in some parts were steep and challenging; now tree roots were becoming slick because of the rain. He lost his footing a few times but managed

The Whiskey Lee

to scramble back up. Blood streamed from his leg where he'd scraped it on a sharp rock.

About halfway up, he stopped to rest, and peered out over the edge of the rock, down to the sea below. He couldn't risk a fall at this elevation. It would be fatal. As he reached the top, he pulled himself up over the ledge. All he could see was the dark, dense forest in front of him. He tried to stay dry under the canopy of trees. He checked the cut on his leg and then did his best to clean it, but it was still bleeding.

Not wanting to waste any more time, he set out in search of the road. He could hear the sound of Mosquitoes buzzing around his ears. They were thick in the forest. He heard some movement off to his left, but he thought it was probably a squirrel. He kept moving and then heard more rustling noises off to his right. It sounded bigger than a squirrel. He was concerned and moved at a quicker pace, frequently scanning the forest. What emerged from the forest appeared to be a gray dog, about the size of a German shepherd—no, not a dog; it was a coyote. They were very common in these parts. The coyote stared curiously at Evans. Soon, there was another one, and then another. A pack of coyotes could be trouble. They appeared to be sizing him up for their next meal. Perhaps they had picked up the scent of fresh blood, or the cookies Evans had stolen from the *Whiskey Lee* before sinking it.

Panicking, Evans stumbled over a vine. While getting back on his feet, he picked up a tree branch. He held the branch over his head to appear taller. The coyotes kept their distance, but still seemed curious. To the right was a fallen tree. The tree was nestled in the fork of a large cedar. Evans scrambled up it and then climbed up into the cedar. He made sure that he was safely nestled on a tree branch, before glancing down at the predators, which were now lurking below him. *Coyotes usually aren't out during the day*, he thought, glancing up at the dark gray sky above the treetops. Blood was dripping from his leg. He was trapped here for a while.

As he sat there waiting for them to leave, he pulled out his pack of cigarettes to calm himself down. Sticking a cigarette in his mouth, he felt his shirt pocket for the stolen silver Zippo lighter which he'd pocketed earlier. It was gone. Fearing that he may have dropped it in the woods, Evans frantically felt all of his pockets for the Zippo. *The lighter's got my fingerprints on it*, he thought.

About twenty minutes later, the coyotes moved on. Evans stayed in the tree a little longer to make sure they'd left the area. He didn't have time to go back and look for the silver Zippo. Time was against him now. He felt a few droplets of rain land on his head and hands. Feeling assured the coyotes were gone, he climbed down from the tree to resume his trek to Coastal Route #1.

After reaching the road, Evans hiked west along the route for ten minutes before thumbing a ride. The accumulating rain was now seeping through his clothing. The lower part of his body was already soaked from wading waist deep in the ocean. Chills were already starting to set in. The first two vehicles passed by him. The third slowed to a stop.

"Why are you out here in the rain all by yourself?" The older driver asked, after pulling his white Lexus over to pick him up. The man was dressed well. He had gray hair and wore glasses.

"Hiking, but I walked too far and got lost," Evans replied.

"Without a backpack?" the older man queried.

"Lost it. I threw it at a coyote that was following me," said Evans.

"That must've been scary. Where are you headed now?"

"Barney's Cove. I left my car there," said Evans.

"You look cold. You can dry off at my cabin if you want to. It's not far from here. Take a shower, or whatever . . ." the man offered.

"No thanks," Evans replied sternly.

The man attempted to make small talk, but Evans tried his best to ignore him.

"You know, it gets kind of lonely out here," the driver hinted. "Sometimes a fella could use some company."

Unbelievable! Evans was taken aback.

The man rambled on that he "would like to have a companion," as he rubbed a hand on the inside of his own thigh. He muttered, "It may be fate how we just met on the road like this."

Avoiding the man's advances, Evans gazed out the window. He just wanted to sit back and have a smoke, but the man's behavior had him on edge. After a few more attempts at seducing him, the man finally got the message when Evans continued to ignore him. He laid his head back and pretended to fall asleep, but attentively left one eye open just in case a stray hand crept over to the passenger side. He shivered at the thought, while his cold, wet blue jeans continued to cling to his legs. Numbness was slowly creeping through his bones. The older man left him alone for the rest of the trip into town.

Wise choice, Evans thought.

38

PRESENT DAY – 2008

Agent Rogan was staring into the mirror when he heard his mobile phone ringing with the theme song of the old British television series, *The Saint*.

"Rogan," he answered, while trying to secure his tie knot in the center of his shirt with his free hand.

"Hi Tom, Flynn here."

"Hi Chief, I was just going to phone you."

"Do you have time to come by the station? I'd like to brief you on a few things," Flynn said.

"Absolutely. How about if I drop by at about half past two? Would that work?" Rogan replied.

"That's perfect. See you then."

***

"I'm glad you could make it on such short notice," said Flynn, "Come on in."

Rogan entered the office and took a seat.

"I have a few things that I'd like to discuss with you, too. But you can go first."

"Thank you," Flynn replied. "First of all, I think everyone has done a really tremendous job in solving this. If it weren't for Brandon's obstinacy I don't know if this investigation would be where is right now. Tom, I wanted to be the first to tell you that Brandon and Chad found the missing *Whiskey Lee* trawler this afternoon, along with some skeletal remains which could turn out to be our missing Captain James Moreland."

"Excellent! Where?"

The Whiskey Lee

"Northeast of Hanlon Cove, past the two small islands. It was resting in between Skull Island and the mainland." Flynn explained.

"That's quite a breakthrough!" Rogan was genuinely delighted at hearing this. "Brandon must be feeling pretty good right now."

"Yes, he is. It's quite the achievement for a civilian," Flynn replied. "But that's not all. I'm sure you heard about the stolen boat. Well, we found it this afternoon at Hanlon Cove."

"Did you catch the person responsible?"

"You mean persons. All three of them are dead. The boat hit something and sank."

"What did it hit?" Rogan asked.

"No clue," Flynn replied. "That's another mystery."

Rogan raised his eyebrows. "Wow. But, now I need to ask why it takes three men to steal a boat. It's too bad you couldn't have questioned at least one of them to find out what their motive was."

Flynn nodded. "I agree, but I can tell you one thing: I don't think one of them would have been able to talk."

Rogan listened attentively, tilting his head. "Why do you say that?"

Flynn continued, leaning his elbows on the desk. "It appears that he may have taken a bullet to the head before the boat crashed. One of my divers said he had a hole in his head which was proportional to a bullet hole."

"This keeps getting better," Rogan said with sarcasm. "How do the other bodies look?"

"We have two coroners working on the bodies now. Our main coroner will be examining the three guys that were found with the stolen boat, and Dr. Sandra Bailey just came on board. She'll be examining the skeletal remains we found on board the *Whiskey Lee* to confirm whether it's Moreland or not. Dr. Bailey's already mentioned to me that it appears that the skull looks like it had been bludgeoned. It could most likely be our cause of death. My divers uncovered a hammer not too far from the sunken *Lee*, but it's unconfirmed at this time if it's the murder weapon," he added. "That stuff's been down there an awful long time."

Agent Rogan nodded.

"That's not all," Flynn added. "There were some other bones near the site of the wrecked cabin cruiser. We found a skull too, which also had been down there a while."

"Do you think those bones could be our John Doe from the photograph?" Rogan asked.

"It could very well be, but I may have a name for our John Doe," Flynn replied, leaning forward to pick up two photographs from his desk and pass them to Rogan.

Rogan's eyes studied the unfamiliar face in the photographs.

"Dennis Cain," Flynn said, "Another missing person case that went cold. Did you come up with any new leads since our last meeting?"

"You'll be glad to know that I've submitted Brandon's photographs to our photo analysis team," Rogan informed him. "I believe your hunch was bang on about Senator Dalton, but I'm still going to wait until the techs confirm it before making my next move."

"Isn't that something?" Flynn shook his head still in disbelief. "I didn't profile him as the killer type."

"You'll be interested in this too: he was only also known as 'Cy' to his boys back then, so Brandon was correct with the two names. It's the same guy. 'Cyrus' is actually his full middle name. You'll be glad to know that Senator Aiden C. Dalton has been under full-time surveillance by my team since our last meeting, when you identified him in the photograph."

"Aiden C. Dalton. Aiden Cyrus Dalton a killer for god's sakes. Cy . . . Who knew?" Flynn repeated. "Wow," he said while still shaking his head. "His ship is sinking fast."

"It's ironic that you used that phrase, but I'd say it sank the day he killed Dennis Cain," said Rogan. "If that's all for now, I really should get back to the office—tons of paperwork to fill out."

"Okay, I understand, and I really appreciate you coming in. As soon as your team has the follow-up on the photo analysis, please update me." Flynn stood to shake Agent Rogan's hand.

"You got it. We'll be in touch. And you let me know as soon as you have a positive identification on those bodies," Rogan said, leaving the office.

***

The Whiskey Lee

The next day, Rogan couldn't wait to share the good news with Chief Flynn over the phone.

"I'm happy to say that my request for a search warrant went through," Rogan proudly announced.

"What did you find over there?" Flynn asked.

"I'll let you know in about five minutes. I'm across the street right now ordering myself a cup o' joe. Would you like one?"

"Sure, that would be nice. Two cream, one sugar," Flynn replied before hanging up.

Five minutes later, Rogan walked in with two coffees. He placed Flynn's cup down on the desk before seating himself in a chair.

"Thanks, what do I owe you?" Flynn asked.

"Nothing, it's on me."

Flynn took a sip of the steamy coffee. "Ah, I needed that. So, what did you find out at the warehouse?"

"Only that we've just successfully put a stop to the biggest smuggling operation since the drug bust in Miami. A search was carried out by my team at Scully's earlier today."

"What kind of smuggling op?"

"You name it. The list keeps growing. Guns, contraband, illegally acquired artifacts, and precious metals from shipwrecks."

"Jeez . . . but somehow that doesn't surprise me." Flynn took another sip of coffee. "Did you find out what was in the oil drums?"

"Yes, I did. As a matter of fact, the hazmat team found toxic waste, gun parts, and spent ammo," said Rogan.

Flynn folded his arms. "Happening right under our noses."

"The oil drums are the reason we were able to acquire a search warrant so fast. We found several empty 55-gallon oil drums sitting out the back of Scully's that matched perfectly with those we found at the bottom of Hanlon Cove. We've already concluded a complete search of the salvage ships *Viper* and *Osprey*. Guess what? We found more of the same oil drums onboard those vessels too," Rogan informed him.

"What about the *Chameleon*? You should probably search that one too," Flynn suggested.

"Yes, my guys are on it as we speak. We already went through the warehouse and their second-level mezzanine offices as well. Guess what else we found?"

"Please tell me you found the original photographs of the shooting," said Flynn, crossing his fingers.

"Yes, all of them—every shred of evidence we need to put that dirtbag Dalton away."

"Yes! Thank you." Flynn smiled, clenching both his fists in victory. "I still don't know why it took me so long to identify Dalton in that photograph. I guess it was his age, the angle the photograph was taken, and that beard. That's what really threw me off: the beard. He always was sharply dressed though, very much like you, Tom."

"Thank you." Agent Rogan seemed to appreciate the compliment.

Flynn's face turned to concern. "So, do you think the charges are going to stick against the senator?"

"I'm confident that Ace, the guy we picked up in Hog's Head National Park, will spill the beans now that we have Dalton to barter with. We know that he can identify him, and I'll bet you six to one he can place him at the scene aboard the *Betsea*, shooting young Dennis Cain in cold blood. I'm counting on our detainee to be the key witness against Dalton," Rogan explained. "He'll do it for a lesser charge, I'm sure."

"Good, I need this to be an open and shut case. Nothing makes me more exasperated than our hard work falling through the cracks of the justice system. Seeing them walk away would open a pit in the bottom of my stomach," Flynn said truthfully. "I'm getting a little long in the tooth for this kind of stuff now. There's way too much doom and gloom. Two more years and I'll be retiring. I just wanted to see this case solved before I walk out that door."

"Don't worry, Ace is going to break really soon. I can just feel it," Rogan assured him. "Everything will be okay."

***

After Rogan placed Aiden C. Dalton under arrest, he returned for another meeting with Chief Flynn.

"The remains found at Hanlon Cove were positively identified as Dennis Cain. He was the victim in the photograph who was shot to death onboard the *Betsea*. The other remains that Brandon and Chad found north of there, with the sunken *Lee*, were positively identified as Captain James Karl Moreland," Flynn explained to Rogan.

"Wow!" Rogan blinked a few times, shaking his head. "Those poor guys didn't deserve that."

"I know. Dennis Cain didn't even see his twenty-fifth birthday. I talked to Dennis's mother personally. She never gave up hope—said he'd left home when he was nineteen years old. They lived in the country, but Dennis always had this obsession with the sea. He worked on a farm until he saved up enough money to travel. After that, he headed for the east coast and started working as a deckhand. It was normal for him not to contact her for three or four months at a time, but when Mrs. Cain hadn't heard from him for a while, she became concerned and tried to find out why.

Someone from the *Betsea* informed her that her son had simply walked out one day . . . quit, 'probably got some work on a different ship,' they said. Mrs. Cain wasn't provided with a forwarding ship name. They said they didn't know where he went and that it was common for guys to just quit and move on. Apparently the first mate did the same thing the summer before that. Someone that I talked to had said one day he was working there, the next day gone . . . quit."

"That's strange. Did you follow that up?" Rogan asked.

"I did go and speak to his landlord at the time. The woman said she remembered him. She said he was a good tenant. He had always paid his rent on time and was never any trouble. One day he returned to his rented room to pack up his things without notice. She'd seen the look on his face. He looked scared. When she asked why he was leaving, he told her that his mom had fallen ill and he had to go home right away. At the time I didn't think there was any reason to follow it up any further. The story checked out. It made sense," Flynn explained.

"Maybe something else scared him," Rogan added.

"That's what I'm thinking now too," said Flynn. "He could've been our mystery photographer who took the shots up on the *Betsea*'s bridge."

Rogan nodded. "It makes sense to me that he'd hightail it after he saw Dennis Cain get murdered," Rogan agreed.

"We won't know until we've questioned him. He could be anywhere by now, and could be our only eye witness," said Flynn.

"My money is on Ace. I'm thinking he may have witnessed it too. He's in the right age group. Would have been in his twenty's back then." Rogan took a sip of coffee. "I'm really counting on Ace's testimony. He'll be promised a lesser sentence if he cooperates, guaranteed."

"Hopefully he doesn't get off too lightly. The charges pending in the attempts on Brandon's life are also on the table," Flynn said.

"Let's hope none of them get off lightly, Rogan replied. "I'm sure the deckhand's family would still like to see some justice for their son."

"You know what? Mrs. Cain said she always kept a framed photograph of Dennis on her mantle. She had it with her when she came to talk to me back then. That's how I got my copy of the photograph."

He picked up the photograph of Dennis, studying it. He then picked up the other photo, of Senator Dalton aiming the gun toward Dennis. Holding the photos side by side, he looked back and forth.

He sighed. "You know, I should have recognized both of them a lot sooner." Flynn placed the photographs back down on the desk.

Rogan exhaled solemnly. "It was a long time ago. Now, at least Mrs. Cain will have some closure. How old would she be now?"

"Late sixties."

"Her husband?" Rogan asked.

"Died of a heart attack five years ago."

"That's rough," said Rogan, shaking his head.

Rogan studied the photographs of a much younger Aiden Cyrus Dalton. It was proof that he had shot and killed Dennis Cain in cold blood. Having this evidence also determined the motive for the brutal slaying of Captain James Karl Moreland.

The most credible witness, of course, would be the person who'd bravely shot the half roll of incriminating evidence of Aiden C. Dalton on 35 mm film from the bridge of the *Betsea*. Rogan hoped the photographer was still alive. There were so many questions that Rogan's superiors would be asking. He hated not having the answers. The media was already crawling at this one.

After an intensive search, Agent Rogan was finally able to track down the first mate, identified as Antonio Martinez. He was relieved to find out Antonio was still living in Maine, in Lewiston. Rogan liked the idea that he could drive there and back in one day. It's not only the most central city of Maine; it's the second largest in the state, and known for its lower cost of living. When he pulled his car up in front of the single detached house, the first thing he noticed was a group of kids playing basketball in a driveway across the street. It seemed like a half-decent community. As he climbed the steps to Antonio Martinez's front porch, he noticed the faded gray wood was in desperate need of a new coat of paint. A few of the old boards needed replacing too. Old rusty deck chairs decorated the porch. He rang the doorbell once. He could hear a dog barking, and then saw the curtain being drawn to the side at the window. A man with glasses, mustache, and a graying, receding hairline peered cautiously through the glass. He looked surprised when Rogan showed him his badge. "Mr. Antonio Martinez? I'm a federal agent. I just want to ask you a few questions," Rogan announced.

A man's voice was heard, firmly telling the dog to go lay down, and then the door opened slowly. "Sorry about that, the dog goes crazy anytime a stranger comes to the door." He looked around warily. "What's this all about?"

"I just want to ask you a few questions about something we've been investigating. Don't worry, it's not about anyone in your family. We're just looking for witnesses. Is it okay if I come in?" Antonio hesitated for a moment, before motioning for Rogan to enter.

A short time later, they sat in the den, chatting, while Antonio's wife and teenaged son allowed them some privacy. The room smelled like smoke, and a full ashtray overflowed onto the desk, beside an oscillating fan and a half bottle of rum.

When Rogan mentioned that he was working with Chief Flynn and that they had photo evidence of a crime which took place aboard the *Betsea* in 1989, Antonio was reluctant to talk at first. He started to squirm uncomfortably in his chair. His eyes darted around, and he fidgeted with his fingers before deciding to reveal everything. His facial expression conveyed a look of worry. Rogan knew that he'd hit a nerve.

"I knew someone would come for me one day. I just hoped it wouldn't be Cy," Antonio said nervously. "I've had a bit of a drinking problem since I witnessed the deckhand get killed. I don't sleep much either. One eye's always open," he admitted. "I was the one who took the photographs from the *Betsea*'s bridge."

When Rogan informed him that Cy became a senator, Antonio's eyes widened with surprise. After chatting for a while, he agreed to testify against Senator

Dalton. "I hope you know I just wanted to protect my family. Those guys really put the fear in me. I've moved three times because I was terrified that they'd come after me and my family," Antonio explained. "My wife and son still don't know anything about it. I guess it's time I fessed up and told them," he sighed.

After gathering enough information, Agent Rogan thanked Antonio before stepping out onto the front porch.

"Don't worry, we'll provide protection for you and your family. We should have all Dalton's men rounded up soon," Rogan assured him, before turning and walking down the porch steps.

The following day, a written statement was obtained from Ace which confirmed that Aiden Dalton had shot and killed Dennis Cain. Both Ace's and Antonio's testimony, along with the photo evidence would help ensure that Aiden Cyrus Dalton was going away for a long time.

***

"*THIS IS ABSOLUTELY LUDICROUS!*" Dalton yelled angrily, as Agent Rogan laid out the list of charges and read him his rights. The senator was carefully placed into the back of a waiting cruiser. He could still be heard shouting from inside the car after the door was closed. "I'll see you in court! You can all kiss your badges goodbye!"

Rogan ignored the feeble threats. He turned to the other agent on his team. "He's never getting out."

"I'll sue all of you!" the senator continued yelling through the open crack in the window of the cruiser.

39

Brandon couldn't wait to phone Gloria and relay the news.

"If you have time, I'd like to update you on the latest in my *Whiskey Lee* investigation. We found it!" Brandon exclaimed, unable to hold back his excitement.

"Wow! That's amazing news. Where?"

"About 150 feet down, just north of Hanlon Cove, between Skull Island and the mainland," Brandon replied.

"Okay, I need to hear the details in person. Come by the Piper & Pelican. You're allowed in here now," Gloria announced delightedly.

"What gives? I thought I was banned from there. What about Red and Mack?" Brandon asked.

"They aren't here anymore," Gloria said. "I'll let you know more when you get here."

"Hmm, okay, I'll be over in about ten minutes," said Brandon, hanging up. "That's weird." He felt perplexed.

"What's up?" Rosie asked.

"Gloria said we can go into the Piper & Pelican now. Red and Mack are gone," said Brandon.

"Gone where?" Rosie asked curiously.

"I dunno," Brandon shrugged. "Gloria said she'd fill me in when I get there."

***

Gloria had a newly hired bartender cover for her while she invited Brandon and Rosie to join her at a booth in the corner. In the daytime it was easier to see the soft brown faded leather which covered the bench seats. Showing many years of use and abuse, it looked worn, cracked and frayed. There was an overly used section in the middle that dipped low. Brandon could also feel how loose the back of the seat was when he leaned against it. Rosie sat down beside him.

"Okay, give me the dirt." Gloria couldn't hold back her eagerness as she sat down on the bench seat opposite them.

Brandon lifted his hand up. "Hold that thought for a minute. What happened to Mack? Why am I allowed back in here now?" he asked.

"Well, this police investigation has opened up a new can of worms, let me tell you. Mack was fired," said Gloria.

Brandon opened his mouth and raised his eyebrows. "Why?"

"When the police started asking questions, our owner, Frank, was also questioned. That's when he decided to make a special 'surprise' trip out here to see what Mack's been up to. It didn't take him long to learn that Mack had been dipping his hand into the company's profits. The owner's still here trying to sort things out."

"Wait, I thought *Mack* was the owner," said Brandon.

"No, actually Mack was the manager. Frank owns this place, as well as five other taverns along the coast. Anyway, to make a long story short, he chose *me* of all people to run this tavern. Once I'm trained as a manager, things are going to change around here."

"A change for the better for sure. I'm really happy for you, Gloria."

Brandon's compliment drew a huge smile from her; she was glowing.

"Congratulations, Gloria! I'm chuffed to bits for you. If anyone deserves to get promoted, it's you." Rosie said.

"Thank you both so much," Gloria replied, still beaming. "I don't think it would have been possible if it weren't for the help of you two crazy sleuths. I'm supposed to start my management training tomorrow."

Brandon looked around the bar. "Where's Frank now? We don't want to get you in trouble before your big promotion."

Gloria laughed. "It's okay. Frank's a pretty laid-back guy. He encourages friendly customer interaction. It's important to make people feel comfortable, so they'll come back."

"He sounds like the complete opposite of Mack," said Brandon.

The Whiskey Lee

"It's going to take some work and changes to get some customers to come back in here, but I'm confident they will. The first thing I'm going to start with is that old tattered awning out front, which Mack should have replaced years ago. That's the first thing that Frank noticed when he arrived. Most of the money for the upkeep of this place went straight into Mack's pocket. No wonder he was driving such a nice truck. Looks like I'm going to have to get that old sign on the roof spruced up and repainted too." She paused. "*Now*, I want some details, Brandon 'Lucky' Summers. Don't keep me in suspense or I'll have to throw you out of here again." She turned her head and winked at Rosie, smiling.

Brandon smiled. "I'm just wondering where to start. Well, first off, Chad and I found the missing *Whiskey Lee* and the skeletal remains believed to be Captain James Karl Moreland."

Brandon then explained the stolen boat and the appearance of the *Whiskey Lee*'s ghost ship, which led them to discovering the wreck and the skeletal remains.

"Wowzer . . ." Gloria shook her head slowly as she absorbed the news.

"It was the ghost of Captain Moreland who was helping us through this all along. He deserves most of the credit for solving his own mystery," Brandon added.

He also told her about Agent Rogan. "I didn't know Tom Rogan then, but he mentioned that he was in your juke joint—uh, respectable establishment—when this stranger, who looked to be in his mid-to-late forties, walked up to the bar and stole your phone. He thought it was oddly bold for someone to do that right out in the open. He guessed the thief didn't think anyone was watching, but Rogan was sitting at the bar right over there." Brandon pointed with his thumb.

Gloria listened eagerly.

"Anyway," Brandon continued, "Rogan followed the thief up to the lighthouse that night; I already explained some of this to you the night it happened. There were actually two guys in the cargo van. I wasn't planning on going anywhere that night. I'd planned to stay in, but I received a text, which I thought came from you, wanting to meet me at the lighthouse. Of course, I went without hesitation. That's when one of the assholes ambushed me at the cliff. No doubt in my mind that he was from Scully's, because I remember he said made a reference to the shipyards." Brandon paused as he recollected, ". . . He said, 'I should have let Mugs shoot you back there at the shipyards,' or something like that."

"Wait! You didn't tell me that before." Gloria replied.

"No, we didn't have much time to talk, and my head still hurt then. A lot was going on that day."

"That Mugs guy sounds like it could be Red's friend, Sammy. I think his nickname is Mugs!" she shrieked. "Did you see him? What did he look like?"

"I didn't really get a good look at him, but this guy was about five feet, eight inches; and had a shaved head, medium build, and wore jeans that were too tight. Yes, I guess Mugs could be a nickname," Brandon said.

"Yes, I'm pretty sure that's him! Sammy's last name is Mugford. The nickname 'Mugs' makes sense. He's got a scar above his left eye which splits his eyebrow in two."

"Yep, that's the guy," Brandon agreed.

"Oh my god! I hope the police picked him up. I don't want him coming in here anymore," she said with a look of genuine fear.

"Yeah, I wouldn't want to run into him now either. By the way, where's Red?" Brandon looked nervously around the juke joint. "You said he's gone."

Gloria explained that Red had been arrested by the police.

Brandon was pleasantly surprised. "That's interesting."

"Yes, the cops stormed in here and paraded him out in front of all my customers yesterday," said Gloria.

"And we didn't get to see it. What a shame," Rosie said half-heartedly.

"He was so embarrassed. His face was completely red. Randy Ballentine is his real name. What do you think they picked him up for? Do you think he had something to do with the *Whiskey Lee*?"

"I'm thinking he may have been too young to be directly involved with that, but he may be involved with the same group of criminals. I need to inform Chief Flynn that we suspect Sammy is the one who drove the white cargo van down from the cliff, and that *he's* the one who'd pursued me, almost forcing me off the road. I'm sure this will be valuable information to the case," said Brandon.

"Yes, of course," Gloria said, still in disbelief. "This is so unbelievable. I feel like I'm in a movie. Someone pinch me; I need to wake up." She frowned. "I might have known Sammy and Red had something to do with this. Those creeps! They were always giving my Benny a hard time when he was in . . ." Something changed in Gloria's face. This time her face showed horror and shock. She gasped, putting her hand up to her mouth. "Brandon, do you think Sammy forced Ben off the road the night his vehicle plunged over the cliff?"

"I wouldn't put it past him or Red to do something like that," said Brandon. "Sammy tried to do the same thing to me. This is all starting to add up now—the way Red reacted whenever I mentioned the *Whiskey Lee*."

"So, now what do we do? Do you think there are more of them out there? Are we still in danger?" Gloria wondered.

"I don't have all the names yet, but you may be surprised who's involved."

"It sounds like you know already," Gloria guessed.

"I'm only going on a hunch, but I can't tell you what that is right now. Just watch the news."

"Oh, snap! Where are my manners? I completely forgot to ask if you two would like something to drink," Gloria offered. "Sorry, I should have offered as soon as you walked in here. I work in a tavern, for god's sake," she added. "It's on the house. My head isn't here today."

"It's okay, we totally understand," said Rosie." That's really kind of you, Gloria. Do you happen to have any coffee ready?"

"Yes, I just made a fresh pot. Comin' right up," Gloria said, jumping up from the table. "Do you take cream and sugar?"

"Yes please. One of each," said Rosie.

"I'll have a—"

"Amber ale?" Gloria asked.

"You got it." Brandon grinned. "Before I forget, could you give this back to Sasha for me?" He handed her a plastic bag.

Gloria looked confused.

"It's the Berretta."

She nodded. "Oh, right. I forgot about that. Did you remove the bullets?"

"Yes, of course," he said.

"Good, thanks. I'll put this in my locker. Be right back." Gloria strode toward the kitchen.

She returned a short time later with their drinks and a cup of tea for herself.

"You know what? Now that I've had time to think about it, I'm almost certain that Red and Sammy had something to do with Benny's death," Gloria said.

"The only thing is, we need to prove their guilt, unless the police have already found something that implicates them," said Brandon, ". . . which leads me to believe that's the reason why they took Red away. Maybe the police arrested Sammy too."

Gloria shook her head slowly. "Red was the link to this all along. He knew Benny was helping me investigate the disappearance of Captain Moreland and the death of Ann Marie. He intimidated the hell out of me." Gloria shivered. "Ugh, that guy really gives me the creeps."

"I didn't like him as soon as I felt him breathing down my neck," said Brandon.

"I'm glad you stood up to him. He deserved that punch in the nose."

"It was an adventure that I'll never forget," said Brandon, peering at Rosie.

"I'll say it was," Rosie agreed, as she made eye contact with him.

Gloria stopped stirring her tea, removed the tea bag with the spoon and then dropped it on the saucer. "Why didn't I see it? I'm thinking about the night those guys ambushed you at the lighthouse. Sammy must have told that other man to linger in here just long enough to grab my phone. I never saw him before and don't even think he ordered a drink from me that night. I would have remembered him. Sammy had probably watched my routine enough times to know where I leave my phone."

"Yeah, that makes sense. I have something else I'd like to share with you too, Gloria," Brandon said.

She stared curiously at him.

"It's my belief that the man who fell over the cliff is the same guy that killed your aunt," said Brandon.

"How do you know that? Did he say something to you?"

"It was as close to a confession as I was going to get out of him. The guy tried to do the same to me: held a gun on me while ordering me to jump. I kept thinking of ways to stall him, hoping that he wasn't going to shoot me down in cold blood. I reckon in 1989 William was in the wrong place at the right time and may have gotten himself killed because he saw what happened to your aunt, maybe even tried to help her."

Gloria nodded sadly. "I think you may have nailed it. Well, I really hope that my aunt, James, and William can all rest in peace now. I know this town is going to be a lot safer. You have no idea how grateful I am—we are," Gloria corrected herself. "*Now,* that horrible man is dead and we have some closure. It would be nice to carry on with our lives normally, without living in fear of these criminals."

"I'm glad I could help," said Brandon.

Before Brandon and Rosie left the tavern, Gloria gave them each a big hug. "Next summer, in honor of my Aunt Ann Marie, Benny, William, and James Moreland, I'm going to hold a special twenty-year commemoration for all the victims. I hope you two can make it."

"We'll try our best. Let's keep in contact," said Rosie.

They exchanged email addresses before parting ways.

40

A bronze statue stood prominently at the entrance of the park. *The Seafarer* was standing at what appeared to be a ship's helm, grasping onto the wheel with both hands. He was clad in a raincoat and a traditional sailor's rain hat, known simply as a sou'wester.

At the foot of the statue was a plaque with a dedication to all the sailors lost at sea. Rosie and Brandon blended in like typical tourists as they strolled up to it.

"Wow," Rosie said with a poignant tone. "This is a really nice memorial. Thanks for showing this to me."

She snapped a couple photos with her camera.

Brandon pulled a silver pen out of his shirt pocket, and then proceeded to use it to jot something down on a small pad of paper:

> *Hi Agent Rogan, I don't think I'll need this pen anymore. We'll be at the lighthouse if you're looking for us.*

"What are you doing?" Rosie asked curiously.

"This pen is bothering me. I just want to try something."

Afterwards, he tore the top piece of paper off the pad and carefully taped the note to the pen. He took the bundle and placed it into a small crevice at the side of the statue, where it wouldn't be found accidentally by a passerby.

They took a self-timed photograph of the two of them in front of the monument and then one with the Senate building behind them.

***

As they neared the door of the lighthouse, Brandon cautiously checked the area to see if anyone was around before using the bolt cutters to cut the lock. He picked up the pieces and then pulled an identical new lock from his pocket. "I'll replace it with this lock after we come out."

"Oh, you are the best!" Rosie gave him an extra-tight hug.

"I'd like to take a look at the electrical shed afterwards too," said Brandon, pocketing the destroyed lock.

He heaved open the heavy door. The rusty hinges groaned and whined as the inside became exposed to the light. When he shone the flashlight around inside, the spiders ran for darkness. Their shadows looked huge on the walls, as they moved across their webs.

"Ladies first." He gestured to Rosie, while holding the door open.

Rosie smiled as she stepped inside to look around. "Aren't you coming in?"

"No, I've already seen it from the inside. I'm just going to wait out here just in case this door decides to slam closed again. That was a little unnerving."

"Pass me the torch," she asked, reaching her hand back.

"We call it a *flashlight* over here." He handed it to her.

After not hearing anything from Rosie for a few minutes, Brandon called out to her. "Everything okay in there?"

"Yes, everything's fine. I haven't seen any ghosts yet."

Brandon turned to see Agent Tom Rogan walking up the hill toward him. "Um, you should probably come back out, Rosie. It looks like we're busted. Agent Rogan just showed up. I guess the pen was a tracker after all."

"Okay, be right down," she said, her voice sounding hollow as it echoed down through the winding staircase.

Rosie stepped outside just as Rogan arrived.

"I might have known you two wouldn't be viewing the lighthouse like the rest of the tourists," said Agent Rogan.

"I see you found my pen," Brandon pointed, noticing the pen's silver clip sticking out of the agent's shirt pocket. A delinquent, yet triumphant smile spread across Brandon's face.

"Yes, that's half an hour out of my life that I'll never get back. Why do you send me on these wild goose chases? Do you not think I'm busy enough?" Rogan's eyes were covered by his mirrored sunglasses. Brandon and Rosie's own reflections stared back at them.

"At least I didn't toss it in a dumpster this time," Brandon reminded him.

"How'd you know the pen was a tracker, anyway?" Rogan asked, as he brushed by Brandon to take a peek inside the lighthouse.

"I didn't really pick up on it until later," said Brandon. "I suppose I was too busy running for my life to notice the obvious. It was right there the entire time. Always with us and you knew exactly where to find us."

"Yeah, but if I hadn't planted it on you, I couldn't have saved your ass out at Hog's Head," said Rogan.

"That's true," Brandon admitted. "Thanks for that."

Rosie appeared from inside the lighthouse. "It's kind of spooky in there," she said.

"Did you find anything extraordinary Rosie? Any ghosts?" Agent Rogan kidded.

"Nope, mostly I just cleaned up some of the cobwebs with my face," Rosie replied.

Brandon chuckled. He turned to Rogan, "I'm curious, how did your commandos get to Hog's Head National Park so fast?"

Rogan moved away from the lighthouse door so Brandon could close it. "I just have to say you're one lucky man." He explained why.

***

Before the incident at Hog's Head National Park Agent Rory had been working on an operation trying to infiltrate a suspected criminal organization connected with Scully's. He was one of the two men airlifted by the helicopter inside Hog's Head National Park. His orders were simple: follow Rosie from her motel and she would lead them to Brandon. At first, they hadn't known about her, but then suspected they were connected after Rosie's knee-to-Red's-groin incident. They just needed to find out who she was and where she was staying. Rory and Ace parked across the street, patiently waiting for Rosie to emerge. When they saw the white SUV pull into the side of her motel parking lot, Ace wasn't even paying attention to it until he saw Rosie step out of the vehicle. "That's her." He straightened in his seat.

A few minutes later, Brandon emerged from the SUV. "That's our target," Ace said. "Brandon must have switched vehicles." The silver sedan waited patiently before easing out into traffic to tail Brandon and Rosie, taking all evasive precautions necessary not to be noticed.

After the silver sedan pulled out, Rogan followed from a distance in his vehicle. He wasn't sure what was going on, but he knew something was about to go down, so he decided to stay within a couple of car lengths of Brandon's SUV. He was careful not to fall too far behind and risk losing them.

***

Agent Rogan paused his story, turning his attention to Brandon.

"You changed vehicles on us, Brandon. It threw everyone for a loop that day," Rogan stated.

"Didn't the pen tracker show you where I was?"

"Yes, but I was focused on following the silver sedan. I needed to stay close, but also had to maintain my distance. If the driver made us, you could have been in serious danger. We actually didn't know who the target was until we saw the sedan follow your vehicle from the motel."

"Wow. I noticed that silver sedan a couple of times too," said Brandon, shaking his head. "I guess my guard was down. I didn't think anyone would know my new ride," said Brandon. "Lucky me to be so popular."

"I guess they didn't plan on you taking them on a road trip that day," said Rogan.

"I shouldn't have underestimated them. I didn't think they knew about Rosie," said Brandon.

"It was only a matter of time before they put two and two together. I must say that we had a really tough time following you once you set foot inside the national park. Time was stacked against us. I had to think of something quick. The terrain was too rough for us to move in, so I decided to pull a chopper team off a nearby military base."

"Tell me about it. We scraped ourselves up pretty good out there on that rough terrain, mostly *because* of that chopper. I didn't know if they were friend or foe," said Brandon.

"Sorry, there wasn't any time for me to candy coat it for you. The driver of the sedan had already devised a plan to terminate you in a remote area. You voluntarily led him to one."

It was then that the gangster name Gloria had chosen for him entered his head: *Brandon 'Lucky' Summers. Yes, that was it.*

Brandon glanced affectionately at Rosie, before turning his attention back to the agent.

"Just so we're both clear on this, I want you to know that neither of the guys on the hike with us was the guy shooting at me near Arthur and Claire's place, *or* at the motel. I would have recognized them right away," Brandon said.

"Duly noted." Rogan pulled a couple of photos out of his pocket. "Was it any of these guys?"

Brandon studied the photos of what appeared to be three deceased men.

"Jeez, they look like they were sent to the hurt locker. This guy—right here!" He pointed to the photograph of Evans. "His head's a little caved, and he's missing the toothpick hanging out of his mouth, but I'd recognize that face anywhere. That's definitely the guy."

"Was he also the man that was shooting at us outside my motel room? In the gray 4x4 truck?" Rosie asked.

"Yes," said Brandon.

"Are you one hundred percent sure that *this* is the man?" Rogan asked.

"Positive," Brandon replied, while looking at another photo. "This guy too." He pointed to Sammy's photograph. "He's the one who chased me down from the cliff in the white GMC cargo van. Sammy Mugford is his name, I believe. They call him Mugs for short. You can verify that though."

"Okay great, That's solid information. I'm glad we wrapped that up. You don't need to worry about these guys anymore," Rogan assured him.

Brandon nodded. "Understood."

"Just curious, Agent Rogan, what happened to them?"

"Karma. They shouldn't have stolen the boat."

"Well, thanks for filling in the blanks and also for protecting us," said Brandon appreciatively.

"You don't need to thank me," Rogan peered over the top of his sunglasses at Brandon and Rosie. "That's just what I do." He pushed the sunglasses back up. "Any time, and thanks for all the information you've provided, Brandon. Maybe you should be working for us," Rogan suggested.

Brandon smiled. "I'm just curious, what about the names I gave you?" Brandon asked.

"Let's just say you were bang on. I still don't know how you knew that, but thanks. It'll be easier to tie him into the rest of it now."

"Him? Didn't I give you *two* names?" Brandon asked.

"Same guy," Rogan revealed.

"Amazing!" Brandon exclaimed.

"You've been a major asset in this investigation and that's the only reason why I'm filling in some of the blanks for you. Thanks to you, we now have motive, and the last missing link that we needed to bring our case to a close. The rest of it was just an added bonus," Rogan said sincerely.

"My pleasure," said Brandon.

"This will be all over the news soon enough. I'll be consulting closely with Chief Flynn. I'm pretty sure there won't be any more threats to you and Rosie. My team is rounding up the rest of the suspects as we speak. Also, you won't be held responsible for the incident which led to the guy falling over the cliff. He was identified as a good-for-nothing named Nash, also a member of Aiden Dalton's dirty organization. We believe that he was directly responsible for the deaths of both Ann Marie and William. I thought you'd like to know that."

"Thanks. Uh . . . What's going to happen now, I mean with me?" Brandon asked.

"Nothing. It was a clear-cut case of self defense. I witnessed the entire incident. It was an unfortunate and unpreventable 'accident' that the suspect fell over the cliff before I could apprehend or question him," Rogan said, producing a small grin. "There's a slight chance you may have to go to court to testify, but I'll do my best to see that you don't have to. We'll talk about that later."

Brandon gave him his business card. "Call me if you need me for anything."

The agent reached for it and then shook hands with both Rosie and Brandon.

"Our highly trained team couldn't crack this case as fast as you did. If we need you for any more questioning, I'll definitely contact you," said Rogan.

"Sure, anytime."

Rogan turned and walked to down the grassy hill to his car.

Brandon looked at Rosie. "There's one more thing I need to do."

Brandon reached into his pocket for something.

"Aren't you supposed to get down on one knee first?" Rosie joked.

"Ha, ha, you are too funny." Brandon removed a shiny new padlock from his pocket and latched it on the lighthouse door. "*Now*, I'd like to check that electrical shed behind the lighthouse. Are you coming with me?"

"Of course, that's a silly question," said Rosie, smiling. Brandon held out his hand for her to take.

They walked hand in hand the short distance to the electrical shed. Brandon cut the lock off the hasp and opened the door. As he glanced inside, he noticed that the electrical panel had been completely gutted. The ends of the wires were just hanging, attached to nothing. It looked like there hadn't been any live current traveling through them for years. The panel was full of spiders, cobwebs, dust, and dirt.

Brandon didn't understand why there was even a lock on the door. When he closed the door, he heard a hum as something powered up. He noticed a glowing light from the corner of his eye. The interior lights were on in the top of the lighthouse and the bright spotlight gleamed proudly out across the bay, as it usually did. *As it usually did? Without an electrical source powering it?*

He'd seen the beam of light many times before, but hadn't really thought about it. He'd even dreamed about that beam of light, but it seemed different now. It was the same light, but different, because now he knew something he hadn't known before. Now, he knew the dark secret. The lights were operating all by themselves. A chill went up Brandon's spine and the hairs on the back of his neck rose up.

It was at that same moment that Brandon saw two images materializing approximately twenty feet from them. The images were that of a man and a woman. Brandon recognized the man as Captain James Moreland. He was wearing the same peaked denim cap, but instead of the navy blue wool sweater, he now wore a red lumber jacket. Brandon remembered he'd been wearing it in many of the photos they'd seen in the cedar chest at Audrey Montgomery's house. Moreland was accompanied by a young woman who appeared to be carrying a small bundle in her arms. There was no doubt in Brandon's mind that this was Ann Marie and their baby, which she lovingly cradled in her arms. He'd remembered her image from the photographs too. He touched Rosie's arm to get her attention. "Look," Brandon whispered, without taking his eyes off the unexpected manifestation in front of him.

"I see them," she whispered back. The two apparitions glided near the heavy lighthouse door. At each step, they seemed to be fading.

The couple appeared to be floating as they simultaneously turned their heads in Brandon and Rosie's direction. Each of them producing a weak but noticeable smile, as if to say thank you.

As they passed by the heavy door, another bizarre occurrence happened. The ghostly couple and their baby were joined by yet another apparition, which floated out beyond the locked door. It appeared as though the lighthouse exhaled him. Brandon recognized this one as William. He looked the same as he did in Chief Flynn's framed photograph. The four apparitions continued to drift toward the edge of the cliff. Before reaching their destination, the three adult apparitions turned to face Brandon and Rosie. Each of them smiled and waved before they each disappeared over the cliff.

Brandon and Rosie bolted over to where they last saw them. "Wow. They just went over the cliff!" Brandon yelled, stopping near the edge to peer down.

"I'm guessing you believe in ghosts now?" Rosie said, staring downward.

"Oh yeah," Brandon whispered, as his eyes focused on the waves pounding against the rocks below.

"Captain Moreland, Ann Marie, and their baby will be crossing over together now. Their souls have finally found peace and closure," Rosie explained.

Brandon nodded solemnly. "William too. Let's step back from the edge now, or we'll be joining them. I've already had my brush with death on this cliff. I'm afraid I'm all out of lives. Agent Rogan won't be here to save me again."

"How many lives do you have left now?" Rosie asked, stepping back from the edge.

"I don't know—lost track. I'd rather not keep tempting fate."

"I'll keep you safe, if you keep me safe," said Rosie, smiling.

"Deal," said Brandon, reaching out for her hand. They walked away together, only to pause briefly at the foot of the tall red and white structure before making their way to the parking lot.

Brandon knew the power would never be restored to the old lighthouse. The days of lighthouses were over. Modern day electronics, such as GPS, sonar, radar, and other navigation technologies had put them and their keepers out of business. No one had any use for them anymore, except as picturesque tourist attractions. Many lighthouses would be restored. Some become museums, to help pay for their upkeep. Others were being torn down, or left empty, dark, and crumbling. Brandon wondered what was in store for this one.

Halfway down the hill, they turned to look back at the lighthouse one more time. The main beam of light which had shone brightly across the bay blinked once, twice, and then switched itself off. It left the lighthouse in complete darkness. All that remained was a huge dark outline of the towering lighthouse as it stood silently at the top of the cliff.

"Lighthouses hold so many secrets. If only their walls could talk," said Brandon.

"Oh, but some of them do," Rosie replied, grinning.

The lighthouse was silhouetted by the sunset, which cast an orange and gray backdrop. It was soon covered by a fog that crept in from the ocean. "Hmmm, it's starting to look kind of spooky now," said Rosie.

"Yeah," said Brandon.

Rosie shivered. "You know what? We've got one hell of a ghost story to tell on bonfire night."

"Yes, we do." Brandon nodded. "I just hope we'll have enough marshmallows."

"Make sure you buy an extra bag, just for me." Rosie grinned. "Let's go, shall we?"

Brandon put his arm around her and gently pulled her closer as they walked toward the parking lot. "This will definitely be one for the books."

"Absolutely," Rosie agreed, snuggling even closer to him. "Now, let's go and celebrate at Brewster's as we promised we would. I still can't believe how Len was spot on with Senator Dalton. He's a great judge of character."

"You know what they say, if you want to find out any dirt in a community, just ask the local bartender," said Brandon.

EPILOGUE:

JULY – 1989

The sharp dressed man with the designer beard stood on the port side of the *Betsea* salvage ship. He stiffened when he noticed the fishing vessel slowly trolling out from behind an island, turning in a seaward direction. Cy grabbed the nearest pair of binoculars affixed to the ship's railing and watched the boat slowly slip away from him. He observed the trawler's captain lower something down from his face. Cy guessed it to be a camera. Shortly thereafter, the captain of the trawler turned his full attention toward the bow and appeared to gun it full throttle in the opposite direction, putting space between the trawler and the salvage ship. He appeared to be fleeing the area. Cy's curiosity was growing with suspicion. *How much did he see?* The red trawler was gradually getting smaller and smaller as it raced north, away from Hanlon Cove. As Cy tilted the binoculars down, he glanced at the name of the boat sprawled across the transom: WHISKEY LEE.

Now, Cy could only watch helplessly as the *Whiskey Lee* fled. He vowed to find out who operated the trawler, and what port it belonged to. *Damn!* he thought, as he gritted his teeth.

He turned and boarded his own vessel after the slain body of Dennis Cain was thrown overboard, attached to an anchor and chain. As he pivoted, he thought he'd caught a glimpse of someone up on the bridge. He knew the captain had gone down to the lower deck to get his lunch. *Who then?* He scanned the bridge for movement. He couldn't see anyone and thought perhaps it was the movement of a flag that was being flailed around by the wind on the upper deck.

Cy turned his attention to the twenty-something-year-old man that stood only a few feet away from him. He waited anxiously while the young man, with a toothpick dangling from his mouth, finished cleaning the blood from the port side of the ship. The *Whiskey Lee* had long since departed the area and had a decent head start on them. The trawler was nowhere in sight now.

Cy's thoughts were interrupted by Lewis's voice drifting up from the private yacht waiting below. "Guys, it's getting really rough down here! I'm getting slammed up against the ship!"

"Come on, hurry up, Evans! We need to go now!" Cy snarled. At this point he reckoned there wasn't a hope in hell of catching the fleeing trawler, but at least Cy would remember the name of it. He'd make sure the trawler's captain was found and taken care of. Cy was impressed by the new guy, Evans. He seemed to be turning out okay, never complained, and was more than eager to do the dirty work for a fair amount of cannabis, or a wad of cash. As soon as they landed back on shore, he'd put Evans on it right away.

"I'm done, boss!" Evans announced dutifully.

"Great! Evans, Ace, let's go! We've wasted enough time on this floating heap of trash." Cy directed the two men to the waiting vessel.

"Weigh the anchor!" He heard the captain bellow shortly afterwards from the bridge, as the larger vessel prepared to get under way. The private yacht was finally free from the hulking salvage vessel; all Cy could think about was how he couldn't leave any loose ends. If this got out, it would surely prevent him from becoming senator. His life would be ruined.

He peered up and noticed the captain on the bridge with a subordinate shadowing him.

Cy hadn't noticed the extra guy on the bridge when he'd arrived. *Of course, the captain would have a first mate.* It was something Cy had regrettably overlooked. He wondered if the subordinate was up there the entire time. *Maybe he saw too much.*

Cy felt a knot tightening in his stomach. He hadn't seen the subordinate descend the ladder for lunch when everyone else did. It was too late to do anything now. The two vessels were headed in opposite directions. Cy would have to settle the score with him later. *No witnesses.*

***

RIDGETOWN, MAINE–2008

It didn't take the media long to put word out that Aiden Cyrus Dalton had been arrested. They were all over it like ants at a picnic.

"Do you see how many reporters are swarming around out there?" Rogan said, peering out Flynn's double-paned office window. "I want to see the look on Dalton's face when he gets handed his life sentence without parole."

"Let's hope he does," Flynn replied, while he closed the lid on the *Whiskey Lee* file.

"Open and shut remember?" Rogan smiled confidently.

"Yeah," Flynn nodded uncertainly. "I'll be glad when all the hype wears down and this town gets back to normal. It's ironic that I left the big city twenty-five years ago to work in a small, quiet town. It's almost as if the crooked bastards followed me here," Flynn rubbed the six o'clock shadow on his chin. "Now that we've busted up Scully's gang, I may have time to shave again."

"All of them are rounded up now; either that or they're in the morgue. I think you'll find lots of time to shave now, Chief."

Flynn nodded contentedly. "Nineteen years and it's finally over. I guess I'd better try and track down Mrs. Moreland and give her the grim news."

"I've already located her," said Rogan, handing Flynn a piece of white paper with her address on it. "Here you go. I thought you'd be the best one to do it. She doesn't know me from Adam."

"Thanks," Flynn replied sincerely.

"Well, are you ready to give the media your statement now?" Rogan asked eagerly.

"As ready as I'll ever be. How do I look?"

"Like shit, Chief," Rogan said, grinning ear to ear.

"Gee, thanks a lot," said Flynn, chuckling. "I'll meet you out there, okay Rogan? I just need to lock up here first."

Rogan walked on ahead. Chief Flynn paused before closing his office door. His fingers gripped the door handle, but his eyes were focused on the framed picture on the wall behind his desk. It was the one of him and William standing in front of the lighthouse. With emotions starting to surface from deep within him, he cleared his throat. "We got him Will," Flynn said softly, forcing a faint smile. It was all he could muster through his somewhat somber mood. Soon afterwards, he pulled the door closed and joined Agent Rogan out on the street a press release.

Flynn remembered something his mother had said to him many moons ago. It was shortly after he'd been sworn in as a young police constable.

She said:

"Let justice be done and the lost souls will find their resting place."

THE END